D1479134

On the Verge BOOK I

R. J. Jojola

Copyright © 2015 R. J. Jojola

All rights reserved

ISBN-13: 978-0986127700

ISBN-10: 0986127701

For Jean Andrews, Reid "the brow" Branning,
Bryanna Antone, Benjamin Antone II ,
and all others
who left this world far too soon.

CONTENTS

NAME PRONUNCIATIONS

Raelle: Ra – yell

Chrishtan: Chrish – den

Sonee: So – nee

Jeanahn: Je - non

Cohlen: Co – len

Oleevar: Oh – lee- var

Olee: Oh – lee

Adreahn: Ah – dree- on

Jenladra: Jen – la – dra

Jabrat: Ja – brot

ACKNOWLEDGMENTS

An enormous thank you goes out to everyone who has supported and assisted me through this project. First, my friends, family, Shelley Martinez, and my husband, for encouraging me. Also, the other veteran authors who offered their priceless advice and mentoring. Ryan Thompson, for introducing me to my fantastic editor, Elizabeth Keenan. Elizabeth, thank you for your wisdom and patience. René Aigner, for allowing me his spectacular, *Master of Birds,* piece for the front cover. Cotey Cerasale, for creating the beautiful owl for the inside cover. Adam Wollet, for the perfect lettering job on the outside cover. And of course, all of my beta readers. Thank you all, so much, for taking this journey with me. I could not have done it without you.

Continent of Mirilan

Ellios

Jassokia

Lake Yerda

Emeda River

Lantern Forest

Lake Fulios

Lake Zalvora

Roessia Forest

Sqmisius

Shimmering Coast

Drasnogite Isle

Liberti River

Abequa

Emerald Meadows

Didumos Plains

Shimmering Sea

Huronus

Didumos River

Didumos Scrub

Didumos Mountains

Sea of Torpaz

Ornz Desert

CHAPTER 1
SAMUEL

Samuel scrambled to pick up as many stones as he could from the lush forest floor, shoving tiny pebbles into his pant pockets before rushing back up the dangling rope ladder to their tree house.

"Here, Browden." He smiled as he emptied his pockets onto the log floor of their tree fort. "We should have enough now."

His brother Browden chuckled, shaking the shaggy brown hair from his face before adding his own collection of pine cones and shards of tree bark to the pile. "I've got these as well. They should work perfectly, Sam."

The two young boys grinned and giggled at one another as they crouched behind the tinder-thatched wall of their stronghold, waiting for their enemy. The delightful and pungent scent of the surrounding pines wafted in with the warm summer breeze, while the echo of an owl hidden among the towering trees seemed to hoot in approval of their strategy. Not much time passed before the enemy arrived.

"Samuel?" A girl's voice called out.

The two young boys stared into each other's big brown eyes and covered their mouths as they tried to hold back their laughter.

"Browden?" The young girl with auburn hair shook her head. "Samuel? I know you're up there. You're not funny."

"We've got you now, Raelle!" Samuel shouted out as his head of wavy blonde hair popped up from behind the fort window. "Now, Browden, now!"

Browden's head darted up even faster than Samuel's. "Get her, Sam. She is an evil sorceress. Keep the evil woman away!"

The two brothers loaded their slingshots and catapulted their collection of small forest items down at their foe. The sound of hysterical laughter echoed through the forest as the tiny sticks and stones bounced off of their older sister's arms that guarded her face.

Browden left the cover of their fortress, rushing out from behind the tinder wall onto the log porch of the stronghold to get a better shot. His messy brown hair hung in his eyes as he laughed out loud at the sight of woodland shrapnel tangled up in Raelle's auburn locks. He leaned heavily into the woven branch railing of the porch to holler at her.

"You'll never defeat us, evil queen. We won't come without a fight!"

The boys' familial enemy had nearly breached their tiny citadel when they all heard it; a horrifying crack echoed through the forest like a bolt of lightning. The porch railing gave way, sending Browden crashing down toward the forest floor. Blood-curdling screams came fleeting from his sister's mouth as she dove toward Browden's shattered body.

Samuel called out from behind the tree house walls, "Raelle? What's happened? Browden?"

The sound of his sister's deep sobs radiated into Samuel's ears as his heart bounded out of his chest and into his throat. He dashed out of the enclosure to see his brother's limp body cradled in his sister's arms. Sheer panic stabbed through Samuel's heart and into his soul.

"Browden!" he screamed in terror as he leapt off the treehouse porch. "Browden, no! Raelle, what's happened?"

Raelle's sobs persisted. "Th–the porch rai-railing gave way a–an–and he fell. I-I—I heard him hit it, Samuel. There was nothing I could do. H–he just snapped. I heard it, Samuel. For the love of The Architect, I can still hear it."

Samuel's eyes grew four times their normal size. "Wha–what do you mean '*he* snapped?' It was the porch that snapped, I—"

Raelle's shook her head as she wept. "No, Samuel,

you don't understand. He—"

Samuel leaned over and shook his brother in a desperate attempt to wake him. "Come on now, Brow, it's me, Sam. Come now, brother, wake up. It's not that far from the top. You've merely had the wind knocked out of you."

Tears barreled out of Samuel's eyes. He barely made out what Raelle said through her hyperventilating. "What, Raelle? Please, I don't understand!"

Raelle's lament only intensified as she moved her bended knees from underneath Browden's limp body. Samuel then realized the horror that lay underneath his brother. It was not Raelle's lap that held Browden's body, but the boulder that had taken Samuel hours to push underneath their fortress to begin building a wall. What Samuel saw made him sick to his stomach. Fresh red blood cascaded down the fragmented boulder where it entered Browden's back. Samuel understood exactly what Raelle meant when she said, *he snapped.*

Samuel shook his brother's lifeless body as tears flowed from his eyes and down his bewildered face. "Browden, no. Please, Browden, wake up. You must wake up!"

Raelle pleaded with him to stop, but he couldn't. Samuel continued in his madness until a tiny owl swooped down out of the trees, landing gently atop Browden's shoulder. The eerie owl stared up at him with glowing red eyes that penetrated deep into Samuel's soul. The piercing glare mesmerized him as the owl cocked its head from one side to the other. Never breaking eye contact with Samuel, the ominous owl hopped along the top of his dead brother's body. Once settled at Browden's lifeless core, the petite owl spoke in an abrasive whisper.

"Murderer."

Samuel held his breath as his heart jumped within the confines of his rib cage.

"Hoo … Hoo," the owl called before its head twitched back the other way. "Yooou killed him Saaamuuuel."

Samuel's lip quivered as he shook his head. "No, I

3

didn't kill him. I didn't know, I swear. I–I never wanted this to happen."

The accusatory owl cocked its head to the opposite side. "Hmmm," its raspy voice continued, "Yooou killed hiiim. Heee's not yoour blood, after aallll. Muurdererrr justifiiied."

Samuel's words tumbled out of him like a broken sack of fruits. "No, I swear. I–I—" He continued to shake his head until he felt a hand grasp his shoulder. It was Raelle. She glared at him with the same glowing red eyes as the owl.

"You did this, Samuel. You know you did," she jeered.

Samuel gasped, "No Raelle, I didn't. He is my brother. I would never—"

Raelle's radiant red eyes looked deep into Samuel's. "He does not share our blood, brother. He is not one of us." Her head cocked to the side just as the owl's had. With a frightening grin she stared down at her palms, painted with the blood of their adopted brother.

"Sheee is right, Saaamuel." The meddlesome owl provoked. "Heee was not your blood. Heee was not your kind. Deeep within in yoooou, yoooou kneeew this to be truuue. Among maaany other things. Yoou knooow this to be the ooonly waaay."

Samuel cried out, "No, I do not. I know none of these things. I want my brother back. I didn't mean for this to happen! The only way for what? What are you talking about?"

His sister raised a bloody palm and turned Samuel's gaze toward her. Her eyes swirled like a whirlpool of fire and blood. "Our blood is the righteous blood, brother. It will rule above all else. You have done well." As Raelle spoke, the glowing red vortex inside her irises faded away, while her pupils grew to enormous proportions. She glared with her completely blacked out eyes as she grinned, exposing teeth as sharp as knives. "This is our destiny, my brother, set before us by the Grand Architect. We mustn't allow anything or anyone to stand in our way."

Samuel shrieked and jumped back from his possessed sister. He backpedaled as fast as his legs could carry him until the trunk of an immense pine stopped him dead in his tracks, pilfering the breath from his lungs. He cringed as the bark tore through his shirt and into the skin on his back. The pain was unbearable. He hyperventilated as tears of agony fled his terror-stricken eyes. He watched in horror as his demonic sister turned to face him. In her claws, she held a crown decorated with glowing blue gems and dripping with gore.

Samuel trembled as the sky grew dark and the wicked version of his sister glided unnaturally across the forest floor toward him. Foreboding whispers accompanied by little red eyes lit up the branches of the massive pines all around him, sending chills down his twelve -year-old spine. His sister grinned, exposing her razor sharp teeth, before placing the bloody crown on Samuel's head. He shivered as warm blood oozed onto his scalp and cascaded off the crown over his face. Samuel froze, unable to move. He shut his eyes tight, and when he opened them again, to his dismay Raelle held a mirror in front of him. Samuel gasped at the reflection of an older, sinister-looking man with his same color hair and eyes wearing the same bleeding crown. The morose reflection sent violent chills through Samuel's adolescent bones.

His sister spoke in a flat and layered tone, "The blood of all shall be none, save one. The blood of the one shall resurrect all and obliterate one. The stone of the one true ruler resurrected."

Fear took Samuel. There was no escape as he pleaded. "No. No please. No. No. I—" He heard someone calling his name. "Samuel, Samuel, wake up. Samuel…"

Samuel woke to find himself hanging over the side of his top bunk. His older sister Raelle pulled on his arm in an attempt to wake him. "Blessed is this day of your birth, brother. Seventeen times around our great star." She smiled.

Samuel rolled over, moving to the far side of his straw-laden bed opposite where Raelle stood.

"Good morning to you too, brother," she muttered under her breath before walking out of their bedroom.

Samuel's head throbbed as if it had been bludgeoned with a hammer. His debilitated body and mind continued to reel from his night terror. He felt certain that he should be used to them by now. But even after five years since Browden's accident, each and every time he had to watch his beloved brother die, it took everything from him. It left him with nothing but emotional and physical pain. And even though it was the same dream each time; it did not lessen the trauma and horror of it all.

As Samuel lay debilitated in his bed, the guilt drove him mad as it always had. He still could not fathom what reason the Grand Architect, the creator of all light and life had for taking his brother from him. Related by blood or not, they were inseparable in life. He needed answers. But his parents only offered him bits and pieces of what he knew to be half-truths and rationalizations. It infuriated him.

The early morning light beamed in through the bedroom doorway adding to his excruciating headache. Samuel scooted across his bed toward the ladder of his bunk and down onto the hardwood floor. He dragged his heels across the creaking floorboards toward the door and closed himself inside his dark quarters. His muscular legs trembled as he walked, causing him to fall helplessly into his sister's bottom bunk. As he sat silently in the dark, thoughts of what the day would bring raced through his troubled mind.

Samuel's mother rapped gently at the door. "Samuel, I've made you breakfast. And on the anniversary of your birth, I've made something incredibly special. Won't you join us, my love?"

Samuel ran his robust hands through his shaggy blonde hair. "Yes Mother. I'll be out in a moment. I promise."

He took in as much air as he could and let it sluggishly drain from his lungs before attempting to stand once more. His legs trembled and the pressure crushing his head intensified. With his hands firmly gripped around the roped perimeter of his top bunk, Samuel lifted himself up off his sister's bed and opened the wardrobe in front of him. He swiftly grabbed his wrinkled clothes that lay wadded up on the bottom of the cabinet. After shaking them out as best he could, Samuel slipped into his brown linen pants and buttoned them before sliding his wrinkly white linen shirt over his muscular frame. He cringed as the movement amplified the pain of his aching muscles.

Samuel squinted heavily upon exiting the shadow of his bedroom into the overpowering light of the morning sun that flooded in through the kitchen and sitting room windows. He raised a hand to his brow in an attempt to block out some of the light that made his head feel as if it would explode at any moment. Once his eyes adjusted to the light of day, he saw his family seated at the table patiently waiting for him to make an appearance.

"Blessed is the day you lived," his father declared.

Samuel's family raised their glasses in unison. "Blessed is the day you lived, Samuel."

Samuel forced a smile before taking a seat at the table where his mother began piling food onto his plate.

"I've got to keep my baby boy fed and strong, haven't I?" She grinned.

"Yes, Mother." Samuel looked down. "You've done your best."

Samuel shoveled the mountain of food from his plate into his mouth as fast as possible. It did not take long for him to finish. He made sure to clear his place before he kissed his mother goodbye and headed out onto the porch to put on his boots.

"But, Samuel, my love," his mother called, "today is the seventeenth anniversary of the day you were born. Are you not going to spend it with the people who love you? Each and every morning you leave and do not return until dinner." She stood. "We hardly see you as it is. Can today not be an exception? I don't wish for you to be alone on such a wonderful day. This is a very important milestone."

Samuel turned to face his mother before stepping out onto the porch. "To me, Mother, today is no different than any other day. Please understand. I need this time to myself each day to find truth and clarity. It is the only purpose I have in this life."

His mother nodded. "As you wish, my son. I love you."

Samuel said nothing and turned back through the doorway and stepped out onto the front porch. A gentle grasp on his arm stopped him in his tracks. He turned to see Raelle.

"I love you, brother," she whispered as a tear escaped one of her soft green eyes. "I just thought you should know."

He felt it, he did, the love for his sister. She had always been there for him. He hated that he could not open up to her. He sensed that it killed her inside, but he reassured himself that he needed to keep everyone at a safe distance.

"I love you too, sister," he said as he took Raelle in his sturdy arms and held her for the first time in years. "I will return, Raelle. And when I do, I promise everything will be better. It will all make sense."

Deep in his heart, he knew that she too had suffered. The last thing he wanted was to let her down. Samuel gently pressed his lips to his sister's forehead, trying to ignore the tears that cascaded down her face. As he walked away with his sister's somber expression still fresh in his mind, his small brindle mutt Sasha followed closely behind, wagging her tail. Samuel paused and turned around to face her.

"Sorry girl, today is mine and mine alone." Samuel reached down and patted his companion on the head. "You'll have to stay here, and wait for my return."

Sasha heeded his word and sat in the tall grass, tilting her head as she watched her master continue down the grassy knoll and into the stable.

CHAPTER 2
RAELLE

Raelle gazed into the clear, blue summer sky above the mountain peaks surrounding her isolated home in the center of the valley. The cool breeze brushing against her face soothed her as she made her way toward her destination. Her long, auburn hair danced in the wind as she looked all around her, taking in the incredible sights and sounds of her homestead. With each step, she uttered silent goodbyes to a land that had molded her into the young woman she had reluctantly become. Raelle tiptoed her bare feet onto the sandy shore of a small serene lake. She took a deep breath and released before creeping into the crystal clear spring water with a grace that she had only been able to muster on this day. But her new found grace felt tainted as the cold water sent chills down her spine. She looked down to see a familiar face staring back at her. Her olive skin was speckled with freckles that could only be seen in the warmth of a summer sun. Her hair sent ripples through her liquid portrait, distorting her bright green eyes, small mouth and prominent nose. To her, the distortions reflected the true agony that had warped her mind.

As soon as she reached her final destination at the deepest part of the spring, Raelle was ready to erase the anguish that writhed inside of her like a restless serpent. She wanted nothing more than to be rid of the physical and emotional pain that ate away at her soul. She reassured herself once more that this was the only way to stop the pain. Raelle exhaled every ounce of air from her lungs before sinking down into the watery abyss. On her journey below, she watched as tiny bubbles escaped her plight and fleeted to the surface. Raelle closed her eyes as the soft sandy bottom of the spring massaged the tips of her toes. The water grew dark as her remaining bubbles floated away into what was left of the sun's rays. Overcome with a sense of peace, Raelle knew that her next breath would surely be her last.

Raelle's eyes jolted open to frenzied splashes above her. She had to get back to the surface. Upon reaching the surface, she saw what looked like a little black bear, scrambling around in the water. It was her dog Pip, struggling to save her drowning master. Raelle knew that Pip could never understand why Raelle would leave her. She would protect Raelle at all costs. Fully aware that Pip was not the best swimmer, Raelle swam as fast as she could toward her furry companion. The poor pup's fluffy coat soaked up every ounce of water it could, weighing the little dog down. Raelle opened her arms and signaled Pip to swim toward her. She and the miniature mutt made it safely to shore just as Raelle saw her father walking down toward the lake.

"Raelle," her father called, "since when do we swim with all of our clothes on? How lazy have you become? It is clearly far too much work to use the appropriate swim attire these days."

Raelle forced a laugh. "No, Father, it's just that… well… uh… Pip… you know how she can be slightly overzealous. She jumped in after something and I had to fish her out. You know how she can be."

Her father chuckled. "Well, keep that foolish little dog in line. She's supposed to protect *you*, you know, not the other way around. I believe she may be more trouble than she's worth."

On the shore of the crystal-clear lake, Raelle and Pip did their best to dry themselves as Raelle's father made his way back to the house.

"I'm sorry Pip," Raelle said as she squatted down and stroked Pip's wet fur, "I let my anguish get the better of me. I feel so lost without him, so empty and alone. I don't want to do that to you girl. I'll never leave you alone. You're all I have now." Pip licked her mistress's face as Raelle embraced her. "Thank you for giving me a reason to stay. I love you."

Raelle did her best to wring out the soaking wet clothes that clung to her body. She squeezed her shirt and watched as the water slowly dripped over her hands and onto the green grass at the shore's edge. The dripping wet imagery triggered her, forcing her mind to flash back to the previous week.

***

"Raelle, you haven't touched your dinner."

"I'm worried mother." Raelle's voice trembled as she looked across the table. "This isn't like him. He didn't even take Sasha with him this morning. He's never done that before. "

Raelle's mother grinned. "Everything is fine, Raelle. Samuel will return home soon enough. He's been staying out later these days. Maybe he just felt like leaving her home today."

"But, Mother." Raelle shook her head. "He's never missed supper before, especially not on the anniversary of his birth. And Sasha never leaves his side. Not ever. Not to mention the fact that he has been disappearing longer and longer every day for the past five years. Doesn't it concern you? It seems that every time I bring it up, you simply dismiss it. We need to go look for him. Something doesn't feel right."

"No." Her mother nodded. "I told you. Everything is fine. He'll be home soon. Just have faith, Raelle. If Samuel says he needs this time to meditate and seek answers from the Grand Architect to gain clarity, then I believe him. He is my son."

Have faith? Raelle thought. *Have faith in what? Faith in what we pretend isn't going on?*

"No, Mother." Raelle pushed back her chair from the dinner table and stood. "Everything is not *fine*. You know it, I know it. Father knows it. Almost every night while Samuel sleeps, he screams and cries and tosses and turns. And if ever I ask him about it, he denies it and pretends as if I'm the crazy one. It's the same way *you* treated *him* after Browden's accident. He came to you for answers, but you offered him nothing, acted as if he had no reason to be devastated. You told him to *have faith*. Ever since then, he's closed himself off to all of us. He's suffering mother! Can't you see it? Aren't you the least bit worried?"

Raelle's mother sighed. "I have faith in my son and faith in the Grand Architect, that Samuel will find the answers he seeks in contemplation when the time is right. The Architect is our maker, and will offer his wisdom how and when he sees fit. It is not my place to meddle in his plan. Everything happens for a reason, Raelle. It is all part of the Architect's grand plan for us."

Raelle shook her head. "The Architects plan? You truly believe keeping us here in this valley away from the rest of the world and ignoring obvious signs that your child is in pain is part of some kind of grand plan?"

"Raelle, I-." her mother's eyes grew wide.

"No mother!" Raelle backed away from the table and threw her hands in the air. "Samuel and I have lived our entire lives in this valley, never leaving or coming into contact with another soul because you and father say that the outside world is a dangerous place. You say our place is here with family, so that we can take care of one another. Exactly how are we taking care of one another when you dismiss everything? You say the outside world is filled with madness? *This* is madness mother. Your denial is madness. I've always believed you and father. I've always trusted you. You're my parents, I love you. But after twenty years of this, I don't know what to think anymore. It's difficult to continue living like this, when you give us no answers. You cannot keep us here forever. You can't just wait for your faith to give you answers. I can't live like this anymore. And I know Samuel can't either. We're losing him! Can't you see that?"

Her mother rushed over and took Raelle's hand. "We are not losing him Raelle. Samuel is a good boy. He's just taking time to get closer to the Architect. He needs more time to heal from his loss than the rest of us. We are safe here Raelle. Samuel is safe here. There is nothing to fear while we are together. This is our home. Please understand. We love you."

Raelle yanked her hand from her mother's grasp. "Understand what mother? You are making no sense. You've told me absolutely nothing! It's been five years since Browden's death. Samuel is no longer a *boy* Mother. He's becoming a young man. And if he is taking longer to deal with Browden's death, it's because *you* dismissed his cries for help when he needed you most. Instead, you let your so-called faith in the Grand Architect take care of his pain for you. Unlike you and father, I refuse to just stand by and ignore his suffering. I'm going to look for him."

"Raelle wait!" Her father pleaded. "You must listen to your—"

Raelle raced out the front door, mumbling her parents' shortcomings under her breath as she stomped toward the forest where her brother had entered that morning. She called Samuel's name as she made her way through the dense woodland. She stopped when she came upon an abandoned tree house hidden among the branches of the surrounding pines. Raelle smiled as tears welled in her reminiscent eyes. She paused to listen for the laughter of her brothers echoing high above her in the warm breeze as they catapulted stones and pinecones down at her. But the only sound she heard was the faint hoot of an owl high in the trees. There was no one else there.

Something on the ground below the deserted tree fort caught her eye.

"Samuel!" Raelle called. She hesitantly approached the object on the forest floor — a solitary bloody ear. She could barely breathe and her heart felt as if it would burst through her chest. Her hands shook uncontrollably as she called out again in desperation. "Samuel?" Her eyes darted back and forth over the forest floor. They froze at the sight of a thick trail of fresh blood leading deeper into the forest.

"Samuel!" Raelle's voice echoed through the trees as she chased the trail of red liquid. She ran ever faster as the trail of blood grew impossibly wide. With each shout, her cries grew shriller. "Samuel! Samuel!"

She had no idea how loud she was screaming until her final shriek cut through the forest like a knife and into her heart. She stood frozen at the base of a massive pine. What she saw within its branches caused her stomach to summersault, sending her dinner up and out onto the forest floor. Raelle wiped the vomit from her mouth before looking up again at her brother's mangled body hanging over a low branch. His face was so badly crushed it was unrecognizable. His entire body was folded in half at the center of his spine where he drooped over the warped bough. At the base of the tree, Samuel's boots, bow, and arrows lay strung across the ground covered in gore. Bright red blood trickled down his arms, over his hands, and off of his fingertips onto the green forest floor.

"Samuel?" Raelle's voice trembled.

She jumped up over and over again trying to grasp at Samuel's brawny arms to pull him down. She leapt and tugged incessantly until finally she pulled his lifeless body to the ground. The sheer weight of Samuel's muscular frame hit the ground with a loud thud, like a giant ragdoll full of sand. Tears streamed down Raelle's face as she struggled to turn Samuel's heavy corpse onto his back.

"No, Samuel, please. Please Samuel no!" she cried. Raelle pounded on his chest in a desperate attempt to restart his heart. In the midst of her futile rescue, she had not noticed the deep slashes covering his entire body, or what was left of it. After a few moments, and what had seemed to Raelle a lifetime, she knew it was over. Her brother was gone, forever. Another life taken.

CHAPTER 3
ON THE VERGE

Raelle stood at the edge of the lake, trapped inside the painful memory of her brother's brutal demise. She snapped herself back to reality and finished peeling away the wet clothes from her body before wringing them out onto the shore. The water trickled into the grass just as Samuel's blood had trickled from his cold dead limbs. The flashback had drained her. Raelle's hands shook violently. Her stomach churned. She felt physically ill. Her trek back to the house felt as if she were climbing one of the enormous snow covered peaks that encompassed their rugged homeland. She did not look forward to explaining her wet clothes to her mother. Raelle knew all too well that the sudden and unforeseen deaths of her two younger brothers did not mean that dirty, wet, or disgusting things could be tracked into the house, that dishes would not be done, or that dinner would not be served at its usual time. Raelle would simply have to set two less places at the table. A seemingly simple task that left her emotionally drained at the end of each and every day.

Raelle often thought that, maybe it would be easier if someone would simply get rid of the other two plates that sit by themselves in the cabinet while the other three are at dinner. Maybe the two plates should be thrown into the lake, or laid to rest next to the graves of her brothers. Maybe, the plates themselves are also dead, just as her parents pretended not to be. It left her with great uncertainty and mounds of questions. The only thing Raelle could be certain of was that she, her mother, and her father were all on the verge. Of what though, remained unclear. Her mother and father had always assured her that someday she would understand, but after twenty years in the valley she was more inundated with confusion than ever. She longed for something more. Raelle convinced herself that her parents must be part of a particular alliance intended to keep secrets from children in order to make their lives more mundane. And with Raelle spending most of her days alone, she had many more opportunities to contemplate the very things that only further amplified her frustration.

As their log cottage came into view over the top of the lush green hill, Raelle eyed the narrow string of smoke that slithered out of the chimney atop the straw-covered roof. *Dinner time.* As Raelle approached their wraparound porch, the memory of her and her brothers as they sat and listened to their father's tales of sorcerers and frightening creatures entered her mind. She had always enjoyed the way her father told them as if he had actually been there, but Raelle knew that it was only fantasy. As she made her way onto the porch, she saw Samuel's dog, Sasha, staring out into the wilderness, patiently awaiting her master's return. Raelle hung her head. It killed her inside that Sasha remained unaware of the tragic and infinite length of her master's journey.

"He left us all behind." She said as she stroked Sasha's smooth brindle coat. "I know how much you must miss him." Raelle turned to Pip who scurried up behind her. "I'll never leave you Pip. I promise." Raelle planted a kiss on Pip's head before sneaking in the front door.

Through her bedroom window, Raelle watched the sun make its final descent behind the mountains. She changed out of her cold wet clothes and prepared for her most dreaded suppertime duty. A burning sensation overwhelmed her body as she entered the kitchen and approached the cabinet. As she opened the door, the hinges emitted a squeak that sounded to Raelle like the loudest, most ear wrenching noise she had ever heard. She felt as if the cabinet was mocking her. With the door open and the sound still ringing in her ears, her heart raced and her body tingled. She reached in and removed three plates, holding them firmly as she took them to the table and placed them at three empty seats. With the table set, she drudged back to the cabinet to close the other two plates inside their tomb.

Across the room, she heard with acuteness, her mother complaining to herself under her breath about Raelle's wet excursion and tardiness. Her father's footsteps on the porch as he approached the door sounded as if they were magnified and in slow motion. Suddenly, Raelle found herself holding the other two plates from the cabinet and smashing them down onto the floor. She screamed at the top of her lungs as a strange array of blue light radiated from her body. The entire house shook, shattering the kitchen window and leaving a pile of glass on the sill. Raelle collapsed to the ground sobbing. Her father and mother stood for a moment, staring at her until it seemed they had recovered from her maniacal episode.

Raelle's father turned to her mother. "Marista."

She glanced back at him. "Lorndan?"

"We cannot hide any longer," he said with serious concern. "We cannot go on like this forever."

"I know," Marista said, shaking her head, "But I prayed that we would see many more moons before this time came upon us. That the Architect would have given us some sort of sign."

Raelle glared up at her parents with disgust. It was true. She knew they were hiding something all along. Now she would find out what it was, no matter what it took.

Lorndan walked over and helped Raelle up off of the floor. She accepted his hand with reluctance as she watched her mother walk over to the window to clean up the mess on the sill. Raelle stared at her mother in disbelief that she had felt the need to clean up the mess at that particular moment.

"Marista," Lorndan said, raising his voice, "I think it's time we sat down."

Marista ignored him. "Ouch," she shrieked before pulling a tiny piece of glass from her hand.

"Marista!" Lorndan shouted.

"Well, fine then!" Marista hollered back at him just before closing her eyes and raising both hands over the glass, prompting each piece to float back to its original position. The window appeared as new.

Raelle thought she must be losing her mind. The window was broken, and it had just put itself back together. Her gaze remained on the window as her mother sat down at the table with them.

Lorndan turned to her, his eyes intent on having her full attention. "Raelle, this may seem difficult to understand, but your mother and I have done everything up until now to protect you from what we are. From *who* we are."

Raelle looked at him with irate eyes. "All right..." she answered. Anger flooded her heart as she attempted to listen to what her father was going to try and explain to her.

Lorndan took a deep breath. "Raelle, do you remember the stories that I used to tell you and your brothers when you were very young?"

Raelle nodded.

"They are not all simply made up stories, but tales of the history of our land passed down in our culture from generation to generation," Lorndan continued. "You, your brothers, your mother and I, we are all descendants of a mage bloodline. You are heir to an entire kingdom, Raelle. And outside the safety of this valley lies a treacherous land that you have only heard about in stories. It is a world that your mother and I have worked your whole life to shield you from, until we felt the time was right. It is why we brought your brother Browden here when he was a baby. He was the son of a dear friend. They were murdered, and it was no longer safe for him, either. Everything we have done up to this point was to protect you, all of you."

Raelle did not blink as her father spoke.

Marista placed a hand on Raelle's before cutting in. "The episode you experienced was produced of an energy known as Lyre," she said. "Our mage bloodline gives us the ability to manipulate our surroundings and amplify abilities. Not everyone is born with Lyre, Raelle, only those originating of these bloodlines. These bloodlines have ruled over our grand world of Lerim and the diverse provinces of our continent of Mirilan for generations. As you know, the Grand Architect is responsible for creating all life and energy. He does not meddle in our life's journey, but gives us only the tools and situations that we are meant to have in order to experience life in our own way. In this way, the Destroyer is different. If given the chance, the Destroyer will meddle when requested by an individual or in a time of individual weakness in order to gain entrance to our living world on Lerim. He would inevitably rescind all that the Architect has created, covering Lerim in the blackness of his void. Just before you were born, Raelle, your uncle, Lochran, called upon the Destroyer and awakened the blackness in order to gain control over our kingdom and eventually the entire continent. We needed to keep you and your brother Samuel safe and hidden until the time was right. It is as your father said. It was not safe. Browden's parents were eventually murdered by Lochran. He would have murdered us too, had we not gone into hiding. Browden was lucky to have survived the ordeal. During one of your father's journeys outside the valley for supplies, he ran into a servant of Browden's kingdom. They begged your father to take Browden with him and keep him safe until the time was right. Had we not hidden you and Samuel, you would have met the same fate as Browden's family."

Raelle heard what her mother and father had said, but it did not make her feel any better. Instead, it only intensified her frustrations. She understood now why she constantly questioned the purpose of her existence. She leaned close and glared at her mother.

"So, Mother," Raelle said in a low monotone, "what you're telling me is that you've kept us inside this bubble to keep us safe?" She shook her head and smirked. "Well, I must say, you have done a splendid job at that considering I'm the only child left." Raelle stood as she raised her voice.

"So is that when you would decide that we were ready? So that the one left alive could carry on the burden of this immense secret?"

"Raelle, I– I'm…" Marista shook her head.

Raelle's hands flailed in the air. "No, Mother! Let me speak. If you had decided a little sooner, is it not possible that either of my brothers could have been spared their untimely deaths? Having the ability to manipulate your surroundings seems like it could have had its benefits. But of course, *you weren't ready.* And I suppose now that your last child left is trying to drown herself in the lake, it must be some kind of *sign* from the Architect that perhaps you should let someone in on this clearly insignificant detail?"

"Raelle," Lorndan said, cutting in. "We truly are sorry. This is not the way it was supposed to be. Your brother Browden's death was an accident. It never should have happened. And Samuel, I don't know. His wounds were indicative of … but … that cannot be because … because we are under protection, and…"

"Indicative of what, Father?" Raelle slammed her fist into the table. "Some insane thing that you decided to keep a secret?"

"Raelle, please," Marista pleaded. "We have been trying to protect you the best we can. Please, do not be angry. You must understand. We did this to protect you. The use of our Lyre would have led the blackness to us and given you and your brothers no chance of survival. The valley is protected by enchantments that break down if we use our abilities within it. There are those that would kill us if they found us. Or use our own Lyre-blood abilities against us—or worse, to do evil. Because of who we are, we could not—"

They all heard it. Something outside knocked over the woodpile on the side of the house. The dogs, who would usually start barking, scratched like rabid animals at the door to get in. Lorndan let them in and signaled for Raelle and Marista to remain silent. They watched as the dogs dashed into Raelle's parents' bedroom to hide.

"Hide, Raelle, right now." Lorndan whispered. "Go hide. Hide in your secret spot."

Raelle hesitated.

"Do it now, Raelle!"

Raelle ran into her parents' bedroom. She flung open the attic hatch and lifted each dog up inside before pulling herself up behind them. She sealed herself and the dogs inside before joining them on the straw covered floor of her sanctuary. Raelle could feel the dogs trembling next to her. She had never seen them act this way. Then they heard it. The dogs' ears perked up as heavy footsteps made their way to the front door, pounding into the porch like giant boulders dropping from the sky. Raelle listened closely as the steps came to a halt. Dead silence. Even the insects who usually played their songs throughout the night did not dare to utter a single note. Raelle did not move or make a sound. Suddenly, the front door came crashing down, allowing a pair of black leathery-skinned legs in metal-laden boots to enter their safe house. Raelle cringed at the knife-like points at the toes of the intruder's boots. A terrifying pair of large black hands with ten centimeter long razor-sharp metal armored claws hung down next to the intruder's knees.

Raelle heard her father's voice. "How did you get here? How did you find us?"

The figure walked toward her father. "Yut fragim hutar," it spoke in a language that Raelle had never heard. Its voice was scratchy and animalistic.

"The plates… the window…" Raelle's mother muttered.

Raelle heard the defeat in her mother's voice, and recalled her saying something about not using their abilities so as to remain undetected. *Tonight, when I smashed the plates, I must have used my Lyre to break the window. Mother also used it to fix the window. This is how they must have found us*, Raelle thought as she trembled above them.

The animalistic voice snickered. "Sisti hutarir Rogue, yem prepim misit unira drosk?"

Her father raised his voice. "I am not weak, Minoti. *You*

are weak. You have sold your soul to Ire Oblitora. You are nothing but a vile creature of the Void, a slave to the Destroyer's foul bidding."

The creature let out a maniacal laugh. Raelle heard her mother spit on the creature. Her father yelled something she could not understand. The creature jumped back to avoid whatever her father had thrown at him. It then moved faster than Raelle could blink. When her eyes opened again, blood spatter dripped from the ceiling. Below her, her parents lay motionless on the floor as deep red blood pooled around their slashed and mangled bodies.

Raelle lay silent; she could no longer see the creature, but she sensed that it had not gone. After a moment, she heard what sounded like sniffing. It was the same sound the dogs made when they picked up the scent of a rabbit. Pip let out a small whimper. Raelle clutched the pup's mouth to shush her. Once the sniffing ceased, it grew dead silent once more. Raelle forced her eyes shut for a couple of seconds and when she opened them again, she saw it through the spaces between the logs of the ceiling. The repulsive creature stood directly beneath her. Its scalp bubbled as if most of its hair had been burned from its human-like head. The putrid smell of gaping infectious wounds wafted from the parts of its body not covered by armor and made Raelle's stomach turn. Its orange snakelike eyes sent chills down her spine. Its face resembled the face of a human, but its nose, lips and ears looked as if they had been cut off. Its black leathery skin looked charred and burned. And as it sniffed around, a long, blood-red tongue, forked like a snake's, slithered out from its mouth.

Raelle let out a silent gasp when she saw the Lyre blood of her parents dripping from its armored hands. The creature looked up directly at her location. Raelle held her breath. Just when she thought she had seen the end of her life, grey, leathery wings flapped out from behind the monster's armor. It took off out the front door casting a shadow of its silhouette onto the full moon. It was the last moon Raelle's parents would ever see.

Raelle was petrified. She did not know whether to move or stay where she was. She had never been so frightened in her twenty years on Lerim. Sasha and Pip lay on the straw with Raelle like a miniature pack of wolves. Pip licked the tears from her mistress's face. Raelle kissed the foreheads of the only family she had left before placing her head in her arms to cry herself to sleep. She hoped that by some miracle, she would not wake up in the morning.

CHAPTER 4
IF ONLY

The entire valley lay completely quiet, as if taking a moment of silence for the recently departed. Raelle had not yet opened her eyes, but the light that woke her turned the inside of her eyelids a ghastly shade of red, reminding her of her parents' brutal death just hours earlier. Realizing that it had not been a bad dream, Raelle shot up with a gasping breath. Sitting on the straw in front of her, the dogs wagged their tales back and forth, as if everything was back to normal and it was time for Raelle to feed them. As Raelle looked down at the horrific scene through the gaps of log and straw, she resented the dogs' ability to live in the moment. She wished that she too could wake up and forget what she had witnessed. Raelle wanted nothing more than to lie back down and sleep forever, but she knew it was no longer an option if she wanted to survive long enough to find answers. She needed a plan. She needed to discover the truth of all that her family had succumbed to.

Raelle dragged her knees across the straw-covered attic to the small door she used to enter her hiding space. She pounded on it several times with her foot before it opened. With the hatch door swinging open toward the floor, Raelle jumped down onto her parents' bed before helping the dogs to the floor. Her body trembled. Her stomach churned and her head throbbed. She had never felt so terrified or alone in her entire life. In one dreadful second, Raelle had lost everything and everyone. She had to remain strong if she was going to succeed, but her body could not hide her true torment.

Trying to collect herself, Raelle went to the washroom and scooped out a bowl of water from the trough to rinse her face. To her surprise, the water that dripped from her wet chin turned a rosy shade of red. Raelle turned toward the window and gasped at her blood-spattered reflection. She was overcome with hate for the young woman staring back at her. How could she not? After all, in her fit of anger, she had released the Lyre that led the revolting creature to her family.

Raelle hung her head as she left the washroom. *If only I had trusted my parents, and trusted in the Grand Architect that all things happen for a reason. Maybe if I hadn't been so selfish as to need to know all the answers and understand everything, then mother and father would still be alive. After all, they would have told me eventually, and maybe we could have done it together.* But now, she was completely and utterly alone, with only pieces of the puzzle that her parents had reluctantly given to her and not a clue what to do next.

The shredded bodies of her parents lying on the sitting room floor forced Raelle's stomach to summersault. She raced outside, trying her best to hold back the dry heaves of her empty and twisted gut. She mustered all of her strength and managed to gain enough control over her body and return to the house. This time, she kept her eyes closed as she walked back through the gruesome scene and straight back to her parents' bedroom. She pulled off the blanket that covered their straw cot and closed her eyes once more on her journey back to the sitting room.

Raelle took a deep breath and held it in before whipping the blanket into the air and covering her parent's mangled bodies. She covered her mouth with her hand and spun back around as tears quickly welled in her eyes. The putrid smell of death made her feel sick again. She raced out onto the porch holding her stomach, where she stumbled upon the dogs fighting over dried meats that had been spilled by the monster. Her gut wrenched as she watched the two little dogs scour the porch as if they had not eaten in days. Raelle did not understand how they could be eating. Food was the last thing on her mind.

She needed a plan, and something to lead her in the right direction. But she had no idea how or where she would attain it. Whatever her decision, she needed to make it soon, before the grotesque creature returned, whatever it was.

Raelle paused in the doorway. She couldn't think straight. She stood motionless, staring off into nowhere waiting for inspiration to strike. Five minutes passed, the dogs had almost finished ridding the porch of its mess, and still Raelle had not struck any kind of epiphany. Out of the corner of her eye she saw the blanket that once covered her parent's bed. She tried to pretend something more pleasant lay underneath it. But she could not lie to herself forever. She could not leave them there to decompose, but she knew she was not strong enough to carry them outside or bury them on her own. She would have to burn them and the house. And even though Raelle did not know where she would go, she knew that she could not stay. Their valley was no longer safe.

The frightening realization overwhelmed her thoughts and made her heart race. She had never been outside the valley before. The only things she knew of the outside world were from her father's daunting tales. She and her brothers always dreamed of leaving on their own adventures and experiencing things that their parents would never allow. And on this day, their dreams would become reality, but in a vastly different way than they had naively anticipated. Instead, it was a nightmare come to life.

A sharp gleam of light entered Raelle's peripheral vision. Her father's wedding ring peeked out from under the blanket, reflecting the light of the morning sun that seeped in through the window. Raelle did not want to leave father's ring to burn up with the rest of her past. Instead, she would hold it safe in her keeping forever. Raelle covered her nose and mouth before walking over to the pale white hand. She closed her eyes and carefully removed the precious ring from her father's cold, limp finger. The metal felt thick and dense in her palm.

Raelle backed away from the dreadful scene before examining the band, which was decorated with small blue gems. She shut her eyes tight and began her preparations, dragging her feet into her and her brothers' room. She pulled the blanket off of her bottom bunk and rolled it up as best she could. She cringed as the thin rope she used to tie the blanket burned into her skin. After putting what belongings and other necessities she thought she might need into a pile, Raelle proceeded to her parents' room.

Upon entering her parents' empty tomb, her hands shook and her stomach churned. She made her way over to the extravagant bureau her father dragged through the mountains and back to the valley years ago. The intoxicating aroma of its dark wood reminded Raelle of her mother, with her sandy-colored hair always pinned to the top of her head and her clothes smelling of the exotic wood that held them. With a trembling hand, Raelle opened the top drawer of the bureau. Inside, she found her mother's brush, hair pins, and ribbons. In the very back, sat her mother's wedding ring. In the light, its white gold gleamed, and the round-cut blue stone at the center dazzled. *Simple, yet beautiful,* Raelle thought. *The stones themselves have a glowing essence about them; it's as if they contain their very own universe.*

The gems mesmerized her. Raelle forced herself from her trance and placed her mother's ring on top of the bureau next to her father's before moving on to the next drawer. Inside, she found her mother's nightclothes. Raelle lifted one of the silk gowns to her nose, breathing in the nostalgic aroma of her departed mother. She gazed back at the rings once more before placing her mother's nightgown back in its drawer. She could not seem to turn her eyes from the two stunning objects. She picked up her mother's ring once more to admire its elegance. Something drove her to move the elaborate band to the tip of her ring finger. Raelle slid the ring over her knuckle and onto her hand. A perfect fit. She marveled at its splendor as it sat on her finger. Raelle felt something peculiar, yet familiar, a sensation similar to what she experienced the night before during her outburst. But unlike the previous day, this felt steady and secure. It did not burn, but instead a warm peaceful energy radiated throughout her entire body. Raelle closed her eyes to feel the vitality flow through her limbs. After a few moments, the sensation subsided and Raelle looked out the window to see the sun's new position in the sky. The sight reinstated her sense of urgency.

Raelle turned around and opened the armoire next to her parents' bed. The shelves inside held her parents' boots and shoes. Her father's pants and shirts were folded up on the very bottom shelf. He had never cared much for clothing and did not have much. He preferred to wear the same things until they were so worn that Raelle's mother would throw them into the fire. Raelle's mouth cracked with a smile as she pictured her mother storming out of the house with the faded clothes, her father chasing her to the fire pit.

Raelle's grin faded. A startling white light glowed from the bottom corner of the armoire. She immediately pulled her hand out. The light disappeared. These days, it was difficult for Raelle to decide whether she was seeing things, or the phenomenon was real. She put her hand back into the armoire. This time, she noticed something else. Not only did the corner glow, but the stones in and around her mother's ring radiated light as well. Raelle had forgotten that she was wearing it. She reached further into the armoire toward the light until she touched the wood where it gleamed, instantly setting something into motion.

A small door formed at the back of the armoire. In its middle was carved a glowing, blue circle. Raelle reached for the handle of the tiny door and pulled, but it would not open. She looked again at the glowing blue circle and then at her mother's illuminated ring. She tugged the ring from her finger and placed it in the circular slot of the miniature cabinet. The light around the slot turned a bright white. Raelle reached for the door handle a second time and pulled it open.

Inside the cabinet she found an ornate box made of dark wood, decorated with silver metal and covered in markings similar to those on the armor worn by her parents' assassin. Raelle fumbled to open the box. A piece of rolled up parchment tied with ribbon and an envelope with a broken blue wax seal lay inside the box. Underneath the envelope sat two more rings similar to those of her parents. After studying the new rings and placing them on the bureau, Raelle untied and unrolled the parchment. It was a map. It illustrated a path from a place called Huronus to an X marked in the middle of a mountainous region called the Didumos Valley. A transparent line lit up the perimeter of the valley. But small gaps made the perimeter incomplete. A blue dot pulsed at the center of the valley. Raelle was not sure what this glowing entity was, but she knew it had to mean something. She rolled the map back up as fast as she could before pulling the envelope from the box. She studied the broken blue wax seal. The stamp pressed into it read *Huronus*. Raelle removed and unfolded the paper inside.

Marista,

If you are reading this letter, it means that the king and I are no more and Lochran has succeeded in his quest for power and the throne. You know what you must do. Leave now and promise me to keep yourselves and the children hidden from Lochran. As heirs to the throne, he may see them as a threat, especially Raelle. But even if he decides not to see them as a threat to his new title and power, he will kill you, and he will use the children to do evil. Inside this box, you will find the contrivance necessary to escape and to stay hidden: a map to safety, our Lyre harness rings, and three orbs containing protective charms. The yellow orb will prevent any entity that is under the control of the blackness from seeing you, the purple orb will prevent any entity under the control of the blackness from smelling your presence, and the orange orb will prevent any enemy from sensing your Lyre. You will need these to get to the valley securely. Once you've arrived you must not use your Lyre or the protective and camouflage charms that shelter and protect the valley will slowly break away and you will be left vulnerable to be detected by Lochran's seekers and minions of the void. While there, you will be able to raise the children without the threat of Lochran and the disintegration of ours and other nations. It is vital that the children remain hidden until the time comes when you are obligated to lead them to their destiny. As you well know, Lochran will be hunting them through their Lyre. You must not disclose their true identities to them in order to prevent the use of Lyre within the protective realm of the valley. Nevertheless, when that time comes upon you, it is of the essence that you travel deep into the Lantern Forest and once again seek out The Lady of the Realm. She will have the answers you seek and the wisdom essential to your mission. Do not forget, it is our bloodline that will allow you entrance into her sanctuary. As you know, the king and I love you both very much and will miss you more than you know. I pray that our heirs to the throne, Raelle and Samuel, will someday return to give the people of our kingdom and this world a fighting chance. Never let your guard down and do not forget all that has happened here. May The Architect bless your journey.

Love Always,

Your Queen, Jowellia

Raelle closed the letter. *This must have been written to my mother by my grandmother, the queen,* she thought. *She would be devastated if she could see her family now. Every one of them dead, murdered, taken, save one.*

Even though Raelle had already made the decision to leave, the letter motivated her in a whole new way. At last, she held a tangible piece of the puzzle in her hand. Raelle shut the enchanted cabinet door and slipped her mother's ring back on her finger, positive that this was where it belonged. Once securely on her hand, it pumped pure warmth and energy throughout her entire body. Raelle grabbed the ornately decorated box and headed back to her room to the pile of items on top of her bed. She shoved it all into a knapsack before racing into the kitchen to gather what little food she thought might keep through the duration of her journey. The dogs looked up at her, begging for scraps as if they had not just finished eating.

Raelle shook her head. "Come on, you silly mutts."

The dogs followed closely behind her as she carried her sacks out the door. In her peripheral vision she could see the blanket lying on the floor where she had placed it hours earlier. She cringed and quickened her pace. The dogs darted out the front door and Raelle marched down after them toward the stable. She could see her white and brown painter horse Winston along with their other two horses pacing around inside the fence. As soon as Winston saw Raelle coming toward them, he trotted up to greet her. Raelle could sense his uneasy energy, but he still seemed to enjoy the touch of her hand as it moved gradually up, down, and around his face.

"It's all right, Winny," Raelle whispered. "We'll figure this out. No need to worry boy." She kissed him on the nose. "You know I love you."

Winston looked at her as if he understood. Raelle's words of comfort to her horse seemed to ease her own mind. She walked around the stable and opened the doors. Once inside, she collected a couple of saddle bags along with a beautiful black leather saddle, a gift from her father. She called Winston into the stable and placed the ornately decorated saddle on his back. Raelle tilted her head as she noticed that the saddle's markings resembled the ones from the box in the armoire.

Winston seemed pleased with the saddle placement and stood proud against the weight of belongings and provisions. With the saddle bags packed, Raelle attached a large, deep basket with a hinged lid and placed a blanket inside. At the back of the stable, Raelle grabbed a pair of linen pants and a shirt that hung on the wall. She removed her dress, leaving nothing but her under shirt and bloomers, and put the brown pants and dirty white linen shirt over them. With Samuel's clothes on, Raelle attempted to sense traces of her brother, but felt nothing. It was as if his ferocious murder had erased him completely. She walked to the other side of the stable and grabbed a belt that sheathed two gemstone-laden daggers belonging to her father. She adjusted the belt around her waist as tightly as possible, but the daggers still hung low around the curvature of her hips.

Raelle released a deep sigh as the departure from the only place she had ever known came hurtling toward her. She did not know what awaited her outside the broken perimeter of their safe zone, but one thing she knew with absolute certainty was that she had no choice but to discover it on her own. Raelle called the dogs, and they came running in with their tails wagging, filled with excitement for the journey ahead. Winston, the wise painted steed, stomped and let out a noise warning the puppy Pip to stop nipping his heels. Raelle let out a deep sigh as she exited the stable and shut the doors behind her, closing what was left of her family safely inside.

Her final task was one that she dreaded most of all. Setting the table was no longer her most formidable obligation. It was time to say her final goodbyes to her parents, who in their fight to shield their children from all that would potentially terrorize them triggered their own demise with their overly cautious conduct. Raelle trudged back up the hill to her family's brush pile. She scooped up as much kindling as both of her arms could cradle and made arduous trips to her home until the floors of their safe house were completely covered. Once finished, Raelle grabbed the two lanterns hanging on the porch and poured their oil all over the inside of her homestead.

As she stood on the porch at the edge of what looked like a miniature brush forest, Raelle breathed in as much air as her lungs could hold, releasing tiny bits at a time in an attempt to put off the inevitable. With no air left in her lungs, she set fire to the small cottage. It did not take long for the enormous flames to engulf the inside. Raelle backed away as she felt the intense heat nearly sear away the peach fuzz that blanketed her soft face. The blaze overwhelmed the modest structure as Raelle struggled to keep her emotions from mimicking the raging inferno. She fell to her knees in the grass, tears dripping down her cheeks. Grief billowed out of her like the flames that now devoured the only place she had ever called home. Her grief-stricken screams and sobs echoed through the valley.

Raelle's grief drained every ounce of energy from her mind and body, but she knew that rest was not an option if she wanted to survive. In a few hours, night would return, and she could not risk being found by the vile beast that murdered her parents. Raelle picked herself up off the ground and headed back to the stable. She wiped her tears as she closed herself inside with her furry companions and prepared to leave. As she leaned down to grab Pip and place her inside the basket attached to Winston's saddle, she noticed the charms on Pip's collar glowing yellow, purple, and orange. The stones in her mother's ring shined along with them.

"The orbs," she said. "These must be the protective orbs that grandmother had written about. This must be why that creature was unable to find us."

Raelle picked up Sasha and placed her in the basket with Pip. "See, you guys have been protecting me all along." Raelle kissed both of them on the head and closed them inside.

Feeling a bit safer knowing that she was protected by charms, Raelle mounted Winston and nudged him on his neck. "Let's go boy."

As they made their way out of the stable, the other two horses followed. They would be free to roam the valley as they pleased. Unlike the horses, Raelle knew that she would not be free. Today, she had been locked into whatever fate awaited her on her journey, no matter how long or how difficult.

CHAPTER 5
THE UNKNOWN

Darkness crept over the sky as the sun sank beneath the horizon. Brisk breezes whipped through the coniferous trees of the forest as Raelle made her way out of the remote valley of the Didumos Mountains and into the wilderness. The rustling leaves and swaying branches sounded to Raelle as if the canopy were crashing down on top of her. Ever since her episode with the plates, Raelle's senses had become enhanced. Every sight, every sound, every touch, and every taste hit her like a punch to the gut.

As she followed the trail carved by her father's many journeys outside the valley, Raelle trembled at the thought that she had never been so far into the forest and that there was no going back. After all, there was nothing and no one to go back to. Fear slunk into her mind. Darkness would soon be upon her, and she did not know what awaited her in the night. She was too anxious to sleep, and did not feel safe enough to close her eyes long enough to blink while the sun was away. She thought it best to travel by night and rest during daylight. Light slipped away as dusk slithered in. The wind died down, transforming the trees into a flat calm. As Raelle's fear and anxiety dissipated, her new ears fixed themselves on the more comforting symphony of nocturnal creatures singing in the night.

Within the vast shadow of nightfall, Raelle's small torch offered her enough light to see the narrow path that lay ahead. The occasional breeze brought a chill that caused the pores across her soft olive skin to rise. Raelle pulled a deep blue velvet cloak out of her side pack and threw it around her neck, pinning it together with a brooch containing a crystal gem that glowed in the dark. As she pulled the hood over her head, she visualized her father coming through their front door just before her fifteenth birthday. He smiled ear to ear as he pulled the stunning cloak from his sack and handed it to her. Raelle's mouth gaped open as she marveled at its beauty. As she remembered hugging her father, the image disappeared into the black of night.

It had been nearly six hours since Raelle set off on her journey into the unknown. The woods grew colder, and she could not seem to find an ounce of warmth within her body. It had become much too cold to continue to travel. Raelle had no choice but to stop and set up camp so that she could warm herself next to a fire. Raelle found a small thicket that would hide her from the path. The grassy area was matted down where deer had once lain together. Both dogs were fast asleep in their basket and did not seem to notice the pause in their journey. Raelle unhitched the basket and placed it on the ground where it would be close to the fire. Using a small hatchet, she gathered enough wood for a small fire. The flames gave off soothing warmth that caused Raelle's eyelids to grow heavy. She could not fight the slumber.

She drifted into dreams filled with images of past and present. Memories blurred together. After a while, the collage seemed to draw in the familiar smell of rotting flesh and death. It smelled so real, causing Raelle's stomach to twist and turn. The painful nausea opened her ears to the sound of the dogs whimpering and Winston stomping his foot on the ground.

Raelle woke, but the sickening scent that haunted her dreams lingered. Her churning stomach jumped into her throat when she saw a large shadowy figure creeping toward them. She rushed to reattach the whimpering basket. Raelle shoved her blanket into her pack and almost lost her footing as she threw her leg over Winston's saddle. Her breaths were so rapid that she was unable to muster the words to Winston to signal their exit. She used her legs instead to squeeze his sides over and over again to gain speed as they whipped through the trees. Struggling to stay on the path, Raelle knew that their only chance was to run.

Whatever chased them was huge and had orange snake-like eyes. As they sprinted on, Raelle turned to look behind her. She could no longer see the creature, but she couldn't be sure it was gone. As she turned back once more, a black winged figure swooped down out of the trees. Raelle pulled a dagger from its sheath as the creature dove down on her like an owl preying upon a mouse. Raelle closed her eyes tight and struck at the heinous beast. The monster's dreadful shriek pierced her eardrums as it crashed to the ground at her side and she pulled away. Raelle opened her eyes to blazing blue light emitted by the gemstones in her father's dagger and her mother's ring.

Her heart rate slowed and she slid the luminescent dagger back into its sheath. She gasped at the sight of the monstrosity's wing stuck in the bindings of her saddle. She had cut it clean off. She cringed as she pulled the black leathery appendage from the cinch strap and tossed it into the darkness. In her panic, she had not recognized the creature, but with her pulse stabilizing, she realized she had seen it before. It had murdered her parents in the blink of an eye. Raelle knew now that they could not stop. Although she had injured the beast, she was not certain how she did it, or if she had the ability to protect herself again. After all, she had minimal practice with the blades and no real experience with them. The only thing she knew for certain was that she was being hunted.

***

After two days of riding through the Didumos Wilderness with only short breaks and no sleep, Raelle felt exhausted and could tell that Winston too felt the strain. Thus far, they had seen nothing but dense forest. At night, loud, unfamiliar creatures howled all around them. Raelle began to think that they might never find a way out. She was not sure if she would ever see or speak to another human being again. She hadn't spoken a word in days and being locked inside her own mind made her feel as if hope had left for good.

Slim rays of sunlight penetrated the forest canopy where they came upon an enormous rock. Raelle tilted her head back and looked up at the gigantic slab of stone that towered over them. *It seems so out of place.* She hopped off of Winston to get a closer look at the object. *It has to mean something.* This whole time she had been looking for a sign, a marker, a signal that she was on the right path. Raelle strolled up to the stone slab and ran her hands between its smooth grooves and over its rough edges. The gems in her ring and daggers glowed blue once again. *This has to be it.* Then, something in the distance caught her eye, an opening in the trees. Raelle smiled. *We've finally reached the end of the forest.* A short distance outside and around the edge of the forest, Raelle saw what looked like a transparent wall. Her gazed turned up. A wall covered the forest like a translucent dome. She walked close enough to the transparent wall to touch it. Her hand reached right through. She felt the wall's energy surge into her arm before pulling it back through.

"This is it, this has to be the edge of the protective field," Raelle said aloud. "That rock must be some sort of generator." The sound of her own voice startled her. Raelle ran back to her companions who waited by the rock. "We found it!" she shouted. "We've finally found it."

At the sound of her eager voice, two pairs of eyes with little wet noses poked their way out of the basket on Winston's side. Raelle could hear the thumping of the dog's tails against the inside of the hamper; a sound she had not heard in quite some time. The thumping consoled her and amplified her small sense of confidence. Raelle reached into the basket and patted her furry companions on the head. Winston turned to Raelle and whinnied, shaking his head up and down to show that he too felt a sense of delight. Raelle stroked the soft brown and white fur on his neck before mounting his strapping structure.

Raelle and her companions cautiously headed toward the translucent dome wall that stood between them and a nameless world. Raelle knew that once they crossed, they would not be coming back through the mammoth shield that had sheltered them their entire lives. But Raelle had no other choice. The grotesque monster was still out there, hunting her. Hope alone could not keep them safe. They had to move on. She closed her eyes and blindly nudged Winston through the force field. As they went, Raelle felt an intense energy flow through them all. It was like nothing she had ever experienced.

Once her eyes readjusted to the bright light of day, Raelle gazed out into a brilliant and unfamiliar landscape. A dazzling scene of rolling emerald green hills seemed to go on forever in front of her. Even the air felt easier to breathe. Raelle closed her eyes as the fragrance of purple wildflowers engulfed her with the gentle breeze. *So this is the dangerous outside world that my parents lost their lives trying to keep us from?* To Raelle, it was one of the most breathtaking sights she had ever seen.

Raelle paused a moment to take it all in before pulling the map out from her ornate box. She noticed the small blue dot that once glowed inside her home in the valley now pulsed just outside the perimeter of the mountains in a place called the Emeralz Meadows. *This dot must be me.* She sighed, relieved she would be able to gauge whether or not she was headed in the right direction. She ran her fingers along the parchment from her location to The Lantern Forest. Once there, she would seek out the Lady of the Realm in the Lantern Forest, just as her grandmother's letter instructed. It was crucial she discover the truth behind all she had lost and how she could avenge her family. Raelle gave Winston a nudge with her heel and they headed out into the gorgeous green uncertainty of the Emeralz Meadows.

***

The flickering light of the brighter stars danced in the purple twilight. Although the sun had not yet completed its journey below the horizon, it would be dark soon, and there was not much shelter to be had in the rolling green hills of their new setting. Tiny clumps of trees appeared here and there, but they would not make a substantial shelter. It was becoming more difficult to see across the infinite number of grassy knolls. Raelle's head hung over her chest. It had been nearly three days since she and Winston had slept. A few times, she drifted off while riding, dreaming while she was awake. She had seen her mother and father and both her brothers. Large spiders that seemed to float down out of the sky had her batting, swatting, and shouting into the air at nothing. Just like liquid, the blades of grass seemed to transform into waves as the wind stirred through the emerald ocean. With the sun in its final descent into the west, Raelle rounded the top of a larger hill and spotted a small group of trees that would have to suffice for their overnight recoup.

Winston galloped toward the clump of foliage that slumped in the direction of the setting sun. The drooping branches held long thin tendrils covered in heart-shaped leaves that looked more blue than green. The shoots hung down almost to the ground, but were too sparse to blanket the tree completely. Near the center of the grouping, a larger tree towered over two smaller ones. Dark brown bark looked almost black as the sun retreated even lower on the horizon, prompting lavender buds on the branches to close for the evening.

With Winston parked underneath the chandelier of blue-green foliage, Raelle unpacked. She unhitched the large basket that sheltered the dogs and let them out. The stunning vista offered Raelle a sense of peace and security as she spread out the dogs' blanket as well as her own on the ground. The restless canines chased each other around the tree growling and barking viciously, as if they were actually intimidating. Pip's fluffy black coat looked like a shadow as she darted in and out of the trees teasing Sasha.

Suddenly, Raelle realized that there was nowhere to get firewood and that after the sun had said its final goodbyes, they would be spending the night in complete darkness. The thought ignited her anxiety. She had no idea what was out there, but her need for rest trumped her terror. She left Winston saddled just in case. He would be ready to go if they needed to flee. She felt awful not allowing Winston the same comforts as she and the dogs, but they could not afford to take risks. With the sun leaving behind only remnants of dark purple, pink, and orange in the west, Raelle made herself comfortable on her blanket next to the dogs who lay panting. Raelle leaned against the trunk of the tree with her arms behind her head and marveled at the night sky through the leafy curtain of their refuge. She gazed out at the stars as they gradually allowed their light to travel through the atmosphere and penetrate the purple sky.

Raelle shifted her gaze northeast to see the enormous golden sphere of the moon make its way over a massive shadow of a hill. Rising up into the shimmering night sky, it appeared as massive as the hill that hid it. Tranquility snuck into Raelle's body and mind. Relieved to discover that they would not be spending the night in complete blackness as they had done the past two nights, she struggled to keep her eyes open. The dazzling moon faded in and out until sleep ensued.

***

An unexpected jerk of her body caused Raelle's eyes to shoot open. The sound of the dogs growling and Winston's stomping his foot sent painful waves of fear surging through her. Then she saw it, the shadow of a four-legged creature standing off in the distance. As her eyes came into focus, she realized there was more than one. At least fifty silhouettes, stood almost a meter taller than a horse, their long, thin legs like twigs compared to their bodies. Spikes longer than Raelle's foot trailed all the way down the creatures' spines to long, whipping tails. Each animal's elongated narrow head had one long, spiraled antler jutting out of its forehead. Raelle lay still, trying not to make a sound. She stroked the dogs until they seemed content that the creatures were not a threat. But Raelle was still not sure. She remained motionless so as not to draw any attention to her pack.

Raelle watched the animals move inch by inch around the hills, their heads facing the ground. *They must be grazers*, she thought. A sigh of relief escaped her and she sat back against the trunk of the strange tree once more, closing her eyes. In the midst one of her minute-long naps, Raelle opened her eyes to see an adolescent grazer standing in front of her. The creature seemed content to munch on a tuft of grass while Raelle studied it. As the awkward-looking animal inched closer, the brilliant light of the moon presented the true image of the fawn, covered in black fur with red-brown swirls that matched the color of its shiny, dog-like nose. Its face resembled that of a deer, but the muzzle was much longer. Its abnormally long tongue wrapped itself around tufts of grass and ripped them from the ground. With the grazer unnoticed by her dormant pack, Raelle closed her eyes once more. Her eyes jolted back open to a harsh swooping noise that pierced through the night air like a blade and reinstated her sense of terror. She was still being hunted. She looked to where the fawn had been, but the grazer was nowhere to be seen. *How could it have just disappeared?* The dogs whimpered as if waiting for a predator to strike. Winston joined their concern and let out a whinny before stepping back as far as he could under the cover of the trees.

Raelle stood and looked out into the moonlight. The other creatures did not seem to notice the incident that had taken place. Suddenly, a large winged silhouette flew in front of the moon. It swooped down and plucked another fawn from the ground. The other grazers perked their heads up in unison. Their large rounded ears swiveled around like satellites as they froze where they stood. Not five seconds passed before another looming silhouette lifted another grazer from the moonlit knoll. This time, the herd of creatures bolted. Their shrill cries reverberated into Raelle's sensitive eardrums. The panicked yelps prompted more winged silhouettes to swoop down and pluck up more of the long-legged creatures. The ground shook as they stampeded toward Raelle's thicket. She fumbled to gather all of their things as the dogs yelped. She tossed them into their basket and threw her leg up and over Winston's saddle.

Raelle did not signal him to run just yet. They stayed quiet, hidden among the strands of tangled branches of their shelter. As the herd charged toward them, more and more of the flying predators swooped out of the sky, plucking the weaker animals with ease. With the stampede only a few meters away, Raelle positioned Winston in line with the trunk of the larger tree. She braced herself as Winston reared up when the herd raged by.

After what seemed like an eternity, the herd and its airborne raiders left Raelle and her tiny pack of mutts behind. After realizing she had been holding her breath the entire time, Raelle allowed the air to finally escape her. Just as Raelle lifted her heel to signal Winton's exit, a soaring straggler passed so closely by their shelter she could feel a draft from its enormous wings. She squeezed her eyes shut, praying that it had not seen them. The colossal creature fixed its piercing, yellow eyes on Raelle and her steed. The scaly beast whipped back around with such force and speed that the branches of their alcove parted, exposing their position. Raelle dug her heels into Winston's sides, and they took off into the blazing blue light of the moonlit midnight. Raelle and Winston's rapid breaths merged into one sound. The soaring silhouette gained on them with every gallop, never taking its eyes off its newfound prey. Its immense shadow hovered above just before it swooped down on them. Raelle pulled out one of her daggers and swung at the beast with all her might. A piercing roar cut deeply into Raelle's eardrums.

She felt her body being lifted from Winston's saddle just before she skidded to the ground alongside a set of toes she had severed from the formidable predator.

Somehow, Raelle summersaulted into a perfect standing position, drawing both her daggers up in front of her chest. The gemstones on her ring and weaponry emanated bright blue light as the giant winged lizard flew at her. When it landed, it stood at least four meters tall. It heaved its long thick neck and head back over its shoulders, flames billowing from its throat. The hair on Raelle's arms singed away as she dodged the blaze, which left only charred grass where she once stood. The beast glared at her with its tallow eyes as it came at her again, this time with its many rows of long jagged teeth. Raelle tucked her head into her chest and rolled underneath the enormous flying reptile to avoid the razor filled trap. She sensed the beast's frustration. Again, it struck at Raelle with its powerful jaws. She closed her eyes and rolled forward. She felt as if she moved in slow motion. Raelle found herself directly beneath the dragon's underbelly. Daggers clenched tight in her hands, she crossed her arms together and uncrossed them, slicing open the smooth skin of the creature's grey belly. Steaming innards spilled out at her feet, and the beast fell forward in slow motion. She nimbly jumped back out of the way as the gigantic, winged, lizard collapsed. It let out a horrific gurgling roar as it hit the ground with an immense thud.

Raelle finally felt safe enough to breathe and let out a sigh of relief. A grin crept over her mouth at the sight of Winston galloping over the hill toward her. She ran to meet him. Her intense speed startled her. It seemed inhuman. She flew up onto Winston's back and dug her heels in.

"Let's go, boy. There may be more of these things. The beast's cry may bring them after us."

They raced off into the immense glow of the moon. There would be no rest again tonight. Raelle could no longer trust her sense of security within the realm of the unknown.

CHAPTER 6
THE LIGHT

The massive sun dwarfed the lustrous moon that illuminated their narrow escape just hours earlier. It blinded her as it inched its way up and over the horizon. Raelle had ridden north all through the night with no end of the grassy emerald hills in sight. The only change in landscape manifested itself in the frequency and number of trees she saw. It felt like an endless desert of green, with no visible end. Her grandmother's map was the only reason they had not gone in circles.

Raelle replayed last night's narrow escape in her mind. *How was I able to kill that enormous and powerful creature?* She had never defended herself before, not really. The only experience she had with weapons was a few dagger lessons with her father and the wooden daggers she and her brothers used to slay one another in their games of pretend. The fact that she had been able to injure the wretched beast that murdered her parents shocked her even more. *How did I know when to strike or where to strike? I have no idea what I'm doing.* In her mind, by all accounts she should have been dead. But somehow, her instincts had saved her.

As they continued north, Winston's pace began to dwindle. They all needed time to recuperate. But Raelle had developed a serious aversion to resting and letting her guard down. Her anxiety told her to keep moving until they reached the forest, but the dogs' cries inside their basket reminded her that she was not the only one being affected by her life's events.

"Ssshh babies, its ok. We'll stop soon. I promise. Hopefully the daytime will allow us more peace than the night."

The daylight offered her only a small sense of relief. After all, they had not yet seen what creatures the sun would bring. After finding a small group of trees resembling their previous refuge, Raelle unpacked the blankets, fed the dogs, and let them play. This time, the buds covering the branches opened their lavender petals to bask in the sun. They too were in the shape of a heart, mimicking the green leaves that surrounded them. A round half-bulb covered in bright blue pollen sat in the middle of the flower. The bloom's scent was intoxicating, reminding Raelle of fresh fruit and sweet nectar. The aroma was comforting, but Raelle told herself that she would not be fooled into relaxing by a peaceful atmosphere. She understood now that a beautiful environment did not reflect the madness that may lay dormant beyond each hill. Raelle sat down on her blanket next to the dogs as they rolled over to expose their bellies and bask in the warmth of the sun.

With her mother's Lyre harness ring secure on her finger, a deep warm energy surged through her every nerve. Raelle lay back and closed her eyes. Somehow she knew she needed to learn to focus her mind, meditate, and reflect. She replayed the attacks of the past few days. As the shock of both incidents began to wear off Raelle could see things more clearly. In her mind, she was back in the woods, riding as fast as she could to evade the repulsive monster that hunted her. She saw the hideous creature swoop down through the trees. She heard with perfect clarity the sound of her own labored breathing as she pressed on through the wilderness. She leaned forward into Winston to minimize air resistance. It was then that she realized time began to slow down. The creature came at her in slow motion. Raelle slowed time even further to calculate her attack. As the creature drew nearer, its energy seemed to disrupt her ability. She swung her right dagger, lacerating half of the creature's wing clean off.

The forest scene faded away in her mind, replaced by the recent memory of a bright, moon lit night. Once again, Raelle rode hard, pushing Winston as fast as she could. Her keen ears magnified each and every flap of the giant lizard's wings as it gained on her. She felt the uneasy energy of the creature above her and pulled out her dagger. It was too late, it caught her cloak. Just as before, Raelle slowed time to get a good look at her options. She seized her closest opportunity, slicing off the creature's toes that held her. They both tumbled to the ground. Raelle could see the black lizard's amputated toes suspended in air as they fell to the ground in slow motion. She pressed her eyelids together as hard as she could and honed in on her intent to survive and to kill.

Raelle moaned in her dreams as the image of the slain lizard transformed. Raelle found herself swallowed into a black abyss. Her arms and legs flailed as she plummeted through the never-ending black hole. Anxiety gripped tight on her mind. Her fear of the unknown magnified tenfold as unfamiliar whispers echoed all around her. She could not make out what they were saying. There were too many and they all ran together. After a time, the falling ceased and Raelle was suspended in nothingness. She used her dangling hands and feet to feel for a floor below her. The surface felt like nothing, but still it was something. Pain coursed through her body as she abruptly dropped to the floor. Her knees rattled as she attempted to stand inside the void. She saw nothing, heard nothing, felt nothing.

She tried to call out, *Hello? Is anybody there?* Her lips moved, but no sound followed. The sound of her own voice echoed inside her head. *Hello? Where am I? Please, somebody, answer me!*

Raelle continued to call out inside the confines of her mind until a tiny speck of light crept into her peripheral vision. It was a small, glowing entity floating in a sea of pitch black nothingness. Mesmerizing voices rang in Raelle's ears once more as she made her way toward the tiny star. With each step, the ball of light grew larger and brighter until its blinding white light consumed every inch of the void. As she traveled further, the whispers faded away one by one, leaving behind one solitary voice. Raelle walked toward the sound, placing her hands in front of her to feel for something, anything. As she did, she felt something indescribable: complete euphoria. Her worries, cares, and traumas seemed to be absorbed by the light. She basked in its utopia until something caught her eye. She gasped at the shadow of something or someone standing inside the light. Raelle squinted at the blurry figure. The lingering voice startled her.

"Raelle," the soft, feminine voice said. The silhouette of a person inched closer, "Raelle, we are here for you…"

"Who… who are you…?" Raelle's voice trailed off into the nothingness around them.

"Raelle," the voice coaxed, "I have loved you since the moment you were born. You were my world. But our world has become distorted. I have only a moment with you here. Our time is running low. A dark truth resides within your future. The murder of your…" the voice trailed off.

"Mother? Is that you?" Raelle could not make out the woman's words and the blurred figure faded as the light started to shrink.

"No! Wait, please!" Raelle pleaded. "I need answers. I need help. I need…" She sobbed as her breath gave no words to her lips. The figure disappeared, and the bright light flew away from her. "No! Please, no."

Despair took her as she cried for help inside her own mind. Raelle felt herself lose control of her muscles just before her legs gave out on her. The light shrank to nothing and Raelle fell backward into the black abyss once more. She braced herself for an end that refused to come. She closed her eyes as she had done before to wake herself from her dream state, but nothing happened. She was powerless to stop it. With her eyes pursed shut, Raelle let go and allowed emptiness to swallow her.

***

Raelle's eyes fluttered open. Her head was propped against a tree in the middle of a rolling sea of green hills. Her face was soaked with tears and her nose sticky with mucus. She tugged on her shirt and pulled it up to wipe away the mess. She gasped as her eyes met the unfamiliar gaze of a complete stranger. She must not have been able to hear anything before. She had not noticed the dogs barking and growling ferociously at the unknown visitor. The stranger, a handsome young man wearing brown leather armor with a hood hanging off the shoulders, danced around in circles as the dogs nipped at his heels.

"It's all right, you tiny beasts. I mean you no harm. I swear it."

Raelle winced at the absurd sight of a grown man begging two little dogs for mercy. Judging by his stature and physique, he would have no problem tossing them both into the grass.

"Who are you?" Raelle asked in a stern tone. She could not trust a soul, not after everything she had been through.

The young man was almost a foot taller than Raelle. A short wave of shaggy brown hair hung over his face that was blanketed with a stubbly brown beard.

"Funny," the stranger chuckled, "I was just about to ask you the same thing. As it were, my name is Chrishtan. I'm a ranger of sorts. And you are?" He barely managed his answer amidst his dance with the dogs.

Raelle flashed him a dirty look. "Well, it is none of your business. It was you who approached me."

The stranger looked back at her with soft blue eyes and laughed as if she had told him a joke. "So, I have replied your inquiry, and you deny me? You see, I know most around these parts, and I have never seen you before. Dark times have fallen upon this land, so when I meet a stranger, I must be sure that they are not a constituent of the blackness."

He tiptoed toward her. "When I came upon you, madam, you seemed to be having some sort of fit. I was sure you were dead until your eyes shot open and your mouth began moving." The young man was snide and flippant.

Unlike the attractive stranger, Raelle saw no humor in the situation at all. "First of all, I have no idea where I am," she snapped back at him. "Second, I am not accustomed to strangers watching me while I sleep. And third, I have been riding for almost four days. I have barely slept." Raelle grasped her right hand around a dagger. She had been through too much to let her guard down now. She said nothing else to the young man called Chrishtan.

"Is that it?" He asked, laughing. "You have no idea where you are, and you have not slept in days? I think you're going to have to do a little better than that. You see, it's like I said, these are dangerous times. And if you want to keep your freedom, you're going to have to give me a bit more than that."

Raelle felt awkward talking with Chrishtan. After all, she had never known anyone outside her immediate family. But her current state did not make the situation easier. She had not slept in almost a week and her disturbing dream had drained all her energy. The only thing keeping her from falling over was the solid trunk of the tree. But worst of all, she felt angry and frustrated. What she wanted more than anything was for it all to end, but she had to stick to her mission. Raelle could not be sure if this Chrishtan fellow was trustworthy, and she had no desire to tell him the details of her family's history and her recent undertaking. Her stubbornness was a signature of her personality and she was not about to lose herself on behalf of this facetious and meddlesome man. She would allow nothing and no one to stand in the way of her journey to the Lantern Forest.

Raelle glared up at the stranger. "I have nothing left to say to you."

Chrishtan shook his head. "Look, I'm just trying to help you. And I'd like to know who you are."

Raelle stood up on wobbly legs and pulled out one of her daggers. Her arm trembled with fatigue as she pointed it at the stranger. "Well then, Chrishtan, you can feel free to leave.

That is the only way you can help me." Raelle's knees quaked as sweat dripped down her forehead, to the end of her nose, and fell into the grass. She eyed the two swords that sat sheathed on Chrishtan's hips. She prayed he did not unsheathe them.

Chrishtan's hands moved toward his hips and up into the air. "I do not wish to fight you," he assured her as he stepped backward. "I only wish to help."

She wanted to believe him. His blue eyes seemed so kind. But she could not take any more chances. "Just leave!" she commanded as she struggled to keep her balance.

"Please," he pleaded, "allow me to help you."

Raelle had never felt this way before, she did not know which way was up or down. She had no idea what she wanted or needed. She felt as if she were losing her mind. Everything started to spin. Sweat crept in between her lips as her body temperature raged out of control.

Chrishtan took one immense step toward to her with his hands out in front of him. "Please, just tell me your name. I promise I will not hurt you. I believe I can help."

He was within striking distance. Raelle stepped out and jabbed at him with her father's dagger. Chrishtan nimbly leapt back to avoid the blade.

"Sorry. I'm sorry," he repeated as he slowly walked backward with his hands in front of him. "But I truly believe I may be able to help you."

Raelle's heart raced faster than ever before. Her sweat-drenched clothing clung to her hot skin. "I already told you, you fool. The only way you can help me is to leave me alone!"

"All right, all right," Chrishtan said as he continued to take steps backward.

Raelle kept the dagger pointed at him in her sweaty, shaking hand while she struggled to round up the dogs and place them in their basket. As she reached down to pick up Sasha, Raelle could barely breathe. In her peripheral vision, she watched the stranger walk to his white horse. As she stood back up, black and red dots appeared in front of her eyes. *Please no*, she thought just before falling to the ground.

CHAPTER 7
A STRANGE FEELING

The up-and-down motion of the horse caused Raelle's head to throb and her stomach to churn in a vicious fashion. Raelle woke to feel a pair of large, heavy arms around her body, holding her up in the saddle. The intense pressure of the dense arms only intensified her nausea. Something was seriously wrong. She had never felt this sick in her entire life. She painfully opened her eyes to see two hands holding the reins of a white horse. Watching the steed's head and mane as it bobbed made her head feel as if it would explode. She had an idea of who the arms belonged to and she tried to express her disapproval of the situation, but only a loud groan escaped her.

She heard a familiar voice respond to her protest. "I'm sorry for the bumpy ride. I know it must feel awful. It's going to be all right though. We'll set up camp soon. Only a few more minutes, I promise."

Raelle looked over her left shoulder to see the sun setting in the west. Her fear of the night intensified the chills that made her teeth chatter violently. Every inch of her body throbbed with intense pain. She wanted more than anything to lie down. She closed her eyes and tried to relax, but the pain was far too great. Each time she fell asleep her head fell forward, causing her to wake abruptly.

Eventually, the torturous up and down motions came to a halt. Raelle was too weak to lift her head. A pair of strong arms plucked her off the saddle and carried her to a blanket on the ground. She opened her eyes to a canopy of enormous trees spinning wildly above her. Chrishtan leaned over her. He was spinning, too. It sounded as if he was asking her a question, but his voice was muffled. She could

barely hear him as his face moved in and out of focus.
Chrishtan gently sat her up.

"How did you get these gashes on your back?"

She finally heard him. *What gashes?*

"Listen, the entire back of your shirt is soaked in blood.
I need you to tell me how you got this injury so that I can
help you."

Raelle did not recall getting injured. She had been so
afraid and pumped full of adrenaline that she felt no pain at
all. Her only focus had been survival. She reached her hand
over her shoulder to feel for the wound. Her shirt was moist
and sticky. As she pressed down, pain shot through her back
like a thousand knives. When she brought her hand back
around, her eyes widened at the sight of her palm, painted
red with her own blood. She immediately reached for the pin
that held her cloak together. *Nothing.* Her beautiful cloak was
gone. *I must have lost it in my struggle with the black lizard. That's
how I got injured.* Raelle recalled the beast grabbing her cloak.
It must have grabbed me as well, and I didn't notice it.

Raelle swayed as she mouthed something to Chrishtan,
"Black … lizard… fire… wings…"

Chrishtan mouthed something back to her before helping
her lie back down on the blanket. His image faded away as
she fell back into unconsciousness.

***

Raelle's nose picked up the scent of something delicious,
prompting her eyes to flutter open. Her stomach churned as
she struggled to sit up against the tree trunk behind her, but
to no avail. Chrishtan stopped stirring the contents of the
metal pot over the fire and hurried over to help her. She
stared deep into his blue eyes. She wanted so badly to thank
him, but she did not have the strength to muster a single
word. Chrishtan gently swept the sweaty hair out of her eyes
and tucked it behind her ears. No one had touched her like
that before. It felt strange, but good. The feeling quickly

dissipated as Raelle felt something boiling up into her esophagus. She turned as quickly as she could to the side. Bile and stomach acid exited her empty stomach onto the jungle floor. She had been under too much duress to eat anything since leaving her home in the valley. Raelle kept her head down. She had never been sick like this before, let alone vomited in front of a complete stranger. She hated feeling so vulnerable.

Chrishtan gently rubbed the bottom of her back. "It's all right." he said softly. "It's going to be okay." He stood up and headed over to a small pot that hung next to a larger one. Using a tiny wooden bowl he scooped out the contents of the small vat.

"Here, drink this. It will help. I promise."

Chrishtan's kind smile eased her humiliation. Raelle lifted her nose to the subtle sweet smell of the blue liquid inside the bowl. The scent made her mouth water despite her nausea. She smiled faintly and pressed the steamy fluid to her lips and drank. The warm concoction soothed her throat. She wasn't sure what would happen when it hit her uneasy stomach, but it tasted so good that she did not care. It did not take long for her to finish it. She was certain her body would reject it and she waited anxiously for the liquid to travel back up and into her mouth, but it never did. Finally, she felt relief.

Chrishtan looked over at her and smirked. "It's helping, isn't it?"

Raelle nodded. "Yes, thank you." Her swollen throat made her voice raspy. It was all she managed to get out.

Chrishtan stood. "It could take over an hour to feel back to normal. You could have died out there all alone, you know."

Tears began to well in Raelle's eyes. He was right. She knew he was right. She had become so overwhelmed with everything that had happened, she lost herself trying to stay strong and focused on her mission. She turned away from him to hide the tears that trickled down her dirty, sweaty face.

Chrishtan walked around to Raelle and squatted down in front of her. "Look, I know you don't know me, but if you could tell me who you are, and whatever it is you're going through, I might be able to help."

Raelle looked at the ground. "No," she said, shaking her head. "No, I can't. You wouldn't understand."

He placed his hand on her shoulder. "Please, allow me to help. I know you think I won't understand. But there is a chance that I might."

Raelle wiped the tears from her stained face and looked up at him. His soft, tan skin, sculpted nose, and gentle blue eyes invited her in.

"Look, I'm sorry, Chrishtan. Truly I am." Her voice was shaky. "I just have no idea where I am, or what I'm supposed to do. I've never spoken to another person outside of my immediate family in my entire life. I wouldn't even know where to begin…" Her voice trailed off as she hung her head once more.

Chrishtan squeezed her shoulder. "Well, why don't you start with your name?" His smile was even more inviting than his eyes.

Her voice trembled. "My name is Raelle."

Chrishtan grinned. "Well, hello, Raelle, my name is Chrishtan. It's great to meet you." He put out his hand to shake hers.

His silly tone made Raelle smirk. She chuckled as she reciprocated his handshake. "Hello, Chrishtan, it's great to meet you as well." His hand felt strong, but kind.

"Perfect," he answered as he clapped his hands together and stood up. "Now, let's get a look at that injury on your back and see if we can't get it cleaned up to prevent infection. Plus, we don't want any more of those toxins slipping into your bloodstream."

Raelle nodded in agreement. As he walked away, she took a moment to admire his physique. He was tall and strong with each muscle in his arms having smooth, definition. The coarse hair covering his forearms matched the short brown beard that incased his face perfectly. She liked how his wavy brown hair hid the very tops of his ears. As he headed back in her direction, Raelle swiftly turned her head away. She felt embarrassed that she felt the need to eye him from head to toe.

Chrishtan returned with a small bowl of warm water and a rag. He mixed a substance from a small pouch into the water. "Okay, Raelle, now I know this may seem inappropriate, but seeing as you aren't able to reach the injury yourself, I'm going to have to clean it for you, if you don't mind."

"It's fine," Raelle said, nodding. "Whatever you need to do."

"All right." Chrishtan moved closer to her. "If you could just lift up your shirt, you can cover yourself with this blanket while I clean it."

Raelle nodded again before taking the blanket and covering her front. She pulled her arms through the sleeves of her brother's shirt, drawing it up and around her neck. She shivered as the chill of a cool breeze slid along the sticky blood of her injury.

"I'm ready. You may turn around now."

Chrishtan dipped the rag in the water and rung it out. "I'm sorry. This may hurt quite a bit, but we've got to get this clean."

"Its fine," Raelle sighed. "I believe I can manage."

As soon as the wet cloth touched her skin, goose bumps rose over her entire body. Chrishtan's touch was gentle as he moved the rag in small circles along the outside of the wounded area. It felt nice to have someone touch her, talk to her, be with her. She closed her eyes as he cleaned her back. Her eyes opened only when she heard his voice.

"Raelle," he said, pausing the circular motions on her back, "I'm going to clean your wound now. I'm really sorry, but this may hurt quite a bit."

Raelle put her head down in her arms and shut her eyes

tight. "Just do it. It needs to be done."

As the rag moved along the inside of her wounds, sharp pain surged through her back and shoulder. She bit down hard, pursing her lips together and covering her mouth with her fist.

"I'm nearly finished, Raelle. You've done quite well. I'm impressed!"

"Thank you." Raelle nodded. "I uh, I'm not sure what would've happened to me had you not shown up."

"Something you need not worry about." Chrishtan shook his head and shrugged. "It's like I said before, I wanted to help."

Chrishtan returned to the fire to stir the larger pot while Raelle carefully pulled her shirt back on under the blanket. It was then that she remembered her tiny pack of mutts. Since fainting back in the Emeralz Meadows, she had only been able to focus on her illness. She looked around frantically until she found Winston wandering the jungle floor, eating small patches of grass alongside Chrishtan's beautiful white stallion. Sasha and Pip's basket sat on the ground near the fire.

Chrishtan saw her eyeing it. "You know, I was going to let them out, but considering their vicious demeanor I experienced earlier, I thought perhaps you would like to let them out."

Raelle laughed. "Indeed." She played along. "Very scary, incredibly vicious. They have been known to kill large beasts with a single bite. It was they who saved me from the monster that gave me this injury."

They both laughed as Raelle opened the basket and the dogs jumped out. Sasha scurried over to Chrishtan and jumped into his lap.

"Well, hello there," Chrishtan greeted the brindle mutt. She stared up at him as if she might say something.

Raelle laughed. "She wants you to pet her. She'll take advantage of anyone who gives her pets or scraps."

Chrishtan scratched behind Sasha's ear. "I bet you like that, huh girl?" Sasha licked his hand, content to stay on her new friend's lap.

Pip, on the other hand, did not seem as sure of him as she cautiously sniffed around the area where they would sleep for the night. Raelle took the blanket from their basket and laid it out on the ground near the fire before doing the same with hers. She sat down on her blanket, still wrapped up in the one that Chrishtan had let her change under. As she sat across the fire from the handsome stranger, she took the opportunity to study the surrounding area. She hadn't the slightest idea where they were.

The last landscape she remembered was a never-ending ocean of rolling, green hills. Now, she found herself under a canopy of enormous colorful trees, some with trunks large enough to turn into a decent-sized house. Others stood so tall that she could not see their tops. The leaves of the trees were not green, but purple, run through with bright green veins. The ground was moist, as was the air she breathed. The remaining light left in the day was blocked out by the larger trees that made up the top of the canopy. Almost all of the smaller, normal-sized trees had flowering buds. More buds awakened the darker it became, ranging in colors from blue, yellow, and red, to pink and purple. Raelle also recognized more of the tendril laden trees that she encountered earlier. They immediately reminded her of her mission. She was now off the path that would lead her to the answers she so desperately needed.

"You seem perplexed." Chrishtan looked up at her while stirring his stew.

"I'm sorry," Raelle said, sighing. "I have a great deal on my mind."

"I see…" Chrishtan scooped the steaming hot, chunky contents of the pot into another small, wooden bowl. "Well, are you hungry? Do you think you might be able to keep some stew down?"

The stew smelled amazing. "Honestly, at this point I do

not care if I'm not able to keep it down. It's been far too long since I've eaten."

Chrishtan handed her the bowl. "Here you are, then. The best stew you will ever taste!"

Raelle smiled as he handed her the bowl. She brought it to her mouth and took a sip of the warm, savory contents. Chrishtan was right; it was the best stew she had ever tasted. Or maybe her starvation tricked her into believing it was. Nevertheless, it did not matter. For the first time in a week, she felt warmth, comfort, and satisfaction.

Chrishtan looked over at Raelle. "You seem to be enjoying your dinner."

Raelle nodded with a mouth full of stew.

Chrishtan looked down. "So, it seems like you've had a rough time. I don't want to pressure you in any way, but I would like to help you. Whatever you might be going through, I may be able to lead you in the right direction. Maybe you could tell me where you're from?" He tapped his foot as he waited for her response.

Raelle sighed, "I–I ugh… I want to tell you, I do, but I'm just not willing to take that risk right now. You just don't understand. It is so important that I continue on my journey alone. You just – look, you simply wouldn't understand…" She couldn't find the right words.

Chrishtan's eyes penetrated her. "You're right. I may not understand at this moment, but I would really like to, if you'd allow me. If you'll just give me a chance."

Raelle wanted so badly to tell him. She felt strangely comfortable with him, as if she already knew him. She felt drawn to him. She genuinely appreciated the way Chrishtan carried himself. His jokes made their situation feel more natural and less awkward. He seemed so carefree and friendly, how could she not allow him to grow on her? But at the same time, the overwhelming fear of making another mistake told her that she could no longer trust anyone or anything, no matter how inviting.

Raelle looked up at Chrishtan's wounded expression.

"I'm so sorry Chrishtan, I –"

She did not understand why it hurt her so deeply to deny his simple request. She wanted to pour her heart and soul out to him. Instead, she simply changed the subject.

"So what caused me to become so ill? How could that injury cause such a condition?"

Chrishtan sighed. "That wasn't just any creature that grabbed you, Raelle," he said. "It's known as a dranogite. For hundreds and thousands of years, they've preyed upon many creatures, from grazers, to people, and even armies of men. Their claws and saliva contain a poison that manifests in humans in the way you had experienced earlier. Dark mages and minions of the blackness have been known to use these creatures as weapons. Using lyre, they can be controlled very easily. However, they are very difficult to catch and extremely deadly. I am curious as to how you were able to survive your encounter with such a notorious beast."

I've only just barely begun to figure it out myself. How could I even begin to explain it to him? She evaded his inquisitive gaze. "I really do not know. Just lucky, I suppose."

Chrishtan laughed. "I hate to be the one to tell you this, but it takes quite a bit more than luck to get away from a dranogite once it has you in its sights."

Raelle shrugged her shoulders and shook her head. "I'm sorry Chrishtan, but that is the only explanation I have and the only one you're going to get. If you don't trust me, it's like I said before, you are free to go on your way and leave me be."

She turned away from him. *He just doesn't understand that I have no other choice. I cannot just tell him about my family. They were being hunted. And who knows what side he's on. I must keep my mission a secret.* At this point, everyone was a potential enemy that could compromise her mission.

She glanced back over at Chrishtan just as he walked around to the opposite side of the massive tree trunk and laid his blanket where Raelle could not see.

"I get it Raelle. I really do." Chrishtan walked behind the

tree where he had spread his blanket. "I think I had better call it a night. I have a long ride ahead of me in the morning. Hopefully I can lead you in the right direction once the sun comes up."

Raelle turned away from the sound of his voice and pulled her blanket over her. "Good night, Chrishtan."

Pip and Sasha found their way underneath Raelle's covers and snuggled against her. Their warm fur and bodies acted as small furnaces. Raelle sighed deeply. She hated the fact that she and her pack would have to leave their new companion and continue their mission to the Lantern Forest alone, but fear told her that she had no other choice. Raelle yawned before closing her eyes. At the moment, she felt safe enough to finally get some rest. But it was only a temporary result of her new and soon to be departed friend. It did not take long for her to fall asleep.

***

The chorus of wild creatures rustling in the trees disturbed her slumber. Raelle sensed that the sun would be coming up soon. She intended to leave before Chrishtan woke in order to avoid his attempts to convince her to stay. It would be much harder to say no again. It was best to leave without saying her goodbyes. The dogs were still very sleepy as she picked up the blanket with them inside and placed them in their basket. With all of her things quietly and quickly packed, she took the blanket that Chrishtan had loaned her, folded it up, and placed it on his pack. She mouthed a silent thank you and goodbye before tiptoeing out of the camp.

Raelle pulled out her map and studied it using what little moonlight that filtered through the canopy. Chrishtan had taken them northwest to a patchy area called the Emeralz Jungle. She could barely make out the glowing dot as it pulsed near the edge of the jungle canopy. It was still dark and the strange howling and shrill screeches that echoed through the treetops reminded her of the terrifying time she once spent in the dark woods just outside her family's safe zone. She felt chills down her spine as she recalled the disgusting smell of the creature that hunted her. After giving the map a second look, Raelle threw her leg over Winston's saddle and hoped that they were headed in the right direction.

**

Raelle had been riding for at least an hour with no sign of an exit. It was hard to see which way she was going on the map with the vast thickness of the giant canopy blocking any and all light. Raelle was lost. Her skills of navigation were not as strong as she thought. She had already lost enough time with Chrishtan. And she hated the fact that she had allowed herself to become so vulnerable. She had become dependent on a complete stranger. Raelle stopped at the base of a gigantic tree to wait for the light of day. She hoped that the sun would ascend over the enormous leafy awning at any moment, but her patience was wearing thin and her anxiety caused her heart rate to skyrocket. Raelle shivered. Without the warmth of Chrishtan's fire, she realized how cold it was.

A half an hour crept by as Raelle curled herself underneath her blanket. There was no sign of the sun, and she could not stand the cold any longer. It was too moist to find decent wood for a fire, so she used all the kindling from her pack. The friction of twine against a dry stick produced smoke that wafted up into Raelle's nose. Just the smell of smoke made her feel warmer. The smolder eventually turned to fire, and tiny flames engulfed the kindling. Raelle sat back against the tree trunk once more, holding her hands out in front of her to steal heat from the fire. The warmth made her eyes grow heavy.

Raelle drifted back into her dreamscape where she found herself trapped inside the nothingness. Once again, the tiny light floated into view. Raelle ran toward it just as before, only this time the light did not grow. Instead it seemed to shrink into the distance. As she ran forward, it felt as if she were moving backward. Raelle reached her hand out to pull herself toward the shrinking ball of light. She heard a voice trailing away from its glow. It was the same soft, feminine voice from before. As the light disappeared, more voices crowded in. They were different than before. They were devious.

Suddenly, Raelle found herself swallowed back into the black abyss. She saw nothing, heard nothing and felt as if the air had been sucked out of her lungs. She gasped to replenish them, but still they felt empty. Panic and terror took over Raelle's mind as she hit the floor. She stood trembling in the empty black void. She sensed something or someone was near. Somehow it casted a shadow in the midst of her pitch black surroundings

Raelle squinted at the shadowy figure. "Who's there? Who are you?" Her mouth opened, but no sound came out. Her voice echoed inside the confines of her own head. She closed her eyes for a moment, awaiting an answer, but heard nothing. Deep, hot breath like boiling steam scorched the back of her neck. Raelle stood completely frozen in horror. She jumped back as a pair of heavy, scorching hot hands grasped her shoulders. She screamed in agony inside her head. A startling voice growled inside her ear.

"We know you," it said. "We are close. You will allow. You belong…"

"Who are you?" Raelle demanded.

"It won't be long now…" the voice trailed off. A pair of red eyes without pupils met Raelle's. She gasped for air that was not there. Suddenly, a pair of large hands grasped around her neck, crushing her throat.

Raelle's eyes shot open to the sound of her own blood-curdling screams bouncing off the jungle's gargantuan tree trunks. Her legs dangled off the forest floor as an enormous black leathery hand in silver armor choked her against the trunk of a tree. The smell of the creature's gaping infectious wounds caused her stomach to churn, but her esophagus was in no condition to allow anything to exit. The monster glared at her with its snake-like eyes as its hot, putrid breath overwhelmed her.

How did it find me? Her mind reeled and raced. The foul creature's strength left her completely defenseless. *This is it,* Raelle thought. *This is how I die. By the hand of the same foul creature that murdered the rest of my family. I have failed.*

Suddenly, Raelle heard something zip through the air. As soon as she heard the sound, she saw it; a broad-head arrow penetrated directly through the abomination's throat. Warm liquid splattered onto her face just before the monster released and she fell to the ground. The furious creature let out a deep and ominous screech. It revealed inch-long canines on both its top and bottom jaws as it struggled to remove the arrow from its throat. Raelle crawled across the ground toward Winston as she struggled to breathe through her damaged esophagus.

She looked up when she heard a familiar voice call out.

"Hey! Over here, Raelle!"

She turned to see Chrishtan holding a bow in one hand while he waved with the other.

Once close enough, Raelle jumped up into Winston's saddle.

Chrishtan rode to her. "Go! Hurry!" he yelled. "We must go now! Run!"

He raised his bow and aimed directly at Raelle. An arrow zoomed past her into the beast that had just finished pulling the first one from its throat. The blood that exited the wound was almost black and looked coagulated. Chrishtan set fire to the next arrow and aimed again. As the fiery arrow struck, the grotesque creature let out a horrific, piercing cry. The blaze took over its entire body.

"Go, go, go!" Chrishtan hollered as he dug his heels into his white stallion.

They took off as fast as they could. Chrishtan pulled

ahead of Raelle before turning around.

"Raelle, you must follow me, or you may never make it out of here alive!"

CHAPTER 8
SECRETS

Deep red and purple vines smacked Raelle in the face as she and Winston pressed on after Chrishtan through the endless jungle maze. Once the sun rose high enough in the sky, Raelle could see the edge of the canopy. She and Chrishtan finally broke through the knotted plants and enormous trees into the sweeping fields of blue-green grass. Only this time, Raelle did not see a vast ocean of rolling hills. Instead she eyed a grand valley painted with purple and white flowers. In the center of the tranquil vale sat a spring filled with crystal clear water. From the west, a pristine creek trickled through the spring and out into the narrow mouth of a waterfall. Raelle had difficulty fathoming the spectacular sight as the crashing waterfall sent a mist into the air that when mixed with the scent of flowers was intoxicating. Groves of the familiar tendril-covered trees grew all around the north side of the sparkling blue spring. Raelle longed to feel the tranquility of the serene estuary. She and Chrishtan slowed their gallop as they came closer to the placid pool.

Chrishtan attempted to catch his breath. "Raelle, you have got to tell me who you are."

"I–I–I can't … I already told you … I—" Raelle stammered.

Chrishtan glared at her. "No, I don't think you quite understand! The Minotirr do not hunt just anyone. I don't think you realize the danger that you're in. You must tell me who you are if you wish to have any chance of surviving."

Raelle looked down, avoiding Chrishtan's penetrating stare. "What–what are Minotirr?"

It was the first time she ever heard him speak with a serious tone. "Something you do not want hunting you. Trust me…"

Raelle sighed and rolled her eyes. "All right. I can obviously see that. Just tell me what it is."

Chrishtan shook his head as he dismounted his white stag. He parted the curtain of branches near the edge of the spring. He calmly sat down against the tree and leaned against its trunk and expelled a long breath

"Look, Raelle, all I want is to help you. But I'm not going to fight with you. You are in serious danger." He threw his hands into the air. "But I can't help you unless you tell me what's going on."

Raelle wanted so badly to tell him, but still was not sure if she could trust him. On the other hand, she needed to know about the monster that hunted her. At this point, Chrishtan seemed just as exhausted and defeated as Raelle. She sensed that he genuinely wanted to help her, but she still did not trust her own sense of security. It had led her blindly into dangerous situations before, almost getting her killed. But at the same time, Chrishtan had been the one to save her life on two of these occasions. The dissonance drove her mad.

Raelle dismounted Winston, landing gently on the ground. She tried not to look at Chrishtan as she walked over to the basket that housed her two small dogs. As soon as she let them out, the dogs ran circles around one another in the gorgeous scenery as if they had not nearly lost their lives in the jungle. Raelle wished she too could forget the morning's horrific events. However, the scene continued to play unremittingly in her mind.

There was something else eating away at her—the dreams. It was the second time she had seen the light in the blackness. The first time, someone in the light had called out to her. She thought it was her mother trying to tell her something. She could barely remember the first dream. The second time, she had no trouble remembering the menacing voice in her ear or the scorching hands on her shoulders. Raelle placed a hand on her shoulder where it had grabbed her. She winced and pulled her shirt down to see a deep red burn covering her left deltoid. Raelle gasped at the enflamed handprint that branded her entire shoulder and finger prints that pressed into her collarbone. *But it was only a dream. How could it have left a mark?*

A friendly voice startled her.

"Interesting brand you have there. Still not in the mood to talk?" Chrishtan looked over at her as he unpacked his saddle bags.

Raelle quickly pulled her shirt back over her shoulder. "Uh–well– I uh–I don't know. It uh–must be from that Minotirr or whatever you call it."

Chrishtan walked back toward the shade of the trees with his belongings. "I've seen Minotirr do many things, but never anything like that."

Raelle knew that at this point she must seem tremendously suspicious to him. She had not told him a single thing about herself aside from her name, yet he still wanted to help her. She felt guilty and ashamed at acting just like her parents, keeping secrets and misleading him. She had already put him in so much danger while she gave him nothing in return. *Maybe, just maybe he could help me.* She shook the idea from her head. Remaining closed off was the only way to ensure that her mission would not be thwarted. Raelle walked back through the curtain of branches and stood in front of Chrishtan.

"You don't have to stay, you know. I appreciate what you've done for me, but I'll be fine now on my own."

Chrishtan winced and shook his head. "Yeah, you know what? I believe I may just do that. You clearly don't need my help escaping near death. You know, you have a very interesting way of showing gratitude to people who save your life."

Raelle felt awful. He was right. But she continued in her defense nonetheless. "Well, I'll just have to be more careful from here on out. I should be fine now that you've killed my stalker."

Chrishtan laughed. "Killed your stalker? I hate to tell you this, but I did not kill him. He'll be back. Trust me. And if not him, then something else. Something even more terrible."

Raelle looked away from Chrishtan's concerned gaze. "Well then, I suppose I will have to figure something out. But I will do it on my own. It's not up to you to save me. My journey is mine alone. Why do you care so much anyway?"

Chrishtan stood. "All right, if that is how you want it. Trust me, I understand completely. Which is part of the reason I care. But I am not just taking off. I plan to stay the night here. It is where I planned on stopping before I came upon you. So, if you'd like to stay and join me, you may. Unlike you, I don't mind a little company, even if it is an ungrateful, secretive, and strange young woman such as yourself."

Raelle watched him walk toward the water. For some reason, even as he struck a nerve in her, she could not take her eyes off him. Something about the way he moved drew her to him. She felt as if she were someone else. The Raelle she knew was a funny, considerate person who longed for the company of others. She knew this, but she also knew that her experiences had imprisoned that part of her. She could not let her tragic human need for companionship get in the way. Yet, she couldn't understand why he would not leave. *Why does he not hate me?* She tried so hard to push him away. This, she decided, would be her last night with the stranger. Tomorrow, she would regain her focus and continue on with her journey on her own. She walked casually over to the pool of water and stood next to Chrishtan.

"I truly am thankful for all that you've done for me, you know. It's just that things are incredibly complicated."

Chrishtan wiped the water from his eyes and looked up at her. It was hard not to stare at his attractive face. His unique lips shielded his white teeth perfectly. And his wavy brown hair gave him such character. She found beauty in his presence.

"I won't bother you anymore about it," Chrishtan said. "I'm sorry. I'm just very concerned for you. Let's forget about these things for a while. What do you say? I'll cook up some more stew, and then tomorrow you can be on your way."

Raelle smiled. "That sounds perfect."

Her eyes followed his every move as he walked away. It occurred to her that she had never really studied a man before. She had seen her father and brothers her whole life, but this was different. The mere sight of him caused her stomach to tingle. And for some reason, it made her smile inside. And even though it felt good, it also terrified her. These days, new feelings were not welcome. She prayed that this particular sensation would put up any easy fight.

Raelle eyed her reflection in the spring water and saw a stranger starring back at her. She hardly recognized herself. Her hair was greasy and tangled. Her arms were covered in dirt and specks of blood. She had worn thin from not eating. Then, she noticed something else. Deep bruises formed a ring around her neck where the Minotirr had strangled her against the tree. She was a wreck. Tears welled up in her eyes. She attempted to hold them in, but they streamed down her face nevertheless. She turned around to check if Chrishtan had seen her, but he hadn't. Raelle quietly made her way to the other side of the pool where she could bathe behind a grove of bushes.

With the sun hidden by the foliage that grew near the spring, Raelle could see tiny glowing fish swimming in the crisp water in front of her. But these were not like the fish in the valley. Their bioluminescent colors were spectacular. Raelle admired their splendor, as they seemed to chase away the tears from her eyes and the sorrow from her heart. Raelle leaned over to scoop water into her hands and splash it onto her sweaty face. She rubbed away the dirt and salty buildup as best she could. With her face somewhat clean, she carefully removed her brother's bloodstained shirt. She cringed as she pulled at the fabric where it stuck to her sticky and sore dranogite wounds.

Raelle removed her brother's pants and her undergarments before sticking a naked toe into the pool before wading into the cold water. She eyed her blurred reflection. She studied the curvature of her figure and wondered if it was attractive. The thought had never crossed her mind until now. It never needed to. *Do I only find Chrishtan attractive because he's the first man I've ever met? What does he think of me?* She could feel herself losing sight of her true mission. She forced herself to put away curiosities and focus on the task at hand.

Each step into the spring brought chilled water closer to Raelle's shoulders causing each and every follicle on her body to transform into a tiny bump. She held her breath before forcing her head under. Finally submerged, she rinsed her hair and body with the pristine water. She shivered as tiny fish gently pressed their lips against her legs, feet, and abdomen like tiny kisses. They too must have thought she needed to be cleaned. After adjusting to the temperature of the water, the bath felt refreshing. She closed her eyes as she dove under the water once more, slicking her long, auburn hair away from her face as she came up. She used her hands to wipe away the salty sweat, dirt, and dried blood that stained her body. As she washed away the physical evidence of her traumatic experiences of the past few days, she prayed that somehow it would rinse them from her mind as well.

With the sandy brown and dark red stains now dancing through the water instead of on her skin, Raelle exited the pool. She wrung the cool liquid contents from her hair as she stepped onto the grass. It did not take long for the heat of the warm summer sun to dry her newly clean olive skin.

Raelle dressed herself again in her brother's filthy blood stained pants and shirt before making her way out from behind the bushes. As she squeezed the remaining water from her hair, she saw Chrishtan running around the groves of trees like a madman. Then she saw her two dogs mimicking him as they chased him in a game of tag. The sight pleased Raelle, forcing her to chuckle under her breath. She was pleasantly surprised by how quickly they warmed up to him. Perhaps it was easier for them to let loose when they did not feel as if they needed to protect her. Raelle wished that her parents could have experienced that feeling. *Maybe they would still be alive. Maybe my life would be different if I hadn't needed protecting.* She knew that the dogs had an innate sense of who needed to be protected and who didn't. She could try and fool everyone else, but her furry companions would not be duped. Raelle envied them. It was her desire to warm up to Chrishtan as well, but it was too dangerous.

As Raelle walked into the peculiar scene, Chrishtan immediately stopped chasing the dogs and turned to face her.

"Well, hello there, stranger," he managed between pants. "I was beginning to think you had abandoned me to entertain these crazy mutts for good."

Raelle cracked a smile. "I'm sorry. I really needed to clean up."

Chrishtan hurried over to a large pot hanging over the fire, sniffed the aroma, and stirred it. "Don't worry about it. It's not a problem. It's not every day that I get the opportunity to be mauled by a miniature pack of canines."

Raelle humored him. "Well it's true, they are quite vicious and not to mention intimidating."

Chrishtan flashed a charming smile. "Feeling better, I see? I'm not sure I've heard you laugh or even seen you smile once before this."

Raelle looked down and walked toward the warm fire. "I'm just trying to make it through the rest of the day. I suppose if I'm stuck here with you, I might as well make the best of it, right?" She tried to match his tone.

Chrishtan shook his head and put more wood on top of the small flames. "Oh, I see how it is. You're just going to tolerate me? Well, good luck with that because I have been known to be a little overwhelming to some. I can't help it. It's just the way I am."

Raelle could tell by the smirk on his face that he was not even going to attempt to be serious. His ironic sense of humor thrilled her. He made her laugh. She missed being able to laugh. It had been a long time since she had done so. The way he walked, the way he smiled at her, and his uncanny sense of humor slowly pulled her in. She tried to fight it with every ounce of her being, but the new feelings exhilarated her. He was far too good to be true. He had to be.

Chrishtan popped up from his squatted position. "Well, it looks like dinner is ready to be served. I hope you're hungry. I personally hunted down the darix that is in this stew, and I must say, I am pretty proud of myself." He winked at Raelle to express the ironic nature of the pompous statement.

Raelle sat on a log near the fire. "This had better be good then. We wouldn't want anything to tarnish your remarkable reputation."

Chrishtan filled wooden bowls to the brim with the steaming stew. The dogs inhaled their food, savoring none of it. They licked their bowls clean before Raelle took her first bite. Once the stew entered her mouth, she closed her eyes and savored every morsel. It had been quite some time since she had enjoyed a meal. The stew tasted delicious. Even though Chrishtan had been joking about his excellent hunting and cooking skills, there was a lot of truth to his facetious boasting. It was the best stew Raelle had ever tasted. It melted in her mouth with each bite.

"I cannot lie, Chrishtan, this stew is very good. So, what exactly is this *darix* you speak of?"

Chrishtan laughed and looked at her as if she were a small child asking a silly question. "*What* is a *darix*, you ask? Are you being serious? All right, where are you from? Because everyone knows what a darix is. You must have seen one out in the Rolling Emeralz? You know, the big animals with the long legs and the spikes on their back? You can't miss them."

Raelle's cheeks felt warm. "Oh… uh… yes. Yes, I know what you're talking about. They are very interesting creatures indeed."

Chrishtan looked at her, puzzled. "Yes, very *interesting*. So, where *are* you from, really?"

Raelle knew this was coming. She felt like an idiot for asking about the darix. *Of course it would give me away.* She was angry with herself for being so naive. She immediately shoved an enormous helping of stew into her mouth. "A vaaw in daat di-re-tun."

Chrishtan stared at her and raised an eyebrow. "What was that? I couldn't quite make out what you were saying with all that food in your mouth. Were you telling me where you're from?"

Raelle swallowed her food, her cheeks burning with embarrassment. "Yes, uh, I said a valley. I'm from a valley in that direction."

"A valley, you say? All right, that really narrows it down. Thank you for that clarification. I feel like I know you so much better now. Well, I guess I can leave now that I have this closure. I have no further questions."

Raelle no longer had the desire to finish her food. Her stomach churned as her muscles tensed up from holding everything inside. She wanted to throw things and yell at this meddlesome man who filled her with even more confusion.

"I'm sorry, Raelle. It's just that I can't get anything out of you. You genuinely interest me and I know nothing about you. I would love the chance to get to know you, considering we have already been through so much together."

Raelle strained to speak, "I can leave, right now. And you won't have to trouble yourself over my identity or my situation any longer." She stood up and walked toward her things.

Chrishtan stood and gently grabbed her arm. "Please, please don't leave. I'm sorry. I know I can be overzealous. And I've been known to be a little impatient. Please, stay here tonight and I promise I won't ask any more questions. I know that there must be a good reason as to why you can't tell me. And I will leave it at that. I know that I don't know you, but I trust you. I just want you to know that."

Raelle did not turn to face him. Instead, she hung her head toward the ground as the tears came. "Its fine," Raelle sniffled. She wiped her wet cheek before turning around to face him. "I would tell you if I could. But I really can't. And I am sorry for being such a burden."

Chrishtan put his hands on her shoulders. "You are not a burden to me, Raelle. You have simply kept me on my toes. It gets lonely out here, roaming around on my own. You've provided me with a wonderful distraction and plenty of entertainment." He smiled. "Trust me, I know what it's like to have to keep secrets."

Chrishtan had a way of making Raelle feel so comfortable, like they were not strangers at all. But she knew this was only her mind tricking her into letting her guard down.

Raelle pulled away and walked back toward the fire. "I suppose that everyone has their secrets."

She could hear the defeat in Chrishtan's voice. "Yes, I suppose you're right."

The glow in his eyes faded. No smile followed his remark. She never intended to hurt him. After all, he had done so much for her. But she could not help it. She felt horrible. Raelle had in one moment caused the positive essence that once surrounded Chrishtan to fade away into nothing.

Raelle sat back down on the log and Pip jumped onto her lap. Her long wet tongue ran up and down Raelle's face, turning Raelle's scowl into a half smile. She stroked Pip's soft, fluffy, black fur. When Raelle looked back up,

Chrishtan was no longer there. Guilt took hold of her. Her cold demeanor had chased him away. She noticed that his horse and belongings were still in their original positions. *Hopefully, he hasn't been scooped up by a dranogite.* The thought made her shiver. She could feel her heart beating faster. She tried to stay calm. *How will I ever make it on my own if my fear is so easily provoked?*

Frustration and confusion dominated her mind. Her current cynical and reticent state was taking a serious toll on her mind and body. She wanted so badly to get it all off her chest. *Maybe Chrishtan could help. No, it is too dangerous.* She hated all of the negative feelings that flowed through her day in and day out. So many traumas plagued her existence that she could no longer tell the difference between her internal pain and her external injuries. She was completely broken.

Startled by the sound of something in the distance, Raelle looked back to see a shadow coming toward her. She squinted to get a better look. But by the time she had finished her squinting game, Chrishtan showed himself in front of the warm fire. He held an enormous pile of branches. She felt relieved to see him, and not something else.

"Are you planning on staying up all night?" Raelle asked.

Chrishtan dumped the wood near the log where she sat. The sound of branches crashing to the ground startled her. "Actually, I may. Would you care to join me?"

Raelle tilted her head. "All night? I really should get some sleep. I haven't been sleeping much lately."

Chrishtan pulled a green glass bottle form his pack and sat down on the log next to Raelle. "Yes, I suppose you must be very tired. But, I tell you what, I have this bottle of Tiznic that I was lucky enough to have gifted to me by a friend. I was hoping that maybe you would do me the honor of helping me drink it."

Raelle had no clue what Tiznic was, but she was not about to ask. She owed it to Chrishtan to humor him and drink the fluid. After all, he had saved her life twice already.

Chrishtan opened the ornate bottle and poured two bowls of the green liquid before Raelle could agree to his proposal.

"Here you are, Milady." Chrishtan said as he grinned.

Raelle nodded. "Thank you, kind sir."

"You are very welcome. So, shall we make a toast?" Chrishtan raised his wooden bowl.

Raelle cracked a half smile. "To what exactly?"

"To anything you'd like." Chrishtan still held his cup high.

"All right," Raelle hesitantly raised her bowl. "How about to *you* saving my life, twice?"

Chrishtan smiled. "Yes, I believe I can toast to that. To Raelle's ability to find trouble."

Raelle raised her cup higher to match Chrishtan's. "To *your* ability to find *me*."

They hit their bowls together and downed the brilliant green liquid. After the words escaped her mouth, she held her breath and looked down. Raelle still was not sure what she had meant by her toast, but she knew it had to mean something. It was completely unfamiliar. She would keep it to herself, along with her other secrets.

CHAPTER 9
THE VOID

The exquisite surroundings of their peaceful campsite engulfed Raelle's heightened senses. The undulating spring reflected the soft glow of firelight onto their faces. The faint sound of water cascading over the cliff's edge eased Raelle's wavering mind. Small insects hummed along with the rhythm of rustling grass. The ambiance deepened the unfamiliar feelings that Chrishtan evoked in her. And each sip of the green liquid appeared to chase away her inhibitions. The more she and Chrishtan talked, the more intense her laughter grew. She felt light and silly, only this time she welcomed the mood. It was as if nothing else mattered outside of her and Chrishtan's banter.

"I'm really glad I got to share this drink with you." Chrishtan laughed. "I was afraid I was going to have to drink it all by myself. All alone, just me and this beautiful bottle."

As the words escaped him, Chrishtan's demeanor changed. His eyes seemed to swell with liquid before he abruptly stood and headed over to the woodpile.

"We're losing heat," Chrishtan said as he threw more branches on the fire. A grin returned to his face as the firelight illuminated his glossy blue eyes.

Raelle could tell he was holding something back, but she obliged him anyway. "Thank you, sir. You are an incredibly gracious host."

Chrishtan reached down and took a lengthy swig of the intoxicating green liquid. The bottle was almost empty. He handed what was left to Raelle.

"Milady, you may have the pleasure of finishing our night off."

In spite of the fact that she already felt far outside her

element, Raelle drank the last sips from the bottle. She closed her eyes and pressed the green glass to her lips. It tasted incredible, like nothing she had ever drunk before. Raelle handed the empty flask back to Chrishtan.

"Thank you for sharing your gift with me. I rather enjoyed it."

Chrishtan took the bottle and held it up in the light of the fire. "Great stuff, isn't it? It's so hard to find nowadays. I mean, when is the last time you've even seen it?"

Of course, Raelle had *never* seen it. She pretended to know exactly what he was talking about, "Oh, yes, I can't even remember. It's–it's been quite some time." She forced a laugh. Her cheeks burned at the thought of Chrishtan catching her in a lie.

Chrishtan looked at her as if he could sense her insecurity. "I miss this."

Raelle heard the deep sentiment in his voice. "What do you mean?"

Chrishtan gazed out into the twinkling night sky. "I miss being able to admire the stars in the company of someone, a friend." He turned his gaze toward Raelle. "It's been so long since I've been able to spend time like this. This night with you is the first time in many a moon that I have genuinely enjoyed, and felt comfort."

Raelle watched as his eyes begin to swell once more. "I know how you feel," she admitted. "It's been quite some time for me as well."

Chrishtan nodded. "I know. I can tell. There aren't many of us out here. Although I don't know where you come from or who you are, what I do know is that you and I are more alike than you might like to believe."

Raelle looked disturbed. "How? How do you know?"

Chrishtan managed a somber smile. "I just do."

Raelle wanted to pry and find out more, but her fear told her it was too risky. *I must keep my secret. No matter what he thinks he knows. He has no idea.* Chrishtan had his back to Raelle when she felt it. She was overcome with dizziness, as though she were falling in spite of the fact that she sat on the log with her feet planted firmly on the ground. The strange sensation had dwelled within her since her first cup of Tiznic and only intensified with every drink thereafter. As Raelle closed her eyes she spun faster, but she did not care. She felt free. Her eyes rolled backward and the falling sensation became more intense.

At once, her eyes burst open to find herself plummeting through a terrifying familiar black abyss. It was no longer the peculiar feeling she had experienced moments earlier. She tried to scream as she plunged through the void. She knew what dwelled within its midst. It had left its signature on her shoulders. Raelle's attempt to take in air to fuel her second scream that left her breathless. She pursed her lips together and closed her eyes tight until she stopped abruptly, suspended on her back in the nothingness.

With her eyes still closed, she reached for a floor. But there was no floor, no light, no walls, only the blackness. Panic took hold of her. Her empty breaths drew closer together as the extreme beating of her heart prompted an excruciating throb in her temples. The throbbing pace quickly evolved into a brutal thumping that felt as if her head would explode at any moment. Raelle screamed in agony inside the prison in her mind. Her eyes shot open as her body hit a floor with intense force. Her face smashed against the abnormally smooth surface. It alarmed her how the black nothingness mimicked a solid surface. A warm sensation trickled into the crevice between her pursed lips. Her tongue caught a metallic taste, reminding her that she was still alive. As she slowly sat up, Raelle wiped the blood from her mouth. She squinted in an attempt to see something, anything, but it only made her head throb more.

She sat with her eyes closed in an attempt to organize her thoughts. But they clashed together in a manic riot as they violently racked her skull. She was so overcome with terror that she could think of nothing else. She needed to escape. She had been starving for air for what seemed like an eternity. The emptiness engulfed her very existence, devoid of all emotion and physiological energy. As if she were nothing, no one. She did not exist.

Raelle's trembling knees caused her to lose her footing as she made her way blindly through the nothingness. After what seemed like hours, a speck of light penetrated the darkness. It looked just as far away as the flickering stars that decorated a night sky. Raelle walked toward the tiny ball of light. It grew in size with each step. Raelle heard something. She paused to listen to the whispers. They reminded her that she had seen this light before. Her pace quickened to a dead run. She was finally able make out her feet in the light as they moved like a flash across the nothingness. As she reached her destination, air flowed back into her lungs. The whispers faded away and Raelle heard a familiar voice inside the light. Emotions, energy, and life surged back into her body. Raelle reached out her hand to touch the silhouette within the light. *This is it. I'm finally going into the light. I'm home.*

It hit her like an explosion. Raelle flew backward as if a bomb had gone off at her feet. Her ears rang with intensity, inviting the painful throbbing back into her skull. It was all she could hear. Her breath had been knocked out of her like a hefty punch to the gut. Nausea ensued and liquid exited through her mouth. She opened her eyes, but it looked as if they were not open at all. The blackness engulfed her once again as her stomach continued to force out all that made her alive. Completely empty, once more. She could not scream, and she could not cry. The emptiness inside of her did not know how. It only knew nothingness, darkness, oblivion.

Raelle bent her neck backward in excruciating pain. With her mouth facing what should have been the sky, Raelle screamed a deathly scream that she did not recognize as her own. Agony surged through her like lightning as a pair of large, black sinister hands grasped her lower thighs. Her captor's ominous silhouette could be seen in the dim light of its scorching hot palms as they branded into her thighs. The animalistic voice silenced her screams, whispering in her ear in a language she had once heard, but did not understand. The heat radiating from its steaming hot breath singed her earlobe. Raelle was paralyzed. She could not escape it. The menacing voice grew louder with each threat and demand. Raelle pressed her eyelids tight; it was all she could do. She tried to find that place with the light, in her mind. She had to go there. As she envisioned it, she reached out. She was there. The startling sound of bloodcurdling screams woke her from her nightmare. Raelle opened her eyes to Chrishtan's panicked face, calling her name over her deafening screams.

"Raelle! Raelle, please! Raelle!"

Raelle shot up, bumping heads with Chrishtan. "What— what happened? Please, tell me what's happening?"

Chrishtan gently squeezed her arms. "Calm down, calm down. You're going to be all right. I'm here. You need to try to relax. We're going to figure this out."

Tears streamed down Raelle's frightened face. "Figure what out? What happened? Where did I go?"

Chrishtan placed his hand on her cheek. "I don't know. You were right here. You didn't go anywhere. I was looking at the stars when I heard something hit the ground. You fell off of the log and started convulsing. At one point you stopped breathing, and I tried to revive you. I had almost given up hope when you finally gasped. After that I still couldn't wake you. The sounds you were making did not sound human. That went on for at least fifteen minutes. Then, just before you woke, you started screaming." Chrishtan looked down at Raelle's thighs. "Then... this happened."

Raelle's pants were burned. It was then that she realized how badly her thighs hurt. Raelle frantically ripped away the burned material. Two more handprints like the ones on her shoulders emblazoned her legs. Forgetting that Chrishtan was there, Raelle pulled her shirt down to reveal one of her shoulders and the matching brand that it bore.

CHAPTER 10
TURNING

The lifeless hole inside her did not replenish when she woke, as if part of her was still trapped within her nightmare. Raelle's soul writhed inside her as she struggled to hold on to consciousness. It felt as if her energy, her lyre, and her life were being stripped away from her very being. Much too weak and dizzy to sit up, Raelle slumped against the log.

"Raelle," Chrishtan called to her. "Please, please don't leave us, come on –"

She could barely speak. "Chrishtan… what… leave? Go where?" Her voice trailed off.

"I–I think you're being turned. Please, try not to sleep. You must stay awake."

Raelle forced her eyes open once more. "Turned?" Her voice was nothing more than a whisper.

Chrishtan swallowed hard. "It is something I learned about once a long time ago in my teachings. I have only seen a turned individual once before. I don't know much, but what I do know is that a person can be turned wraith using the Destroyer's dark energy. There are a number of different ways that a person can be turned. I can't recall exactly what they are. I was very young when my mentor taught me, but once you've been turned you could become a minion of the blackness."

Her eyes grew twice their normal size. "What?" She coughed. "But how—why—wha—what are you talking about?" Raelle used up her remaining energy to muster her distress.

Chrishtan looked frustrated and overwhelmed. "Do you have a mirror, anything reflective?"

Raelle's hand trembled as she pointed to her pack beneath the tree. Chrishtan rushed over and rummaged through its contents. He pulled out an ornate mirror before running back to her.

"Look." Chrishtan turned the reflective side of the mirror toward Raelle.

She gasped at the reflection that looked nothing like the young woman she had seen in the spring hours earlier. In its place was a sickly and pale young woman covered in bulging, purple veins that ran though her virtually translucent skin. The pupils of her once green eyes had grown so large that only a thin ring of new ghostly grey irises could be seen. A look of terror crept over Raelle's face. She hyperventilated as she gazed down at the protruding veins covering her arm.

The beautiful ring Raelle wore on her left ring finger caught Chrishtan's eye. He studied it before watching Raelle's head drop back against the log. "Where did you get this ring Raelle?"

Raelle did not respond. She could not respond.

"Raelle, please," Chrishtan repeated. "How did you get this ring?" He gently shook her. "You must tell me about this ring."

Raelle's eyes fluttered open as a faint whisper slipped from her lips. "I–I–It was a gift," she lied.

Chrishtan's patience waned. "A gift from whom? Who gave this to you?"

Raelle lied once more. "A friend, a friend gave it to me." Her voice grew raspier with each word.

Chrishtan shook his head. "Raelle, I need you to be honest with me. You are going to turn if you do not let me in. We need to get you help. But I don't know who you are, where you are from, or how to help you. Please, I want so badly to help you. Trust me, to become a phantom, a minion of the darkness, is much worse than death. I don't know how you came upon this ring, but it could have something to do with your condition. Please, Raelle, allow me to help."

Raelle strained to speak. "Map... there–there is a m–

map—" She pointed back at her pack once more. "Box… inside… wooden…"

***

Chrishtan rummaged through her pack. Inside the ornate box, he found a rolled up map and what looked like a letter. As he studied them, his thoughts were interrupted by the sound of Raelle moaning in pain. He quickly pulled out the map and shut the box before rushing to her side.

"I've got the map." He opened it. "Where do we need to go? Where are you trying to get to?"

Raelle's shaky finger pointed to the Lantern Forest. "Lady… of… the… Realm," she managed to push out.

Chrishtan nodded.

"All right," Chrishtan said. "We need to leave now. I don't know how long you have with these handprints on your body and the process so far along."

Raelle's trembling hand grazed the branding on her shoulder. The touch seemed to send excruciating pain surging through her extremities. Chrishtan watched as her irises turned red for a moment, then back to the ghostly grey. A tear glided over Raelle's cheek and down her face.

Chrishtan shuddered at seeing the sheer helplessness in Raelle's expression. She needed him, and he wanted to take care of her more than anything. He was not sure how, but something inside him told him that his sole mission from here on out was to help her. Chrishtan knew exactly what this meant, and it sent shivers down his spine. It meant that he would have to remember. He would have to try to recollect things from before, things he had worked so hard and so long to forget. But he had no other choice if he wanted to save her.

Chrishtan drug his feet toward his pack and opened the flap to a square compartment. He gingerly removed a thick black book covered in ornate markings similar the ones on Raelle's box. The leather-bound book looked dusty and unused. Chrishtan brushed the filth from the cover, exposing an intricate metallic symbol with a glowing prism in the center. Once his hand left the cover, the prism's light faded away into the black leather cover. He thumbed through hundreds of pages until he came upon a heading marked with five handprints, one on each corner of the page, and one in the center. On the page directly opposite sat an image of an anatomical man with his arms and legs spread. Each shoulder and each leg was branded with a handprint. In middle of the man's chest sat an even larger handprint.

The top of the page read: *Tonitin – Viat Penitarin isk Contisan Bitrim Ralmari.*

Chrishtan translated the text written in a different language than he and Raelle spoke, "Turning, Through Penetration of Consciousness between Realms." He interpreted the text that followed aloud:

In order to be turned through penetration of consciousness inside the space between realms, also known as the Verge, a blood relative of the Lyre must be willing to make the ultimate sacrifice. This will fill in the gap between realms. To do this, a Lyre-blood mage must pledge a sacred commitment to the Destroyer. Without Lyre, it is impossible to bridge the gap between realms. The two realms that one must fall between are of the living (the Light) and the eternally dead (the Void of Blackness).

Chrishtan moved down to the next heading: *Virtom ek fut Lyre.*

Victim does not possess Lyre —If the turnee does not possess Lyre, it can prove difficult to turn them. First, the turnee must possess an object given to them by the Lyre blood turner and must contain a portion of the turner's soul (see soul severing). This object must be worn by or have direct physical contact with the turnee, such as a gemstone, trinket, or clothing. The state of the turnee must be docile and vulnerable, and may require that the turning be done while the turnee sleeps. This ensures that consciousness and awareness do not interfere with or block the connection between the two realms within the Verge.

Chrishtan moved onto the next heading, *Virtom fut Lyre:*

Victim Posses Lyre —If the victim also possesses *Lyre*, their *body-Lyre* connection must be completely open (see *opening Lyre connection*). This enables the turner to anonymously connect with the turnee. This connection, in most cases, is made not only through blood relation, but through the victim's gemstone. Once the gemstone and mage touch, their *Lyre* connection is open. With the *Lyre* connection open, their consciousness can be altered at almost any time. However, turning is most successful when the state of the turnee is docile and vulnerable, and may need to take place while the turnee sleeps or is sleep deprived. This ensures that consciousness and awareness do not interfere with or block the connection of the two realms within the *Verge*.

Chrishtan moved on to the text preceded by the anatomical man, *Ire Fint Trom Hoorfir*.

The Five Torrid Hands —The turning process requires direct contact with the Destroyer, and or one of his demons. Once the victim has received the first set of torrid hands by a demon, the turning process begins to take place. *Torrid Hands* deliver a demonic poison into the body and soul of the victim. With each torrid hand, the poison gradually traps the parts of the victim's soul in the blackness of the Void while their physical body remains in the living world. The turning process requires five *Torrid Hands* to be complete: two above the heart, two below, and one in the center of the chest perpendicular to the heart. The final hand is branded by the Destroyer himself. Then, and only then can the victim's soul completely pass over into the black realm of the Void, whilst still physically residing within the realm of the living world of Lerim. Once fully turned, the victim is neither living nor dead, and is subject to the bidding of the Destroyer and his demons. Lastly, those victims who do not complete the turning process will inevitably die. However, they will not go into the light. Instead, their souls become trapped in the blackness of the Void for all of eternity.

Chrishtan slammed the book closed, coming to terms with the fact that he did not know enough about the phenomenon to help Raelle on his own. *If only I had kept my promise to my mentor.* The only way he could help at this point was to temporarily close the connection between Raelle and her perpetrator. Frustrated that he knew nothing about her, Chrishtan shoved the book back into his pack before pressing his hands into his face and pulling back on his hair. He had no idea who would want to turn her, or why someone of her own blood would do this to her. But he had no time to waste figuring it out as Raelle's labored breathing and sporadic choking reinstated his sense of urgency.

Chrishtan sighed as he watched Raelle fading in and out of consciousness. Unsure whether she possessed Lyre or not, Chrishtan decided to part her from any object or Lyre gemstone that could potentially harm her. He immediately remembered the ring and extracted the striking jewelry from her hand. He had no problem slipping it from her emaciated finger. He took a moment to study the striking object before placing it in the box he found in Raelle's pack.

As he searched Raelle for other objects, he recalled what the book said about clothing. He closed his eyes and turned away to remove her shirt and pants. It was not his intention to disrespect her, but he could not afford to take any chances. Raelle's naked body shivered in the chill of the night. Her lips turned purple, and Chrishtan felt her skin turn cold. He wrapped her in a blanket, picked her up, and laid her next to the fire. He rubbed her arms outside of the blanket in an attempt to warm her. Raelle's two small dogs rushed the stranger who stroked their master. But once the condition of their owner became clear, they offered their help. Pip licked Raelle's face while Sasha curled up in her lap.

While the dogs watched over Raelle, Chrishtan packed up their belongings. He saddled both horses and tied Winston's reins to his stunning white stallion, Boone. Once finished packing, he dressed Raelle in his spare clothes, which were much too big for her, before wrapping her back up in her blanket.

With the dogs safe in their basket and the horses all set, Chrishtan scooped Raelle up in his powerful arms and carried her to his horse. With incredible ease, he lifted Raelle's limp body and sat her up in a proper riding position in Boone's saddle. He followed right behind. With Raelle safely propped in one arm, he reached for her map with the other. With both arms around her, he unrolled the map to find that the glowing dot in their location had disappeared. He knew it had been her mark on the map. *She does possess Lyre.*

It was not that long ago that he too possessed a similar map. The familiar sight prompted a flood gate of suppressed memories to burst open. The intense guilt of his past hit him like a slap to the face as flashbacks of his childhood enveloped his anxious mind.

CHAPTER 11
CHRISHTAN

Soft candlelight of the palace bedroom glowed inside the small boy's striking blue eyes as they swelled with tears that crept down his soft tan cheeks. "I don't want to go, Mother. I want to stay here with you and Father. Please don't make me go, Mother, please."

Queen Jeanahn's kind chestnut eyes mirrored her son's glossy gaze as she sat down on her bed. "Chrishtan, we have no other choice. You must go with Framin. It is no longer safe for you here. He will take good care of you as he always has. And when the time is right, your father and I will come to you, and we'll be together once more."

Chrishtan smoothed his hands over his mother's silky brown hair where it covered her ears. "But, Mother, please, I can help. I want to stay and fight. I can help you and Father, and the kingdom." Tears rolled down Chrishtan's face and dripped onto the floor.

Queen Jeanahn forced a smile as she gently tucked her son's wavy brown hair behind his ear. "You are very strong and I have no doubt that one day you will be an amazing warrior, but right now you are only a boy of ten years and have much learning to do. You cannot do that here, with enemies closing in on our doorstep. I know this must be hard to understand now, but this is the only way to ensure that you are safe and that our legacy lives on. It is the only way that you can become the brave, good, mighty warrior and king I know you were meant to be."

"No, Mother!" Chrishtan cried. "I do not understand, and I will not go. I will stay here with you and fight. I am no longer a small child. I can do this." His tears grew faster. "I will miss you too much. I don't want to leave you and Father. I don't want to miss my new baby brother or sister." Chrishtan embraced his mother, nestling his head in her large, pregnant belly.

His mother held him tight, allowing the tears to run freely from her eyes. "I know, my prince. I will miss you too, more than you know. You are my everything. And I know how badly you want to meet your new baby brother or sister, and you will. Once we make sure our kingdom is safe, we will be together again, all of us with the new baby. But first, your father and I have things we must sort out. It is better that you and Framin go on ahead of us."

Chrishtan pleaded one last time. "But, Father is the ruler of this nation. Why can he not tell them that we do not wish to be with them? Why can he not tell them that the nation of Abequa does not fight for the Destroyer? Why can he not tell them that we wish to be left alone?"

Queen Jeanahn sighed and looked down at her son, her long hair falling into his face. "One day, my son, you will learn that things are not that simple, though it would be a better world if it were. Your father must first negotiate with King Lochran to save our nation, and when this is finished, we will be together again. You know what King Lochran is and what he will do if he finds you. Lyre children are no longer safe, especially those of royal bloodlines. This is why you must promise me that you will go with Framin so that you will be safe, and I will come to be with you as soon as I am able, after the baby arrives."

Chrishtan pushed the words out with apprehension. "Yes, Mother, I will go, and I will wait for you. I will wait for you and the baby." He quietly walked out of his parents' chambers and into the hall where his mentor, Framin, waited for him.

Just as every young mage had done before him, Chrishtan had trained with his mentor since the age of five. In that duration, Chrishtan had spent more time with him than anyone else. Framin was to teach Chrishtan the ways of the Lyre and how to become a great warrior and king. Framin had also trained Chrishtan's father. Framin was old enough to be Chrishtan's grandfather, and he thought of him as such.

"I am very sorry, Chrishtan." Framin placed his hand on the boy's shoulder. "Please, you must understand. They are doing this for you, for your safety." Framin followed as Chrishtan headed inside his bed chamber without acknowledging him. "It is the best thing for you right now."

"I know, Framin, I know. Mother has already told me. I told her that I would go with you. But I am only going because she wants me to go, and she is going to come and get me when things are safe again. You'll see. We won't be gone very long at all, will we, Framin?"

Framin smiled. "That is right, Chrishtan. We will be with your family again soon enough. But as you know, we must leave tonight if we are to make it far enough before the arrival of the Huronians."

Chrishtan humored his mentor. "Right, right, *Huronians*."

Framin turned to leave the room. "We leave at nightfall, young prince."

Chrishtan put his head down. "*We leave at nightfall.*"

***

With nightfall less than an hour away, fear bombarded Chrishtan's mind. He had never been away from his family overnight before, let alone for an extended and unknown period of time. He was the son of the king, after all, and believed his rightful place to be beside him.

A slight rapping at his door drew Chrishtan's gaze to the arched entryway of his chamber. "Chrishtan," Queen Jeanahn spoke in a tender voice, "are you ready, my love?"

"Yes, Mother," Chrishtan nodded. "I suppose I'm as ready as I can be."

Queen Jeanahn smiled. "That's a good boy. You are so brave Chrishtan and so strong. I am so proud of you. You will make a great king one day, and an even more amazing warrior."

92

To Chrishtan, the idea of having to leave his kingdom was a clear contradiction to ever becoming a great king for his people. He attempted to hide his disappointment. "Thank you, Mother. All I do is for you."

Queen Jeanahn rushed to hold her son. "I know that, my beautiful son, and I am so thankful for your love and devotion to me and your father." She pulled him in as close as she could to her pregnant belly. "You, my son, are the reason I live. The reason I breathe. You are my everything. You will be forever strong, wonderful, and great, no matter what lies ahead." She lifted his chin so that his gaze met hers. "Promise me that you will never, ever forget that. No matter how hard things get. Even when all hope seems lost, promise me." Her smile did not easily mask the sadness behind her eyes as a tear rolled down her cheek and fell onto her son's arm.

The wet sensation of his mother's tear on his skin triggered a deep despair. "I won't, Mother, I promise. I love you so much." Chrishtan backed away as he gazed into his mother's eyes with uncertainty. "I will see you again, Mother, won't I? Won't I?"

Queen Jeanahn wiped the tears from her face, and smiled. "Of course you will, my love. One day, no matter what, we will be together again, I promise. And always know in your heart that no matter where you are, I will be right here, always." She placed Chrishtan's hand over his heart, and then to his head. "Here, I will remain with you forever and ever, until the end of time."

Chrishtan wiped what tears still lingered on his cheeks as he nodded in agreement. He sniffed the last bit of fluid back into his nose just before Framin walked into the room.

"Are you ready, my young king?" Framin bowed.

Chrishtan nodded to signal *yes*.

Queen Jeanahn nodded toward Chrishtan's mentor. "Let us go meet your father, then. He will guide you both to the woods." She placed her hands on her son's shoulders and guided him through the doorway with his belongings.

Chrishtan's father, King Sonee, met them at the stables wearing a black hooded cloak. On either side of him stood two saddled and packed horses. One was a tall brown mare, and the other a brilliant white stallion that Chrishtan knew to be his father's horse, Boone. As Chrishtan entered the stable, his father stopped him before placing an ornately decorated ring with red gemstones inside his son's palm.

"I wish you to have this, my son."

Chrishtan nodded as he squeezed the ring tightly in his small hand.

King Sonee was a tall man and so squatted down to his son's level to look him in the eyes. "This is the Lyre harness ring of a very powerful mage warrior, your grandfather. In your training, my son, you will learn to harness all of the power and will of your Lyre, and when you do, this ring will be a perfect fit. For now, wear it as you learn and as you grow into it. With each new day and each year, and every bit of knowledge and skill you acquire, you will grow not only in age and size, but in wisdom as well. Keep it close, keep it safe, and never forget where you come from. You are my son. You are my world. Of that, I am sure. One day, this will all make sense. But until that time, stay strong and most of all, vigilant. Listen to your mentor, hang on his every word and teaching. And most of all, my young king, do not ever give up hope."

Chrishtan stared deep into his father's blue eyes, but said nothing. King Sonee's message overwhelmed him. The only thing Chrishtan was able to discern from what his father had said was that he had a great deal to live up to. The pressure of it all began to crush him, as if he held the weight of the world on his young shoulders. King Sonee wrapped his arms around his son, embracing him with a force that Chrishtan knew meant that his father loved him very much. Once the hug ended, Chrishtan slowly backed away from his father the king, nodding in promise and reverence to him.

King Sonee turned to Framin and handed him an extravagantly decorated wooden box.

"Inside, you will find the map. You know where to go. If things go as planned, we will meet you there in less than one month's time, depending on when the baby arrives. There may be others there as well, but I'm not sure how many have already fallen. It is pertinent that this map stay hidden and does not fall into the wrong hands. I'm sure you understand this, Framin." The king embraced his son's mentor and patted him on the back. "Good luck, my friend, and thank you for all that you have done and continue to do for our family."

As the King backed away, Queen Jeanahn approached Framin, holding him in her arms and closing her eyes tight. "Thank you, my friend, thank you so much." Jeanahn let go and turned to face both Chrishtan and his mentor. "We love you both very much."

Framin nodded before heading over to his brown mare and pulling himself up onto the saddle. "It has been a pleasure, Queen Jeanahn, and I am sure we will be reunited soon enough."

Chrishtan, who was still unsure of how he felt about the situation, stared at the adults with bewildered eyes.

"All right, my little king." Queen Jeanahn motioned for Chrishtan to mount his father's white stallion. "It's time for you to embark on your journey."

As he approached Boone, the stallion's proud and confident stature felt slightly comforting. But it was not enough to dull the pain and intense fear that gripped him so tightly.

"You take good care of him, my son," King Sonee said as he walked over to where Chrishtan stood and patted Boone on the neck. "He's a great companion to have. Boone has always led me in the right direction, and now he will lead you."

"I will, Father." Chrishtan nodded. "I promise."

The king lifted his son up into the saddle. With Chrishtan safely on the back of his white stallion, the king walked around back and brought out a beautiful black mare that belonged to Queen Jeanahn. King Sonee mounted the black beauty and patted his son on the back as he rode by.

"Let us head out, shall we?" the king motioned toward the woods and the three set out on their journey. Chrishtan hung his head, grimacing at the idea that only one of them would be returning home from their ride, and it would not be him.

CHAPTER 12
THE MENTOR

Lerim's great star hung high in the afternoon sky, pushing out immense heat that caused both the boy and his mentor to drip profusely with sweat. Nonetheless, they continued to ride on through the hot and desolate Didumos Plains. The scorched plains were blanketed with dead grass and the occasional warped leafless tree every now and again. It had been nearly three days since Framin and Chrishtan set out into the unknown. Chrishtan missed his parents dearly and prayed to the Grand Architect each and every night that his parents would meet them soon. Framin assured him that his father was *a strong man and mage warrior who would never let anything happen without a fight.* But that was precisely what Chrishtan was afraid of—*a fight.* If his father had to put up a fight, then that meant that someone would potentially be hurt or killed. Chrishtan was young, but he was not naive. He was a born and bred warrior of a royal Lyre bloodline. He knew that every fight or battle meant that a soldier or leader might not make it home to their mother, father, brother, sister, wife, or child. There was a strong chance he may never see his parents again.

Framin did his best to help take Chrishtan's mind off his family, especially the concern that his new sibling would be born any day now. He kept the boy busy with usual lessons in the sorcery of Lyre manipulation as well as the warrior practices of their culture. In addition, they studied out of a thick, black leather-bound book that Framin had assured the young prince contained *all knowledge of things that you will need to know in order to defeat the Blackness if it should ever make its way into our living world on Lerim.*

***

On their fourth day of travel, Chrishtan became uneasy, fidgeting in the saddle. He could tell that his mentor too was not himself. A disturbance that he had never felt before bombarded Chrishtan's Lyre. The energy surrounding them felt slightly disrupted. It made him fear for his parents. He tried to connect with them through his thoughts as he had done every day since their departure, but could not feel it the way he had before when he had his grandfather's ring on. The day before, Framin made him take it off, painstakingly explaining to him that it was no longer safe to wear. Once again, Chrishtan prayed for the safety of his mother and father and unborn sibling. As he prayed, Framin urged him to ride faster. They did not stop to learn on this day. Instead their pace only accelerated toward their destination, the Lantern Forest.

Chrishtan trotted Boone alongside his mentor. "Why must we run, Framin? What's the matter? What's happening?"

"We must hurry. Do not panic. We will be safe where we are going, but we need to get there quickly." Framin dug his heals into his brown mare, forcing her into a gallop.

"Framin! What is going on? Please tell me," Chrishtan begged as he and Boone ran alongside his paranoid mentor.

"Just ride, my boy, ride as fast as you can."

"But why? What's happening? Framin I need to know. Please," Chrishtan pleaded as they galloped across the plains.

"My boy," Framin answered, his breaths growing shorter as their pace quickened, "I believe we are being hunted. Now, ride!"

Hunted? By whom? Chrishtan thought. *What about my mother and father? What about the kingdom? Who is hunting us? How do they know where we are?*

Chrishtan looked all around for those who supposedly hunted them, but saw nothing and heard nothing. He thought for a moment that his mentor must be losing his mind. *There is no way that someone could be hunting us. No one knows where we are. Plus, Mother and Father would never let anything happen to us.*

***

Hours passed with the boy and his mentor on the run. Still, Chrishtan saw no one and was not sure how much longer Boone could ride at this pace. The stallion was beginning to foam around the mouth. Chrishtan knew that the horse might die if he did not rest. This was his father's horse. And his father had charged Chrishtan with Boone's care. He would not allow him to die.

"Framin, Framin! We must stop. Boone is not going to make it. He could die. Please, Framin," Chrishtan pleaded, slowing down so that Boone could recover. "No one is behind us. No one is hunting us."

"We cannot, Chrishtan. We must keep going," Framin yelled back at Chrishtan. "They will be more likely to find us if we stop now."

"No, Framin, I will not go. I will not hurt Boone. I can't. He is my family. He belonged to my father. I will not do it!" Chrishtan pulled the reins of the magnificent horse. The horse finally came to a halt. Chrishtan felt his horse's side. He was burning up. Chrishtan jumped down with his water pouch, pouring water into the mouth of his white companion. Chrishtan watched as his mentor continued into the distance.

Chrishtan was still watering Boone when he saw Framin whip his horse around and race back toward him. He was yelling something, but Chrishtan could not make out what it was. Chrishtan smelled something disgusting. He and Boone both raised their noses to the air. Suddenly, Boone reared up. Chrishtan screamed as his own feet left the ground. Something held him and scooped him up into the air. Chrishtan turned his head to find that he was in the arms of a repulsive winged creature.

Only meters away, his mentor cried out in desperation as Chrishtan was carried away by the grotesque beast. Its large leathery wings flapped as Chrishtan screamed. The creature held him tight in its humanoid arms, with metal-clawed hands. Framin grabbed his knife. The gemstones on the handle of the blade glowed a vibrant red, matching the gemstone on the ring he bore on his left hand.

"Framin! Help me!" Chrishtan screamed.

Framin closed his eyes, and then opened them to throw the knife at the creature. The monster cried out with a shrill, ear-splitting scream as it dropped Chrishtan and came crashing to the ground.

Chrishtan hit the ground hard. He back pedaled on his hands and feet away from the beast as it violently pulled the blade from its body with incredible force. It raged through an animalistic scream.

Framin swiftly pulled out his sword. With his red gemmed sword held high, Framin ran toward the beast with incredible power and speed. The revolting creature, with charred, black, leathery skin drew a large machete adorned with elaborate designs and black gemstones in the handle. It limped toward Chrishtan.

"Framin!" Chrishtan screamed.

Framin ran toward the monster, his speed much faster than any normal human being. Just as the beast grabbed Chrishtan, Framin jumped up into the air at least four meters with incredible ease. He landed with a loud thud in front of the creature, striking down on the Minotirr with his enormous sword. With Chrishtan kicking and screaming in one arm, the monster blocked Framin's strike with his machete in the other hand. The beast backed away from the mage warrior, defending each blow with its black jeweled weapon.

Chrishtan cried out as Framin closed his eyes and focused his Lyre. When he opened them again, his sword came down in a clean slice through the arm of the beast that held Chrishtan.

Chrishtan shrieked as he and the wretched creature's enormous arm fell to the ground. Black coagulated blood oozed from the wound where its arm had once been. Chrishtan hyperventilated and watched in awe as Framin wielded another high, double-handed swing clean through the neck of the beast. Chrishtan closed his eyes. He heard the creature's enormous body hit the ground. When he opened his eyes, they were met with the dead gaze of the headless beast where it had landed beside him.

Framin reached for his hand. "Chrishtan, we must go now."

Chrishtan looked up at his mentor and nodded profusely as he pointed out into the distance. "Framin!" he screamed.

Just as Framin turned, the tip of a metal blade came through his sternum, sending blood dripping onto his boots.

Chrishtan squealed in terror. "Framin, no!"

Framin's sword was still drawn. Once again, he struck at yet another repulsive winged monster as it ripped its machete blade from his chest. As blood poured from Framin's torso, he struck the beast again. His sword clashed against the creature's blood-stained machete.

Chrishtan watched the battle through pouring tears. The last blow from the beast knocked his mentor to the ground. Framin's glowing sword fell from his hands as the beast stabbed him again, this time through the stomach. With its weapon in Framin's stomach, the grotesque monster placed one foot on the mentor's chest and slowly pulled the blade up toward Framin's sternum, cutting him clean open. As it did, the revolting creature looked into Framin's eyes as if it enjoyed watching his suffering. It grinned as it watched the energy and life drain from Framin's face and body.

As soon as Framin took his final breath, the putrid-smelling brute turned around to gather the boy, but he was gone. The vile Minotirr turned to look for him. As it did, a sword sliced partially through the monstrosity's neck, severing most of its head from its black leathery body. Chrishtan stood above the creature, his mentor's large sword in his small, quivering hands. He immediately dropped the enormous blade and fell to his knees next to his mentor as he sobbed. Tears cascaded from his eyes and down his cheeks. His weeping continued until he heard a familiar voice.

"Chrishtan…" the voice called.

Chrishtan looked around to see who it was, but saw no one. "Who is it? Who's there?" His voice trembled.

The voice echoed once again inside his mind.

"Chrishtan, it is Framin. You must listen to me. Please, make a promise to me, Chrishtan. Promise me that you will not stop. Promise me that you will go to the Lantern Forest and that you will not forget the things I have taught you. Promise me that you will continue to read, study, and practice the ways of the Lyre and the Blackness. Take the box with the map and my ring. It now belongs to you. Promise me that you will continue on our journey and seek out the Lady of the Realm of the Lantern Forest. Do not give up, my young prince. Promise me." The voice faded away.

"I promise, Framin," Chrishtan managed through sobs. "I promise." He listened for the voice to speak again. "Framin? Framin, are you there?" He heard nothing. Chrishtan murmured to himself as he cried on the dead shoulder of his late mentor. "This is all my fault. I'm so sorry, Framin. If it weren't for me, you'd still be alive. What have I done?"

CHAPTER 13
PROMISES

Three times the moon came and left since the brutal death of his beloved mentor. Chrishtan lay curled up on the crunchy dry grass of the Didumos Plains next to his mentor's dead body. His small frame shivered as the chill of a stormy breeze lifted his clothing and slithered inside. Far off in his dreams, he could not feel the effects of the unforgiving environment on his pitiful body. Deep inside his coma, he was somewhere else. He had flown away from the horrific scene that had taken his beloved mentor. Far outside the edge of his planet's atmosphere, he floated through the galaxy. As he drifted through the unknown of an endless universe, he gazed out at the billions of lustrous balls of fire and energy far off in the distance. Although space seemed void and empty of life, he heard many voices. Though they were faint, they were calling to him.

Chrishtan followed the melodious voices away from Lerim toward a large mountain of colorful gases. The closer he swam to the nebula, the louder the voices grew. Chrishtan propelled himself as close as he could to the beautiful arrangement of purple, pink, and green gases. Once inside the hazy birthplace of stars and worlds like his own, he could finally make out what the voices said.

"Chrishtan, do not stray," they hummed. "Do not give up."

Chrishtan glided through the vibrant gases in search of the chorus that sang to him. Toward the center of the nebula, he saw a swirling black entity. He propelled himself toward it, leaving a trail in the sea of flamboyant gases behind him. Once close enough, Chrishtan reached out his arm to touch the swirling void. He gently laid a finger to the fluid like structure as it whirled around. His fingers sent ripples outward, like a rock hitting the surface of a pond.

Chrishtan paused for a moment before pushing his hand directly through the whirling waves. His eyes grew wide as a force pulled on him from the other side. Before he could pull back, Chrishtan found himself plunged into the vortex. Bright stars and familiar vibrant gases passed by as he soared. The amazing sight washed away his sorrows and made him feel at ease. With a sudden, yet slow jerk, the singularity softly spit him out into a pitch black abyss. He could see nothing, no floor, no ceiling, no walls, only darkness.

Chrishtan floated down until his feet landed on an indescribable surface. He squinted hard trying to something, anything at all in the pitch black setting.

"Hello?" he called, but heard nothing. His voice sounded muffled inside his head. He tried again. "Hello? Is anyone there?" Again nothing. Chrishtan called out once more as he walked toward a tiny light off in the distance. "Hello?"

As he walked toward the tiny lustrous pin prick, it grew. The faster he walked, the larger it became. When he approached his destination, the voices returned. They too were muffled and too numerous to distinguish what they were saying. Chrishtan moved even faster toward the light that now beamed onto him. In a dead sprint, he raced toward the light. It transformed into an oval doorway. As soon as he approached it, the chorus consolidated into one clear and familiar voice. The sound of it brought tears to Chrishtan's eyes.

"Slow down, my precious prince. Do not be in such a hurry to come here." the voice called.

The light was so bright that Chrishtan felt as if he had run into a wall. He could not get any closer. Chrishtan shielded his eyes with his hands. "M–mo–mother? Is that you?"

"My precious boy, why have you come here? Please, do not travel any closer." The voice echoed.

Chrishtan squinted hard. "Mother, wh–where are you? I can't see you."

"It's all right, my prince. I am here."

Chrishtan tried once more to look directly into the light, but it blinded him. "Mother, where are you?" He tried to find his mother within the brilliance. As his eyes gradually came into focus, the silhouette of a woman stood in front of him. The shadow moved closer, reaching out with a translucent hand. Chrishtan felt its cool calming touch as it gently grasped his palm.

"Oh my prince, how I've missed you so."

A tear trickled down Chrishtan's cheek. "Mother, where are we?"

"My precious boy." She squeezed his hand. "You have traveled into the Verge, the space between the living world and the spirit world. It is not safe here for you at this time, my little warrior. You must return to our world. You must return to Lerim."

"Are you coming with me, Mother?" Chrishtan wept.

"No, Chrishtan, I am sorry. I cannot. I am so sorry, my precious prince."

"Bu—but why not mother? If I can come here, then you can come back with me. We must have come the same way. I can show you."

"I am sorry my love," his mother explained. "But we have not come the same way. You see, my spirit is all that is left of me now. My body, my vessel, is no longer living. And I am no longer a part of Lerim."

Chrishtan did not want to believe what he heard "Wh—what do you mean mother? Aren't you, father, and the baby going to meet me at the Lantern Forest?"

"No, my son, I am afraid that your father and I have come to be with the Grand Architect. Here we shall remain for eternity. It is up to you now, my prince. It is up to you to bring hope to our world Chrishtan. Bring hope to Lerim."

Chrishtan shook his head as he pleaded. "Mother, I don't understand. Are you saying that you and father are … dead?"

"Yes, my son. I am so sorry. Your father and I fought as hard as we could, but Lochran and his forces were much too powerful. They were not interested in negotiations."

Chrishtan fell to his knees, clutching his mother's shadowy hand before bursting into sobs. "No, Mother, no. How could this happen? We were supposed to be together again, all of us, in the Lantern Forest. You promised. You, me, Father, Framin, and my new baby brother or sister."

Chrishtan felt a hand on his face. It tenderly traveled to his chin and lifted it. "Brother. Your new baby brother."

Chrishtan opened his burning eyes. As he wiped away the tears, he saw her, as clear as he had seen her the day he left for the Lantern Forest. "Oh, Mother!" He wrapped his arms around her neck and squeezed like he would never let go. "I have a baby brother?" He smiled. "Where is he? Is he here with you?"

"No, no, my love, he is not. Your father was able to get him out of Abequa before the worst hit. I do not know where he is now, but I know he is alive and safe. I can feel it."

Chrishtan rose from his knees and hugged his mother. "I must find him, Mother. I must."

Queen Jeanahn embraced her son. "Yes, my little warrior, you must, in time. Lerim is a dangerous place right now, as many evils have been allowed to enter it. When you return, you must remain vigilant and you must stay hidden. You must try your best to get to the Lantern Forest and seek out the Lady of the Realm. She holds the key to your success."

Chrishtan nodded up at his mother as he tightened his embrace. "Yes, Mother, I will do as you ask. I swear it."

Queen Jeanahn stroked her son's cheek. He could feel her soft hand against his face. "I am so proud of you, my warrior prince. I know that you will bring hope, not only to the people of our continent of Mirilan and the people of our nation of Abequa, but to the entire world of Lerim.

Tears escaped Chrishtan's eyes once more. "I love you, Mother. I miss you so much."

Queen Jeanahn squeezed her son tight before kissing him on the forehead. A tear glided down her face and landed on his. It became dark once again, but Chrishtan could still feel a multitude of tears dropping onto his face. They came more and more, until it felt as if they were showering him.

The startling crack of thunder and flash of lightning woke him. His eyes shot open to see ominous grey clouds overhead pelting his body with rain drops. He was soaking wet. And in an instant, reality struck him as he looked over to see the body of his dead mentor lying next to him. Chrishtan carefully crawled out from under Framin's limp arm before struggling to stand on his trembling legs. *I must have been asleep for days.* The rumbling of his stomach made him aware of the painful starvation that had set in. He looked around for shelter, but it was difficult to see through the dense curtain of pouring rain. In the distance, he was able to make out a large tree with a white blob underneath it. *It has to be Boone. He's found shelter.*

Chrishtan looked at his mentor, then back at Boone, and back to his mentor once more. It pained his heart to leave Framin's body there, but Chrishtan was not yet strong enough to move or bury him. As he knelt down on the muddy ground to pay his last respects to his best friend and mentor, he noticed Framin's gold ring on his left ring finger. It was adorned with red Rubiz gemstones. Heavy raindrops smacked into his face and soaked through his clothes. Chrishtan removed his mentor's Lyre harness ring and placed it on his left thumb before dashing over to Boone's refuge.

Chrishtan found Boone standing under the enormous tree. The thick foliage provided the orphans with plenty of shelter. Its long, wispy, dead branches hung almost all the way to the ground like a tent of intertwined foliage. Chrishtan dug through one of Boone's packs and yanked out a large blanket to wrap himself in. He sat at the base of the tree shivering violently. He would have to take off his wet clothes if he wanted to get warm. Terrified of what might be hiding in the storm, he slowly and diligently undressed before wrapping himself in the blanket.

Once swaddled, Chrishtan crouched down at the base of the tree. His teeth chattered violently as he wept, contemplating what was to come and the promises he had made to Framin and to the spirit of his noble mother. Tomorrow, he would set off into the unknown in another attempt to reach the Lantern Forest. He had no one left and no other choice.

CHAPTER 14
NOT ALONE

The ruthless thunder and brutal lightning of the merciless storm raged on for days. Monsoon season had arrived. Chrishtan knew that once it began, there was no stopping it. The unremitting winds and rain staggered Chrishtan and his white stallion as they drudged through the Didumos Plains. Chrishtan hunched over in Boone's saddle every so often to examine the map Framin had given him. The distance on the map seemed infinite, and Chrishtan's spirits dwindled. He wanted more than anything to give up, to lie down in the dead, muddy grass of the open plains and allow the Grand Architect to reunite him with his recently departed family. But deep within his heart he could not forsake them. He made a promise that he intended to keep.

As he and Boone labored on over the vast Didumos Plains, the brutal scene of his beloved mentor's murder played unrelentingly in his mind. The repulsive smell of the revolting Minotirr lingered in his nose with every meter they gained on the Lantern Forest. Vivid images of the creature's snakelike orange eyes glared at him every waking moment. The memory of its blood-red forked tongue looked even more repulsive against its charred black skin when it hung from the side of its lifeless mouth. Chrishtan dwelled upon the gigantic sword he had used to decapitate the vile beast.

Chrishtan thought he would be relieved once the monsoons took a break, but the heat of the summer gave way to a whole new kind of suffering. There had been almost no shelter in the barren wasteland of dying grass and mangled trees. His heart beat like a snare drum. Sweat poured off his forehead, gliding down into his despairing mouth. He had run out of water nearly twelve hours earlier. Both he and Boone breathed hard, drenched in sticky sweat. Mentally and physically exhausted, he cringed knowing that it would be dark within the hour. The sun began its final descent over the distant horizon as Chrishtan continued his journey north. Off in the distance, he noticed a tree wiggling in the mirage of heat. He wasn't sure if it was real, but he felt desperate enough to nudge Boone toward the tree.

A ten-minute ride landed them in front of another strange-looking tree. Its long tendrils hung down to the ground from all sides and looked more like strands of thick hair than branches. Chrishtan carefully dismounted his recently departed father's grand white steed and walked over to where the tendrils began. He slowly raised the curtain of dead branches to make sure there was enough room to house both him and his equine companion. The tree, which sat at the base of an enormous hill, looked eerie as the sky behind it in the east turned a deep, dark purple in contrast to the western sky which held a rather large red sun in an orange and pink sky.

Chrishtan slowly slid down to the base of the lifeless tree, bringing down shards of dead bark as he went. He watched Boone search the dry, crisp grass under the tree for any sign of green to munch on. To Chrishtan's surprise, the stallion was somewhat successful along the eastern side of the tree closer to the hill. Chrishtan's legs and back hurt terribly from their travels. He rolled toward Boone. For some reason, it felt cooler over there. Chrishtan closed his eyes and tried to slow his heart rate just as his mentor taught him. He needed to recharge his energy, his Lyre.

Chrishtan slowly took in breaths and eased them back out, focusing only on the rise and fall of his chest. As his heart rate began to slow, he heard with keenness the sound of his companion's mouth as he masticated small pieces of vegetation and swallowed them down through his long esophagus into his empty gut. It sounded as if he were right inside the horse. As he focused further, he could hear the soft whisper of the wind as it traveled through each of the dead branches of his shelter. He could hone in on the smallest detail of the smallest sound, down to a mouse crunching on a seed in the distance. Chrishtan took it all in as he processed the week's traumatic events. He needed to rest in order to recharge his Lyre. The success of his promises depended on it.

Chrishtan gained a new sense of confidence as he honed the skills that the Grand Architect had given him. Every mage, no matter their Lyre's specific strength and ability, had the aptitude to amplify their senses. The ability to hear what could not be heard, to see what was too far away to see, and to sense any disturbance in his surroundings. His sense of smell was so keen that he could pick out the individual ingredients in a recipe if he wanted to. As a mage of the warrior Lyre bloodline unique to his nation of Abequa, he would be able to harness incredible strength, stamina, agility, and endurance. Though he was not even close to realizing his full potential, this was how he had been able to defeat the repulsive creature that had slain his mentor, his best friend. He missed him greatly. Memories of Framin slowly crept in, interrupting his meditation.

***

Chrishtan raced into the king's chambers. "Father, father, look!"

King Sonee did not flinch. He continued reading the parchment in his hands.

"Father! I'm a real warrior. Look!" Chrishtan plunged his miniature sword through his father's parchment.

"Chrishtan!" King Sonee yelled. "What is wrong with you? I'm in the middle of reading an incredibly important document. I do not have time for your silly games!"

Chrishtan stopped dead in his tracks. His eyes grew wide as he stared into the king's fuming glower. "I–I–I'm–" Chrishtan dropped his sword and ran out of his father's chambers.

"Chrishtan, my boy! What's the matter?" Framin called as Chrishtan ran down the hall and rushed into his arms.

"Slow down my prince. What's happened?"

Tears streamed down Chrishtan's face as he gazed up into his mentor's compassionate eyes. "I–I–I've ups–" Chrishtan hyperventilated.

"Ssshh, my boy. It's all right." Framin rubbed Chrishtan's head as he held him close. "Try and breathe. Focus on the rise and fall of your chest. Listen closely to the air as it flows in and out."

Chrishtan closed his eyes and did as his mentor instructed. Finally, he was able to contain his emotions. "I've upset father again. He hates me Framin. I'm always in the way. He said he doesn't have time for my silly games." Chrishtan stammered. "I–I– I just wanted to show him that I finally received my sword. I wanted him to see how far I've come. How I'm on my way to becoming a true warrior."

Framin squatted down and wiped the tears from Chrishtan's face. "I know my boy, I know. Your father *is* very proud of you. He just has a great deal on his mind right now."

Chrishtan shook his head. "He's not proud of me. He's angry with me. I didn't mean to upset him. I just wanted him to see–" He broke into tears.

Framin embraced him. "Ssshh my boy. It's all right. Your father is going through a lot right now. I am sure if you show him later on when he is not dealing with matters of the kingdom that he will be more than willing to see what you have accomplished. He loves you very much."

"No." Chrishtan cried. "He sees me as a bother. I only get in his way. He doesn't have time for me. I wish I had a different father. Why can't you be my father, Framin?"

"Your father loves you more than you know Chrishtan." Framin looked deep into his pupil's eyes. "He is your king *and* your father. That is not any easy task. The life of a king is filled with many tough decisions. Keeping his people and his kingdom safe can be a difficult task. But most of all, your father's job is to keep *you* safe. And with the enemy so close to infiltrating our good nation, much more is on the line."

Chrishtan looked down. "But Framin, I feel as if it's always been this way. Even before the Huronians threatened our kingdom. He does not wish to be my father. He only wishes to be king. That is all he has time for. This is why I want *you* to be my father. Why can't you be my father?"

"My boy." Framin shook his head. "One day, you will become king and you will understand why your father is the way he is. Being king is a task that is never complete. Being a father is similar. Your father is doing the best he can under the circumstances. You must understand that his anger and frustration has nothing to do with you. It is his fear of losing this kingdom and losing *you* that plagues him. His anger stems from the evil that knocks at the gates of his kingdom and his loved ones' doorstep. You must try to understand this."

"But Framin." Chrishtan shook his head. "You are a mentor and that is a big responsibility and you still take the time to listen to me. You take me seriously. And you laugh at my jokes. I know you love me, Framin. With father, I am never quite sure. You would make a great father, Framin."

Framin sighed, "Thank you ,my boy."

"Framin?" Chrishtan asked.

"Yes?"

"Framin why do you not have any children of your own?"

"Well." Framin answered as he walked Chrishtan to his chambers. "When you chose the life of a Lyre mentor, you vow to devote your life solely to the Lyre. This means that a mentor must vow never to marry or have any children of his own. It is the way of the Lyre. Those who teach about the Lyre require the most pristine and unclouded view of it. The intense emotions associated with family and relationships only cloud this knowledge. A mentor must have unclouded priorities in order to become the most effective teacher possible. After all, we are responsible for the growth of individuals who could potentially become powerful enough to destroy life on Lerim. Therefore, in order to protect life, me must provide the most effective, responsible, and enlightened training possible, for the good of our world and the protection of all."

"That sounds much harder than having to be king." Chrishtan shook his head. "Not being able to have a family or loved ones sounds like the hardest thing in the world. Doesn't it get lonely?"

Framin smiled. "My boy, being able to devote myself to the development of such a spectacular warrior mage such as you, is more than satisfying. I have committed my life to you and your family. That is all I need. I do it because of my love for the Lyre. That is all the love I need."

***

Framin's face faded away and Chrishtan opened his eyes to see Boone standing in front of him underneath their tree shelter. He ran his hand up and down Boone's lowered head. "You know boy, I used to think not being able to love others must have been the hardest thing in the world. Now, I wish I had never been able to get close to anyone."

He sighed deeply as his adolescent mind dwelled on his losses. He wished that he had never loved his mother so dearly, his father so profoundly, and his mentor so intensely. He regretted ever bonding with a single soul. It would have spared him the anguish that currently resided inside him. Somehow, it would nullify any promises made to those whom he loved so deeply. Then he could simply surrender. He would lay down to die, relieving himself of the pain, heartache, and memories that haunted him. He would be with his family again.

No. He thought. *I have to survive. I must find my baby brother. He's still out there and he needs me.* It was the only thing that kept him going.

Chrishtan closed his eyes to meditate once more. Finally in tune with all of his senses, Chrishtan began to feel at ease.

He took in only the elements of his surroundings and their life energy. His body temperature slowly decreased as he dozed off. He leaned against the tree. A cool, refreshing sensation brushed over the fibers on his arm. It carried the moist smell of grass and flowering vegetation. He had not yet slipped into slumber, which meant that the sensation was real. As Chrishtan drifted back into consciousness, he honed in on the moist botanical scent. It was close, less than a kilometer away.

Chrishtan winced in pain as he stood to gaze into the direction of the bountiful smell, but the enormous hill blocked his view. As he closed his eyes once more, he focused on the individual scents of grass, tree bark, flowers, and moist soil. Chrishtan grabbed Boone's saddle and the rest of their packs.

"Boone, Boone, come on!"

Boone paused his search for grass and trotted back over to Chrishtan, cracking the curtain of dry branches as he entered.

"Boone, we're getting out of this inferno. Just beyond that hill, I think there is water, life!" Chrishtan quickly saddled and packed his companion. "Real grass for you to eat, and a cooler place to rest. I can feel it!"

Chrishtan shoved his foot into the stirrup and threw his leg over Boone's saddle before heading up the gigantic hill. It was the steepest hill they had ever ridden. Boone was tired and his pace slowed. But Chrishtan refused to give up. He was desperate for water and good shelter. As they reached the top of the knoll, the most amazing sight lay before them. For kilometers, all Chrishtan could see was a waist–high, rolling sea of emerald green grass. The hills were vast and spotted with large, blooming trees that resembled the dead tree that he had meditated under. Only these trees were thriving and covered in blue-green leaves with soft, purple flowers. It was the most breath-taking sight he had ever seen. Off in the distance to the northeast, a golden moon leisurely rose over a grassy, tree-topped hill. As he turned to the west, he waved goodbye to the sun as it sunk below the horizon in the fuchsia sky. Although he had suffered a great loss and knew nothing of what was to come, a sense of hope gently came over Chrishtan. He and Boone trotted into the whispering sea of green grass accompanied by a wondrous scent that Chrishtan had never before encountered. It was cool, fresh, and salty.

Before heading north toward the Lantern forest, Chrishtan decided that they would first travel east and discover the source of the mysterious salty scent. But before he did anything, he needed to rest, or else he would never make it. Although his new setting was filled with astounding beauty, Chrishtan knew that looks could be deceiving and the night could bring danger. He would have to remain hidden among the vegetation. From atop the hill, he saw a trough between a smaller hill and an enormous one. The vibrant, ascending moon lit his way. It reflected off the shimmering blades of emerald grass and shined a spotlight on a large tendril-laden tree within the trough.

Just before reaching the tree, Chrishtan dismounted Boone and signaled for him to hush. He did not know what hid beneath the curtain of aromatic foliage, but he did not wish to take any chances. He removed a small polished sword from his pack. It was just his size. The hilt was covered with Rubiz gems that, like his mentor's ring, lit up as Chrishtan's hand gripped tight. He crept toward the strands of luscious branches, closing his eyes to connect directly with his Lyre and honed in on his senses. Straight away, he detected a presence. He wasn't alone.

He felt its energy gently bounce off his. His keen nose picked up the familiar scent of human hair and skin. He acutely listened to the nervous breaths moving in and out of the entity's lungs. Though the presence did not feel hostile, Chrishtan remained vigilant. He held his sword high, ready to strike at any moment. He carefully parted the floral tendrils to see a small silhouette of someone crouched against the base of the tree. As he moved in closer to the figure, he heard a slight whimper. Chrishtan dug into his pocket with his free hand to pull out an ornate metal piece that housed a large crystal. Chrishtan closed his eyes and used his Lyre to bring in energy to light the translucent rock. In the light of the crystal, Chrishtan saw a young boy, much smaller than him, with red hair and tall pointy ears, shielding his face from the light of the transparent gem.

"Please, please don't hurt me, please!" the boy cried out.

"Who—who are you?" Chrishtan asked.

"I—I my name is Cohlen. Please, don't hurt me," the small boy pleaded.

Chrishtan lowered his Rubiz-studded sword. "I'm not going to hurt you. My name is Chrishtan. I'm not from around here. Do you live here?"

The boy stood up against the trunk of the great tree. "N—no, I—I don't live here. My brother and I are lost. We're hiding here."

Chrishtan moved closer to the boy. "How old are you? Where did you come from? What, may I ask, are you hiding from?"

The look on the boy's face shifted from scared to sad. "I—I've been around the great star six times. My brother and I are from the kingdoms of Samisius and Ellios. We were sent out by our parents with our mentor before the Greedy One tried to take us. But, our mentor began acting strangely, so we ran away from him, and now we are lost. We've been hiding here for a few days. At night we have to sleep here so that the flying monsters don't eat us. How old are you?"

Chrishtan knew this story already. When the boy mentioned monsters, he thought for sure that he was talking about the same hideous beast that had killed his mentor. "I'm ten. I have been around the great star ten times. I too am on a similar mission. So, uh, these flying monsters, what do they look like?"

"Well," Cohlen explained, "they are gigantic, eighty times taller than me. They are like giant lizards. You know, dragons. They are scaly and have big leathery wings. My brother calls them Dranogites. He learned about them in a book. He loves to read books. They live on an island not far away, and they come here every night to eat the animals that forage in the meadow. You know, those ones with the horns and the long legs. They eat grass."

Chrishtan knew what Cohlen was talking about. "Yes, I learned about them last year in my studies. They're called darix. So, we must be in the Emeralz Meadows." Chrishtan pulled out his map. "Yep, sure are. That means I'm getting close."

"Close to what?" the boy inquired.

"To the Lantern Forest, of course. Isn't that where you're headed?"

The boy anxiously looked at Chrishtan. "How, how did you know that?"

Chrishtan walked to the trunk of the leafy tree where the boy stood and sat down against it. "Because, I think we are in the same predicament. Everywhere is under siege. We children were sent to the Lantern Forest for some kind of protection, I think, but I'm not sure."

Cohlen slipped down the trunk next to Chrishtan. He looked up with sad blue eyes. "Yes, we don't know what we're supposed to do. I'm scared. Me and my brother, we're both scared."

"So, where is this brother of yours?" Chrishtan probed.

"He went out to find a place to fill our canteens with water. We were all out, and he wanted to wait until it was cooler. He should be back any moment."

Just as Cohlen finished his sentence, his brother slipped under the tent of branches. He aimed a bow with a knocked arrow directly at Chrishtan.

"Who are you? What are you doing here? Get away from my brother!"

Chrishtan jumped up, threw his sword on the ground, and raised his hands in the air. "I'm sorry. I'm like you. I'm headed to the Lantern Forest, too."

The brother, who looked nothing like Cohlen, aside from

his tall, pointy ears, had light brown hair and eyes. He appeared to be about the same age as Chrishtan. With his arrow still knocked, he continued to interrogate. "Who are you? Where did you come from? Where is your mentor?"

The last question transformed Chrishtan's mouth into a frown. "My mentor was killed, murdered, by a disgusting and vile beast. I am Chrishtan, and I come from the nation of Abequa."

With a heavy sigh, the brother lowered his bow and returned his arrow to the quiver on his back. He reached into his satchel and threw down four strange-looking birds with long, skinny, white beaks and deep blue feathers.

"Dinner is served. Well, sort of. I'm Oleevar. Great to meet you, Chrishtan. Sorry about the hostility. We have been on the run for quite some time now." Oleevar spoke formally and eloquently.

"I understand," Chrishtan said. "I have been on the run as well. I believe a terrible creature is hunting me." A haze of tears came over Chrishtan's eyes. "It murdered my mentor. It was terrible." The gruesome scene played once again in Chrishtan's mind, causing him to shiver.

Oleevar sat down next to him and put a hand on Chrishtan's shoulder. "It was one of the Minotirr. They are truly disgusting."

"What is it called?" Chrishtan asked as a tear rolled down his cheek.

"My mentor told me all about them when he found out they were hunting us," Oleevar continued. "He said that they were once men and women too. Greedy men and women of Lyre-blood who lusted for power, too much power. To gain their power, they sever their souls and give them to the Destroyer. With their lust for power always unsatisfied, they split their soul until it can no longer be reconciled. That is when the Destroyer claims them. He takes them into the Void, into the fire. He burns them until their bodies and souls are completely demolished. That is why their skin is so

119

black and leathery. They are burned people. He cuts their tongues down the middle and replaces their soul with evil that makes their eyes glow orange and gives them wings. It is some kind of demonic transformation."

"That sounds terrible." Chrishtan's eyes grew wide. "Why would anyone want to go through that?"

Oleevar shook his head. "I don't know. I suppose it is because they are so blinded by their lust for power in the beginning that they truly believe they are invincible. The Minotirr are hunting us, too. They would come when our mentor fell asleep. He began talking in his sleep, screaming, crying, and speaking in the old language of our people. Within a short time, the Minotirr would come for us. It was like they were attracted to him when he slept. Our mentor was able to fight them off, but something else happened, something dreadful. His eyes became cloudy, and then black. His teeth became sharp. It was as if he did not know us any longer. After every nap or night of sleep, it got worse. In the night, during one of his naps, we snuck away. We could not get the map because he had it. So, we left without knowing where we were going. Now here we are, lost."

Chrishtan grinned as he pulled something out of his pocket. "Not anymore, you're not. I have a map right here."

A gigantic smile came over Oleevar's face. "Thank the Architect! Let me see that."

Chrishtan handed Oleevar the map. "It's the real thing, I swear it."

Oleevar's eyes grew wide. "This is outstanding. Cohlen, you must come look at this."

The young boy with red hair scurried over to his older brother. "Let me see, Olee!"

"It's genuine, little brother. Look!"

"I told you it was the real thing," Chrishtan boasted. "Now we can all go together. We don't have to be alone any longer."

Oleevar agreed. "We are truly blessed by the Architect to have you delivered here tonight. We should leave first thing in the morning."

"Well, here's the thing." Chrishtan looked down and shrugged. "Earlier today the most interesting and fragrant smell flooded my senses, and I would really like to see where it leads."

Oleevar tilted his head. "Did it come from the east?"

Chrishtan nodded. "Indeed."

"I can tell you where it leads." Oleevar smiled. "It leads to the Shimmering Coast. Have you never been to the sea?"

"No, I can't say that I have." Chrishtan shook his head. "My father promised to take me there one day, but now he is gone."

Oleevar immediately hung his head. "Well, how about *I* take you there?"

Cohlen grunted in disapproval at his older brother.

Oleevar swiftly retracted. "I mean *we. We* will take you there."

Chrishtan grinned with one side of his mouth. "That would be fantastic, thank you." He so admired his new friend, Oleevar. He was so articulate, not like Chrishtan. Chrishtan was the joker, the comedian. He was the boy who would say anything to put a smile on someone's face, but as of late, he had completely forgotten this. All he could think about was Framin, his beloved mentor, and how much he missed him. But now, he had a distraction that put him precisely where he loved to be, in the company of friends.

CHAPTER 15
THE SHIMMERING COAST

Each blade of emerald green grass glittered with cool refreshing dew in the morning light as the boys woke from their slumber. The warmth of a new summer sun took the place of the dark clouds of the monsoons. The change brought smiles to their young faces. With the comfort of the sun lending them a hopeful energy, the boys packed and headed east for the Shimmering Coast. The unanticipated heat of one of the last days of summer made their trek a bit warmer than they would have liked, but with their bellies satisfied and their canteens full, they were able to take the high temperature. The moist blades of grass tickled their ankles as they rode on horseback through the Emeralz fields. As they rode, Chrishtan watched as Oleevar honed in on his Lyre ability. He could sense animals that hid within the grass and when he would spook them, he seemingly without effort, plucked them from the sky with arrows from his bow adorned with green jewels. Oleevar's skills with a bow and arrow were amazing. Chrishtan thought they were as good as his skills with a sword, maybe even better. Oleevar explained to Chrishtan that most of the inhabitants of their two kingdoms of Samisius and Ellios had much different Lyre abilities than Chrishtan's people.

"You see Chrishtan, everyone in our nations of Samisius and Ellios is born of Lyre-blood, not just a select few. This is because we are much more closely related to our Lyre-blood ancestors than your people are."

Chrishtan grinned. He had heard that elves were pompous, but Oleevar's discourse offered him a prime example of this behavior. "I see, so your people are hunters and rangers, correct?"

"Yes," Oleevar answered, "that is correct. The Lyre

bloodline of my people harnesses abilities of stealth, camouflage, mimicry of animal sounds, animal transformation, as well as the ability to communicate directly with animals. We are remarkable hunters and trackers."

Along the way, Chrishtan admired Oleevar as he shot their future meals with ease. When the boys would stop to rest for a short while, Oleevar allowed Chrishtan to practice shooting the bow, teaching him the keys to becoming a respectable hunter and ranger. Oleevar gave him tips on how to use his Lyre to find his target without even looking at it. Chrishtan was incredibly grateful, and so promised to teach Oleevar and Cohlen how to wield a sword once they arrived at the coast. Chrishtan admired how, despite his age, Cohlen excelled with his small bow. And though he was not yet as gifted as his brother, he had no problem hunting enough birds to feed himself. With each kill, the elvish boys said a prayer to the Grand Architect to bless their meal and free the spirit of the animal.

After a few hours of riding in the heat and humidity, the three boys finally made it to the coast just as the sun had reached its highest point in the sky. What Chrishtan saw left him speechless, which was a feat for him. He had never witnessed anything so grand in his entire life. He stood in awe at the pure white sand decorated with sea shells near the surf. His gaze drifted over to the north side of the beach, where an enormous shale rock cliff towered over the sea. His eyes followed the angle of the cliff up and out into the ocean. There, small waves bumped into enormous rock formations in the midst of a shallow sandbar. Through the crystal clear water, Chrishtan could see the white sandy bottom of the sea. The sun hung high in the southeastern sky, sending rays of light bouncing off brilliant blue-green water. Not far beyond the rock formations, the water transformed into a much darker turquoise. Chrishtan assumed it dropped off to much deeper depths.

Chrishtan closed his eyes and took in a deep breath to focus his senses. The smell of the salty air was intoxicating.

The soothing sound of the gentle waves in the silky breeze made him want to cry. He wanted so badly to share this moment with his family and his beloved mentor. But instead of shedding a tear, Chrishtan took in a huge breath and sprinted down the grassy hill toward the surf with his arms spread out like a pair of wings. He stripped off his pants and shirt before dashing into the warm turquoise water. He splashed and played wildly in his undershorts. His laughter echoed over the brilliant white sand and off the elevated coastal cliff. Oleevar and Cohlen stared slack jawed at the peculiar sight, exchanging hesitant looks. But it did not take long before the two elven boys followed suit, leaving their clothes behind as they dashed into the surf after Chrishtan. It was as if the sand, sun, and water had freed them from their journey and allowed them to behave as children once more.

In the moist, warm atmosphere of the sea and surf, the boys wrestled, swam, and bathed in the sun until it bid them goodnight over a deep green horizon. Chrishtan was taken aback by the stunning scene that presented itself as the great star made its daily descent. He gazed to the northeast as an enormous champagne moon came up over the jutted cliff. With the sun setting behind him and the moon welcoming them into the evening, the warm coastal water now reflected a powder blue color. It looked icy against the grey sky with hints of deep purple and blue. The light of the enormous ascending moon gave way to the night. Chrishtan could still see through the water to the white sand that stretched out among the spectacular rock formations. The ocean waves had eroded the largest formation into what appeared like an arched entryway. Chrishtan wanted so badly to swim through the doorway and see where it would lead. In his imagination, it led him to his family. To a life where he, his mother, father, baby brother and mentor splashed around on the sand bar together.

"It's absolutely stunning, isn't it, Chrishtan?"

A hand on Chrishtan's shoulder startled him from his

familial fantasy. Chrishtan turned his head to see Oleevar smiling at him. "Yes, it is probably one of the most beautiful sights I've ever seen. Thank you, so much for bringing me here."

Oleevar patted Chrishtan once more on the shoulder. "Please, call me Olee. It was my pleasure. Everyone should get a chance to see something like this in their lifetime."

Olee removed his hand from Chrishtan's shoulder. The boys headed up to where they had decided to set up camp for the night. Although the recently departed sun invited cooler temperatures, the boys continued to laugh and play as they set up camp. They joked and poked and prodded one another as they dried off and slipped back into their clothes. They behaved as if the traumas of the past few weeks had never occurred.

The cool ocean breeze that rolled in with the night air prompted the boys to build a fire. As they waited for the coals to burn down to a more modest flame for cooking, Oleevar brought out a few of the birds from his pack and began plucking them. Chrishtan found himself eager to help . He had never plucked a bird before. With the birds' feathers removed, Chrishtan felt a sense of accomplishment as he, Olee, and Cohlen roasted their dinner over their perfectly constructed cooking fire. Chrishtan had never prepared or cooked his own dinner before. As the boys consumed their bird feast, they continued to do what they were best at: coming up with silly jokes and scenarios that would make no sense to anyone but them. The three young boys laughed until they could no longer breathe. It did not take long before Chrishtan put on comedic acts to entertain his friends. It was his favorite thing to do. In the midst of one of his standups, he suddenly hit the ground as if ducking from something. "What was that?" Chrishtan panicked.

"What was what?" Oleevar answered. A large shadowy figure crossed over them, accompanied by a whooshing noise.

"That! What was that?" Chrishtan shrieked.

Oleevar chuckled as he helped Chrishtan back onto his feet. Chrishtan shook the sand off of his body and out of his pants.

"Those are the dranogite," Olee explained. "They are small dragons—"

"Oooh, okay, right," Chrishtan cut him off. "I know what those are. Scared me to death! Will they hurt us?"

Oleevar smirked as he shook his head and spoke to Chrishtan like he was a small child. "No, we should be fine. Although, their claws do contain a toxin that causes immediate infection and in some cases even death. It's all right though. They really stay away from humanoids. They leave their island at night to eat. They go out and feast on the darix from the meadows. So, as long as you don't attempt to go over and eat a grassy snack with the darix, you should be fine."

"That's good to know. Okay, I'm okay. Nobody panic…" Chrishtan poked fun at himself, and the other boys laughed.

The rest of the night was dedicated to the boys mimicking Chrishtan's ridiculous plunge to the ground, with the boys tumbling into the sand screaming and laughing over and over again. They finally fell asleep in the soft cool sand of the Shimmering Coast.

***

In the morning, the boys woke to the sound of gulls squawking and pecking at small minnows and crustaceans in the surf. Every now and again a seagull swooped down and plucked a creature from the surf closest to the boys. As they shook out their britches, Oleevar called out to Chrishtan.

"Have you ever eaten food from the sea?"

"Um, yes, I think I have… possibly…" Chrishtan laughed.

"I believe we may have some sea creatures for breakfast this morning. What do you say? Cohlen, how about you?"

Cohlen smiled and nodded *yes* with intense excitement.

Oleevar waved his hand in the direction of the gulls. "Come, this way. We're going to catch some small surf dwellers. If the birds can do it, so can we!" He ran toward the surf, chasing the gulls out over the sea.

The boys spent over an hour trying to catch little creatures in the surf, but it was not as easy as the gulls made it look. The surf dwellers were fast and could bury themselves beneath the sand very quickly. In the end, their breakfast was small, but the fun they had catching it made up for any losses. In the afternoon, Chrishtan attempted to teach Olee and Cohlen how to use a sword—how to be a *true warrior*. They found sticks to use as swords and battled along the bright white beach as the heat drove them into the sea and back out again. They spent the entire day swimming and practicing combat until the sun hid away in the west and the moon lit their tranquil refuge once more.

That evening, Cohlen set up a target for Chrishtan to practice his archery. Meanwhile, Oleevar constructed another impeccable fire and boiled up some fowl in a stew for dinner. Oleevar clapped as Chrishtan's archery improved with every shot he made. His Lyre blood made for a rather different learning curve than a normal human. Cohlen laughed with excitement as Chrishtan allowed him to be the teacher. Chrishtan constantly had the young red-headed elf in stitches, rolling in the sand with laughter. Outside, he chuckled along with Cohlen, but inside it secretly pained him to think of the baby inside his mother's belly that he never had the chance to meet.

I wish I could laugh and play with my new baby brother. One day, I'll get the chance. After I find him. I wish I knew where he was now. Chrishtan held in the tears and went back to playing with Cohlen.

***

At dinner Oleevar and Chrishtan discussed the different philosophies behind both of their Lyre bloodlines. Oleevar, the archer and hunter, and Chrishtan, the warrior. It was customary in both kingdoms to take on the trade of their land and Lyre bloodline. Oleevar spoke of his nations of Samisius and Ellios, which bred archers, hunters, and rangers, in addition to a new line of elves known as contrivers.

"So, the elves have evolved further? You say you have a new trade?" Chrishtan asked.

Olee nodded with his mouth full of stew. He swallowed before answering. "Yes, it has happened over the past one hundred and fifty years or so. Our province of Ellios has experienced vast technological advances. The way the Ellosioans live is almost contradictory to how Samisians live. Ellosioans were the first to harness and engineer Lyre technology using a rare gemstone that can be found only in the lakes surrounding Ellios. Essentially, the Ellosioans are our industrialized descendants. In Samisius, our elven people reside deep within the Roeesar Forest."

Chrishtan interrupted. "So, in Samisius, where you live, people live in trees?"

Olee nodded, "That's right. We use only what nature provides us. Unlike humans, we do not fabricate material things. All of the furniture in the palace where Cohlen and I reside, was gifted to our people long ago by the humans. It is the only place in Samisius with such things. This is why some elves left Samisius and settled in Ellios, because they wished to have more material possessions. Someday, Chrishtan, I am going to live in Ellios. Not only that, I am going to be their leader. Cohlen can rule over Samisius. I want to do more for my people. I want to research and create technology that will keep us safe against our enemies. No one will have the ability to defeat or control me and my people. You'll see."

Chrishtan smiled sadly at Oleevar as he tried to hide his feelings, knowing that his kingdom had already been destroyed. He and his family had ultimately failed at keeping their people safe.

"That sounds fantastic, Oleevar. I know you'll be able to do anything you set your mind to. So, you and Cohlen are elven royalty, then?"

Oleevar put a hand on Chrishtan's shoulder. "Yes, royalty just like you. When we are old enough, we will protect our people together. We can be allies. You can come home with Cohlen and me after we meet the Lady of the Realm. You will be one of us, you'll see."

Chrishtan forced a smile. "That sounds wonderful, Olee. I would like that very much. Thank you."

Oleever smiled. "No need to thank me. We are brothers now."

With Chrishtan's spirits somewhat lifted, the boys continued their discussion regarding the different Lyre bloodlines and nations. They spoke of the amazing power bred by the Abequan warriors of Chrishtan's homeland. Lyre-blood Abequans had the ability to wield a sword with power and ease. They were extremely strong, fast, agile, and in peak physical condition. Chrishtan knew that one day, he would be a true warrior. He had no other choice. His family and his people were counting on him. Chrishtan put his head down as he watched the flames from the fire dance in his sword's reflection. "I don't want to let anyone down the way I let my family down. The way I let my mentor down."

Oleevar looked Chrishtan in his eyes. "You won't. I know you won't. I am sure of it. What happened to your family and mentor was not your fault. You must know this."

Chrishtan was far from sure, but nodded in agreement with Olee nonetheless. "I used to think that Huronians bred the most incredible faction, but now I just see them as breeding evil."

Oleevar nodded. "Yes, the rogues bred by Huronus are incredible. They're so elusive and clever. Maybe it makes them more vulnerable to dissatisfaction and leaves them wanting more? But I don't know what more a rogue could want. They're agile, dexterous, and quick. I mean, they have the ability to use their Lyre to slow down their perception of time, which makes them almost invincible. Their ability to distract and stun enemies makes them formidable. They are flawless assassins. Though a great deal of reform has taken place over the past hundred years or so in Huronus, leaving many a pure Lyre-blood restless and unsettled."

Chrishtan shook his head. "It's not an excuse to ruin the lives of others and destroy other nations, especially those that were your allies. Abequa and Huronus have been allies for centuries. It makes no sense to me why they would destroy us."

Oleevar sighed. "Yes, you're right. It does not make sense. But many of the things that humans do don't make sense. Which is why we elves try to stay out of your business."

Chrishtan rolled his eyes. "Yes, I noticed that. The Jassokians of the northwest refuse to interact with humans at all. They think they're so high and mighty because of their connection and affiliation with the Grand Architect. I understand that breeding priests is important, but it does not make them better than us."

Oleevar smiled. "Well, in a way it does. Communicating directly with the Grand Architect is a rare gift and is central to their power. They breed great healers who harness their Lyre in connection with the Grand Architect to benefit the ill and injured. If evil has taken someone, a Jassokian priest has the ability to rid the person of evil and bring them back to the light. This ability can take up to one hundred years to train properly. "

Chrishtan nodded. "Which is why it is so important for them to share their gifts with the rest of us. To help those that need it, not just their own."

Oleevar grinned. "Maybe you're right. I think that it has just become culturally acceptable for us elves to stay away from humans because we fear their sometimes meddlesome and overemotional ways. I am not saying that I feel that way personally, but I know many elves do."

"I understand," Chrishtan smiled. "So are you going to show me these amazing Emeralz gemstones of yours?"

Olee and Chrishtan oohed and aahed as they showed off the gemstones of their nations. Chrishtan's a deep red Rubiz, and Oleevar's a deep green Emeralz. Regardless of what kingdom or trade, all Lyre-blood factions were dependent upon the specific gemstones of their weapons and rings to harness their Lyre energy and render a more stable connection. Each trade or ability matched with a particular gemstone. The crystal light wielding gem Chrishtan possessed, known as Diamoz, could only be used to harness light energy.

Into the night, the boys shared all the things they had learned regarding the kingdoms and trades with one another, filling in each other's gaps. Cohlen was intrigued by the conversation, taking it all in as he looked on with admiration at the two older boys and their vast knowledge of it all. When the two older boys spoke of the Ornz Desert, Cohlen's eyes grew wide. Oleevar and Chrishtan took complete advantage of it, telling Cohlen scary stories of the crazy warlocks that dwelled in the deserts and how they would eat his brain if they ever caught him. To Cohlen, this was not funny, but Oleevar and Chrishtan seemed to really enjoy taking advantage of the small boy's naiveté.

"So, Olee," Chrishtan asked, "do you know why they call it the Shimmering Coast?"

"Yes, I most certainly do," Oleevar boasted. "You know that Diamoz light you have?"

"Yes." Chrishtan nodded.

"Well," Olee explained, "those can only be found here on the Shimmering Coast."

"Really? Where are they?" Chrishtan asked.

Olee pointed out into the ocean. "Out there, under the sea. They used to wash up on the shore long ago, but not anymore."

"Wow, seriously? Can we get to them?" Chrishtan stood.

"No, not really." Oleevar shook his head. "First off, you

can only find them at depths that are too deep for us to swim to, and, second, they belong to someone.

This only further intrigued Chrishtan's curiosity. "Who? Who do they belong to?"

"To the merpeople, of course." Oleevar patronized. "Diamoz were brought out of the ocean thousands of years ago when our original Lyre-blood ancestors decided to leave the sea to dwell on land. And when they did, they brought with them the Diamoz crystals. But those who stayed behind to dwell in the sea were not happy with those who left. Therefore, they never allowed them to return or have any more crystals. And so the people of our continent have evolved into what we are now. Some of us more human like you, and some of us more merpeople like Cohlen and I. Regardless, none of us have the ability to morph into our previous sea-dwelling forms any longer."

Chrishtan jumped with excitement. "Really? Merpeople? You say elves used to be merpeople? Have you ever met one?"

"No, I cannot say that I have." Oleevar shook his head.

"I think we should," Chrishtan chuckled, "We could swim out there and say hello."

Oleevar continued to shake his head. "I really do not believe that would be a good idea."

"Well, why not?" Chrishtan threw his hands in the air. "Are you afraid?" he taunted.

"No. Well, yes, as a matter of fact I am, and rightfully so," Olee said. "You don't know what is out there, or what they would do to you."

"I am going to do it anyway. Are you coming or not, Olee?"

"No," Oleevar said, his voice growing louder, "I most certainly will not be coming."

"All right, then. Suit yourself." Chrishtan stripped off his clothes and ran toward the surf. "I'm going for a swim." He stopped and turned around to holler at Olee. "I'll tell the mermaids you said hi!"

Oleevar mumbled under his breath. "You must be joking." He slowly stood and looked at Cohlen.

Cohlen shrugged his shoulders and raised his eyebrows at his brother.

"Oh, all right. I'll be right back. You stay here, Cohlen," Olee instructed.

Oleevar stripped off his garments and ran off after their companion. "Chrishtan! Chrishtan, wait!" Olee called as he ran to meet him in the surf.

Chrishtan turned to mock him. "I thought you *most certainly will not be coming.*"

Oleevar splashed Chrishtan as they waded into the sea. "Ha ha, very funny. I can't very well let you be out here all by yourself, now can I?"

Chrishtan splashed back. "I knew you wouldn't be able to resist. I mean, think about it, when will you ever be able to do this again?"

Oleevar swam behind Chrishtan. "The probability is rather low. I will give you that. But it is extremely dark out here. This is very dangerous. I cannot see a thing."

Once out past the rock archway, they swam out to even deeper depths. Chrishtan stopped to pull something from his pocket.

"Maybe this will help." The Diamoz light shined bright and reflected off the top of the water all around them.

"I still can't see what's underneath us. This is incredibly dangerous." Oleevar's eyes darted all around.

"Look, it'll be fine, come on." Chrishtan held the light out in front of him before diving under the water. He immediately rushed back to the surface, sputtering water from his mouth. "You're right. This is not helping." Chrishtan used his Lyre to put out the Diamoz light, and the dark of night engulfed them once more.

All of the sudden, something in the darkness caught Oleevar's eye. He softly patted Chrishtan on the shoulder. "Look, down there. Look, what is that?"

Chrishtan jerked his head in the direction Oleevar was

pointing. "It looks like a light, but it's hard to tell."

Oleevar swam in front of him. "It is most definitely a light. Look, there's another one."

Chrishtan looked down. "You're right. And they're moving closer and fast."

Oleevar tugged at Chrishtan. "Maybe we should head back now."

Chrishtan threw Oleevar's hand from his arm. "No, not just yet. Wait, I think I see something else."

"And what if what you see is going to kill us?" Oleevar screeched.

"I don't think so. Hold on." Chrishtan squinted to get a better look. Multicolored specks radiated around the two balls of light as they drew closer. "Olee, look." Chrishtan grabbed the cautious elf, "I think I see a face!"

A young girl with light green skin and bright red hair popped up in front of them. She held a Diamoz crystal in front of her that lit the area.

"Hello," she said in a strange accent as she tilted her head and smiled.

"Hello there," Chrishtan stammered. He looked down into the water to see an enormous scaly, deep red fin instead of legs. She was the most beautiful being he had ever seen.

Oleevar gasped at the sound of giggling behind him. Both he and Chrishtan turned around to see another young mermaid with violet skin and bright blue eyes. Her white hair floated across the top of the water as she moved closer.

Oleevar greeted the beautiful creature with a lump in his throat. "How do you do, Miss?"

She answered in her strange accent. "I am good. You?"

"Uhh, very well. Thank you. I think?"

Chrishtan wrapped an arm around his friend. "This is my friend, Olee. He's a tad bit frightened."

The two mermaids cocked their heads as if they were confused by what Chrishtan said. "He's just a very cautious person, you see. Not really one for taking risks."

The girls giggled. "Then why you call us?" the red haired mermaid replied.

Oleevar's voice cracked. "Call you? Whatever do you mean?"

The red haired girl pointed with her green, scaly hand to Chrishtan's Diamoz crystal.

Oleevar laughed. "Oh, that. Well, that was not our intention."

The girls looked at one another. "Then you wish us to leave?"

Chrishtan hurried in front of Olee. "No, no, please don't leave. We did call you."

The girls smiled. The mermaid with white hair spoke this time. "You came for light?"

The boys looked at one another. Chrishtan spoke up first. "Um, yes. Yes, we came for light. How do we go about getting it?"

The girls laughed. "From us, silly."

Oleevar stared at the beautiful young mermaids. They were naked above their shimmery fins.

"All right," Oleevar said, clearing his throat. "So, may we have the light, then?"

The girls giggled. "Yes, but what you give us?"

The boys exchanged confused glances. "Well, what do you like?" Chrishtan spoke up.

"Shiny. We like shiny," the mermaid with red hair and pink eyes answered. Her blue-skinned partner nodded in agreement.

Chrishtan thought for a moment. "I think I have something you might like. Just wait here," he replied before taking off back to the beach.

Oleevar called out to him. "Where are you going?"

"Just stay there. I'll be right back!" Chrishtan shouted.

"Yes, of course," Oleevar mumbled under his breath. "I will just stay here in the middle of the black sea all alone with two creatures that could potentially drown me. Sure thing."

It didn't take long for Chrishtan to return. Even as a young warrior, his bloodline gave him the strength and agility to swim quickly and with ease. He placed Framin's Rubiz-studded dagger in the green palm of the red-haired mermaid. "Here, what about this? Is this shiny enough for you?"

The pink-eyed mermaid squeezed the dagger tight as she grinned from ear to ear. She held the knife up in the light before glancing over at her white-haired companion. They nodded in unison.

"Yes," she answered. "Yes, very shiny."

Chrishtan smiled. "So, may we have the light?"

The girls conversed using voiceless facial expressions. The red-haired girl with green skin answered, "One thing more."

Oleevar rolled his eyes. "Dear Architect…"

The red-haired mermaid smiled. "Love."

Chrishtan shook his head. "Love? What do you mean love?"

The girls smiled at one another and then at him. "Your love. You give love to us."

The two boys shot confused glances at one another. Oleevar cleared his throat. "I'm afraid we don't understand what you mean."

The red-haired girl closed in on Chrishtan. "We show you."

She grabbed Chrishtan's face with her scale covered hands and pressed her soft pink lips to his as she pulled him under. As they sank down, her lips remained tightly pressed to his. Chrishtan immediately looked over to see Olee in the same predicament with the blue lips of the white-haired mermaid. As they sunk deeper, Chrishtan allowed himself to relax as he took it all in. The kiss felt magical as the mermaid opened her mouth just enough to let her tongue enter and softly massage his. He reciprocated the gesture and realized that he was breathing under water. The life altering ordeal lasted for only a few moments, and when it was over, both girls placed their crystal lights inside the boys' hands. The two boys popped up from the water at once.

"Holy Architect!" Chrishtan shrieked. "That was amazing!"

Oleevar, blushed. "We could have drowned."

"But we didn't. We had the most phenomenal experience ever!" Chrishtan grinned and shook Oleevar by the shoulders.

Oleevar shook his head. "Whatever you think, Chrishtan. I'm going back to the beach now, if I may. It's getting cold out here." Oleevar turned around to swim back toward the beach when they heard the two girls pop up behind them.

"Thank you, Oleevar Jurlorn of Samisius and Chrishtan Vilgare of Abequa," They sang in unison.

"They know our surnames and our kingdoms. How do they know that?" Chrishtan shouted at Oleevar.

The girls giggled as they waved goodbye. "We know great deal of much, young warrior prince."

Oleevar sighed. "Great, just wonderful."

"Wait," Chrishtan hollered at the mermaids, "before you leave, what are your names? In case we ever bump into each other again? You know, in the future?"

The girls smiled. "I Balee and this Somya," the redhead answered.

Chrishtan bowed his head. "Thank you, Balee. Thank you, Somya. Thank you so much!"

As the mermaids dove into the dark sea, Chrishtan returned to the beach. When he finally reached the shore, he found Oleevar waiting for him. His teeth chattered violently as he spoke. "I am freezing, Chrishtan. I will never do that again."

Chrishtan laughed as they both put their shirts back on. "Oh please, Olee, you loved it. I guess we know for sure now why they call it the Shimmering Sea. I will never forget this."

Oleevar shook his head in a feeble attempt to sound serious. "Nor will I."

Both boys laughed.

The sudden burst of laughter woke Cohlen from his slumber in the sand next to the nearly burned-out fire. "Where did you guys go, Olee?" he mumbled in a sleepy voice. "What happened?"

The two older boys looked at one another and grinned as they pulled the Diamoz crystals from their pockets.

Cohlen's eyes opened wide. "Wow! How did you get those? Tell me please," he begged as he jumped up and down.

Oleevar squatted down to Cohlen. "Mermaids, Cohlen Mermaids."

Cohlen jumped a foot off the ground. "Really? Mermaids? What were they like?"

Chrishtan and Oleevar looked at each other and smirked. "Let's just say, they were very, very nice to us," Chrishtan answered.

The two older boys laughed. The thought of their lips pressed to the young mermaids' was exhilarating.

Cohlen threw more wood on top of the fire before blowing on it. "Wow, you guys sure are lucky! I wish I could have seen a mermaid."

Chrishtan and Oleevar walked over to Cohlen. Chrishtan put his hand on the young boy's shoulder. "You will one day, Cohlen, I promise. When you're a little bit older, you'll see."

Cohlen seemed content with what Chrishtan said and went back to huffing and puffing at the fire. They spent the rest of the night sleeping on top of the sand next to a warm fire with dreams of mermaids and shimmers in the sea.

CHAPTER 16
ON THE RUN

The sound of squawking gulls and crashing waves woke the boys from their dreams of magical mermaids and crystal stones. The gulls swooping into the surf reminded the boys that they too needed to have a hardy breakfast before setting out for the Lantern Forest. This breakfast would be no different than any other meal they had spent together, filled with laughter and silly pantomimes as they enjoyed a stew of crustaceans and fowl.

After finishing their morning feast, the boys sat together in the sand. They looked at Chrishtan's map to plan their route to the Lantern Forest. Chrishtan showed the other two boys where he had traveled from and they showed him the short length of their journey. On the map, a small yellow dot glowed on the northeastern side of the Lantern Forest. Chrishtan was not sure what this glowing dot was, but he needed to know.

"Would either of you happen to have any idea what this is?" Chrishtan pointed to the lustrous gold dot.

"That, my friend, is the *light* entrance to the Lantern Forest, where we will find the path to our Lady of the Realm of Mirilan," Oleevar answered buoyantly. "My mentor told me that it is the only entrance that is somewhat safe. All other ways in are dangerous and should not be attempted. In fact, our land of Samius resides directly across from the southwest borders of the forest. People are forbidden to enter or go near it. I do not know exactly why, but it is said to be extremely dangerous."

Chrishtan's puzzled look slowly transformed into an attempt to hide his fear. "Well, then I supposed we had better enter at this light entrance. It's not that far. It is around the other side of the bay. It should only take us about a day and a half to get there. Don't you think?"

Oleevar nodded. "Yes, I agree. If we don't make too many stops, about a day and a half. If we do not stop at all, maybe only a day. We should be able to follow the coastline directly to it."

Chrishtan stood and rolled up his map. "It sounds like we have a plan. We had better head out before it gets any later. I would feel much safer traveling by day with those dranogites so close by."

Packing up their tiny camp did not take long with the three boys helping one another. But a distant rumble from the east accelerated their progress. Ominous storm clouds over the sea were headed in their direction. Oleevar looked at Chrishtan and grimaced. "We had better be on our way before this storm rolls in, or else it may take a week to get there."

Cohlen dashed over and wrapped his arms around Chrishtan's waist. "I'm scared, Chrishtan. I don't like storms."

Chrishtan rubbed Cohlen's head. "It's going to be all right, Cohlen. Olee and I won't let anything happen to you. I promise." Chrishtan reached in his pocket and pulled out an ornate amulet. "Here, Cohlen, I want you to have this. My father gave it to me a few years ago when I needed to be brave. I call it my courage stone."

Cohlen cupped his hands together as Chrishtan slowly poured the chain into Cohlen's palms until the amulet lay atop a small mound of white gold. Cohlen lifted the amulet by the chain, admiring the teardrop-shaped talisman with his light blue eyes. In the center of the teardrop sat a large Diamoz stone surrounded by smaller dots of Diamoz, all threaded together by ornate designs. "Wow, this is amazing Chrishtan. Does it really work? Does it really make you brave?"

Chrishtan put his hands on his hips and stood up straight. "Of course it does. Would I lie to you, Cohlen?"

Cohlen grinned from the corner of his mouth before

giving a huge smile. "No, I don't think so. You're very brave. Not like my brother. He is always so scared and too cautious. He is no fun. Not like you. How do you use it?"

Chrishtan took the amulet and placed it around Cohlen's neck. "Whenever you're scared, close your eyes and hold the amulet tight while you say, 'I am brave.' Do you think you can do that, Cohlen?"

Cohlen smiled as he nodded *yes*.

Oleevar was packing up their things when he overheard his little brother. He turned around with a scowl on his face. "Very nice, Cohlen, very nice. I will have you know that I am not overly cautious. I am logical enough to know that you don't just dive into situations that could be potentially dangerous. To me, *that* is brave, being smart enough to stay out of trouble." Oleevar fiercely continued his packing.

Chrishtan and Cohlen looked at one another and broke out in laughter over the seriousness of Oleevar's response. They cracked up so hard that they could barely muster the words to mock him.

Oleevar spun around at the amused sound. "What?" He shrugged. "What may I ask is so funny?"

The two boys looked at each other once again, holding their bellies as they laughed hysterically.

Oleevar, tried to keep a straight face as he replied. "Look, this is not a joke. I was being serious…" As the last couple of words left Oleevar's mouth, a smile overcame him. "I'm very serious…"

Chrishtan threw a hand over his own mouth as he chuckled.

Oleevar could not hold back any longer. Laughter escaped him as he shook his head. "You two are absolutely terrible."

All three boys fell into the sand giggling. Chrishtan and Cohlen continued to point at Oleevar to mock him.

"Oh yes, I am superbly brave. Look at me. I am ever so safe," they teased as tears flowed from their eyes.

Chrishtan felt proud that he was able to lower Olee's

guard and get him to laugh at himself. He had done what he does best. He brought joy and laughter to those he held most dear.

Once packed, the boys mounted their horses. Only this time, Cohlen decided to ride with Chrishtan. He was convinced that Chrishtan knew more than his brother about being brave. As they reached the top of the dune and rode out onto the grass, the blades of vegetation whistled in an intense wind that brought a menacing storm closer with every gust. Thunder cracked in the background, forcing Cohlen to grasp his hands tightly around his new amulet. A dim light shone from the stones of the talisman as he squeezed.

With the map in hand, Chrishtan and his companions headed north toward the glowing yellow dot. They planned to stay atop the dunes in the grass along the shoreline and follow the path around the bay to the entrance. Their current situation allowed Chrishtan and his newly found friends a sense of relief. First, for finding one another, and second, having a map to guide them.

**

Hours dragged past as the boys followed the shoreline north to the Lantern Forest. With every kilometer they gained, the ominous storm over the bay drew closer. Thunder crashed more often and gusts of wind nearly blew the boys off their horses. Cohlen clung so tightly to Chrishtan's amulet that it left welts in his skin. And even though he was not yet one hundred percent brave, he seemed content enough not to cry or complain.

Oleevar gripped the map tightly as he led the way. He turned around to check on the other two boys. "I knew this storm was traveling fast, but not this fast. We should pray that the lightning does not come any closer and the rain does not fall on us today."

Oleevar barely finished his sentence when a sharp bolt of

lightning struck the beach accompanied by the loudest, most ear-splitting crack the three boys had ever heard. The horses reared up. Cohlen squeezed his talisman as tight as he could. *I am brave. I am brave. I am brave. I am so incredibly brave*, he whispered. Oleevar stopped his horse Elliot, and waited for Chrishtan to ride up next to him.

"Whoa!" Chrishtan hollered. "Did you see that, Olee? Look at those glass shards where the lightning hit."

Oleevar smiled at Chrishtan as if he were a small child. "Indeed, it was hard to miss it."

As the boys stared at the shards of sand glass, lighting struck once more, prompting rain to crash down violently on top of them.

Cohlen hunched over, using Chrishtan as shelter. "Ouch, it hurts. This rain hurts, Chrishtan."

The two older boys covered their heads with their hands as they sputtered the rain from their lips. Oleevar yelled over the sound of heavy drops that slammed into their bodies and packs. "We need to find shelter. Good shelter. These trees near the beach here are not sufficient. They'll leave us exposed on one side. We'll need to move a bit further west to find a proper shelter."

Fat drops of rain bounced off Chrishtan's head. He nodded in agreement with Oleevar and nudged Boone in the proper direction.

At a galloping pace, the boys slowly angled away from the safe entrance of the Lantern Forest. They had no other choice. The weather was too extreme for them to continue on their intended path. Fifteen minutes of drenched riding led them to a tree large enough to house all three boys and their horses. They swiftly dismounted and ran toward the tree, dragging their horses by the reins. They forced their way through the branches of the enormous tree and led their animals inside. As Oleevar and Chrishtan peeled off their wet shirts, they paused at the sound of chattering teeth behind them. Cohlen sat on the ground, shivering viciously from the cold. Chrishtan and Oleevar rushed over to help the trembling boy remove his wet clothing.

"So cold. Why is it so cold, Olee?" Cohlen managed through his quivering lips.

Oleevar yanked Cohlen's shirt over his head and tossed it onto the ground. "Because you are soaking wet, Cohlen. We need to get these wet clothes off you and get you dry."

Chrishtan helped Cohlen remove his wet pants while Oleevar searched the packs for a dry blanket. He unfolded a quilt and motioned for Cohlen to come over. Cohlen, wearing nothing but his undershorts and his teeth still chattering, dragged his feet toward his brother. Oleevar wrapped his younger brother tightly and sat him against the trunk of the gigantic tree. With their wet pants still dripping, Chrishtan and Oleevar unpacked the horses before stripping down to their under shorts and swaddling their own shivering extremities. All three boys huddled close together inside their blankets.

Chrishtan's blue lips shuddered as he gazed at Oleevar. "Now what, Olee?"

Oleevar, put his arm around Cohlen and looked over at his bow leaned up against the trunk of the massive tree. "Well, I suppose once we are dry enough and warm enough and the rain lets up a bit, I should go out and get us some food before it starts pouring again. Who knows how long this is going to last. It's monsoon season in this area, and the storms will be moving west toward the Didumos Plains and flooding them. Did you manage to take the extra wood and kindle from the beach for a fire?"

"Yes, I brought it. It's back there," Chrishtan answered. He wrung the water out of the hair that hung in his face. "So, do you think we should stay here for the day, maybe the night until this storm blows over?"

"Yes, I suppose it's not safe to travel in this type of storm. We really lucked out those two days on the beach. Tomorrow we may get lucky again. All we can do is wait and see. While we wait, I'll make us a fire to warm us and dry our clothes." Oleevar said as he dried his wispy brown hair with his blanket.

The three boys napped under the great tree next to a small fire as the rain fell steadily. Once they rested their heads on one another, they realized how tired they were from their journeys and staying up so late the night before. If it weren't for Oleevar, Chrishtan did not know how he would have eaten after his rations were gone.

An hour passed and the rain finally let up enough for Oleevar to go out hunting and fill their canteens with fresh water. Chrishtan felt Olee ease his way out from under his blanket so as not to wake the other two boys. Cohlen lay fast asleep on his side using Chrishtan's leg as a pillow. Chrishtan napped with his mouth open and his head against the trunk of the tree. The rattling of Oleevar's arrows inside his quiver prompted Chrishtan's eyes to flutter open.

"You headed out?"

Oleevar nodded. "Yes, I need to go now before this storm picks up again."

Chrishtan whispered. "I wish I could go with you. That I could help you hunt for us."

Oleevar laughed under his breath. "Well, I would say that you could go, except for I wouldn't want to wake Cohlen, as he is using you as a pillow. He hasn't been sleeping well since we left home. He really needs this."

"I understand," Chrishtan said. "Maybe some other time I can go with you. You can teach me how to be an archer, a *real* hunter."

"I would like that very much. I enjoy teaching people things." Oleevar grinned before walking through the curtain of foliage and out into a sea of freshly watered grass.

***

Oleevar had been gone for over an hour when Cohlen finally woke. "Chrishtan, where is Olee?"

Chrishtan stood and stretched his limbs under the blue green leaves of their colossal shelter. "He went to find us some food to eat."

Cohlen re-wrapped himself in his blanket. "Chrishtan, I'm scared."

Chrishtan grabbed Cohlen's dried pants and shirt and helped him put them on. "What are you afraid of, Cohlen? Everything is fine. The thunder is over."

Cohlen shuffled toward the outskirts of the branches as if looking around for something. "No, nothing like that. More like, a bad feeling. I feel something bad, but familiar." Cohlen continued to search with his eyes, nose, and ears.

Chrishtan walked up behind him and placed his hands on the boy's shoulders. He closed his eyes and harnessed his Lyre to see if he too could sense anything. As he fixated on his senses, he first smelled the familiar scent of Oleevar and birds. *He must be close.* His acute ears picked up footsteps that squeaked against the wet grass as they tramped across the field. But something sounded off. Chrishtan focused further. *His footsteps are a mess. It sounds more like four feet than two. As if one pair is being trampled by another.* Chrishtan sensed a disturbance and delved deeper into his Lyre to find an aura, a feeling. Fear came over him. *Danger is near. It's near Oleevar. Or maybe it already has him. But why can't I smell it?*

Cohlen screamed. Chrishtan snapped his head around to see a sinister-looking individual with short, black ,greying hair holding Oleevar's arms in place against his body with the other hand over Oleevar's mouth. Olee shook his head from side to side as he tried to wiggle loose. The demonic-looking elf glared at Cohlen. Its eyes held no iris or white, only pitch black. The hand that covered Oleevar's mouth had sharp, triangular claws that matched the shape of its serrated teeth. Its skin was so pale that each and every vein seemed to protrude from its face and neck. Chrishtan recognized an Emeralz ring on its left ring finger.

"Kyre! Kyre, please." Cohlen screamed. "Please don't hurt Olee! Please, Kyre."

This must be their possessed mentor, Chrishtan thought as he grabbed his sword from where it leaned against the tree. He stepped in front of Cohlen. He pointed the miniature blade at the elven wraith. "Let him go!" he demanded. "I said, let him go, now!"

With one hand still grasping Oleevar, Kyre lunged for Cohlen. The young boy casted a blood-curdling scream. The possessed mentor glared at Chrishtan. "These children are mine. Give them to me!" Kyre's voice sounded raspy and layered, as if there was more than one.

Kyre leaned forward to threaten Chrishtan, and Oleevar lifted his leg high enough to pull a hunting knife from his boot. As Kyre lunged at Chrishtan and Cohlen, Oleevar plunged a large, serrated knife into Kyre's ribcage. The possessed mentor crashed to the ground, smashing his face into the grass. With Kyre injured and immobile, Oleevar jumped over the moaning body to join Chrishtan and Cohlen. The three boys mounted Boone bareback. Without any reins, Chrishtan used Boone's white hair to steer through the tree's long branches. Kyre's shrill screeches echoed behind them as they galloped away. Chrishtan had no idea which direction they were going. All he could think about was getting away.

As Boone raced through the grass with the three boys, Oleevar let out a distinct whistle several times. After a number of whistles, the boys saw Elliot, Oleevar's black steed, ride up beside them saddled with all of Oleevar's packs and all the canteens. As Elliot galloped closer to Boone, Olee leaned toward his magnificent horse. Once close enough, he grabbed the saddle with both hands and hopped onto Elliot, hanging off the horse's side as they ran. After a few moments, Oleevar found his footing and mounted him completely. The boys breathed hard in terror. They knew what the mentor had become, but had no idea what he was capable of. Their only goal was to get away, no matter where. They were on the run once again and would not stop until they knew with certainty that they were safe.

CHAPTER 17
LOST IN THE DARK

Chilly rains fell from the dark, dense clouds of the monsoon as the boys searched tirelessly for a safe place they knew they would never find. Their horses had been running for over two hours, and their physical condition dwindled. Thick curtains of rain made it difficult to see, but the boys could not stop. In spite of their cold, rain-soaked bodies, they had to continue on. They slowed to a walk to try and regain some of the horses' strength. Cohlen shivered fiercely as he clung to Chrishtan and the courage stone. The small boy fell over each time he drifted off to sleep on the back of the horse. Chrishtan did not want Cohlen to fall off, so he paused their journey to wrap Cohlen in a somewhat dry blanket and moved him up front so that he could hold Cohlen while he slept.

More hours passed with Chrishtan and Oleevar finding it hard to keep their heads up. It was time for a break. The rain finally shifted to a light drizzle. The boys dismounted their horses, allowing Elliot and Boone to graze for a few minutes. The rumbling of the boys' empty stomachs could easily be heard outside their lean, growing bodies. They had not eaten since breakfast over six hours earlier. While the horses snacked, Oleevar collected clover buds. He passed a handful to Chrishtan.

"It's too risky to go out hunting. Here, eat these. They taste good, trust me."

Chrishtan took the blue buds from Olee. He picked out a good-sized bud from the handful and put it in his mouth. "Hmm, not bad Olee, not bad. Thank you."

"You're very welcome." Oleevar grinned as he handed the rest to his little brother. Cohlen was so hungry he ate them all without question. "We had better get moving again." Olee motioned to the horses.

Although Oleevar had stabbed Kyre, they all knew he was not dead. All three of them had heightened their Lyre since the attack. They knew they were still being hunted. The disturbance in their Lyre was weak, but ever-present. They had to keep moving. All three boys re-mounted their horses and rode on. As they reached the top of an enormous grassy hill, a vast forest lay before them far off in the distance.

Oleevar pulled the map from his pocket. "It looks like we're heading right toward the middle of the Lantern Forest, right between the southwest and northeast corner. We need to turn east, toward the storms to get to our safe entrance."

Chrishtan looked to the east at the menacing clouds headed in their direction. "I would hate to rush right into those storms. We should just continue north until we are just outside the forest border and then follow the forest line east to our entrance. Maybe by that time the storms will have died down."

Oleevar nodded. "All right, that sounds like a plan. It will take us a bit longer, but hopefully by that time it will, as you said, allow the storms to drop over there instead of right on top of us."

The boys headed north toward the Lantern Forest. Soft sprinkles and fat pelting drops from the storms intermittently splashed on the trio. Cohlen was still wrapped in his blanket, although it no longer served its purpose due to its rained-soaked fibers. Five hundred meters out from the tree-line, the boys eyed the amazing trees that made up the Lantern Forest. With enormous trunks and branches, the giant trees towered over the grass on the edge of the forest. Their massive leaves acted as giant umbrellas. It wouldn't be long now. All they needed to do was follow the tree line around to their safe entrance. Finally, there seemed to be hope within view.

Each thunderous crack seemed to send more raindrops tearing down from the clouds, hammering into the boys at an alarming rate. Cohlen groaned as he tried not to cry from the pain of the assaulting precipitation. He held the bravery amulet firmly in his hands. They could barely see through the storm when they heard gruff, labored breathing followed by a horrifying snarl. Oleevar turned around just as Kyre lunged onto Boone, clawing at Cohlen and digging his claws into the horse's hind end. Boone screamed and flew into a dead run, trying to escape whatever had latched onto him. Oleevar took off after Boone and the other two boys as fast as Elliot could carry him. He pulled up next to them just as Chrishtan pulled his small sword from its sheath.

"Oleevar, take this. You know what you need to do!" he yelled as he tossed the sword into Oleevar's hands.

The Rubiz gems on the hilt glowed bright red as Oleevar rode up next to his crazed mentor. Kyre climbed the back end of Boone, digging in his razor sharp claws. Oleevar got close enough to strike the wraith. He raised the sword and struck the left arm of his mentor. The creature's severed arm flew backwards, and a demented scream exited Kyre's purple mouth. Dark, dense, coagulated blood oozed from Kyre's wound. Still hanging onto Boone with his one arm, Kyre clawed deeper into the backside of the horse. Chrishtan hoped that Kyre would fall off. But even if he did, he would not be dead. They had to kill him, or he would stalk them forever. Kyre was no longer human and did not need his arm to hunt them.

Oleevar turned toward the other boys. "My knife, Cohlen. My other hunting knife! Take it from my boot. Hurry!"

Cohlen leaned as far down as he could, reaching for Olee's knife.

Oleevar yelled over the pounding rain. "This sword isn't large enough to cut through Kyre's neck Cohlen! You're going to have to stab his head! You can do it. Just a little further!"

Cohlen swallowed hard and reached as far as he could toward Olee, almost falling off Chrishtan's horse before finally snatching the knife.

"His head," Oleevar demanded. "Go for his head!"

A look of horror came over Cohlen's face. Tears cascaded from the little boy's soft blue eyes and over the tiny freckles on his face, mixing in with rain. Cohlen took the knife with both hands and brought it up over his head. Closing his eyes, he brought the knife down into the center of his mentor's skull. He was not strong enough to break through. Cohlen broke into sobs. "I can't do it, Oleevar!"

In an instant, Oleevar came around the other side,swinging Chrishtan's sword into the neck of the wraith as hard as he could. The boys heard another monstrous scream as they watched the sword lacerate the back of Kyre's neck. The mentor instantly let go of Boone, falling into the grass and sliding along for a few meters.

Chrishtan turned to Oleevar. "You've done it, Olee!"

Oleevar said nothing in return. His expression had glazed over. Suddenly, Cohlen let out a blood curdling scream. The other two boys turned around to see the mentor, with coagulated blood oozing from both sides of his neck, sprinting toward them at an impossible rate. His legs moved so fast that the boys could barely make them out.

Chrishtan squeezed Boone's sides. "Go! Go! Go!"

With fear and urgency taking over, the boys rushed over the hill and ran their horses straight into the forest. They did not stop until the light of day vanished. The absence of light in the forest caused the boys to stop dead in their tracks. It was dark as night. They couldn't see two meters in front of them. The deathly silence made them shiver. Chrishtan felt Cohlen's intense shaking as he hyperventilated in the dark. He could barely make out the light from the bravery amulet with Cohlen's hands wrapped around it so tightly.

Chrishtan brought out his Diamoz stone and lit it with his Lyre. "Where in the name of the Architect are we?"

Oleevar shielded his eyes from the glow of the crystal. "We must be inside the Lantern Forest. We weren't supposed to enter here. I'll get the map and figure out where we are. We need to find a way back out as quickly as possible."

Chrishtan passed the light stone to Oleevar as he fumbled to open the map.

"What in the world?" Oleevar glared at the map, his eyes bulging.

Chrishtan grasped the parchment. "Let me see." He eyed the map with the same wide eyes as Oleevar. "There's nothing here. It's completely blank. How does an enchanted map just erase itself?"

Oleevar shook his head. "I'm not sure. Chrishtan, do you recall where we came in?"

Chrishtan winced as he looked around. "I don't know. Somewhere near the middle, I guess."

Oleevar's eyes darted around. "No, that's not what I mean. I need to know where we entered this space we are standing in right now. From which direction did we enter? I can't see any light from the outside."

Chrishtan shook his head. He could just barely see what the light from his Diamoz stone touched. "I'm sorry Olee, I don't know. We weren't thinking. We were just trying to get away from—"

Oleevar put his hand up to silence him. "Ssshh! Listen."

Chrishtan leaned in and whispered. "What is it? What's the matter? I don't hear anything."

Oleevar shook his head. "That's exactly it. Here we are, in the middle of a forest, and there isn't a single noise to be heard. No birds? No insects? No breeze? No nothing? This isn't right."

Chrishtan listened to the silence. "What do you think is going on?"

Oleevar leaned in even closer to Chrishtan. "I think we are being watched. There is a reason our map no longer functions. I think whoever is watching us wants it that way."

Chrishtan gazed all around him trying to spot anyone watching them. "What do you plan to do, Olee? Do you want to choose a way that *you* think might be the way out and go in that direction? Or do you want to just stay here, forever?"

Chrishtan looked back down at the map, praying that it was just a simple malfunction and it would decide to reveal itself soon. But still nothing had reappeared. Even more alarming, the edges of the parchment looked as if they were disintegrating.

Oleevar quickly rolled up the parchment and handed it back to him. He gave Chrishtan his Diamoz light. "Well, first we should use our Lyre and see if we can sense a way out. Then we will go from there."

Oleevar hopped down from Elliot and extended his arms out to help Cohlen dismount Boone. Chrishtan followed behind with his Diamoz light. He studied the forest floor. It did not look much different from the Emeralz Meadow, except the grass was shorter and littered with small, blood-red flowers. Oleevar pulled a blanket from his pack and spread it out onto the forest floor. They would need to partake in some serious meditation in order to use their Lyre in a way that could help them to find a way out of the forest. The two older boys tied their horses to a large bush with deep purple, heart-shaped leaves adorned with bright red buds. The bush was covered in thorns, but it was the only thing close by that was low enough for them to tie up to.

With their blankets spread out on the lush forest floor, Oleevar and Chrishtan sat on either side of Cohlen. They were soaking wet and famished. The incessant grumbling of each other's stomachs was hard to ignore, but they did their best to focus on their Lyre. Oleevar lit his Diamoz stone to give them more light. Cohlen followed suit, uncovering the glow of his bravery amulet.

Oleevar cleared his throat before taking both Cohlen and Chrishtan's hands in his. "Cohlen, Chrishtan, it is vital that we work together on this one. It is imperative that we harness as much Lyre as possible in order to gain a clear sense of where we might find a way out. In order to do this,

I think we must first attempt to discover the location from which we are pulling the light energy for our Diamoz stones. Once we have done this, we can use our feelings to sense the direction from which the energy is coming. If at all possible, we must discern the aura of this place and sense any location that has an aura different from this. It may be coming from an exit. Lastly, it is very likely that it is still raining. Focus hard on your scents and try to discover the location of rain-soaked grass and soil. Search for the sound of wind blowing through the leaves of the trees. Wind may also lead us out of here. I truly believe we can do this. We have all been taught to accomplish tasks such as these. But never before has so much depended upon it. We must do it, for our mentors."

Chrishtan and Cohlen held hands and repeated the phrase. "For our mentors."

"For our families," Chrishtan added.

"For our families," the other two repeated.

The three boys held hands and closed their eyes. As they slowly pacified their minds, they focused solely on their senses in search of a way out. With their minds completely locked, they reached deep within themselves to harness as much Lyre as possible. Nearly an hour of meditation had gone by when Chrishtan opened his eyes once more. Oleevar immediately followed before Cohlen opened one eye to see if he was the only one having trouble.

Cohlen frowned. "Oleevar, there is nothing."

Oleevar looked at Chrishtan. "How about you?"

Chrishtan diverted his eye contact and shook his head. "Nothing, I can't hear anything. I can't smell anything. I can't even taste anything, let alone sense anything. This place is devoid of energy, of life."

Oleevar looked down as he shrugged his shoulders. "It is the same for me. The only thing I can hear is the gurgling within our bellies. The only thing I can smell is the stench of our rancid breath, and the only thing I can taste is the dry roof of my own mouth. I sense despair within each of us."

Cohlen laid his head in his brother's lap and began to cry.

"I'm so hungry, Olee. I miss Mother and Father. I don't want to die here."

CHAPTER 18
FRIENDS IN THE FOREST

The pitch black fog of the Lantern Forest hid all that the boys feared surrounded them within its depths. The dead silence nurtured the fears that grew inside their young minds. Not a single glimpse of light could be seen outside the boys' Diamoz crystals. Oleevar cradled his brother's head in his arms.

"We're not going to die here, Cohlen. We will figure this out. I promise."

Chrishtan looked over at the small red-haired boy and felt terrible. He wished he could make him feel better. He wished he could see his joyful smile once again.

"You know, Cohlen," Chrishtan said, touching him on the shoulder. "We *will* make it out of here. I know we will. And when we do, we'll be so brave that no one will be able to hurt us. You'll go back to your family and show them what a grand hunter and ranger you've become. I promise."

Cohlen closed his eyes and nodded. Chrishtan could tell Cohlen was exhausted and had nothing left to give.

"Chrishtan," Oleevar sighed, "perhaps you and I should try once again, just the two of us. Cohlen is too weak and may have altered our abilities. Let's try one more time."

Chrishtan presented Oleevar with both his hands. With Cohlen asleep in Oleevar's lap, the two older boys meditated once more. Only a few minutes passed when an owl's hoot broke through the silence. They instantly opened their eyes. Cohlen lay fast asleep as Olee and Chrishtan listened closely for the owl. It hooted once more. Olee and Chrishtan raised their Diamoz stones high to search the trees for their hooting visitor, but saw nothing. Once again, they heard the owl's call. It sounded as if it were right behind them. The boys jolted around to see a tiny owl flying directly at them.

They ducked as it swooped overhead and landed on the ground in front of them. They held their breath as they stared at the peculiar owl. Mesmerized by its glowing red eyes, the boys froze in place. The owl stared back, studying them as it cocked its head from side to side and back and forth. After a moment of review, the owl hopped in their direction. The boys leaned back and gasped.

"Hello," it said in a small scratchy voice.

The boys' eyes grew two sizes. Oleevar's mouth opened, but nothing came out.

"H–h–hello," Chrishtan barely managed.

The owl hopped toward him. "Whooo are yoou?" a hoarse voice scratched out of its little mouth.

Oleevar seemed to be stuck, staring at the bird. Chrishtan, wide eyed and terrified opened his quivering lips. "Uh. W–well, Uh I am Chrishtan a–and this is Oleevar and his b–brother Cohlen."

The owl twitched its head from side to side. "Chriiishtan, Oleevaaaar, Cohleeen. Are you huuuman?"

Chrishtan nodded. "Y–y–yes. I am human, and they are elves."

The owl hopped onto Chrishtan's legs and stared up at him. "Ah, yes. Very niiice. Very nice indeeeed."

The boys exchanged terrified expressions. Oleevar finally managed to clear his throat. "Who are you? W–w–what do you want?"

The owl rotated its head toward Olee. "Whooo am I? I am friend. I help yoooou."

Chrishtan sat up straight. "How can you help us? Who are you? What are you?"

Revolving its head back toward Chrishtan, the owl glared. "I told you. We are friend. We are all your friends. We can help yoooou."

Oleevar raised his voice. "What do you mean, *we*?"

The owl looked up and around before starting again in its scratchy tone. "I mean aaall of us. Weee are friend. Weee help yoooou."

Chrishtan and Oleevar looked up. What they saw left their mouths hanging wide open. Lanterns hanging from the branches lit up with soft red light all around them. Additional pairs of red eyes surrounded them and faint whispers filled their ears. Some whispered *welcome,* while others said, *little boys* or *yes.* Chrishtan looked down at Cohlen to make sure he was still asleep. They did not dare wake him in this frightening moment.

Oleevar glared at the meddlesome owl. "What are you? Where are we?"

"Weee are the Red Owls. Weee are friend. Weee help yooou young ooones."

As the red owl spoke, a few glowing balls of red light floated out from the lanterns and down toward the boys. Once close enough, the boys discovered that they were not actually floating balls of red light, but tiny pixies with wings. Their bodies were painted in red, and their solid black eyes angled upward into their odd-looking faces as they surrounded the three intruders. The black-haired fairies pulled and sniffed the boy's hair and pinched the skin on the boys' faces.

Chrishtan heard the fairies murmur to themselves, *Yes. Very good. Mmm, yes. Very nice indeed.* With the fairies so close, the boys noticed their sharp, lengthy fingernails.

"What do you want with us?" Oleevar trembled.

"We want to help yooou," the eerie owl reiterated.

From the corner of his eye, Chrishtan watched the fairies poking and prodding him. "Help us how?"

The owl turned around and hopped down Chrishtan's leg onto the blanket before transforming into a red fairy. "Come, little Chrishtan. I show you."

The fairy that had once been a small owl waved its hand, signaling all the others to follow as they left the boys behind. Her voice transformed into something much more inviting as she waved. "Come, come. This way. I show you now."

The swarm of fairies giggled as they gestured the boys in their direction. Oleevar and Chrishtan exchanged equally anxious glances. They heard moaning and looked down to see Cohlen waking from his deep slumber. As he sat up, his eyes bulged with surprise. The fairies reciprocated the intrigue as they watched the small boy wake in front of them. In unison they greeted him, floating toward him in one big ball of glowing red light.

"Hello, little one. Welcome to the Red Lanterns."

Cohlen glanced at Chrishtan for reassurance before saying anything.

Chrishtan nodded.

"Hello. Who are you?" Cohlen waved. He looked around to see that they were no longer in the dark. Red lanterns exposed red vines and deep purple leaves all around them.

"We are the Red Owls. We are friend. We help you," they answered.

The sound of his starving belly broke through the silence. "I am very hungry," he cried.

The lead fairy smiled with her lips closed. "I can help, little one. Follow me."

"Follow us," the pixies chimed as they flew off into the forest.

Famished and desperate for food, Cohlen ran off after the red fairies. Oleevar and Chrishtan shot up after him, calling his name through the trees as they chased the brilliant choir of lustrous red balls further into the forest. Not far from their location sat a glorious picnic in the middle of a clearing. Cohlen was the first to run toward the astounding array of breads, cheeses, and fruits atop a red silk blanket. Chrishtan and Oleevar tried their best to put a stop to Cohlen's race toward the spectacular feast, but were unsuccessful.

"Cohlen, wait. Slow down!" Oleevar called.

As the two older boys got closer, the pungent aroma of food dissolved any and all apprehension. They were all starving and could not resist the mouthwatering buffet laid so elegantly before them. The red fairies perched on tree branches all around as they smiled with their lips, savoring the sight of three young boys filling their empty bellies with food. Faint whispers echoed through the trees as they shoveled food into their mouths. *Yes, eat. It is delicious. Have as much as you'd like. You will never go hungry here.* The boys stuffed their faces with breads, cheeses, and fruits until they could eat no more. Once finished, a pair of red fairies brought out small pastry pies filled with a strange red fruit the boys had never tasted before. Oleevar, who claimed to be too full to eat any dessert, lay back on a pile of red silk pillows as Chrishtan enjoyed a single pie. Colin finished the rest. With their stomachs full, the crumb-covered boys rested their heads on the red silk pillows before them and dozed off to sleep. Inside their dreams, horrific memories disappeared and joyful images of families and loved ones moved in as if nothing had ever changed. Their woodland friends had cured all that ailed them. They no longer had to fend for themselves. Finally, someone was taking care of them.

CHAPTER 19
OLEEVAR

The Lantern Forest glowed with the rosy light of the Red Owl Fairies. The once eerily silent wood echoed with the laughter of three young boys finding joy away from the rest of Lerim. They had no idea how long they had slept before waking from their blissful slumber. But once they did, they felt at ease and perfectly content. They laughed, and played as if everything wrong with the world had been made right. They were finally able to live in the moment and were content to do so. Thoughts of their mission, their families, and lost mentors no longer loomed over their adolescent heads. It was as if they had no recollection of their purpose or experiences. Nothing else mattered.

The red fairies grinned and nodded, seeming pleased by the blissful antics of the three young boys. When the boys got hungry, the fairies would feed them. When they got tired, they would watch them sleep. But as time passed, Oleevar's logic started to seep through the ignorant bliss that flooded their minds. Finally, he became fully aware of their plight once more, reminding him that they were still lost. He called Chrishtan away from a stick battle with Cohlen.

Out of breath, Chrishtan plopped down on the soft, silken blankets of their giant grass bed and placed a hand on Oleevar's shoulder. "What is it, my very astute friend?"

Oleevar shot him a dirty look. "Don't even begin to poke fun at me, Chrishtan. Something is not right here."

Chrishtan answered with a sharp twinge of anger in his voice. "What do you mean 'isn't right?' We've found the Lantern Forest. We have food, drink, and fun. What could possibly be wrong?"

Oleevar looked down and shook his head. He contemplated Chrishtan's strange reaction. "There is no need to get angry, Chrishtan. I've been sensing something.

Something feels off to me."

Chrishtan's typically gentle blue eyes appeared wild. "We have everything we need right here. We don't need to overthink this, Olee. We did what we set out to do, just as our parents sent us to do. We are here, and we don't need to worry about anything anymore. No monsters, no one trying to kill us." Chrishtan's voice changed. "So leave it be, Oleevar!"

Oleevar's eyes grew wide as he backed away from his fuming friend. The depraved voice from Chrishtan's mouth terrified him.

Chrishtan's eyes bulged as he slapped a hand over his own mouth as his eyes darted back and forth. He turned around to see if Cohlen had witnessed the frightening anomaly, but he hadn't. Chrishtan uncovered his mouth and leaned in to whisper to Olee. "I am so sorry Olee. I–I–I don't know what came over me. I'm so sorry. Please forgive me."

Oleevar looked around to make sure the fairies were not listening. "It's all right, Chrishtan. It's like I said. There is something not right here. We've been here for I don't even know how long. There is no sense of time here, and the fairies watch our every move. Every day they feed us, but where are they getting the food? It doesn't make sense to me. It all seems fabulous, but it doesn't add up. They have answered no questions thus far and have made sure to keep us plenty occupied. Something feels horribly wrong. I don't know what yet, but something is up."

Chrishtan looked down and ran his hand across the silk beneath his legs. "You may be right, Olee. Ever since we came here, I haven't had a single thought about all the horrible things that have happened, and in a way, I prefer it. I haven't had to think about anything at all. I had forgotten everything. The only thing I have thought about is getting more and more food. I'm constantly waiting for the next meal. I crave and long for it. Nothing else matters."

Oleevar leaned toward his friend's ear. "I've had the same

experience. It's as if they're trying to distract us. We were supposed to find the Lady of the Realm. I haven't seen her. Not to mention that this is not anywhere near where we were supposed to enter the forest to begin with. I think these fairies are up to something. I need to figure out what."

The boys remained close together as an owl glided down between them. It spoke in a sharp and raspy voice. "Are youu not satisfiiied? Do yoou neeed more fooood? I can briiing yooou desserts. Yoooou can have mooore if yoooou'd like."

The boys backed away. They exchanged dismayed glances before faking smiles at the owl that glared up at them.

"No, we are not hungry," Oleevar answered. "However, we are also not satisfied."

The tiny owl cocked his head to one side before hopping toward the unsatisfied elf. "Not satisfiiied? Not huungry? What doooes this little prince requiiiire?"

Oleevar mustered a firm tone. "What I require, my tiny little friend, is answers. Not like the ones you have already given us, but *real* answers."

The owl twitched its head back to the other side and continued forward. "Ansssswers? Quessstions? Whaaat for? You are happy heeere. Are yoooou not?"

Oleevar swallowed hard. "We greatly appreciate all you have done for us. Please don't misunderstand. We cannot thank you enough for your accommodations. However, we have no idea where we are or who you are. We cannot stay here forever. We have somewhere we must be."

The owl eerily tilted its head to the opposite side and back again. "Yoooou do not liiiike us? Yoooou are not sssatisfied with our fooood, drink, and bed? You want to leave?" Its voice cracked.

Chrishtan jumped in to defuse the conversation. "Of course we like you. You all have been great. You have given us plenty of food and a soft bed to sleep on. We like you very much." Chrishtan shot a look at Oleevar urging him to play along. "I think what my friend was trying to say is that we are still lost. We are looking for someone. Maybe you can help us, yes?"

Oleevar humored his friend and the vexed owl. "Yes, precisely. I was just asking for your help. You see, since you all are so helpful."

The owl had not caught onto Olee's tone and moved its head upright. "Yeesss. We are helpfuuul. Weeee will help yooou. Yooou will be satisfiiied. Yooou are not loooost. Yooou are with the Red Lanterns. Neeever lost with the Reeed Lanterns. Weee are friend. Weee help yooou find what you search fooor."

Chrishtan smiled. "That is fantastic. We are looking for the Lady of the Realm. Do you know where we can find her?"

The red owl paused for a moment as its head moved back and forth before glaring up at Chrishtan with its red eyes. "Yeees, I knooow the Lady. I can bring her too yooou."

The boys grinned. "You can?"

The petite owl spoke in a more pleasant tone. "Yeees, I can. I will fly to herrrr and invite herrr for dinner. Yooou will seeee. I can help yooou. Yooou will be satisfiiied."

The eerie owl flapped its wings and flew off into the pitch black of the surrounding wilderness. With the suspicious owl gone, the boys felt safe enough to continue their discussion. Cohlen ran over to join them, swinging his stick as he skipped.

"What are you guys doing? Chrishtan, aren't we going to play more swords?"

"Not now Cohlen." Oleevar snapped.

Cohlen dropped down to his knees to join his older brother and friend before setting his makeshift sword on top of the silken sheets. "Olee, I can talk too, with the two of you. I don't want to be left out anymore. You can tell me too, you know!"

Oleevar barely acknowledged his little brother's muttering. "Oh, all right... all right..." He continued to talk to Chrishtan as if Cohlen were not there.

Chrishtan cleared his throat. "Do you think it's true? Do you think they can help? I mean, bring the Lady of the Realm to us?"

Oleevar looked down and shook his head. "I just don't know. Something still doesn't feel right. Did you see the way it reacted to us wanting to leave? It was as if we had said the very words that we weren't supposed to say. Also, the answers given were more like questions. They never tell us anything. I suppose we shall see at dinner."

Cohlen was still determined to be a part of the conversation. "See what? What is happening at dinner?

"Cohlen, you need to keep your voice down or they will hear us." Oleevar shushed.

Cohlen spoke in a loud whisper. "Who will hear us? What is wrong?"

Oleevar sighed. "You must talk more quietly. I am not sure who these fairies are or what they want with us. We need to be cautious. Do you understand?"

Cohlen instantly stood up, his lip quivering as he yelled. "What are you talking about Olee? These fairies are our friends. They are helping us. More than you have helped us! We were starving, and now we have food. We were stuck in the rain, and now we have a safe, dry place to sleep. My tummy doesn't hurt anymore. Why would you say that, Olee?"

Chrishtan pulled Cohlen back down to the sheet as he looked around at all the fairies and owls in the trees. "No, no, no, Cohlen. It's all right. Uh, your brother is just tired. I think he stayed up too late last night. He wasn't saying that. He was simply saying that he wanted to get to know our new home and the fairies better." Chrishtan nodded at Oleevar, giving him a *you'd better play along* look.

Oleevar eyed the owls and fairies that spied on them from the trees. "Yes, Cohlen, what I mean is that I would like to get to know our new friends better."

The red eyes that scrutinized the scene seemed satisfied

with Oleevar's words.

Cohlen beamed in approval. "Good. They are our friends. They help us. We are all safe now."

Oleevar was profoundly upset by his little brother's outburst and so spent the rest of the day by himself until dinner. Chrishtan, on the other hand, was not as perturbed as his elven friend. He opted to play bows and swords with Cohlen until meal time. It was the only measure of time they had. They never knew whether it was day or night, morning or evening. They based their days on their sleep cycle and meal patterns. When they were tired, they slept and assumed it was night. When they woke and played, they assumed it was day. Some fairies slept when the boys slept and others when the boys were awake. Either way, no matter what time, day or night, someone was watching them.

To Oleevar, it meant control, manipulation, and loss of freedom. To Cohlen, it meant he was safe with someone always looking after him. He could tell Chrishtan was torn. They all wanted so badly to believe that they had succeeded in their task and located the Lady of the Realm. And with all of the terror they had experienced over the past couple of weeks, Oleevar understood why they longed for stability. He knew there was nothing outside the forest for Chrishtan. But there was a good chance that Oleevar's parents could still be alive. Cohlen seemed to have forgotten all about them.

Oleevar, on the other hand, had not forgotten anything. *I will complete this mission and return home to my family. I know they're still alive and waiting for me in Samisius. I refuse to forsake my dreams and aspirations of ruling over Ellios. The life and safety of my people depends on it. I can save my people. All of them. I will defend Samisius and Ellios if it's the last thing I do. I refuse to stay here in this awful place.*

***

Oleevar twiddled his nervous thumbs as he awaited the arrival of their dinner guest. He was still uncertain of what to believe and did not wish to invest himself in a lie. Chrishtan spent the day with Cohlen to give Oleevar his space. With Chrishtan and Cohlen still battling swords, the fairies prepared for a special dinner. A group of twenty or so fairies conjured a table and chairs to eat on instead of their usual picnic. Watching the fairies conjure furniture out of thin air astounded Chrishtan and Cohlen. Oleevar on the other hand, acted as if it did not impress him in the slightest. *I just do not understand how they can be so awestruck with a place that could potentially be the death of them.*

The fairies conjured a red silk table cloth, a candelabra, plates, glasses, and silverware. Usually the boys ate with their hands, but this was a special occasion. The Lady of the Realm would be joining them, thus allowing them the ability to complete their mission, save their kingdoms, and return home. Or so Oleevar hoped.

The pixies rushed over to the boys and hurried them along to the ornately carved round table. It was set for a fabulous dinner. Oleevar dragged his feet the entire way as the fairies flew in with fruits and appetizers. He grudgingly sat down at the table with his brother and Chrishtan.

Cohlen was thrilled to have such a fancy feast. He gently draped the red material of his silk napkin across his lap. "Look at all this," he smiled. "Isn't it wonderful? The fairies are so nice. They've made a special and fancy dinner just for us. What great friends they are."

Chrishtan smiled in agreement with Cohlen and then at Oleevar. He smoothed his napkin over his lap as Cohlen had. "Actually, Cohlen, this is a special dinner because we have a special visitor."

Oleevar shot Chrishtan a dirty look. He did not want Cohlen getting his hopes up if they were going to be duped by a ring of conniving fairy folk. He felt as if Chrishtan was trying too hard to be nice to Cohlen. The two of them had been getting on his nerves the entire afternoon. *How are they able to play around when their lives are being held in the balance and they may never get back to their homes?*

The thought infuriated him. As he ignored the excited conversation of the other two, his eyes wandered the surroundings, studying the trees, leaves, bushes, and creatures around him. The tallest and largest of the trees were tall enough and wide enough to block out all sunlight. He could not see the tops of them, but assumed this was the case. In the candle light, he was able to see that it was not just the red lanterns that made the leaves look red. The entire forest around them was laden with different shades of deep red and purple leaves.

A shadowy figure startled Oleevar. It glided out from under the trees along what looked like a narrow path. It was difficult to make out what the figure was until it stepped into the light. It was a woman garbed in an ornately decorated dress with a hood. Her gorgeous red gown with black designs fit tight around her waist and bosom. Its neckline plunged low enough for the boys to see much of her cleavage. A red silk train slithered along behind her. At the waist, her dress was laced tight with a black rope that looked as if it were made of hair. Hanging from her neck was a dark metal chain holding an ornate amulet set with a large black oval stone in the center. On her hand sat a ring to match the necklace. Her fingernails were long and matched her black jewelry. Her waist-length black hair made her deep red lips stand out even more on her porcelain face. Her puckering lips lay perfectly over her teeth. She was the most beautiful woman the boys had ever seen. They stared into her eyes. Her irises gleamed with a red brown hue on either side of her petite nose. It came to a flawless slope.

All three boys followed the woman with their eyes as she glided toward the table. Chrishtan rushed over to pull a chair out for her at the head of the table. She smiled with her mouth closed. Chrishtan gave her a nervous and silly grin as she removed her hood. Oleevar and Cohlen stood as the stunning lady gracefully took her seat. With the woman seated and her chair pushed in, the three boys sat back down. A discreet crowd of fairies and red owls watched the dinner party's every move.

Chrishtan was the first to speak. "Hello, I'm Chrishtan. Are you the Lady of the Realm?"

The woman smiled with her mouth closed. "I am." She nodded.

An enormous grin came over Chrishtan's face. "I knew it. It *is* you!" Chrishtan beamed at the other two boys. "We did it! We found the Lady of the Realm. We've completed our mission all on our own."

Cohlen grinned ear to ear as he hugged Chrishtan. "We did it, Chrishtan. We can go home now. I can go home to see my mother and father."

Oleevar was not convinced. "So *you* are the Lady of the Realm? Then please do tell us what it is we have come here to do so that we may return to our homes."

Still harboring a closed mouth grin, the woman turned to Oleevar. "*This* is your home now." Her voice was soft and smooth as she wove the words together like the silk of her dress.

Before Oleevar could reply to the undesired answer, Cohlen's voice rang out in an even higher pitch than before. "But what about my mother and father? I want to see them. I miss them."

Oleevar sat up straight in his chair. Once again, he was interrupted, only this time by the seductive tone of the beautiful black haired woman. "Do not fret, little one. You will see them soon enough."

This time, Oleevar would not miss his chance to speak. "So, you're saying we get to leave, correct? Our parents are in our homeland. That is the only way we will see them."

Oleevar took a deep breath before continuing his explanation just as the fairies brought out the first course of dinner, filling his nose with an intoxicating aroma. All three boys salivated at the enormous feast. As they devoured each course, another was fetched, all the way through dessert. Each bite was heaven, and each savory morsel rendered Oleevar's questions further from his mind. Each taste led the boys closer to rapture. With their ravenous minds focused solely on the flavors inside their drooling mouths and satisfied bellies, no one noticed that the Lady of the Realm did not share in the feast. Instead, she watched intently as the three gluttonous boys piled food into their mouths, completely ignoring the silverware the fairies had set for them. Their hands were much more efficient for the rate at which they devoured their delicious meal. Their voracious behavior brought a hint of a grin to the woman's deep red lips.

When dessert finally arrived, the boys' eyes opened wide at the pile of small pastries with red fruit filling. A mouthwatering aroma wafted from the pastries, inciting the boys to grab at the silver tray as it dropped in front of them. The boys demolished the pile of tiny pies, leaving noticeable remnants of red goo all over their faces. The three boys shared a look of disappointment at their mess. They wiped the stains away using the red silk napkins from their laps. And although the boys had eaten more than their fill, they still yearned for more. An insatiable hunger loomed inside their bellies as they sat in front of their gorgeous guest.

Chrishtan smiled broadly at the gorgeous woman. "Dinner was delicious. Thank you so much."

The woman closed her eyes and nodded. "You are most welcome, Chrishtan."

Oleevar and Cohlen rushed to thank her in unison, jumbling their words as they spoke over one another.

"It was my pleasure, young princes, I assure you." Her luscious lips puckered as she grinned.

Cohlen smiled at the lady with all of his teeth. "It was very good. The best. When do we get to see Mother and Father?"

The woman pushed her chair back to stand. "In good time, little one. All in good time."

With their bellies full, Oleevar and Chrishtan faded in and out of drowsiness. They struggled to keep their eyes open as they waited for the woman to answer Cohlen's question. All three boys passed out at the table, each of them pulled into an abysmal sleep that struck them faster than a bolt of lightning.

Off in his deep dreamscape, Oleevar lived out his deepest desires. He was finally headed off to the Ellios Academy to harness his skills in the most profound and proficient ways possible. He had become the most efficient hunter and archer in order to join his kingdoms' forces as an officer, the most decorated of his faction. His little brother cuddled with his mother in the living area of their palace as she told him stories of fairies and dragons. His father accompanied Cohlen to archery practice with the other boys, and Oleevar took time out of his busy schedule to spend time with him and help him get better.

Their hopeful dreams allowed them to travel along the fork in the road that had been washed away by evil. Their families were whole once again and their relationships repaired. It was their life without tragedy. What could have been. What should have been. A life without the selfish egos of men lusting for power and breeding evil.

***

The tremendous trees hummed with whispers of fervent fairies and eager owls who watched three young boys sleep deep inside the Lantern Forest. Their whispers faded as the boys stretched and woke from their serene slumber. The boys' stomachs ached with insatiable hunger, and they wondered how long they had slept. Although they had no recollection of putting themselves to bed, the boys found themselves blanketed by a heavy silk sheet. Their bodies were dressed in the same red material. As they stood and stretched, they carefully studied their new attire. They *oohed* and *aaahed* as they touched the gentle fabric of their long pants and matching shirts. Their new wardrobes reminded them of the Lady of the Realm's dress of long bell sleeves and red silk. Like her, they now wore long necklaces of silver that held a black oval gem in the center. And though their gems were not as large as the Lady's, they admired them with great appreciation, feeling like princes once again.

Before they had a chance to speak of their dinner experience, the smell of tantalizing food wafted through the air and into their noses. They snapped their heads around to see the same ornate table and chairs as before set with a plethora of wondrous foods. All three boys rushed to the table in unison and sat down. Once again, they neglected their silverware as they brutally attacked the meal before them. It was as if they had not eaten in months. In the middle of stuffing their faces, a red fairy floated down to the center of the table. It took a few tries to gain the attention of the gluttonous boys before they gazed at her with crumbs and remnants of food stuck to their faces and mouths.

"Satisfied, are you not?" the fairy giggled, "Yes, I told you. I told you that you would be satisfied. I did not tell a lie, did I?"

The lethargic boys nodded their heads in agreement.

"I am glad you are satisfied," the fairy continued. "It makes me happy. You will always be very satisfied. You will want to stay here. You will not leave. Yes, you will be satisfied."

The fairy flew away and left the boys to finish their meal. After they devoured their main courses, they waited eagerly for dessert.

"This sure is delicious," Cohlen managed through a mouth full of food. "I was very hungry. I can't wait for dessert. That lady is so nice. She really takes care of us. Don't you agree?"

Chrishtan turned to his surrogate brother. "Absolutely the best meal I have ever had. We'll never go hungry again. I feel like a prince. A real prince, not like before in Abequa."

The mention of *before* caused Oleevar's drooping head to snap up as he gaped at Chrishtan and Cohlen. "Before," he muttered. "*Before, before this*. Cohlen, we cannot stay here. This is not our home." It was as if a light turned back on

172

inside Oleevar's head. He had not forgotten his home and his life. His real life awaited him outside of the dark, red forest trees.

Cohlen leaned forward and glared into Oleevar's eyes. "You are ungrateful, brother. You do not appreciate what has been given to you. You are selfish." His raspy voice sounded as if it were layered with another, much deeper voice.

Oleevar leaned back. His eyes opened wide and his eyebrows moved high above his browline. Cohlen was now pleasantly sitting back in his chair, but Oleevar noticed something unusual. Cohlen's pupils were dilated. The black circles had almost completely taken over the blue of his irises, and the whites of his eyes were overrun by thinly braided rivers of blood.

Cohlen and Chrishtan conversed with one another as if Cohlen's outburst never occurred. As they discussed the food and their anticipation of dessert Oleevar noticed that Chrishtan's eyes looked exactly like Cohlen's. Oleevar desperately needed to see his reflection. It was possible that he too displayed these symptoms. He abruptly got up from the table. *My pack, it has a mirror inside.* His mother had given it to him in the hopes that when he missed her, he could look into it and see her in his own reflection. Oleevar rushed over to where they had been sleeping and threw up the blankets and pillows in search of his pack. It was nowhere to be found. In an instant, he realized that his pack was still with Elliot. When they had run off to follow the fairies, they left the horses tied to the bushes. Oleevar panicked in the realization that they were still lost and had no idea where they were. They had been so desperate for food that they had forgotten everything else: their belongings, their homes, their horses, and even who they were.

In a frenzy, Oleevar searched for a solution that was nowhere to be found. He looked back to see Cohlen and Chrishtan passed out, face-down at the messy, crumb-covered table where they had just finished desert. In spite of his fear, Oleevar knew he had to pull himself together and come up with a plan to escape their charmingly deceptive captors. *We're not guests here. We're prisoners.* He had no idea what purpose they would serve to their wardens, but his gut told him it was something sinister. And somehow, it had crept into their souls, forcing them to forget anything rational or familiar. *I must get us out of here, no matter the cost.* But first, he needed to find his Lyre harness ring and search his packs for anything else that could assist them with their escape. With the other two boys trapped in their food comas and unable to question his absence, the time was now.

Glowing red eyes watched his every move as Oleevar snuck toward the tree line surrounding their grassy knoll. As he inched closer to his exit, the volume of whispers steadily increased. He knew it would not be long before a fairy tried to question him, and so he quickened his pace as he slipped into the blackness of the trees. Unable to see anything in the darkness, he reached for his pocket to pull out his Diamoz light. But his new silky attire had no pockets, which meant no light to guide him. Oleevar's fear and panic magnified. No one had tried to stop him on his way back into the forest. *Is it because they know I don't stand a chance? No,* he thought, *I can do this. I must take control of my emotions and hone in on my senses, harness my Lyre as best I can, meditate, and come up with a viable plan.*

Oleevar sat down on the grassy floor of the pitch black forest and focused on his Lyre. With the dark energy of the forest working against him, Oleevar knew it would be an incredible challenge. And since he could not see, he honed in on his senses of hearing and smell to lead him to the horses. *It's my only chance. I must remain strong.* As he closed his eyes, he felt the heavy necklace around his neck that he remembered housed a black stone similar to the Lady's. He ripped it off, breaking its chain, and threw it deep into the forest. He immediately felt a twinge of his Lyre energy flow steadily back through him. His body grew lighter and his drowsiness began to subside.

After a while, Oleevar was able to stabilize the slightest bit of Lyre and catch a whiff of Elliot and Boone. Following the hint of odor, Oleevar carefully and instinctively tracked his way to the horses. The journey seemed endless as he tramped blindly through the trees. When he finally reached them, they whinnied with pleasure as he patted their backsides. They too were overcome with fright in the wicked darkness of the forest. Oleevar felt around inside one of the packs for one of the Diamoz stones. He used his Lyre energy to light it. After spending so much time in the murky shadow of the forest, the light nearly blinded him. As his eyes adjusted, he desperately rummaged through his packs in search of his Lyre harness ring. He would need it to connect directly with his Lyre and could not recall whether he had taken it with him or not. His search through the packs left him empty handed.

Oleevar sighed, and all hope seemed to flee with his breath. He slunk down the side of his horse and onto the ground. He tossed the Diamoz light across the forest floor. Never before had he felt such frustration. He was smart, calm, collected, and logical. It was beneath him to feel this way. *Come on Olee, get it together. Think, think, think.* And just as he stood to retrieve his Diamoz light, a glint of light reflected off the ground. As he stepped closer to the Diamoz stone, the glimmer came into focus. Oleevar smiled at the sight of his and Chrishtan's Lyre harness rings lying on the ground near the light. *I don't recall leaving them here,* he thought. *They must have slipped off. So strange.*

Olee slipped his ring on, bringing another glimmer of hope. He knew full well that he was not yet well practiced at animorphism, but it was the only chance he had of escaping their devious captors. He sat on the forest floor, once more, to harness his Lyre. He focused as hard as he could to connect with it as the insidious forces of the Lantern Forest worked against him. Just like before, a large chunk of time went by before Oleevar was able to feel anything. It took every ounce of his being to harness enough Lyre to begin making the transformation. He knew exactly what he would become. He would morph into a tiny owl.

He took his mind back to the moment the first red owl landed on his leg. As he focused further, he drew on the energy of the meddlesome owl until what occurred in his mind became physical reality. When he opened his eyes again, he found himself standing on the forest floor looking up at the enormous horses. The Diamoz light glowed brightly in front of him. Oleevar hooted with pleasure at his success. After the Diamoz light faded away, he was still able to see through his new red owl eyes. It was vastly different from his usual elf vision. Everything around him was red, and he could easily make out the white outlines of trees and objects. It was as if he was seeing everything through a red film.

The thought of being able to fly excited him. Oleevar hopped and flapped his wings and flew off toward the grassy knoll where he left Cohlen and Chrishtan. As he landed, Oleevar saw Chrishtan fast asleep on their bed of deep red silk. Cohlen was nowhere to be seen. Oleevar landed gently on the chest of his sleeping friend, letting out a loud hoot to wake him. Chrishtan shot up from his slumber with wide panicked eyes, panting heavily. Oleevar stood over him, inhis elvish form, with a heavy frown.

"Where is my brother?" he demanded.

Chrishtan met Oleevar's fuming gaze with a confused one. "What? What do you mean? He's here, isn't he?"

"No, he is not here." Oleevar cringed.

Chrishtan's fully dilated pupils searched for the boy. He was nowhere to be seen. "But...well, then... where– where did he go? You were here Oleevar. We were eating, and then I don't know what happened. That's all I remember. Where were you?"

Oleevar knew he should not have left his brother, but he had no other choice. The guilt he felt came out as anger toward Chrishtan. "I had to leave this evil place to come up with a plan to get us out of here. I thought Cohlen would be safe with you, but you clearly do not know what it means to look after someone." Oleevar could tell this cut Chrishtan deeply.

"You think you are so much better than me because you are an elf?" Chrishtan spoke in a raspy layered voice. "Because you speak with your fancy tongue and talk down to me? You elves always think you're better than men. Treating us as if we're nothing. *You* are the one who left your brother here while you selfishly tried to figure out a plan to escape a place that does not need escaping. That does not make you more intelligent than me. It makes you a fool."

Oleevar smirked. "Well if that is what you truly believe, then you are the fool, my friend. Since we've met, I have done nothing but be of assistance to you. I have hunted food for you, listened to your obnoxious jokes and incessant mockery, and humored you in your meddlesome adventures. You're naiveté and unrealistic perception of the world is what led my brother to go missing and left us stranded here in this evil place. It is time you grow up, Chrishtan, and see that the world is no longer a safe place where you can fulfill your desires to be childish. And if I am the only one who is intelligent and mature enough to see this, then maybe it is best we part ways. But first, I must find my brother."

The sinister nature of their surroundings ate away at their souls, replacing their open minds with narrow and resentful ideas. Overcome with anger for one another, they left all reason behind. It took everything in Oleevar's being to remain vigilant and not allow the blackness to take him any further. He could see his friend slipping away. Chrishtan's black pupils continued to grow as they flooded into the bloodshot whites of his eyes. His skin had become pale and grey, and in spite of the huge meals they had been eating, his fingers and face appeared bony and emaciated. Even his voice had begun to sound animalistic, inflected with a deep growl.

Oleevar shook off his resentful state of mind caused by his surroundings, allowing logic and reason to return. He knew that Chrishtan did not mean what he had said. He was clearly being possessed or transformed in some way. Oleevar felt bad for what he had said to Chrishtan. He had allowed the evil to take him for a moment. It would take everything he had to keep his vigilance in order to find his brother. But he needed Chrishtan's help, and Chrishtan was no good to him in this demonic state. Oleevar eyed the black stone amulet hanging from his friend's neck.

"Chrishtan, I am very sorry. I didn't mean the things I said. I am just very upset, and I think you are, too. You are not yourself.

Chrishtan scowled. "What do you mean? I'm fine. It's you who has become such a nagging, naysayer. All you want to do is cause trouble. You're never satisfied. And now you've lost your own brother."

The words cut deep, but Oleevar knew it was the evil speaking. "You're right. This is all my fault. I have been ungrateful, and because of that, I have lost my brother. But do you think you could find it within yourself to forgive me and help me find him?"

Chrishtan glared at his friend with his enormous black eyes. "If you are truly sorry, and you promise not to meddle with things that ought not be meddled with any longer, then, yes, I can forgive you."

Oleevar smiled as he stepped closer to his friend. "Thank you. May we embrace?"

Chrishtan nodded and Oleevar put an arm around him. As they hugged, Oleevar carefully snuck a hand in between their bodies, grasping Chrishtan's amulet tightly. An animalistic screech raged from Chrishtan's mouth as Oleevar yanked the amulet from his neck, breaking the chain and throwing it deep into the woods. Oleevar covered his ears. The deafening screech billowing from his friend's lungs finally faded away, rendering Chrishtan unconscious on the forest floor. Oleevar dove to the ground, cradling Chrishtan's head in his arms.

"Chrishtan, Chrishtan, wake up. Please wake up."

178

Oleevar patted his friend's cheek.

Chrishtan coughed before gasping for air. "Where am I? What's happened?" Tears welled up in his bloodshot blue eyes before slithering down his cheek.

Oleevar sighed with relief. "It's going to be all right. Here, put this on." Oleevar slipped Chrishtan's Lyre harness ring onto his thumb.

As the bloody rivers in his eyes returned to white, Chrishtan's hyperventilating dissipated. Oleevar looked into his friend's brilliant blue eyes before holding him tight. "Thank the Architect you're all right. Chrishtan, how do you feel?" Oleevar could see the terror in his friend's eyes.

"Where did I go, Olee? Where have I been? What's happened?"

"Chrishtan," Oleevar said, helping his friend to sit upright, "it's all right now. You're going to be all right. I believe there is an evil here that aims to hurt us. I am not sure exactly what it wants with us, but I know it is of a vile and menacing nature—a demon perhaps. This is why we must find Cohlen as quickly as possible."

Chrishtan gasped. "A demon? Oh Grand Architect, where is Cohlen? What do you mean we need to find him? We were just at dinner, weren't we?"

Oleevar looked directly into the eyes of his mortified friend. "There is no time to explain. We must find Cohlen as quickly as possible and get out of here."

Chrishtan stood. "All right, let's find him. But this place is so dark. Where do we look?"

Oleevar searched their surroundings. "I do not know yet. First we must check the perimeter and see if there are any paths or signs of entry or exit from this area."

The two boys scoured the perimeter of their dimly lit knoll. After only a few minutes of searching, Oleevar called Chrishtan over to where the dinner table usually sat. "Chrishtan, come here. You must see this."

Chrishtan rushed over and squinted into the dark forest to see where Oleevar was pointing.

"I think it's some kind of path. Look!"

It took a moment before Chrishtan was able to see exactly what Oleevar was talking about. A few meters into the forest, flat stepping stones, glowing red, hovered above the ground.

Chrishtan pointed. "I see it. I see it. It looks like a path or something. You truly are a great tracker. A fine specimen of your people."

Oleevar nodded. "Thank you. I think that is precisely what this is. It is the only lead we have right now, so we must follow it, and quickly."

CHAPTER 20
HAZALE

Countless whispers scorned Chrishtan and Oleevar's trek through the forest as they tiptoed across slabs of levitated pathway. In the black depths of the woodland, they could see nothing outside the red incandescent perimeter of each stone slab as it led them closer to a nameless terminus. But it was the only lead they had to find their missing brother.

"I can't see a thing," Chrishtan whispered.

"I know," Oleevar replied. "I can't either. But we must keep going. I have a feeling that this will lead us to Cohlen. We must trust it."

Chrishtan shed a hefty sigh "Yes, Oleevar, I know."

The boys continued along the twists and turns of the pathway until they noticed the floating slabs of rock ascend upward like a staircase. Chrishtan's eyes followed the floating steps up toward a doorway carved into the center of a large tree. The bottom half of the door remained closed, while the top half hung open. Both the open door and the window next to it flickered with the orange glow of a fire. The boys shuddered as they watched the shadow of someone or something move around inside.

Oleevar motioned for Chrishtan to stop behind him as he studied the scene above them. "Wait. We don't yet know what's in there, and it is more likely to be foe than friend. Or a foe acting as a friend. We must be extremely cautious. Do you understand?"

Chrishtan nodded. "I agree, but we need to find out if Cohlen is actually in there."

"I know. We will. Listen, I think we should go to the door and see if we can peek in and see what is in there. Then we'll go from there. But we absolutely must not be seen, all right?"

"I get it, Olee, I get it. Let's do this. But what if Cohlen isn't in there, then what?"

"I truly believe Cohlen is in there," Oleevar reassured him. "I can sense it. But if he isn't, then we will reassess and come up with a new plan, all right?"

"All right," Chrishtan sighed. "But I don't know about this. I have a bad feeling."

Oleevar sighed. "This whole place is one big bad feeling."

"You're right about that." Chrishtan shook his head.

The two boys crept up the levitated staircase trying not to draw attention to themselves. As they got closer to the door, they heard a disturbing voice chanting a tune.

Precious and dear to lose is fear
So sweet and soft pleasure is oft
When little ones come and beat my drum I
shriek with content for my gifts are sent
Sleep now child for you will soon be wild
And thirsty for gore of this I am sure
Precious child
Precious Gift
I live for your soul

Olee and Chrishtan froze dead in their tracks as they played audience to the grotesque voice of the nameless songster. Both boys slunk down before inching toward the door to sneak a peek at the anonymous poet. Inside they eyed a young child dressed in red silk, his neck ornamented with a black stone necklace, lying on a wooden table. The nameless figure prepared for something as it chanted its horrid rhyme over and over again. Black gemstones, like the one on the boy's necklace, enclosed the child's perimeter. The dim wavering of the fireplace made it difficult to make out the face of the boy on the table.

"The child is his size. It could be Cohlen." Chrishtan grabbed Olee's arm. "What do we do?"

Oleevar slapped a hand over Chrishtan's mouth.

"Quiet, or it will hear us."

Chrishtan frowned. "Sorry."

Oleevar shook his head. "It's fine," he whispered. "If it is Cohlen, he's alive. I can see his chest rise and fall. That is a good sign. Hopefully he is unharmed."

The boys held their breath as the cloaked individual stepped out of the shadows to collect the black gemstones surrounding the comatose boy. Olee and Chrishtan gawked at the back of a small molting head that looked like it had once had feathers. Three lengthy, talon-like fingers used their claws to pluck the stones from the table. Its grossly emaciated wrists were bony, bald, dry, and cracked, with equally withered hands. As the creature stepped back into the firelight, Olee and Chrishtan shuddered. Its humanoid head did not harbor the appearance of a person. Instead, it took on the face of a barn owl with big black eyes. A long, slender nasal cavity stretched far down to a long skinny bill that looked more like a clawed finger than a beak. Tufts of down feathers flaked away over its browline, while most of its head and face was covered in bumpy and wrinkly pink skin.

They gasped as the creature spread its arms and they caught a glimpse of the grotesque being's bald, emaciated body. Its mid-section looked completely human, with a bony rib cage, while its legs did not look human at all. The long, skinny limbs bent backward at the knee like the legs of a bird. Overall, it looked to be part human and part owl. But the boys knew exactly what it was. It was one of the numerous demons of the Destroyer.

Chrishtan held back tears as he muttered under his breath. "What do we do? It's a demon of the Void. We don't stand a chance."

"Ssshh," Oleevar whispered. "Be quiet. It'll hear you."

But it was too late. The demon shifted its gaze in their direction as the boys ducked behind the door. There was nowhere to hide. Oleevar and Chrishtan waited for the demon, but they did not hear any footsteps and the door did not open. Chrishtan covered his mouth as he looked up to see an eerie owl face with black eyes looking out the window directly above them. Then the demon headed back to the blind spot of the tree house.

Oleevar nudged Chrishtan. "I think it's gone."

Chrishtan slowly peered back through the window to see where the creature had gone, but could only see its shadow. He watched as its silhouette suddenly transformed into a more attractive figure. It stepped out from behind the blind spot to reveal the beautiful woman with black hair, once again garbed in her red, hooded dress. Chrishtan glared at her as she glided over to the boy on the table and covered him with a red silk cloth. When she looked back over at the window, the boys ducked back down as her footsteps shuffled toward them. Still crouching, they turned to exit down the floating stairs whence they came. They made it half way when the sliver of light from a creaking door shined over their escape.

"Leaving so soon, are we? You have not yet come in to say hello."

The boys slowly turned around to see the stunning woman from dinner standing in the doorway of the tree house.

"You have come to visit me, have you not?" Her gaze mesmerized them as it pierced through their souls.

The boys froze, speechless. They were caught with nowhere to run, left to the mercy of the Grand Architect to provide them a way out of their blunder.

"Uh, well, yes, Milady, we have." Oleevar answered.

The woman smiled as she always did, with her lips closed. "Splendid," she nodded. "Come in, come in. I have treats for you."

The boys swallowed hard as they entered the tree house. Inside, they found the table that once held a small boy set with dessert plates, goblets of juice, treats, and appetizers. A mouthwatering pile of goodies sat atop a three-tiered platter made of solid yellow gold to match the plates and goblets. Behind the table, a fireplace crackled with flames. Chrishtan eyed the sconces holding lit candlesticks that decorated the walls along with child-sized weaponry, such as small bows, swords, daggers, and staffs. He paused his gaze on an arched door to another room. He could not help but wonder what was behind it.

The lady turned to address the boys as they sat at the table. "You boys must be hungry. Please, have a seat. You may have as much as you'd like."

The woman's closed-lip smile became more unnerving each time they saw it. They knew exactly what she was, deep down, and it was certainly not what she appeared to be.

Oleevar humored the demon in disguise. "Oh yes, we are very hungry indeed. You see, we got lost looking for our little brother, Cohlen. We are so glad that we found you. Maybe you can help us to find him?"

Chrishtan shot Oleevar an uneasy look to say that it was *too much too soon.*

The woman did not make eye contact as she answered. "Your brother, you say? And he is missing? Do you have any idea what may have happened to him? Perhaps he ran away."

As he sat at the table, Chrishtan studied the miniature weapons hanging on the walls, wondering where they had come from. Simultaneously, he listened as Oleevar attempted to placate the deceitful woman once more.

"Perhaps he did. Is there any way you could help us to locate him?" Oleevar's voice trembled slightly as he did his best to camouflage his fear with ignorance.

Neither of the boys had touched the food, afraid of what it might do to them.

The deceitful woman cocked her head. "I thought you boys said you were hungry. Is my food not good enough for you? And what happened to the necklaces I gave to you? Those were a very special gift."

"Oh no, we are hungry," Chrishtan stammered. "And we, um, lost the necklaces on the way here. They… uh, slipped off… must have gotten caught on some bushes…" He answered as he reached for a small meat pie at the center of the arrangement. He gestured at Oleevar to do the same.

The demon in disguise glared at the boys as it waited for them to take a bite of the appetizer. They sluggishly used their forks to cut off a very small piece of the meat pie and shove it into their mouths. The demon still did not appear satisfied, prompting both boys to make disingenuous noises of pleasure to appease her.

"Yum, yes very good. Very good." They exaggerated.

The woman flashed her dishonorable smile and took a seat at the table with the boys as she watched them eat. "Well then, I suppose I will need to help my young princes find their necklaces and get them back to you."

The boys continued to eat knowing that they had no other choice. There was no escaping her now. Chrishtan studied the walls of weaponry as he drudgingly ate his meal. Suddenly, he spotted a small bow that hung behind Oleevar. He immediately recognized the markings carved into it. It was Cohlen's. *How did Cohlen's bow end up on that wall?* Chrishtan wondered. The woman glared at them with such intensity that Chrishtan did not risk pointing the bow out to Oleevar. It killed him inside that he had to remain unaware of it.

With their stomachs full and their goblets empty, the masqueraded demon grinned with approval. "Would you boys like more to drink or eat?"

Even though Chrishtan grew groggier with each moment that passed, he needed to find some way to distract her, to get her to leave or turn her back if even for just a moment. "Oh yes." Chrishtan smiled. "I would love some of your special red fruit pies. They are so delicious. Do you have any of those?" Chrishtan knew she didn't. She would have to summon the fairies to make them.

The demon smiled through plump red lips. "But of course. I will call the Red Owls straight away. You will not be displeased. Here, have some more to drink while you wait." The gorgeous woman topped off the boys' goblets. They grinned and pretended to drink before watching her open the door and walk out into the wilderness to summon the fairies. Chrishtan knew he had only seconds to grab a dagger from the wall; he needed something small enough to hide underneath his shirt. He spun around and grabbed a rogue's dagger and tucked it under his shirt before the demon returned. Oleevar stared at him in disbelief.

"Just trust me," Chrishtan whispered.

The boys immediately lifted goblets to their mouths and pretended to drink as soon as the demon walked back through the doorway.

She sat back down at the table with them. "You will have your desserts very soon, young princes. You will see."

Chrishtan smiled. "Thank you very much, Milady."

The boys sustained their make-believe sips until they saw floating red lights off in the distance. The demon glided away from the table to greet the fairies and take the pies. Chrishtan had eaten the pies many times before and loved them, but his new knowledge of this demon had his stomach doing summersaults. He knew that whatever filled those pies was not fruit at all, but a vile, disgusting, horrid substance.

Chrishtan's eyes trailed the demon's every move toward the door. He waited for the right moment. As he watched the red fairies retreat, he called upon his Lyre and jumped directly from his chair, with incredible ease, to the point where the demon stood with a tray of red pies. The gem on the hilt of the dagger radiated blue light as Chrishtan drove it deep into the demon's belly. A vile and deafening screech billowed from the demon's mouth as it dropped to the floor smashing the pies, splattering blood-colored filling everywhere.

Oleevar remained in his seat with his eyes wide open and his jaw hanging as the wounded demon writhed on the floor.

"Hurry, Olee," Chrishtan called. "Through that door!"

Oleevar hurdled over the table as fast as he could to meet Chrishtan on the other side. They flung the curious door open and scurried inside, locking it behind them, using the ornate key in the keyhole. To their dismay, the boys had not entered another room. Instead they found themselves outside on the edge of a giant bird nest. From the light of the torches that lit its perimeter, they could see child-sized Lyre rings of all different gemstones scattered within the intricately woven branches of the gigantic nest.

Chrishtan's eyes darted around the area. "My Architect, what is this place?"

Oleevar shook his head. "I do not know, but I believe it preys upon children. These are all the Lyre rings of very young mages." Oleevar pointed at the jewelry left behind. "Look at them all. They are everywhere. There must be thousands of them."

Chrishtan pulled his hair with both hands. "Hazale, it must be Hazale. I remember reading of him in a book I found in our library that Framin told me not to read. It's said that he feeds from the souls of children, turning their bodies into demonic wraiths who feed off the bodies of adults who wander into Hazale's keep. What are we going to do, Olee?"

"I do not know—" Oleevar gasped.

"What was that?" Chrishtan's eyes grew wide.

Both boys jerked their heads toward the chilling sound. It came from underneath a red silk sheet in a far corner of the nest. The sheet growled again as Chrishtan inched closer. Assuming that something sinister resided underneath, he broke off a large stick from the nest and used it to pull the red tablecloth off whatever hid beneath it.

"Chrishtan, please be careful!" Oleevar pleaded.

The exposed entity glared at Chrishtan with blacked out eyes as it snarled and hissed, revealing rows of razor sharp serrated teeth. It foamed at the mouth and twitched its head back and forth as it studied him. The possessed boy was smaller than both Oleevar and Chrishtan. His red hair was faded, and he wore the same red silk pajamas.

"Chrishtan," Oleevar's voice quivered. "Chrishtan, who is that? Answer me."

Chrishtan hung his head as his knees hit the nest floor.

Oleevar called over Chrishtan's sobs. "Chrishtan, please. What is it? Who is it?"

Tears streamed down Chrishtan's face. He could not muster the words to tell Oleevar what was underneath the blanket. In his heart, he prayed that maybe if Oleevar kept on asking, then a different answer would come to his lips. That he would say it was another strange creature, or that he didn't know who it was. But Chrishtan knew exactly who it was. They both did.

Oleevar fell to his knees. "No, please no. Please, oh grand designer of all things. Please do not let this demon, the Destroyer, take my brother. Please, I beg you." Tears flowed from the young elf's eyes.

Chrishtan could not bear to look at him. It killed him inside to see Oleevar in such pain and anguish. Chrishtan knew that Cohlen was gone. What was left of him had been transformed into a demonic shell. Cohlen was nothing and no one. He was now a monster who would feed on the flesh of any grown man or woman that wandered into Hazale's keep. Chrishtan knew it would not be long before the demonic boy became hungry. They needed to leave, and fast.

"Olee, we must go. We can't stay here. The demon is not dead and will be here at any moment."

Oleevar pleaded as tears rushed over his cheeks. "I can't leave. I will not leave my brother. We must take him with us."

"Oleevar." Chrishtan grabbed his friend by the shoulders as he attempted to appeal to his logical side. "You must listen to me. That is no longer Cohlen. I am so sorry, but Cohlen is gone. That is not him. You know this, Olee. I

189

know you do." Chrishtan found himself in tears once again. "I'm so sorry, my friend. I truly am. But we must leave now if we are to have any chance of surviving."

Oleevar hyperventilated at the sound of the demon, Hazale, pounding on the door. "No, I can't leave him. I won't leave him, Chrishtan!"

Chrishtan raised his voice. "Cohlen is gone, Oleevar. You cannot save him now. We must leave, or we too will suffer the same fate."

Oleevar rushed toward the black-eyed boy with pale, veiny skin and razor-sharp teeth. "Come, Cohlen. It's all right. You must come with me." Olee cradled his brother in his arms. "We are going home now, brother."

The demonic boy hissed and tried to bite Oleevar before slicing into his cheek with its claws. Oleevar jumped back. He touched his hand to the injury and pulled it away to see blood painted across his palm. Oleevar had no choice but to accept the agonizing truth of what had happened. It was no longer his brother. They were too late.

Chrishtan sprinted across the nest and pulled Oleevar away from the wraith. Once again, the demon child lashed out at both boys. Chrishtan knew it would be hungry soon and had no desire to be its first meal. With the demon, Hazale, breaking through the door, Chrishtan grabbed a torch to defend himself and Oleevar against the possessed boy. Cohlen's demonic shell snarled and clawed at them until Chrishtan landed a hit and burned the small wraith. The young demon let out a torturous squeal before running on all fours with unnatural speed and leaping onto the nearest tree. The boy skittered up its trunk like an insect, disappearing beneath the foliage.

Chrishtan raised the torch toward the great tree to make sure their wraith brother was backing off. What he saw hidden among the branches petrified him. The tops of the trees were filled with wraith children. They climbed and twitched like bugs as they scattered. They hissed and screeched in unison at the bothersome light of the flame.

Chrishtan's heart sank with the realization that all these children had all been taken from their families and loved ones, never to enjoy life again. Never to be with the Grand Architect. So many innocent lives taken.

The startling sound of the door crashing down behind him brought Chrishtan's mind back to the danger of their current situation.

Oleevar waved him over to the edge of the giant nest. "Over here, Chrishtan. We can climb down using these branches and vines. Hurry!"

In an instant, Chrishtan used his Lyre ability to jump with ease directly from where he stood to where Oleevar climbed down, following directly after him. As Chrishtan steadily made his way down after Oleevar, the staggering grip of talons pierced the skin on his back. Chrishtan screamed with pain. He looked up to see that Hazale had him by his red silk shirt. It squawked and screeched and tried to pull him back into the nest.

Oleevar shrieked as he watched the horrifying scene above him. "Just slip out of the shirt, Chrishtan. You can do it!"

Chrishtan struggled and tried to wriggle out of the blouse. A final jerk forced Chrishtan out of the shirt and sent him tumbling toward the forest floor. He feebly reached for branches as he plummeted. Suddenly, a hand grasped his wrist, putting an end to his deadly descent. It was Oleevar.

"Are you all right?" Oleevar managed through rapid breaths.

"I'm not sure." Chrishtan wheezed in pain. "I hit a couple of big branches on the way down. I think I may have broken my other arm." It took everything in him to keep from crying.

Oleevar squeezed his wrist tight. "It's going to be all right. We're going to get out of here, I promise. And we will never have to come back here ever again. Not ever."

Oleevar carefully helped Chrishtan to the ground. Once their feet hit the forest floor, Oleevar managed to find the trunk of a tree hidden among a bed of thick brush to lean Chrishtan against.

"Chrishtan, you are hurt too badly to come with me to get the horses," Olee whispered. "You need to stay here while I retrieve them. Do you understand?"

Chrishtan groaned as tears seeped from his fearful eyes. "I don't want to be alone. This place is wretched. I'm so scared, Olee."

Oleevar nodded. "I know, Chrishtan, I know. But it is the only way. I won't be gone long, I swear it. Please stay here. I'm going to mark you with my Lyre. This scent will allow me to find you more easily once I have the horses."

Chrishtan cringed as his friend transformed into a small owl and flew away. The thought of being left alone in such an evil place horrified him, but he knew Oleevar had to go. The pain of his broken arm worsened with each second that passed. Before he was able to respond to Olee, he fainted against the trunk of the hidden tree.

***

"Chrishtan, Chrishtan?" Oleevar shook the shoulder of his friend. "Wake up. Please, wake up. I've got our horses."

Chrishtan could hear Olee's voice, but was unable to speak. The shock and pain of his injury would not allow him.

Oleevar checked Chrishtan's pulse and his Lyre energy. He was still alive. But before waking him again, Oleevar tore a piece of red silk from his shirt and fashioned a sling to support his friend's broken arm. With Chrishtan's injured limb stabilized, Oleevar shook him much harder.

"Chrishtan, you must wake up."

Chrishtan still offered no response to his friend's requests. Oleevar placed both his hands on his friend's chest, and pumped a surge of his own Lyre into his body. Chrishtan's eyes jolted open.

"What's going on?" Chrishtan cried. "Where are we?" It was too dark for him to see Olee directly in front of him.

192

"It's me, Olee. I've brought the horses. It is finally time for us to leave this horrid place."

Chrishtan still felt very weak from his injury and the toxic food they had eaten. He fell forward with exhaustion. Olee caught him in his arms.

"Chrishtan, I need you to try and remain awake until I get you up onto my horse with me, all right?" Olee propped his friend up straight in his arms. "Are you able to do that?"

Chrishtan nodded. He struggled to stand even with Oleevar's help. He had even more difficulty getting onto Oleevar's horse. It took a few tries to get him safely into Elliot's saddle.

"I think I can sense a way out, Chrishtan. Hold on tight."

With both of them in the saddle and Chrishtan's horse Boone tagging along behind, Oleevar rode as fast as he could in the first direction that gave him the slightest sense of energy outside the demonic void.

CHAPTER 21
A SECOND CHANCE

Bright beams of sunlight creeping in through an arched window roused Chrishtan from his hibernation. His eyes fluttered open. He found himself snuggled in unfamiliar sheets of an unfamiliar bed inside an unfamiliar room filled with unfamiliar things. He squinted in the warm light of morning that poured through the window and onto his skin. The heat and energy of day sent a surge of vitality flowing through him as he stretched. He looked down at his left arm to see it wrapped in a white linen bandage with a splint underneath. *It hadn't been a nightmare. It was all real.* Flashes and vivid memories of the sinister forest prison overwhelmed him as he cried out.

"Mother? Father? Framin? Anyone?" He called out until a familiar face rushed into the room and bounced onto the lavender sheets next to him.

"You're awake!" Oleevar cheered.

"Yes, I believe I am." Although he was happy to see his friend Oleevar, his heart sank with disappointment. His mother and father would never again wake him.

Chrishtan stretched once more as he studied the cave-like walls of the room. They were decorated with wooden sconces that held lavender candles. A small table against the wall opposite him held an elaborate bouquet of purple and pink flowers. The beautifully carved matching tables on either side of the bed housed the same exquisite arrangement. He ran his hands over the smooth linen sheets covering his body. He looked down to see the same fabric in the outfit that he wore.

Chrishtan sighed. "So where are we anyway?"

Oleevar gazed out the window of their beautiful castle carved into the cliff rock of a massive waterfall on the edge of the forest. "We are home, Chrishtan. You are in the grand elven palace of Samisius, home to my family and capital to the people of this beautiful nation. You are free to live with us now. This can be your new home. I promise that you will love it here. Our exquisite community inside the Roeesar Forest is untouched by all things unnatural. Unlike humans, we do not commandeer building materials here. We simply live as we were intended within the natural confines of whatever the land provides to us. Here in Samisius, we do not build homes or structures, but simply dwell within the hollows of our trees and rock formations provided to us by the Grand Architect himself. It is truly a wonder. Before the influence of humans, we elves did not even use furniture. We saw no purpose in chopping down and killing living things in order to serve our own stylish purposes. All of the furniture in this palace was gifted to us by your kind. "

Chrishtan did not wish to insult his gracious friend's pride, but he had to know. "Well what about my home in Abequa?"

Oleevar did not turn to face his friend. "Abequa has fallen, Chrishtan. Lochran has taken it. I am so sorry."

Deep in his gut, Chrishtan already knew this to be true. His parents had been killed, which meant that their nation had most likely fallen along with them. "Well, what about Samisius? Is it safe here?"

Oleevar faced his friend with confidence. "Yes, we are very safe here, I assure you. Our contrivers of Ellios have designed a technology that can keep out any enemy, a sort of force field if you will. As soon as the kingdom of Huronus fell to Lochran five years ago, our contrivers spent every waking moment developing technologies to keep our nation safe. And one day, I will attend the academy there and help to design even more weaponry and defenses for my people."

Chrishtan turned his gaze toward the bedroom doorway. A stunning woman with long, silky, red hair pulled half up behind her tall pointy ears, strolled in. Her porcelain face, sprinkled with freckles, instantly reminded him of Cohlen. Tears welled in his eyes.

"How is our guest settling in?" she asked as she sat down on Chrishtan's bed. "I am Queen Lamoore, Oleevar's mother, and this is King Adreahn, Oleevar's father."

Chrishtan sat up straight in the bed to address the beautiful queen. "Very well, thank you. This room is perfect. Thank you for having me. How long have we been away?"

Oleevar's father, who was the spitting image of Olee, remained standing as he spoke. "You were trapped in the Lantern Forest for over six months, my son. But you are home now. You are safe with us. Oleevar told us your story. We are so very sorry for your loss. I assure you that our nations of Samisius and Ellios are working hard to establish a sturdy resistance against Lochran. I also wanted to say, thank you, for getting my Oleevar out of harm's way. He told us how you saved his life and got him away from the demon, Hazale. We cannot thank you enough. You are family now. Anything you need, we will provide it to you. You are now an honorary prince of Samisius and Ellios."

Chrishtan watched as tears welled up in Lamoore's soft blue eyes. Like the freckles, her eyes reminded him of Cohlen. He had been the spitting image of her. Chrishtan knew that Oleevar's parents were mourning the loss of their younger son. Chrishtan felt like he should say something to comfort them. He took Queen Lamoore's hand. "I am so sorry, Queen Lamoore. We tried so hard to rescue him. We really did." Tears glided down his face. He struggled to gain his composure. "Cohlen was a wonderful boy who brought me great joy while I knew him. I will miss him so much."

King Adreahn hung his head while Queen Lamoore leaned forward to embrace Chrishtan. "Thank you Chrishtan. We are so proud of both you and Oleevar. We know you did everything you could to try and save our Cohlen. He will be with us forever in our hearts; may we never forget him. We have all suffered great losses during this dark time. Therefore, we must stick together and have hope for the future if we are to prevail. May your generation be the answer to our prayers. A light in the blackness. A glimmer of hope in a time of war waged by evil and selfish men."

Her words made the tears flow from Chrishtan's eyes. "But why, Queen Lamoore, why is this happening? Why does Lochran want to destroy us all? I hate him so much for what he has done."

Lamoore grasped Chrishtan's hands as she looked deep into his moist eyes. "It may be difficult for you boys to understand, as it is difficult for most to understand. You see, sometimes when bad things happen to us in our lives, we look for someone to blame, someone to turn our anger and frustration toward. By doing this, it allows hate to enter our hearts and the Destroyer an entrance into our soul. When this occurs, it is easy for us to forget how to love. Hatred and anger for those who we believe have wronged us overwhelm all that we are. This is what the Destroyer wants. By fueling this hatred further, the Destroyer no longer allows us to think clearly or reasonably. When this occurs, one begins to objectify their perceived enemy, and ignore any context, explanation, or understanding of them. This anger and hatred allows those individuals to partake in heinous and seemingly unnecessary acts of oppression and violence under the guise of revenge, elitism, or false power. The Destroyer poisons them with a lust for power. He promises that power will heal all that ails them and avenge all that has wounded them. This is what happened to Lochran."

Chrishtan sat up straight in the lavish canopy bed. "But what happened to Lochran to make him so mad? Why is he so angry with us? We never did anything to him."

Lamoore nodded. "I realize that. We all realize that. But Lochran does not. He blames the people of Huronus and their close ally, Abequa, for the death of his father, whom he never had the chance to know. And after his mother, Princess Ginevir Jowellia, remarried to a man who was not of Lyre blood, it caused uproar. Elitist Lyre-bloods convinced Lochran that his father's death had been a conspiracy. He never forgave his mother, or the king and queen for allowing the marriage. And as he grew older, he became more resentful. He wanted nothing more than to become the ruler of his nation and other human nations. He and other elitists intended to do away with unclean marriages, such as his mother's. But you see, Lochran was not heir to the throne. His older sister was to inherit it. She did not see eye to eye with Lochran and his elitist ways. Thus, Lochran took the throne by force. He intends to do the same across our great continent, enslaving those born without Lyre. Somehow he has justified his behavior as a means to avenge his father. The Destroyer has taken advantage of this, and so Lochran traded pieces of his soul to gain power from the Destroyer, allowing evil to twist his mind and enter our realm."

Oleevar interrupted from his perch and moved to the bed next to Chrishtan. "But that is ludicrous! How can one person blame an entire population of people for the death of his father? It makes no sense to me. Believing that ruining the lives of others is going to somehow heal your own wounds is absolutely absurd and illogical, not to mention unreasonable."

Lamoore placed a hand on her son's cheek. "I know, my son. You will never understand these things because you are not human. You are an elf. Your mind does not work in the same way that a human's does. We are, for the most part, unclouded by our emotions. Though we still feel them, we do not allow them to hold dominion over our logic or action. This is a human trait. Also, every elf is born with blood of the Lyre so we do not categorize our people in classes. We are all equal."

Chrishtan hung his head in shame of his hideous human trait. He understood perfectly well what Lochran had felt for his stepfather and his people. And he understood how that had led him to the Destroyer. It was the exact same feeling that tore Chrishtan apart inside when he thought of Lochran and what he had done to the people *he* loved. It terrified him to think that one day his hatred and anger might also push him into the open arms of the Destroyer.

Queen Lamoore picked up on Chrishtan's guilt-stricken demeanor. She gently lifted his chin and looked deep into his eyes just as his own mother would have done. "You are not doomed, my child. Just because you are human does not mean that you will fall onto the same path. It only means that you will have to work much harder to avoid it. We all have a choice in this life, which the Architect has granted to us. Do not waste your precious time or energy on Lerim in hatred and judgment of those who have wronged you. Instead, feel for and attempt to understand them if possible. Do not be so quick to judge the choices of others so easily in order to place blame upon them. This, my child is the easy route, the dangerous path."

"But if I am not judging them, then how do I assess their intentions? How do I know if I am doing the right thing?" Chrishtan asked.

King Adreahn sat down on the bed. "You see Chrishtan, it is much easier to judge another in an instant than it is to understand them and forgive. We will never truly know the experiences and traumas of those around us unless we open our hearts to them and acknowledge them. Also, we must acknowledge our own fears and downfalls if we do not wish for our fear of *the other* to break us. Nor can we allow the anger of misunderstanding and victimization to waste our precious time and energy. Instead, we must rise above and attempt to understand those that have wronged us and use our energy to thrive even more in compassion. We must rise out of the ashes of our experiences and learn to love again. Chrishtan, in spite of your seemingly tragic plight, I truly believe with my whole heart and soul that you are a young and innocent soul, full of love that I have faith will one day be the answer to all of our prayers."

Tears fell from Chrishtan's eyes as he leaned forward to embrace his new mother and father. *This is my home now. I must try not to think about all the bad things. I want to make my new family proud. I don't want to let the anger and darkness take me.* "I will do my best to help bring light back into a world hidden in darkness."

CHAPTER 22
THIS TIME

The salty sea breeze tangled the waves of Chrishtan's shaggy brown hair as he galloped along the coastline on the back of his white steed. The possessed girl hunched forward in his arms. She had been incoherent since the morning, only expressing herself every now and again in the form of indiscernible moans. Chrishtan knew he was running low on time. It was pertinent that he get Raelle to the Lantern Forest as soon as possible. He would not allow her to suffer the same fate as his beloved friend Cohlen. He had worked most of his life to erase the past from his mind, but his current circumstances flooded him with memories, landing him back on the road to a mission long forgotten. Only this time, he was determined not to allow such horrific events to repeat themselves. Even if Raelle was a stranger, in his eyes she was much more than that.

Unlike his last attempt to seek out the Lady of the Realm, Chrishtan remained on their original route to the safe entrance of the Lantern Forest. Although the coastline made for a serene setting, Chrishtan knew that it did not reflect the menacing danger that lay ahead of them. Hopefully, this safe entrance would not mirror his past experiences in the Lantern Forest. It had tainted every ounce of innocence within his soul. Even though he never expressed it to Oleevar or his parent's, in his heart, he blamed himself for what happened to Cohlen. *If only I hadn't been so human, so easily manipulated by the demon, allowing my judgment to become clouded, then we would have found our way out of the forest before the demon had a chance to take Cohlen. But this time, things will be different. I'll make sure of it.*

The sun dipped below the rolling hills of the western horizon as Chrishtan made his way to the top of an immense sand dune. Once at the crest, he looked to the north toward the edge of the Lantern Forest where it scattered out onto the beach. To the east, a familiar scene of deep purple sky holding up the crown of a golden moon calmed his nerves. The frost-blue water of the Shimmering Coast reflected the golden light of the moon exactly as he remembered it. A flood of emotions swept over him, but he did his best to dam them up. He needed to stay strong for Raelle. Using her map, Chrishtan checked his route once more. This time, he would not enter anywhere but the light entry.

"Have we arrived?" Raelle managed in a hoarse voice.

Chrishtan leaned forward to speak softly in her ear. "It won't be long now, I promise. We are very close. We're taking the beach the rest of the way. But promise me, whatever you do, do not look into the forest. It is a wretched place that will play tricks on you if you allow it."

"Yes, Chrishtan," Raelle sighed as she switched from her hunched-over position to sit up straight in his arms. "I will do my best."

Chrishtan felt pleased with her new found ability to sit upright. "How are you feeling? Do you think you can make it another hour or so?"

Raelle nodded. "Yes, I think I can," she managed before returning to her hunched-over position.

Chrishtan took a moment to rub Raelle's back before squeezing Boone's sides and trotting toward the shoreline. Raelle faded in and out of consciousness as they made their way along the sparkling sand.

"It's not fair," Raelle moaned. "I can hear the ocean, but I want to see it. I want to see the sea. But every time I try to open my eyes, the world starts spinning again. My head is pounding."

Chrishtan understood her frustration. He knew what a beautiful scene she was missing out on. "You're right. It isn't fair. And when you are well again, I promise to bring you back here. And you *will* be well again Raelle, I promise. If it is the last thing I do."

Chrishtan's heart thumped. The light entrance would be around the corner at any moment. Finally, he would make it to the Lady of the Realm, and she would cure Raelle of her depraved ailments. As he rounded the next group of trees trickling onto the beach from the forest, he saw it. A colossal cliff jutted straight out from the forest and into the sea, far out past any sand bar. His heart sank and he shook his head in disbelief. The cliff had to be at least thirty meters high and composed of solid rock. Chrishtan's pause in their journey prompted Raelle to lift her head to see what was going on. As she opened her eyes, she too tilted her head back to look to the top of the immense rock wall.

"Is this the way in?" Raelle muttered.

"I think so. The entrance has to be somewhere just beyond this wall. But I'm not quite sure how we're going to get there."

"What do you mean?" Raelle asked. "Isn't there some kind of door or entryway?"

Chrishtan shook his head. "The map is showing the entrance on the other side, but I see no door. I need to check it out. Let's move closer so that I can take a look."

Chrishtan rode as close as he could to the gigantic cliff wall and hopped off of his horse into the white sand. He opened his pack and pulled out a book. The center had been carved out and fitted with an ornate wooden box like Raelle's. Chrishtan opened it to reveal a gold band decorated with one large Rubiz stone surrounded by smaller ones around the ring's perimeter.

Chrishtan slipped Framin's ring onto his finger, closed his eyes and harnessed his Lyre. It was the first time he had worn a Lyre harness ring in over a year. It had helped him remain undetected by enemies, but today he would need the deepest connection with his Lyre. He would be ready for any sinister foe in the Lantern Forest. With the ring perfectly settled on his finger, the memory of his promise to Framin slunk into his mind. Emotions surged through him as the image of his beloved mentor faded away. He had to find a way to the light entrance. He had already let Framin down and was not about to let Raelle down.

Raelle watched as Chrishtan pressed his hands along the outside of the cliff wall in search of a door, using his Lyre to sense any energy or evidence of a secret entryway. After a few minutes of scouring the rock barrier for clues, Chrishtan returned to Raelle. By this time, she was able to keep her eyes open and sit up on her own.

"Did you find anything?"

Chrishtan shook his head. "Nothing. I can't sense anything. I don't know what we're going to do. I need to figure this out. We're much too close to give up now, and it's far too dangerous to risk going into the forest, especially in your condition."

Chrishtan squeezed his hands around Raelle's thin, malnourished waist and helped her down off Boone. Raelle's knees buckled as soon as her naked feet hit the soft, cool sand of the beach. Chrishtan caught her just in time. He cradled her in his brawny, warrior arms.

"I've got you, don't worry." He looked into her ghostly irises as he carried her to where he intended to set up camp. Her abnormally large pupils were even larger than before.

Raelle sighed and shook her head. Her voice was so raspy and weak that Chrishtan could barely make out what she said. "I'm so sorry, Chrishtan. I am truly a burden. I do not desire to be. I want to be strong enough to take care of myself."

Chrishtan set Raelle down in the sand as she hung her head in shame. He lifted her chin with a gentle hand and gazed into her eyes. "Raelle, you are not a burden to me. I offered to help you. I want to help you. Please don't ever feel like you're a burden because you aren't."

Raelle mustered a smile and nodded. "Thank you, Chrishtan."

Chrishtan saw the despair in Raelle's expression. He wanted nothing more than to make her feel better. He popped up from the ground and clapped his hands together.

"Well, I am going to go get our things and set up a small camp, cook us some food, and figure this thing out."

Raelle smiled at him as she laid her aching body in the sand. Her eyes grew heavier with each undulation of the salty sea over the shore.

"Raelle, Raelle!" Chrishtan's paranoid face loomed over her. "I'm sorry. But please try your hardest not to fall asleep." He helped her rest against a log he had set behind her. He had already taken care of everything while she slept. She managed a laugh as the dogs chased each other in and out of the sea, but her demeanor quickly changed.

"What is it?" Chrishtan asked.

"How long was I out for? I thought I had only shut my eyes for a moment."

"Maybe fifteen minutes," he answered. "I'm sorry, but I can't allow you to sleep. That is when you are most vulnerable."

Raelle shook her head as she glared at her unsteady hands. Her breaths were still quite labored. As she broke into sobs, Chrishtan put his arms around her.

"I feel so lost Chrishtan. What's happening to me? Why is this happening to me? Everything is falling apart. I don't know who I am anymore. I feel so broken."

Chrishtan loosened his embrace and backed up enough to gaze into her despairing eyes. "I know you feel lost, but I'm here with you. I promise with every fiber of my being that I will not let anything happen to you. I will not allow this demon to take you."

Raelle sniffled. "Demon? What do you mean? What's happening to me?"

"Raelle, someone is trying to turn you. They're trying to take your soul and enslave it to the Destroyer. I'm not sure who it is that is doing this to you, but I know the Lady of the Realm can help."

Dread infiltrated her eyes as tears ran down her pale veiny cheeks. "Turn me? What do you mean? I don't understand. Who is doing this?"

"It's complicated, but I am certain that it's a blood relative of yours. Do you know of anyone in your family who would wish to hurt you?"

Raelle nodded. "Yes, there is one possibility." She cleared her throat. "But I don't understand how he could be doing this to me."

"Well," Chrishtan shook his head, "who is it? Who do you think it is?"

Raelle swallowed hard as she looked into Chrishtan's kind blue eyes. "He is my uncle. A man called Lochran."

Chrishtan's heart sank. Fifteen years of suppressed pain and anger ignited within him. The mention of Lochran triggered his hatred. The young woman whom he had come to care so much about was the niece of the one man he hated above all. Lochran had ruined his life and caused him great suffering. The thought flooded him with bitterness and rage. He said nothing in return to Raelle.

"What is it, Chrishtan? What's wrong?" Raelle sat up and grabbed Chrishtan's hand.

Chrishtan pulled his hand away as sordid images of his past flashed through his memory. His mind drifted off elsewhere, back to a world of trauma and torment.

***

"Please, what's wrong? Have I done something?" Raelle's head was reeling. It finally became evident to her how much she needed and depended on him. Without him, she would surely be dead or lost to the blackness. He was her only hope, her only friend, her survival, her everything. In that moment, she realized how much she cared for him. Raelle gently turned his gaze toward her. "Chrishtan, please. Whatever it is you can tell me."

This time, he did not offer her his kind and gentle eyes. "You wouldn't understand. And why should I? You have refused to tell me anything about yourself."

Raelle was overcome with guilt as she tried to explain. "Chrishtan, I'm so sorry. I should not have been so secretive, but I didn't know who to trust. The truth is, I have no idea who I am. I have lived my whole life never knowing anyone outside of my mother, father, and two brothers. We were never allowed to leave the valley where we lived. The only reason I left was because I had no other choice. Both of my brothers were killed in accidents. And my parents were murdered just over a week ago by that vile Minotirr that is hunting me. I was all alone with no answers and only a letter and a map I found hidden away by my parents. I was scared. I'm sorry, Chrishtan. I truly am. Please try to understand."

Chrishtan pulled a parchment from his pocket and opened it.

"Where did you get that? That is my letter." Raelle asked.

"I found it next to your map. I thought it might be of importance, so I brought it just in case. I didn't read it because it is not mine to read."

Raelle nodded. "I think it may be best if you did read it. Maybe it would help you to better understand my situation."

Chrishtan opened the letter and read it. Once finished, Chrishtan shook his head as he folded the letter back up, and placed it in Raelle's trembling hand.

"Are you able to understand a little better now?" Raelle sighed.

Chrishtan cleared his throat. "What I understand is that a foolish queen allowed Lochran to alienate himself from her while she clearly remained selfishly ignorant of it until it was too late. And then, to top it all off, this blatant denial led to the death of many others, including my family. And better yet, they take off with their children, you and your brothers, to keep you safe, leaving the rest of us at the whim of a deranged and vengeful dictator. I understand that it is not your fault, but at the same time, I am so infuriated and taken aback by the selfish and ignorant actions of your family. My family and everyone I loved had to die so that you and your family could live in secret. Hiding from a mess *they* created?

That does not seem right to me. This whole time, everyone thought you and your family dead."

Raelle, who grew weaker with every second that passed, felt helpless and confused. "I am so sorry. Please understand. I knew nothing about this. What happened to your family? Please tell me. I want to understand."

Chrishtan did not make eye contact with her. But Raelle could still see the tears welling in his eyes. "Well, it's fairly simple. After your parents left, Lochran demolished and took over their kingdom. But after two years, he decided that Huronus alone was not enough and so tried to convince my mother and father, to join him or die. They tried to reason with him, but he was not interested in reason, only power. He murdered my family and many of my people. Then, he sent one of the vile Minotirr after my mentor and me. On our way to the Lantern Forest my mentor was killed trying to save me from two of those abominations, and I was left alone in the middle of the Didumos Plains at the age of ten. So forgive my ten-year-old self for not understanding why his family was taken from him and left alone to die so that your parents could hide from what *they* created."

Raelle felt awful for being so selfish in thinking that she was the only one who had experienced tragedy. "I'm so sorry, Chrishtan. I had no idea. I realize now that so many people, other than myself, have been affected by my family. I wish I had known sooner. I wish my parents had not hidden the truth from me. I wish we would have stayed and found a way to help you and your family, I really do. I am so sorry for what happened to you. It must have been much harder at such a young age. I feel terrible for what happened to you, Chrishtan."

Chrishtan finally made eye contact with her. "Raelle, I'm sorry for being cross with you. I've let my anger and frustration get the better of me. It's not what I want. I want to be reasonable and strong. This is what my adoptive parents taught me. It's just that, sometimes it's very difficult, considering the circumstances. I'm not angry with you. This whole thing has brought up many painful things that I have tried for a very long time to forget."

Raelle knew exactly how he felt. Although her tragedies had struck her later in life, she knew how terribly he must be hurting inside. "You were adopted? So you must have been strong enough to make it out of the Didumos Plains. Only a very strong boy could do that at the age of ten."

Chrishtan nodded. "Yes, I made it out, but not completely on my own. You could say that I was 'rescued.'"

"By your adoptive parents?"

Chrishtan shook his head. "No, by my brother, Olee. He and his younger brother—"

Raelle put her hand on his shoulder. "It's all right, you don't need to tell me if it's too difficult."

Chrishtan tried to control his emotions. "No, it's fine. I need to tell you. It was Oleevar and his younger brother Cohlen of Samisius. They were in the same predicament I was. We were going with our mentors to the Lantern Forest. But we never made it, and Cohlen was lost to the blackness along the way. It was entirely my fault."

Raelle had no idea of the tragedy in her new friend's life. She could not believe how easily he had made it seem like he was so strong when he first rescued her. She admired his strength and humility. After all, he had been able to make both of them laugh even as he carried around the pain and anguish of his tragic past.

"I'm so sorry, Chrishtan. I know what it's like to lose a younger sibling. It is the most horrendous thing I can think of. Even if they aren't blood, they're still family. I am sorry to hear about Cohlen."

Chrishtan nodded. "I know you understand. You have lost your family as well. You had two brothers?"

"Yes, Samuel and Browden. Samuel is my brother by blood, and Browden was adopted. When I was five years old and my brother Samuel two years old, my father brought home an infant boy after traveling outside the valley. He said that he was the son of dear friends of theirs who had passed away and that the boy needed a safe home."

The story of Raelle's adopted brother triggered a curiosity in Chrishtan. "Do you recall who these people were that died? How old are you now?"

Raelle's eyebrows raised at his query. "Um, he never told me their names. Just that they had been dear friends and allies. I am twenty now. Why? How old are you?"

Chrishtan mumbled in contemplation. "So, if you're twenty now and you were five when your father brought the baby home, that would mean that was fifteen years ago, which would have made me around ten at the time…"

Raelle did not understand why Chrishtan was going on about their ages, but she listened intently as if waiting for him to strike some sort of epiphany.

"Raelle?" Chrishtan looked at her with glistening wet eyes.

"What is it, Chrishtan?"

"I—I know this may seem a bit difficult to understand, but I think that your adopted brother Browden may have been *my* baby brother."

"What do you mean? How do you know?"

"Well, I don't know for sure, but it makes sense." Chrishtan nodded. "There is something I didn't tell you earlier because I was clouded by anger. You see, before you were born, you and I were betrothed. I was five and your mother was to have a baby very soon, you. At least that is what my mother told me. They thought our marriage would strengthen the bond between our two progressive human nations. But with whispers of Lochran's takeover. They set it aside. They never told me your name."

Raelle frowned. "Something else my parents kept a secret?" She shook her head. "But what does that have to do with Browden being your brother?"

"Well," Chrishtan sighed, "fifteen years ago, right before Abequa was attacked by Lochran, my mother was due any day to have my baby brother. I know that she was able to give birth to him before they were killed. So, the way I see it, since our families were very close, when my parents died they made sure that Browden was in a safe location with people they trusted. Someone must have recognized your father and asked him to take the baby. My mother spoke of this in the Verge. She told me he was safe. Plus, I was ten years old when my brother was born, and that is precisely when your father brought him home to your family. You and I are five years apart. It makes sense." Chrishtan's voice trembled as he tried to hide his face. "But it also means that I will never get to meet my brother, because he is dead."

Raelle was blown away by what she heard. It was as if fate had brought her and Chrishtan together, but at the same time was tearing them apart with all it had taken from them. Raelle wept as Chrishtan's head fell into his knees. She knew he must be reeling with pain. She ached to comfort him in their mutual loss. It took everything in her not to break into sobs as she spoke.

"Chrishtan," Raelle said, placing a hand on his shoulder. "Browden was a wonderful person, he truly was. In fact, you remind me so much of him. He was comical and carefree. He had the same gift of laughter that you have. He was adventurous and full of life. He wasn't the type of person who followed the rules and led a boring life. He was the light of my, Samuel's, and my parents' life. He brought the most valuable thing to our lives that anyone could ever bring, joy and laughter. He was a lifter of spirits and a bringer of happiness. I promise you this. We loved him very much."

Chrishtan lifted his head and forced a smile against the tears. "I am glad to hear that. I know I would have loved him just as much as you, if only I had been given the chance. I've been searching for him for years. It's part of the reason I was out here on my own. How did he die? How old was he?"

Raelle had never spoken of Browden's death to anyone out loud before. It had played unremittingly in her mind for so long. "I wish I could say there was someone to blame or that there was a reason for it, but there simply wasn't. It was not a death caused by malice or the evil of the Destroyer. It was purely a freak accident. He was ten years old when it happened. He and Samuel were playing in our tree fort when Browden fell onto a large boulder. He died instantly. There was nothing we could do. It was a tragic accident."

Chrishtan shook his head. "And to think, for the past five years I've been traveling this great continent in search of a brother who was not only dead, but hidden in a place I would have never thought to look. Sometimes I swear the Grand Architect has cursed me. Though, I am not sure why. It is as if almost anyone I love is destined to suffer or die."

Raelle attempted to reason with him. "I know it feels that way. I too feel the same. I have lost everyone I love, the same as you. So either we are both cursed, or we have been forced to live in a time of suffering and malevolence. I know that you must have put your heart and soul into searching for your brother, but I assure you it was not in vain." With frail, shaky hands, Raelle placed Chrishtan's hand on her heart. "You have found him, Chrishtan. Your search is over. He is right here, and this is where he will live on forever. I promise." A tear trickled from Raelle's eye and down her face.

Chrishtan stroked her cheek and gently wiped the tear away before pressing his lips against hers. It was the most incredible feeling Raelle had ever felt. It was as if she and Chrishtan were one entity in that lingering moment of pure connectedness. In that moment, she was at peace. She had never felt safer, or more connected to anyone in her entire life.

Chrishtan's Lyre flowed through her as they embraced. The serene sound of gentle waves against the shimmering shore in the light of an ascending moon only intensified the euphoric feelings and energy that ran through them. She felt completely healed, as if her ailment had been lifted.

As they slowly pulled away from the passionate kiss that seemed to bind them for eternity, Raelle smiled with humility. Chrishtan wiped the tears from her face as he looked deep into her eyes. "Thank you."

Raelle wiped away the rest of her tears as she forced herself back to reality. "For what?"

"For leading me back to the path I was chosen to travel. For giving me peace. For letting me in. For helping me remember, and not allowing me to forget my purpose here on Lerim."

Raelle did not see how she had done all these things. In her mind, it was Chrishtan who had saved her, who brought her back to her chosen path. After all, it was he who had rescued her multiple times. "No, it is I who should be thanking you. If not for you, I would be dead, or worse, trapped in the blackness by now. I never would have made it here to this place if you hadn't found me. It is you who has saved me. It is you who has opened my eyes and helped me to see and understand what I could not before. It is you who has given me an experience I will never ever take for granted. You are my savior, Chrishtan."

Chrishtan laughed. "Well, then I suppose we can call it even now? We are both in debt to one another."

Raelle giggled. "Yes, I suppose we are. Although I don't know how you can look at me. I'm a monster."

Chrishtan smiled. "When we kissed, somehow my Lyre brought the light back into your green eyes. I know what your true beauty is. I am not fooled by this mask that the Destroyer has covered you with. You are beautiful, Raelle. You truly are. Inside and out."

Raelle had no idea how to feel or what to say. No one had ever called her beautiful before. Especially not like this.

Chrishtan smiled. "Has no one ever told you that before?"

Raelle shook her head. "No, never. It is strange to me. When I think of beauty, I think of the sunset behind the mountains, or the flowers that blossom in the spring in the bright green grass after a rain shower. I do not think of myself. Nature is beautiful. Lerim is beautiful, not me. I am simply human."

Chrishtan grinned. "Embrace it, because you are truly beautiful, especially to me. Because of you, I am no longer alone. You are *my* savior, Raelle. And *that* is beautiful. Do not ever forget it."

Raelle blushed as she looked down. "Thank you, Chrishtan."

"You are very welcome, Raelle."

Raelle gazed back up at him. She was still curious about the man who had given her so much in such a short period of time without asking for anything in return. "Chrishtan..."

"Yes?"

"You said you've been on your own for a while. Why were you alone? Did you not have anyone to come with you to help you find your brother? That doesn't seem right."

Chrishtan shook his head. "I know it doesn't. And I guess in hindsight I might be able to see now how ridiculous I may have been."

"Ridiculous? How so?"

"I did it to myself. I just didn't want to see anyone else hurt or killed because of me."

"Who? Who was going to be hurt or killed?"

"The mission troops and my people." Chrishtan sighed. "I was a part of the mission troops formed by Samisius and Ellios to bring aid to those who had been cast out of Huronus and Abequa. We provided refugee camps for those who were able to escape Lochran. There was no room left in Samisius or Ellios, so we set up camps for them in the outskirts near the Didumos Plains. It is the first army of its kind, containing members from all Lyre bloodlines. Rogue mages from Huronus and warrior mages from Abequa came together with the elvish hunter and ranger mages of Samisius and Ellios to form the most diverse army ever created. I was a captain before I went on this search. My brother Oleevar and I helped to develop these armies at the Ellios Academy of Interlyre Studies."

Raelle was perplexed. "If you were captain, and an

investor in this army, then why did you leave?"

Chrishtan shrugged. "Because I was endangering the lives of my men and the people in the camps."

"But how?" Raelle shook her head. "What could you have possibly done? It was your idea. Your army."

"Because Lochran wants me dead, that's why. He wants all of us human Lyre royalty dead. For most of my life, my adoptive parents, Queen Lamoore and King Adreahn, were able to keep my identity a secret. And for most of my life, the people of the other nations assumed me dead, along with my family and mentor. But after a few years of traveling with our forces in search of my brother and people who needed help, rumors and whispers of me being alive quickly spread. Eventually, the rumors made their way to Lochran. Since then, he has done everything in his power to find and destroy me, threatening everyone I care about in the process."

Raelle scowled. "But why? Why you?"

"Because Lochran knows there is a chance that together, those of us who were children sent to the Lantern Forest during the time of his uprising could still defeat him. He knows he cannot lay a hand on Oleevar, because he is protected by his elven people. Because they are all of Lyre blood, they are still more powerful than he is at this time. He has tried to negotiate with them to come to his side, but they refuse. Lochran claims that he is only allowing the elven nations to remain unharmed because they are all of Lyre blood and so are in line with his beliefs and practices, but I think he is just scared of the elves."

Raelle's eyes grew wide. "So, do you know why we were sent to the Lantern Forest?"

"I wish I did. What I do know is that our parents were instructed to do so. The Lady of the Realm came to Lamoore in a dream. Queen Lamoore passed that message on to all other Royal families of Mirilan. According to her, whatever waits for us there, may help us to defeat him when the time comes. Therefore, he needs to either kill us, or control us to ensure his own safety."

"That makes sense." Raelle nodded her head.

"You see Raelle, the more of us that remain alive or out of his control, the more likely we are to be able to defeat him. Because he knows this, Lochran threatened our armies, the refugee people, and the elves of Samisius and Ellios. He gave them an ultimatum. He declared that anyone who came into contact with me and did not capture and send me to him would die. He threatened to attack the elven kingdoms until they gave me up, to kill anyone he could until they surrendered me. This was a year ago. My parents told me they would stand and fight for me and I didn't need to leave, but I couldn't do that to them. I didn't want anyone else dying because of me. So I left my home, my people, my troops, and never looked back. And I have been searching for my brother in secret on my own ever since."

Chrishtan's explanation captivated Raelle. "So, there is a chance that those of us who are royalty born during that time could still destroy Lochran? I suppose he must know that I am still alive. He probably thinks that my brothers are, too."

"Yes, I suppose he does." Chrishtan nodded. "Which is why he has sent his Minotirr after you and is trying to turn you. It's so he can have control over you and add you to his army of minions. I haven't worn my Lyre ring since I left so that he couldn't use my connection to find me. Tonight, I put it back on because I wasn't sure what would be waiting outside the forest. I may need full connection with my Lyre to defeat it."

Raelle sighed and shook her head. "If only I had known that my mother's ring would open my connection and allow Lochran to locate me, I never would have put it on. Something else I suppose my parents kept a 'secret' in order to protect me."

"I'm sorry, Raelle. But the good news is we have made it to the Lantern Forest and hopefully the Lady of the Realm will be able to help us turn you back. I just need to figure out a way to get in."

Chrishtan stood and stirred their dinner before using one of his wooden bowls to scoop out its contents and place it in Raelle's unsteady hands. "But for now, you need to eat and keep your strength up as much as possible. I'll meditate and search my Lyre for a solution while you eat."

Raelle nodded. She leaned back against the log and sipped the delicious stew from her bowl. She eyed Chrishtan's every move as he sat down next to her and closed his eyes. The process of methodically connecting with Lyre intrigued her. The large red gemstone of Chrishtan's ring began to glow as he focused. Raelle wished so badly that she too could close her eyes, relax, focus, and hone her newfound energy as well, but it was far too dangerous. However, this concern did not keep the warm liquid from offering her some sort of relief as it trickled down her throat and into her empty belly. Her eyes grew heavier with each soothing sip. Before she knew it she was awakened by the whisper of a familiar voice.

Raelle's eyes burst open to see Chrishtan still sitting next to the fire, deep in meditation. The familiar voice continued to whisper to her from a distance. It sounded as if it were coming from the forest. She sat up and peaked over the log to see if she could see anyone, but there was no one else nearby. Once again, she heard the familiar voice calling to her from the forest. *Raelle, I am here. Come on an adventure with me. I have missed you, Raelle...*

The voice trailed off. Raelle struggled to stand on her weak, wobbling legs. She wanted to get a better view of the forest to discover where the voice came from. With Chrishtan still deep in meditation, she painstakingly walked around him toward the forest. As she did, the whisper grew louder and clearer.

"Raelle, I have been waiting for you," it said.

Close enough to the forest, Raelle saw a familiar figure standing inside the trees. "Raelle, you are home now. We are together once again."

Raelle tilted her head as she stepped closer. "Samuel? Samuel is that you?"

"Yes. Sister, it is I," he hissed. "Come, join me. Here we shall be together forever."

Samuel's tantalizing voice put Raelle into a trance as she inched her way toward the woods.

***

Raelle had nearly reached her brother when Chrishtan sprinted up behind her, pulling her back before she was able to enter. Raelle struggled in his sturdy arms.

"Let go of me, Chrishtan! What do you think you're doing?"

It did not take much for Chrishtan to restrain the fragile, possessed woman in his robust warrior arms. "You must not enter the forest. It's not safe. There are evil entities inside that wish to harm you."

Raelle wriggled and writhed, trying to escape Chrishtan's embrace, but to no avail.

"What are you saying? I must go in there. My brother Samuel is in there." Raelle pointed into the trees. "Look, see he is waiting for me right there. He wishes me to come with him. He has been waiting for me."

Chrishtan looked where Raelle pointed, but saw no one. He swiftly turned her around to look into her eyes that were nothing but black pupil.

"Raelle, your brother is dead. He is not in there. The forest is filled with evil enchantments. It's playing tricks on you to pull you in. You must fight it. Do you understand?"

A devious grin came over Raelle's face, exposing razor sharp teeth. "Oh, I understand perfectly well," She snapped as her pupil took over her entire eye, leaving no white to be seen. "I understand that *you* are no one and have no business telling me what I can and cannot do. So get your hands off me and allow me to fulfill my mission with my brother."

Chrishtan tightened his grasp. "I cannot do that Raelle.

You are not yourself right now. You are being possessed by a demon of the Destroyer. I will do whatever I must to save you."

Raelle tilted her head with a menacing look that was not her own before continuing in a disturbingly wicked tone. "You think you can stop me, boy? You are nothing, no one. You are a pathetic shred of existence that got his entire family, mentor, and friend killed. Everyone you come into contact with is cursed by your weakness. You are worthless. You will not stop me. You do not have the strength. You are pathetic, human."

Chrishtan clenched Raelle's arms and the demon within her. "I will stop you if it is the last thing I ever do. Do you hear me? If it is the last thing I ever do!"

The possessed girl snickered. "You are weak, Chrishtan. You are nothing compared to the power of the Destroyer. You will fail. I promise you that, you filthy human."

Chrishtan breathed hard as the words cut him deep. He knew he had to pull his feelings together. He could not allow this demon to get to him, or else all would be lost. He closed his eyes, harnessed his focus, and pulled in every ounce of energy he could to fuel his Lyre. The Rubiz gems on his ring shined brilliantly as a bolt of energy surged from him into Raelle. She instantly collapsed unconscious in his arms.

"I'm sorry, Raelle, truly I am. But I cannot allow this to happen. Not again."

Chrishtan eased Raelle's limp, frail figure over his shoulder and rushed back to their camp in desperate need of a plan. This time, he promised himself that he would not be weak. This time, he would remain vigilant and never let his guard down. This time, he would not allow them to steal someone from him. Raelle would not be counted amongst the taken.

CHAPTER 23
NOT MUCH TIME

Neither the soft glow of the moon nor the placid sound of waves brushing over the surf of the Shimmering Coast eased the panic in Chrishtan's mind. As Raelle lay unconscious in the sand, he paced back and forth in front of the enormous cliff wall that stood between him and salvation. He desperately needed to get to the Lady of the Realm. At this point, nothing was out of the question. Time was swiftly running out.

Chrishtan stepped back several meters from the wall and paused to harness his Lyre before sprinting at the stone face with incredible speed that only a warrior could muster. Just before the wall, he jumped straight up in an attempt to grasp the cliff's ledge. Even though he was a warrior with the ability to spring incredible heights and distances, the stone wall was much too high. Chrishtan slid back down to the ground, scraping his hands and arms against the rough edges of the rock face, leaving a trail of blood behind him.

As Chrishtan hit the ground, a sense of despair overwhelmed him. His bloody and shredded hands and arms reminded him that although he was a well-trained warrior of the Lyre, he was not invincible. He hung his head and mumbled under his breath as he dragged his feet back to camp. As he reached the site where Raelle lay, he noticed her letter lying on the ground next to her. Suddenly, it struck him that the letter could hold a clue as to how to enter the realm of the Lady. He picked up the folded parchment and sat down to read it, scrutinizing each and every word. One phrase in particular stuck with him. *Do not forget, it is our bloodline that will allow you entrance into her sanctuary.*

Chrishtan was not entirely sure what it meant, but he knew it had to mean something. He looked back toward the wall that had defeated him so easily moments earlier. Only this time, he noticed something that had not been there before. Where his blood stained the rock face, the surface seemed to shimmer and glow. Chrishtan folded up the letter and tossed it into Raelle's lap before rushing to the wall to examine the new phenomenon. Chrishtan raised a hand to the glowing marks left behind by his blood. A steady Lyre energy flowed through him as his hand went directly through the once hard surface. It was as if his blood had disintegrated the cliff rock.

"Do not forget, it is our bloodline that will allow you entrance into her sanctuary." He repeated aloud. "That's it! Our Lyre blood gives us special entry into the Lady's realm." Overwhelmed with eagerness, Chrishtan cringed as he used the fresh blood on his hand to paint a doorway into the face of the cliff. With the trails of his bloodline now connected in the form of a circle, the glowing blood line disintegrated the wall, transforming it into a tunnel. Chrishtan peeked inside. To his surprise, he gazed upon a walkway lit with torches to a moon-lit staircase.

Fueled by a new found sense of hope, Chrishtan ran back to their camp site to bandage his wounds and pack up their things. With the dogs safely in their basket attached to Winston's side and Boone ready to go, Chrishtan cradled Raelle in his arms. He led their steeds to the light entrance of the Lantern Forest. Once he and his party entered, the door he had created with his Lyre blood transformed back into a wall, closing them inside the torch-lit tunnel. As they made their way toward the stone steps, Chrishtan stopped his party before they could enter the stairwell.

"This stairway is much too narrow for you, Boone. You horses will have to hang back while Raelle and I go on from here." He secured their mounts to a couple of iron torch posts before cradling Raelle in his sturdy arms once more. His warrior muscles bulged from his vascular skin as he made his way to the top of the stairwell. At the top, a lush field of green grass littered with white silky flowers welcomed him. Chrishtan paused to admire the serene vista and noticed that the forest looked vastly different from the one he had left behind the wall. Instead of an eerie jungle, tall trees with violet leaves and pale grey bark swayed gracefully in the coastal breeze. At the very edge of the woods, Chrishtan watched as tiny balls of white light flickered and floated around two white flame torches.

"That must be the entrance." Chrishtan readjusted Raelle in his brawny arms before traipsing across the flowery field toward the entry. In between the torches sat a tranquil path covered in wispy green grass and purple flowers. As he placed his first boot onto the path, tiny voices echoed concern all around him.

Oh, no. No shoes here. Step lightly. You are on the light path.

Chrishtan kicked his foot back from the path and back onto the field. "Hello? Is anyone there?"

Tiny whispers among white floating orbs answered his query. "Yes. We are here. You must tread lightly on the light path, young warrior."

Chrishtan looked down at his boots and back at the path. *All right.* "I suppose I should remove my boots then, yes?"

The voices giggled. "Yes, please. Please tread lightly on the light path. Walk softly, young warrior."

Chrishtan laid Raelle in the grass while he unhitched his boots and placed them in the sand next to the grassy entrance of the forest. As soon as he finished, the whispering orbs of light flew out from the trees and surrounded him. As they encircled him, he eyed the albino pixies' soft white hair and skin. Their violet eyes glowed bright as their soft pink lips puckered against his skin like fish in a pond. As Chrishtan sat motionless, they tugged on his wavy hair, echoing whispers of approval at this male specimen. Chrishtan shuddered. The last time something like this happened, he was led into a trap where he and his friends were held prisoner and nearly lost forever. Chrishtan was still unsure whether to trust them. This time, he would not be fooled so easily. As soon as the petite pixies seemed satisfied with their examination of Chrishtan, they did the same dance over Raelle. Unlike Chrishtan's assessment, the pixies whispered concerns and apprehensions as they clustered around the unconscious girl. Her skin was ghostly white and covered in prominent blue veins.

Chrishtan scooted toward them as they examined her. "I believe she is being possessed. Can you help her?"

He listened closely for an answer and managed to pick up only whispering echoes of the phrases. *Oh dear, this is not good. Get Jabrat, we must. Take her there, we shall. He will know.*

Chrishtan squeezed in amongst them. "Take her where? Who is Jabrat?"

The pixies did not acknowledge him as they discussed the severity of the situation amongst themselves.

Chrishtan raised his voice. "Hello? Could somebody please tell me what is going on? I need to find the Lady of the Realm. This woman is being turned. We must help her."

A chorus of whispers started again among the pixies. *Yes turned. Five hands. Four here. No time. Jabrat, yes, Jabrat. We shall call on him and he will take you to her. You will see. Please, wait here, young warrior.* And in an instant, the lustrous entities took off back into the stunning lavender forest.

***

It did not take long for the pixies to return. Their whispers overwhelmed Chrishtan's ears as they darted in. *Come you must. Come, come. Jabrat is waiting. Please come. Step lightly on the light path, young warrior.* Heeding their message, Chrishtan scooped Raelle from the meadow and followed the albino pixies onto the path. He ogled at the stunning trail. It was lit with torches of brilliant white fire and littered with purple flowers that closed their petals each time his naked feet disturbed them. The surrounding trees of the elegant forest whispered in the cool ocean breeze as lavender leaves fluttered from their branches onto the forest floor.

Glowing lanterns made of white coral and adorned with purple pearls hung from the branches of the exquisite trees. Inside they glowed from the light of the pixies residing within them. Chrishtan thought the white vines that crawled across the forest floor looked as if they belonged underneath the sea rather than on land. It was the most remarkable sight he had ever seen. He listened closely to the pixies' chatter as they moved along. *Almost there. Yes, Jabrat is waiting. Yes, he is. Very soon, yes.*

Chrishtan stopped in his tracks as the spectacular sight came into view. Through the purple leaves of the immense, grey-barked trees, the moon shined a light on an incredible palace made of white coral. They had finally made it to the chateau of the Lady of the Realm of the Lantern Forest. Chrishtan gazed up in wonder. The convex windows of the citadel looked as if they were actually massive transparent pearls. An enormous waterfall behind the coral structure spilled into a moat of frost-blue water surrounding the stronghold. In the center, the coral chateau sat on top of a white sand island. As he drew closer, Chrishtan watched as dazzling, reflective fish darted through the cool blue waters of the lake. He marveled at the front door made of a gigantic, pearlescent oyster shell. As he stood with Raelle cradled in his arms at the edge of the remarkable structure, the pixies sang another message. *Welcome to the chateau of our Lady of the Realm, Jenladra. Lady of land and sea and elven empress of the old world and the new.*

Chrishtan looked into the water once more to see a mermaid-like creature with green skin and purple scales and fins swimming toward them. As it swam closer to the white sandy beach, its fins transformed into legs before it exited the water and walked in their direction. The tall creature's face looked somewhat human, but with features of a deer, in particular its nose and ears. A pair of fuzzy antlers sat atop the creature's head of long white hair. Though the creature was naked of traditional clothing, white fur covered it from just below its navel down to its green, human-like ankles and feet.

Chrishtan gawked at the being. It stood at least a head taller than him and spoke in a smooth assertive tone. "Welcome young mages, rogue and warrior. I am Jabrat, the spirit of the Lantern Forest and your guide. I welcome thee to the chateau of our Lady of the Realm, Jenladra. The lady of both land and sea and elven empress of both the old world and the new. Our Lady of the Realm of the Lantern Forest and of the coast that shimmers with Pearlz sands and the sole guardian of the Opalz gemstone. May I ask what brings two humans so far from home?"

Chrishtan's blue eyes gazed deeply into the purple irises of their spirit guide. "We are here to see the Lady of the Realm. We are looking for answers and in dire need of assistance."

The creature tilted his head and adjusted its tall pointy ears in a way that was not human. "*Assistance,* the human warrior says. What help do you require?"

"We were sent here years ago as children, but were thwarted in our attempt. I am Chrishtan Vilgare, son of King Sonee Vilgare of the warrior nation of Abequa. And this is Raelle Jowellia, of the rogue nation of Huronus. She is being turned and needs your help."

The creature stepped forward and lifted Raelle's chin with his green hands, prying open her eyelids to expose the blackness beneath them. He continued to swivel her head around as he examined her.

"*Jowellia,* he says. Yes, *Jowellia.* She is friend of Our Lady, brought to us by Lamoore of Samisius twenty years ago. You are late I should say, very late indeed. We have been expecting you, both of you." He continued to inspect her. "I should say, this one here is tainted. We have a demon within."

Raelle's black eyes opened. Her hand shot up, clutching the wrist of the spirit guide. Her demeanor completely transformed as she spoke in a familiar layered voice. "Jabrat, you filthy, disgusting animal. You will not dare to lay a hand on my vessel. It is too late. She belongs to me."

Jabrat leaned in close to the demon. "You shall not be allowed to take this soul, Azmodil, prince of blackness. Of that I will make sure. We will return you to your desolate abode of the black abyss and save this soul."

A frightening laugh echoed as a menacing grin came over Raelle's tainted face. "You will try. But you will fail. Her soul resides with me in a chasm where it can never be found."

Jabrat touched one of his hairy green hands to Raelle's forehead. His rounded black claws gently stroked her face. "We shall see about that." A burst of energy surged from Jabrat into Raelle. The demon screeched with a wail that resonated through the trees, and Raelle collapsed, unconscious.

Jabrat took Raelle's limp body from Chrishtan and cradled her in his arms. "We do not have much time, Chrishtan, human warrior of Abequa. We must act fast if we are to find her within the depths of the Void."

Chrishtan swiftly followed after the lanky green creature as he headed toward the water surrounding the coral refuge. "Find her? But where has she gone? She's right here."

"Yes, young human," Jabrat nodded. "Her shell is here, but her soul is not. It is being held captive in the black chasm of the Destroyer's realm by the demon Azmodil. He is a foul and menacing demon. He is one member of a group of demons who reside over the Destroyer's minions. Using his Five Torrid Hands, he has forced Raelle's soul from her shell."

Chrishtan's voice trembled. "How much time do we have? She already has four Torrid Hands."

Jabrat turned to face Chrishtan. "It is as I said, young prince, we do not have much time."

As the spirit guide turned his head back in the direction of the coral chateau, a strange noise echoed from deep within his throat. Chrishtan thought it sounded similar to the chatter of a dolphin. With his call, the enormous oyster shell door of the citadel lowered across the lake. Chrishtan followed the spirit guide across the pearlescent drawbridge to the white sand island. They were finally entering the chateau of the Lady of the Realm.

CHAPTER 24
INTO THE VERGE

The sound of water trickling down the white coral palace walls into a narrow river running along the edges of the citadel eased Chrishtan's weary mind. He admired the colorful anemones, starfish, and choral that decorated the inside of the palace like paintings on a wall. The soft, cool, white sand that blanketed the floor felt soothing underneath his feet and in between his toes. As he followed Jabrat through the citadel, little white crabs scurried along the porous walls and shimmering seascape. They passed through rooms with giant clams filled with pearls. Strings of lights made entirely of purple sea vines and Diamoz crystals hung from the ceilings. Enormous pearls sat like furniture, some large enough for Chrishtan to sit on. Chrishtan followed Jabrat through the aquatic sanctuary and down to the bottom of a narrow stairwell.

"We will be with our lady soon." Jabrat turned to Chrishtan. "She has told me to bring the girl, and she will give you what you need to find her." Jabrat stepped back and motioned Christian through doorway at the bottom of the stairwell. "Please enter."

Before entering, Chrishtan noticed a translucent substance covering the shell-rimmed archway. It was as if the doorway were sealed by a curtain of water. He first put his hand through the clear substance to see what he could make of it. It felt like putting his hand through a bubble. He looked up at Jabrat for reassurance.

"It is safe, human. You may enter. Go on."

Chrishtan forced his naked foot through the bubble seal into a long corridor lined with elaborately carved columns of white marble. Through the wide spaces of the columns and the transparent ceiling of the long passageway, Chrishtan saw that they were underwater. He surveyed the ceiling. Spaces in between the columns were sealed with the same translucent bubble material he had entered through. Once again, white sand covered the floor of the walkway, where two long narrow pools of water ran along either side. Sconces holding Diamoz crystals carved in the forms of different sea creatures lit his way through the amazing passageway. Fish of diverse shapes, sizes, and colors scuttled by in the surrounding water. Chrishtan made sure to be very careful not to step on pearls and sea shells that slept in the white sediment of the walkway. The grand design of the palace astounded him. The only reason he had for turning around was to make sure his guide followed close behind, carrying what was now the most important thing in his life, Raelle.

As they reached the end of the marvelous corridor, they came upon a sealed oyster shell door. Just as before, Jabrat opened his mouth to emit dolphin-like sounds, prompting the pearlescent shell to lower. Chrishtan stepped onto the mouth of the shell and through the doorway to find himself at the top of an enormous spiral staircase constructed of the same elaborate columns and translucent bubble walls of the corridor. The depth of the lake seemed endless as they traveled down the spiral staircase. It grew darker with each and every step. Chrishtan and his guide used the light of the elaborately carved diamoz stones to guide them. At over one hundred meters below the surface, the types of sea life viewed through the bubble sealed windows of the stairwell began to change. Bioluminescent creatures swam by, pulsating a multitude of colored lights as they moved. Chrishtan could not believe what he saw. In that moment, he knew exactly what Raelle meant when she defined *beauty* and *this* was it. He wished with all his heart that she could share the incredible view with him. He spun around once more to check on her. "How is she doing back there?"

Jabrat answered frankly. "She is slipping away with every moment that passes. We will be with the Lady Jenladra very soon. She will be of assistance to us in this matter."

Chrishtan sighed. "I pray you're right."

"Well, of course I am right." Jabrat snapped at the young prince. "I am Jabrat. I am always right."

Chrishtan dropped the subject and increased his pace. He wanted nothing more than to reach the Lady of the Realm and save Raelle. He was prepared to do anything.

At the bottom of the dark stairwell, Chrishtan was met with another oyster shell door. Just as before, he stood back and allowed Jabrat to call it open. Jabrat entered first, signaling for Chrishtan to follow him into a pitch black room. "She is in here, warrior. You must enter."

A twinge of fear came over him as he stepped through the arched doorway into the dark room. He could see nothing. He had no idea what to expect and so put both of his hands on the two swords scabbarded on his hips. His Rubiz ring and gemstones of his hilts blazed as Lyre surged through him. The sound of Jabrat's voice startled him. "You will not be needing those, warrior."

Chrishtan ignored the spirit guide, leaving his hands right where they were, gripping his weapons tighter. He would not be so easily manipulated this time. He would be ready to take on whatever evil hid in the darkness. This time, he would not be weak. With his eyes adjusted to the darkness, Chrishtan gazed up and around at the seemingly spherical walls and ceilings of the large room. They looked as if they were blanketed in stars, just like the ones he admired in the sky every night before he fell asleep. He felt as if he were standing in the center of the galaxy. The magnificent sight calmed his nerves as he eased the grip on his blades. Suddenly, Chrishtan's head snapped down at the sound of a startling feminine voice.

"Welcome, my son. We have been expecting you."

Chrishtan squinted hard and focused his Lyre to get a better look at the bioluminescent figure. She sat on a giant pearl throne a few meters ahead of him. He tightened his grip on the swords as he cautiously made his way toward the blue figure.

"Are you the Lady of the Realm of the Lantern Forest? Are you the one they call Jenladra?"

The frost-blue woman nodded. "I am the one you seek."

Chrishtan studied her as he inched closer. He saw that she was not clothed, but instead allowed her long hair to cover most of her body. Chrishtan opened his mouth. "I am Chrish-"

"Chrishtan Vilgare, son of King Sonee Vilgare and mage warrior prince of Abequa. Yes, we have been expecting you." The woman nodded.

Chrishtan made his way up the steps to Jenladra's pearl throne. She held out her luminescent blue hand decorated with glowing green fish scales. Chrishtan dropped to one knee and kissed her hand in reverence. He stared into her green eyes, which emitted the same glow as the scales ornamenting her neck, abdomen, and her lower legs and feet. "Yes Milady, I have been on my way here for quite some time now. Approximately fifteen years. I am sorry. It seems that I got lost somewhere along the way, in more ways than one."

"Indeed, my young prince, you have been lost. You have lost yourself and been taken by fear, but now you shall be found."

Jenladra closed her eyes and raised her hands above her head. Enormous, milky gemstones with rainbows of many different colors lit up all around them. Chrishtan had never seen a gemstone like it. With the room dimly lit, he could see the gorgeous creature much better. He stared at Jenladra's tall, pointed blue ears that stuck out from her incredibly long, purple hair. Long ribbons of green seaweed intertwined with her long locks of pearlescent hair. Jenladra's features were different from anything Chrishtan had ever seen. It was as if ornate, leaf-shaped pieces of cartilage had been molded around her eyes and brow line. Her enormous green eyes seemed to float within her rounded eye sockets. Unlike his eyes, hers had no white at all. She was the most elegant creature he had ever seen. Her splendor rendered him speechless.

Jenladra gracefully stood in front of him. She tucked her hand beneath Chrishtan's chin and raised it. "You have seen much pain and sorrow, my young warrior. You have become jaded. You have been taken by the darkness within your mind. Please rise."

Chrishtan did as the striking woman requested without question. He felt ashamed that she was able to identify his human weakness so easily.

Jenladra glided down the stairs toward a large treasure chest of white wood and gold. "You believe that by saving this woman you will somehow rid yourself of all that haunts you? That somehow it will right what wrongs you believe you have done? That this act alone will rid you of the guilt that plagues your human soul and allows the darkness to capture the innocence of your childhood?"

Chrishtan had no idea how, but somehow Jenladra had managed to reach into the darkest depths of his soul and uncover the harsh truths that haunted his very existence. "Milady, I simply cannot allow this to happen again. I have already lost so much. I'm stronger now than I was before. I was weak. That weakness allowed things to happen that could have been prevented. I will not allow this woman to be taken like so many others. I refuse to let it happen again."

Jenladra opened the ornate treasure chest to reveal gemstones of all bloodlines in addition to more milky gems like the ones that lit the room. She looked through the stones until finally finding one that pleased her. She elegantly plucked the small gem from the pile, shut the chest, and returned to Chrishtan.

"It is your human guilt that tells you these things, Chrishtan. Surely your reason must tell you otherwise. We cannot control the things that happen to us in our lives. We are not to blame for the things that wound our very being. It is true that we must learn from our experiences and adapt our behavior accordingly in order to survive in this world, but there is a difference between adapting and allowing fear and guilt to drive our every action and feeling. It is true that our world is filled with perils and evils that will take a piece of us if we allow them to overshadow what good and beauty remains on Lerim. You must accept that you are not to blame for the evil that has devastated your soul and taken from you that which you loved so deeply. It is not a reflection of you or your self-worth. You were only a child. Only evil is to blame for such things. The only thing you have the ability to control now is how you interpret and react to this evil. You must move on from them and live your life in this present moment if you are to rescue Raelle. It is time for that young boy who lost everything to let go and rest eternally in peace. It is time for Chrishtan, the warrior mage, to rise above it all and bring peace, not only to himself, but to the people of his nation who so desperately need him."

Jenladra placed the unique gemstone in Chrishtan's palm and eased his fingers around it. She lifted his drooping head. "Can you do this, Chrishtan Vilgare, son of Sonee Vilgare and heir to the warrior mage throne of Abequa?"

Chrishtan nodded *yes* as a tear glided down over his cheek. He gazed at the distinctive white stone. A spectrum of colors flowed through its milky solidarity.

Jenladra continued. "Good, my son. What you are looking at is known as the Opalz gemstone. It is a rare gem that is only kept here in my safekeeping. The ability that it bears is much too dangerous to fall into the wrong hands, which is why it has not left this sanctuary for thousands of years. You will need it to save Raelle, and you all will need it if you are to stand a chance against Lochran and the Destroyer."

Chrishtan studied the smooth, rounded gemstone that reflected a colorful spectrum in his hand. "What sort of ability do you speak of?"

Jenladra sat back on her pearl throne. "The ability to travel between worlds as you please. The ability to enter and leave the Verge at any time undetected, thus allowing you the unique ability of astral projection."

Chrishtan winced. "Astral projection? Isn't that practiced solely by Jassokians? Their soul is able to assume the existence of an astral body. They can separate from their physical body here on Lerim and travel outside of it."

"Indeed." Jenladra nodded. "It is a skill that must be practiced for hundreds of years. But with this stone, an unpracticed mage, such as yourself, is blessed with this same ability. You can now travel into that space between our world of the living and that of the dead. This ability is gifted to you by the stone along with one other gift. It can reach into the most intense portions of your Lyre and magnify or create a new ability for its user. However, this ability is chosen by the Opalz stone alone, not its user."

Chrishtan looked perplexed. "But I've experienced this once before when my mentor died, and I didn't have one of these stones."

Jenladra nodded. "Yes, you did indeed. This is because you attached yourself to the soul of your dying mentor. You were able to astral project in this way. It is uncommon, but not unheard of."

Chrishtan shrugged. "But how is this ability going to help me to save Raelle? To save our nations? What sort of new ability will this stone give me?"

"It will allow you to enter the realm of the enemy and find Raelle. It offers you ways of defeating the enemy within their realm. You will be able to take from them what was stolen from us and embedded with evil so long ago. Access to the Verge is key to ridding our world of this evil once and for all. With the aid of your fellow mages, eventually you will be able to capture and imprison the emperor of darkness himself, the Destroyer."

"But how?" Chrishtan shook his head.

"Inside the Verge, you and your cohorts will be the weapon against evil. The Verge is a place where your Lyre-blood abilities can meld together, allowing young mages such as yourself to do things that no other mage has the ability to do." Jenladra paused, and leaned forward to Chrishtan. "In regards to your new ability, only time will tell, and only the stone can yield it. You will discover it without intending to. This is the gift I gave to you and the remaining heirs of the continent of Mirilan so many years ago when Lochran first brought such darkness into our world. You are the answer. You are the key. You are the hope, Chrishtan, not the despair that you have hidden yourself beneath for so long."

Chrishtan stood. "If only I had known this sooner. Why did Lamoore not tell Oleevar and me?"

Jenladra took Chrishtan's hand. "Because she understands that for things to happen the way they are intended to happen, she must not meddle in the Grand Architect's plan. You had to make this journey on your own. Your first attempt was thwarted and thus not meant to be. Now, your time has come, and you will fulfill your destiny. You made it here when you were meant to, you and Raelle both."

Chrishtan shook his head as he walked down the steps of Jenladra's throne. "But what about the other heirs? What about Oleevar of Samisius and son of Lamoore? What about Karaleste of Jassokia and Lanadia of the Ornz Desert?"

Jenladra smiled. "Many times, the only way we are able to undoubtedly find our own way is when we are truly alone and have no way out. At this point, when we are without distraction, is the only time our true path can become clear to us. We have no other choice but to either find our own way, or give in and perish. You and Raelle both chose not to give in when you had nowhere to turn. You were truly lost and alone and thus have found your way back into the light during a very dark time. In a way, you have both adopted the task of holding the lantern for one another as you walk a smoke-filled path of darkness and evil. In time, it will be the two of you who will guide others, such as Oleevar, Karaleste, and Lanadia to this path. And they will hopefully travel alongside you. Together, inside the Verge, you will all become a penetrating beam of light in the black void of evil."

Chrishtan walked back up the steps to sit. "Yes, wise Lady of the Realm of nature, light, and beauty. I find strength in your words and will not forsake them. It is clear to me now that I have clouded my own mind with fears and insecurities. I promise from this day forth that I will no longer allow these entities to rule my life, and instead become a key player and advocate for my own destiny and the fate of our beautiful world of Lerim. Thank you Jenladra, for your wisdom is priceless and shall never be forsaken."

Jenladra nodded. "Then you shall proceed into the Verge and find Raelle within the Destroyer's void. But first, I will need your Lyre harness ring and the Opalz gemstone."

Chrishtan did as the Lady of the Realm requested and dropped both items into her cool, blue luminescent palm. Jenladra took the objects and pressed her hands together. As she closed her eyes, small rays of bright blue light beamed from her hands. A blast of energy flashed from her palms, sending the ring into Chrishtan's hand. Chrishtan examined his altered Lyre ring. It was now studded with fragments of the Opalz gemstone embedded in the band.

"You are ready." Jenladra stood and gestured toward her throne. "Please, take a seat here. Your physical body will remain here while you are away. Remember, while you are inside of the Verge in your astral form, you cannot be harmed. The only way to perish within the Verge is to allow your fears to take over and trap you within the Void. The demons that reside there will play upon those fears in order to make you more vulnerable. Do not believe everything you see. Search your energy, your Lyre for truth and you will find it"

"Yes Milady." Chrishtan nodded.

"Also" Jenladra sat Chrishtan on her throne, "I have arranged for you to have a guide along the way. Please remain mindful of what you have learned today, and carry yourself with the confidence that only a mage warrior can. In the name of Abequa, travel forth into the Verge and return with hope. You may be able to spare more than one soul today."

"For the people of our nations and the souls of those who have lost so much or been taken into darkness, I shall do my best to prevail."

With Chrishtan seated in her throne, Jenladra grasped his wrists. "Now, you will need to focus deeply on your Lyre and harness an energy that will allow you to travel very far. You must clear your mind of everything and focus only on the task at hand. You have done this many times before in your training. It is very similar. You know where you need to go. You have been there once before, which will make it easier. Remember, your guide awaits you on the other side. Use your Lyre to search for truth in his energy, and he will guide you through the darkness."

"Yes, Jenladra." Chrishtan closed his eyes and harnessed his Lyre. Only this time, he was intent on leaving his physical body behind to travel into an unknown world that would swallow him up if given the chance.

CHAPTER 25
THE TAKEN

Glistening balls of burning gases gleamed in the vast distances all around him. A familiar sense of peace came over him as he swam through the vast oblivion of the galaxy toward the stunning nebula he had visited what seemed like a lifetime ago. Vibrant purple and green gases engulfed him as Chrishtan entered one of the many birthplaces of stars, energy, and life in the galaxy. This time, he felt confident of his entry, filled with a new sense of purpose as he propelled himself into the wormhole at the center of the nebula. Just as before, he plummeted into a vortex of diverse stars and familiar effervescent gases. It was just as breathtaking as he remembered it to be. And with a sudden and gentle jerk, the wormhole spit him out into another abyss. Only this time it was not a black void. Bright, white light had taken the place of the blackness from his previous visit.

Chrishtan's head toggled back and forth and up and down as he looked for something, anything in the brilliant white space. He squinted at the hint of something very small in the distance. It looked like a growing black dot as he tried to focus. After a while, the dot transformed into the shape of a person, like a mirage in the middle of a hot desert. *This must be my guide,* Chrishtan thought. As his guide came into view, Chrishtan saw a young man, no older than his early twenties. His brown hair looked messy and un-groomed, but at the same time seemed to suit him perfectly.

"Hello," the young man grinned. "You must be Chrishtan."

Chrishtan nodded. "Yes, I am Chrishtan. And you must be my guide."

The young man's smile grew over his plump lips and big teeth. "Yes, that I am indeed. So I hear you've lost your girl."

Chrishtan chuckled at the guide's matter-of-fact tone. "Well, I guess you could say it like that. Her soul has been taken hostage by the demon Azmo—"

The guide leaned in awkwardly close. "Hush, my friend. We do not speak their names here in the light."

Chrishtan nodded. Something in the young man's eyes made him feel safe and comfortable. His behavior and mannerisms reminded Chrishtan of a person much younger than his early twenties.

The guide raised his eyebrows. . "Shall we head out then?"

Chrishtan sighed. "I suppose we should. Where exactly are we headed, anyway? I don't see anything around."

The guide wrinkled his button nose and tilted his head. "I presume you're right. I guess we will have to close our eyes and use our good old imaginations to get there. You still know how to use it now, don't you? You haven't forgotten it with age, I hope."

Chrishtan managed a smile. "I will try my best. Where do we begin?"

The guide cleared his throat and attempted to replace his silly expression with a more serious one. . "You begin by closing your eyes and allowing your most horrific fears to connect you with the darkness. At the same time, you must not allow those fears to take over your mind and forget who you are and where you really are, which is safely inside the keep of our lady Jenladra's chateau."

For some reason, Chrishtan had no reservation about his task. He trusted his guide with his whole heart. He felt safe with him, like he had known him his entire life. Chrishtan closed his eyes and reached for his Lyre. Memories of a sordid past swept his mind into darkness. When he finally opened his eyes again, he and his guide found themselves standing inside the ominous, rosy glow of the Red Lantern Forest. Chrishtan started to hyperventilate. He turned toward his guide, who seemed calm and collected.

"Why are we here? What are we doing here?"

The guide chuckled as if Chrishtan had said the dumbest thing he had ever heard. "Well, I don't know. It's your nightmare, not mine."

"Nightmare? What do you mean?"

The guide shook his head and laughed. "It's like I told you before. You are allowing your most horrific fears to connect you with the darkness. This must be one of your fears, is it not?"

Chrishtan looked around. "Yes, a horrible memory from my past."

The guide threw his hands in the air. "Well then, there you have it. You have chosen the setting. Remember what Jenladra told you. *You can only be imprisoned by your own fears. The demons that reside there will play upon those fears in order to make you more vulnerable. Do not believe everything you see.* We are in the Void of the Verge where demons reside, but what we are seeing is projected by you. This is your nightmare, and somewhere within it is Raelle. We need to find her soon. You know this place better than I. You must lead the way."

Chrishtan examined his surroundings for anything that would lead him in the right direction. Off in the distance, he eyed a daunting horde of red fairies. He knew they liked to gather in the bald spot of the forest where he, Oleevar, and Cohlen slept in the grass and ate their lives away. He would need to head in that direction to get his bearings.

Chrishtan gestured to his guide. "Come on, this way."

Chrishtan stopped behind a grove of trees just outside the clearing where the Red Owl fairies flocked.

His clumsy guide snapped a branch as he moved in closer. Chrishtan motioned for him to stop.

"Sorry, I am no good with paying attention, you know," the guide whispered.

Chrishtan scowled. "Ssshh. They'll hear you."

The guide grimaced. "Sorry, won't happen again."

For being a guide, he's not very good, Chrishtan thought. *Why would Jenladra send* him, *of all guides?* Then, he heard it. The dreadful whispers of the Red Owls reverberated in his ears.

You have returned, friend. Come, come and stay forever. You will like it here. We promise.

Chrishtan squirmed as glowing balls of red light swarmed him and his guide. They tugged and pulled on the two young men, dragging them into the clearing.

Chrishtan flailed and thrashed as he screamed. "No, I will not go with you. Not this time!" He swatted the demonic fairies, trying to release himself from their menacing grip. Pure terror engulfed him. He continued his struggle as he looked into copious pairs of red eyes that sat above tiny mouths filled with rows of serrated teeth. Blood dripped from their voracious lips as they tore into Chrishtan's flesh. Chrishtan's eyes pursed shut as his pain-stricken screams rang through the trees. Amidst the overwhelming whispers of the evil fairies and the sound of his own shrieks, Chrishtan heard another voice calling to him.

"Chrishtan, remember what Jenladra told you. *You can only be imprisoned by your own fears. The demons that reside there will play upon those fears in order to make you more vulnerable. Do not believe everything you see.*"

It was his guide. Suddenly it dawned on Chrishtan that the young man was not there to guide him physically, but mentally. He trusted his guide with every fiber of his being, though he was not sure why. Chrishtan pressed his eyelids tight and then opened them to find himself unharmed, lying in the grass of the clearing in the middle of the Lantern Forest. His guide stood over him with a look of serious disappointment.

"Dear Architect, you sure do have a wild imagination. For a moment there I thought you were going to blow the whole thing."

Chrishtan brushed himself off as he stood. "Sorry, it must be that 'imagination' thing you spoke of earlier."

"Yes, it surely was." The guide laughed.

Chrishtan surveyed his surroundings once again. "So, what is it exactly that I should be looking for?"

"First off," the guide squeezed Chrishtan's shoulders,

" you will need to try to connect with Raelle."

Chrishtan shrugged. "How exactly do I do that?"

The guide sat down in the clearing and folded his legs. "It will require a bit of focus, which I am not very good at. So *you* must harness your Lyre by focusing on a particular moment. It should be a moment with Raelle when you felt the deepest connection. This should allow you to reconnect and get an idea of her location."

Chrishtan sat down in the grass with his guide. He knew exactly what he would focus on. Chrishtan closed his eyes and flashed back to an intimate kiss beneath the light of a golden moon on the beach of the shimmering coast. Overwhelming feelings of comfort, joy, and passion flooded his body. His mind lingered in the experience until it gradually transformed into disturbing images of Raelle shivering naked in the dark below a pair of menacing red eyes. Chrishtan could barely make out her figure in the blackness, but he knew it was her. Suddenly, the fiery eyes changed direction as if looking directly into Chrishtan's mind. A sinister and demonic voice echoed inside his skull. *She is mine, weakling. And soon, you will be too.*

The horrific imagery faded away, replaced by a familiar setting that Chrishtan had tried to erase from memory so long ago. Images of a stairway of levitating stones leading to a treehouse infiltrated Chrishtan's mind. A disturbing melody echoed in the trees, sending shivers through his entire body.

Precious and dear to lose is fear
So sweet and soft pleasure is oft
When little ones come and beat my drum
I shriek with content for my gifts are sent
Sleep now child for you soon be wild
And thirsty for gore of this I am sure
Precious child
Precious Gift
I live for your soul

But this time, he heard another voice hidden somewhere within the daunting song. A familiar voice, one he had not heard for a very long time. It called to him.

"Chrishtan, please teach me. You promised you would."

"Teach you?" Chrishtan answered.

"Yes, Chrishtan," the small voice said. "You promised to teach me how to use a sword. Don't you remember?"

"Cohlen? Cohlen is that you?" Chrishtan cried.

"Of course it is silly," the voice answered. "Who else would it be? I've been waiting here for you to teach me."

Hazale's tree house and Cohlen's voice dwindled away as Chrishtan's mind traveled back to the clearing with his guide. He opened his eyes to see the young guide still sitting in front of him. The young man's dimples decorated his enormous grin.

Chrishtan cleared his throat. "Did you see what I saw?"

The guide continued to beam as he nodded, *yes*.

Chrishtan looked into his eyes. "Is it possible that since we are in the Void within the Verge, that other trapped souls may reside here as well?"

His guide flashed a toothy smile. "Yes, that is a fact. Those souls which have been trapped or are being held captive by a demon reside here within the Void. Many of them are hidden. But if you know exactly where to look, then they are much easier to find."

Chrishtan struck an epiphany. "So, since my mind has led us to my demon here in the Red Lantern Forest where Cohlen was lost, then is it possible his soul is still here and we can bring him back?"

"Yes, if his soul has not yet been consumed by the demon. Very good, Chrishtan. It is as Jenladra said to you before beginning on this journey. *You may be given the opportunity to spare more than one soul.* And so you shall."

Chrishtan stood as he revealed a long awaited smile. "Then by all means, we shall go there now." He took off toward Hazale's tree house, with his clumsy guide following closely behind.

Looming trees echoed with the irritated hoots of owls and angry whispers of unsatisfied fairies as Chrishtan and his guide moved as fast as they could over the levitated pathway. Once they reached the base of the stairway, Chrishtan motioned for his guide to stay quiet as they tiptoed up to the treehouse door. Chrishtan drew the sword from his right hip. He looked through a small window carved into the arched door of the tree house, but he saw no one inside. Chrishtan eyed Cohlen's bow, still hanging on the wall behind the table where Oleevar and Chrishtan had eaten their last Red Lantern Forest meal with the demon. Chrishtan grasped the ornate door handle and pressed down to enter the demon's den. He raised his weapon as a precaution, but found no one inside. The sound of his guide's voice startled him.

"It seems no one's at home."

Chrishtan covered his guide's mouth. "Quiet." He whispered. "There is another door. We don't know what lies behind it."

The flustered guide scowled. "Sorry, bad habit. I never could seem to hold my tongue."

Chrishtan put his hand up to signal a pause. Sound seeped out from behind the door where he and Oleevar once found a giant nest filled with child-size Lyre-harnessing rings.

"Do you hear that?" Chrishtan motioned.

The guide stopped to listen. "Yes, it sounds like the voices of children."

Faint childlike voices filled the ears of the two young men in the tree house. Chrishtan's hand trembled as it reached for the door. He slowly turned the handle and entered to find the same nest from before. Only this time it was not littered with the Lyre rings of young children. Instead, hundreds of children lay fast asleep in their avian prison. Each spoke out in their sleep, as if living in a dream world.

Chrishtan turned to his guide. "What is this? Why are

they sleeping here?"

The guide hung his head. "These are the trapped souls of the children who have wandered into the Red Lantern Forest over thousands of years. The demon Hazale feeds off of their souls, but he only needs to feed once for every time Lerim travels around the great star. So, he traps them here in the Verge and feeds on them when the time comes. He uses this nest as a sort of pantry, if you will. After he has devoured a soul, it is lost for all eternity. The souls that you see trapped here, some of them are children born a hundred or a thousand years ago. They have not yet been devoured."

Chrishtan closed his sad eyes and shook his head. "But how does he trap them? How does he keep them here?"

"He traps their souls within their Lyre harnessing objects, such as rings or weapons which contain their Lyre gemstone. He keeps them as a sort of trophy."

Chrishtan turned around to view Cohlen's bow hanging on the wall in the other room. "So that is how he trapped Cohlen. His soul is bound to his bow?"

The young guide nodded. "Yes, but it is also bound to the demon and to this place." The guide pointed to the enormous tree across the way.

Chrishtan flashed back to Cohlen's demonic razor sharp teeth, black eyes, and pale, veiny skin. He remembered how the boy used his claws to scurry up the tree like an insect to join others who looked just like him.

"His physical body, like the bodies of many others, is still in the forest as well. Though, it is not the same body you remember. He is a sort of wraith now. These wraiths feed off adult flesh and blood that comes wandering into the forest."

Chrishtan shrugged. "So then how do we return his soul and his body to the living world?"

His guide looked him directly in the eye. "We must find Hazale and destroy him. It is as Jenladra said. We must take back from the darkness what was stolen from the light so long ago and allowed these demons to have a place on the living world of Lerim."

Chrishtan lowered his brow. "What do you mean? What was stolen?"

"You see, thousands of years ago, when the merpeople left the seas to reside on land, they created what we now know as elves and Lyre-blood humans. Before this time, Lerim was covered mostly by water and had little land. But as the geological surfaces of our planet changed, merfolk used their anamorphous ability to form legs and come out of the seas to settle on land. With them, they brought the ancient magic which we refer to as Lyre, as well as the gemstones we use to harness them, including the most powerful stone, the Opalz gem. There were six leaders of the first merfolk settlers. Each as a pair, one male and one female, claimed one of the three continents of Lerim and so became the keepers of those realms. Jenladra and her mate Hazale were the founders and keepers of Mirilan. But when they settled here, they did not realize that the land was already inhabited by a native species very similar to theirs known as humans—or man as we are called. You see, when merfolk first morphed to come out of the waters of our planet, they did not look like elves do today. They looked like Jenladra. Jenladra has been living on land as the keeper of this realm for thousands of years."

The history of their world intrigued Chrishtan. "So then, if Jenladra and Hazale were mates, how did Hazale become so evil? Jenladra seems so virtuous."

"As the story goes, once Jenladra and Hazale discovered the human race, they saw them as the weaker species and wished to hold dominion over them. Therefore, Jenladra and Hazale conquered and enslaved them. In the beginning, Jenladra did not intend to enslave the human race, but desired only to reside over them as their leader and teacher to give them a more civilized way of living. It was Hazale who enslaved them, and it was then that he and Jenladra began to part ways in philosophy. Jenladra felt a deep sense to nurture and teach the humans, and Hazale's thirst for power over them grew even more with her defiance. However, his love for Jenladra led to compromise. He allowed her to teach his human slaves and enlighten them to more civilized ways. It was there in one of Jenladra's many teaching sessions that she met and fell in love with one of her human students, a young man named Jorland. As legend has it, Jorland and Jenladra shared an incredibly passionate relationship that lead to a secret affair behind Hazale's back. Inevitably, Jenladra became pregnant with the first half human and half mermaid child. That was the first decedent of the elves and Lyre-blood humans we know today."

Chrishtan shook his head. "So, clearly Hazale must have found out about this after the baby was born."

"Well," the guide nodded, "Jenladra had come clean about the affair months before the baby was to be born. She knew that once the child came, she would not be able to keep it a secret."

"So how did Hazale react? He must have gone mad."

"Yes, Chrishtan, he did at first. He was overcome with anger, rage, and jealousy. And the hurt of Jenladra's betrayal made his lust for power even more extreme. He told her that she would have the child, but that the child would be a prisoner. And with his newfound knowledge of the two races' ability to reproduce, he intended to create and imprison a slave army of these humanoid mermaids to take over the other continents. He mated with only the most beautiful young human slave women, using them as his concubines and punishment for his wife's indiscretions. From then on, his rage and lust for power only intensified, allowing the Destroyer an open door into Hazale's mind and soul."

"But how did the Destroyer get to him?"

"He visited Hazale in his dreams, using the power of the Opalz gem to bring his soul into the Verge, where he would teach him the ways of the blackness and convince Hazale of its undeniable power. Hazale wanted nothing more than to rule all of Lerim. The Destroyer knew this, and so played upon his thirst for power. He offered Hazale a power which could not be matched in exchange for the one thing that the Destroyer did not yet have—the ability to enter the realm of the living and possess the bodies of the living on Lerim. In order to do this, he would need the Opalz gemstone. That is exactly what Hazale sacrificed to gain his power. It is now known as Black Opalz. It is worn by each demon residing, whether within the Void or the living realm on Lerim."

Chrishtan's eyes grew wide. "I recall seeing this stone around Hazale's neck. He also gave us stones to wear around our necks."

The guide nodded. "Yes, these necklaces allowed the Destroyer and Hazale to access to your mind and soul while you wore them."

Chrishtan sighed. "The Demon also laid a perimeter of them around Cohlen when he had him lying on the table."

"Yes, this is how the Destroyer has power in the world of the living. How he is able to take a soul hostage, so to speak. Even when you wore it for that short time, Hazale and the Destroyer were able to damage parts of your soul."

Chrishtan hung his head. "I know. I've always known. It's haunted me my whole life." He tried to change the subject. "But what about Jenladra? What happened to her? She obviously still lives in the forest."

"You see, Chrishtan, because Jenladra's indiscretion made it possible for evil to enter the living world of Lerim, the Grand Architect cursed her with immortality, banishing her to the eastern portion of the forest and Hazale to the western portion. Eventually, all of her people migrated out of the forest and settled over the continent, leaving Jenladra by herself. "

Chrishtan rubbed his forehead. "So, how is Hazale still living? And why does he look the way he does?"

"Well, technically he is not still *alive*. He is a demon. After being banished to his half of the forest, the Destroyer made a deal with him that he could live as an immortal and rule the continent from the forest as long as he agreed to one thing, never to seek out Jenladra. But it didn't take long before loneliness enveloped him. He morphed into an owl and visited Jenladra in the eastern woods. When Jenladra turned him away and he was forced to return to the western woods, the Destroyer punished him. He took Hazale's soul, trapping him in a demonic shell that was half owl."

Chrishtan and his guide whipped their heads around at the sound of a wicked voice.

"We usually elect to stay hidden within the void, but as you have called my name on so many occasions, I could not stay away with you offering yourself to me so freely." The demon, Hazale, stood in the doorway of his tree house. His balding barn owl head twitched back and forth. His solid black eyes penetrated deep into their souls as they studied the two young men who wandered into his home.

The shrill sound of metal rang out through the trees as Chrishtan swiftly slid a sword from its scabbard. "Stay back, demon!"

Hazale did the exact opposite and stepped through the doorway. His black cloak blew open to reveal his emaciated half bird figure. The talons on his avian feet made an eerie noise as he stepped out onto the nest. "You have come to take my children from me?"

Chrishtan stepped into his defensive stance. "These are not your children. You took them from their rightful families. We have come to set them free."

The demon screeched as his head twitched back and forth. "Free them? They cannot be freed. They are *my* children. They belong to me. They wanted to be with me. They entered into my dominion willingly. They were not happy with their families."

Chrishtan repositioned himself to be ready to strike. "You manipulated them. You made them believe things that weren't true. You took advantage of them!"

The demon's head twitched again. "Oh no, my boy. You

know precisely what I am talking about. As I recall, you loved stuffing your face with my goodies and treats. You did not complain when it was I who gave you a home and soft bed of silk to sleep on. You are the liar, boy. It is you who took advantage of my hospitality. It is you who enjoyed yourself so much that you forgot to take care of your beloved Cohlen. So ungrateful."

Tears welled up in Chrishtan's eyes as he shook his head. "No! *You're* a liar. You tricked us. You are to blame. We were just children. We didn't know. You twisted our minds!"

A familiar voice wafted into Chrishtan's mind. It was his guide. *Remember what we came here for. You know what you must do, how to destroy him.*

"Your time here is through, Hazale!" Chrishtan yelled as he leapt forward and sliced the black Opalz from the demon's skinny bald neck.

Hazale's demonic screech reverberated through the trees as Chrishtan caught the necklace in midair.

"Give me my stone, you filthy human!"

Chrishtan held a sword at the demon's throat. "It hasn't been your stone for thousands of years, Hazale. You lost that privilege when you traded it to the Destroyer for power. I'm retuning it where it belongs, and I am setting these children free!"

The demon chuckled. "You cannot set them free while I exist. Not while their souls belong to me."

Chrishtan tucked the Opalz stone safely in his pocket before reaching for his second blade. With both blades in hand, he pointed directly at the demon. "Which is why I have come to put an end to you!"

Before the demon could respond, Chrishtan lunged forward. In one rapid motion, he extended his blades out and swiftly brought them back together at the base of the demon's skinny neck. A final horrifying screech exited the mouth of the owl demon. Its head crashed to the twig floor of the gigantic nest. Small twigs crunched underneath its dead weight.

Chrishtan spun around as more screeches sounded off within the branches of the trees that surrounded them. Like a swarm of insects, wraith children skittered down the trunks of the enormous trees. Chrishtan and his guide ran toward the treehouse as the demonic children poured into the nest where their souls slept. As they met their sleeping counterpart, they instantly became one before disappearing into a flash of light.

Chrishtan turned to his guide. "What's happening to them?

His guide smiled. "The souls of the children whose lives have been over for quite some time now are going to be with the Grand Architect, where they belong. They are going into the light, Chrishtan. You have freed those that had been taken."

Chrishtan felt like a burden had been lifted as he watched hundreds of souls of hundreds of children disappear into the light. After the last remaining soul vanished, only one child remained on the outside corner of the nest. Chrishtan crouched down beside the young, red-headed boy curled up in a ball. "Cohlen, its Chrishtan. It's time to wake."

Cohlen did not stir. Chrishtan turned around to seek guidance from his escort. "What's wrong with him? Why won't he wake?"

"You must be patient. He will come to. It may take a little more time, seeing as he is the only soul that still has a whole life to live. He's been stuck inside a loop, reliving his short life over and over again. It may take him some time to be able to move on to the next part of his life, especially since he has missed so many years."

Chrishtan's guide was right. Cohlen eventually opened his eyes and turned over. "Cohlen, it's me, Chrishtan. Are you all right?"

Cohlen studied Chrishtan's face and looked deep into his blue eyes. "Chrishtan?" He pressed his friend's beard. "Why are you so old?"

Chrishtan held back tears of joy as he embraced his long

lost friend. "Yes, it's me. You're safe now. You've been asleep for a very long time. It's time for you to go home now."

Cohlen's look of confusion remained. "How long did I sleep for? Where is Olee?"

Chrishtan helped the small boy to his feet. "Olee is safe at home with your family. You have been asleep for fifteen years, but you're awake now, and that is all that matters."

Tears welled up in Cohlen's eyes. He leaned into Chrishtan's waist.

"I can't remember what happened, Chrishtan. But I know it was bad. I feel so sad. It hurts so much."

Chrishtan rubbed Cohlen's head and back. "It's all right, Cohlen. It's all over now. Nothing can hurt you now."

CHAPTER 26
CONNECTIONS

With the evil that once resided there vanquished, for the first time in over a thousand years, a quiet peace swept over the Red Lantern Forest. Still inside the giant nest of the recently departed demon of the realm, Chrishtan's guide promptly reminded him of his original purpose in the Verge.

"We must find Raelle before it's too late. Search something, anything to tell us where the demon, Azmodil, has hidden her within the Void."

Chrishtan took Cohlen's hand. "Cohlen, you see this nice young man here?"

Cohlen nodded.

"He is going to be your partner for a little adventure we're going on. Does that sound all right?"

Cohlen nodded.

The guide smiled whimsically and held out a hand for Cohlen. Chrishtan made his way toward the edge of the nest to look out into the forest. His mind replayed the memory of plummeting from the nest through the trees and breaking his arm. Closing his eyes, Chrishtan honed in on his Lyre to redirect his focus on the current mission. Five minutes of meditation passed before he opened his eyes. When he again looked into the forest, something new caught his eye. Off in the distance an unfamiliar log cabin with a wraparound porch sat inside a clearing. The modest homestead looked out of place in the midst of the Red Lantern Forest.

Chrishtan waved his guide over. "Come look at this. There, do you see that? Out in that clearing there's a cabin that was not here when Olee and I were here before. It doesn't belong."

The guide beamed as if looking at a familiar sight. "You've done it. You've connected with her. She must be there."

Chrishtan patted his guide on the back. "Come, we must hurry. Cohlen, hold onto our guide's hand and do not let go, all right?"

Cohlen nodded and squeezed his chaperone's hand.

Chrishtan paused. "So, how are we going to get her? I mean, won't the demon be in there?"

The young guide shook his head. "Were you not listening to the Lady of the Realm when she explained this to you? They cannot harm you within the Verge because you are among the living on Lerim. Only your soul can be injured in the Verge. But now that we have Hazale's Opalz stone and the Opalz in your ring, you have the power to destroy the demons that reside here, if you can find them. They cannot hurt you unless they take control of your soul, as they have done to Raelle. But even that had to be instigated by a living relative on Lerim. Demons are powerless without access to the living world."

The guide grasped Chrishtan's shoulder. "The demon will most likely be hiding. Watching, but hiding. He will not have full control over Raelle until the turning process is complete, and that process is in the hands of the turner who is alive on Lerim. I think that our turner, whoever it is, might be having second thoughts and that is why she has not yet been completely turned."

"One can only hope." Chrishtan patted his guide on the back before heading back through the tree house. Cohlen followed close behind.

***

As they approached the cabin, a gruesome spectacle appeared before them. Chrishtan's eyes darted around the brutal scene until they became fixed on the body of a mutilated young man dangling backward over the branch of a large pine. The tree was unlike any others in the Lantern Forest.

"What is this place?" Chrishtan shook his head.

His guide stopped dead in his tracks as tears welled up in his eyes.

Chrishtan followed his guide's gaze. To his dismay, he saw the wilted body of a young boy lying lifeless over a large boulder. A treehouse loomed above. Chrishtan's heart sank. He grasped the guide's shoulder. "Are you going to be all right?"

The guide nodded, wiping tears from his somber face. "Yes, I'm sorry. I'll be fine."

Chrishtan continued to scrutinize the horrific scene. "What is this horrible place? What happened here?"

The guide sniffled. "This is Raelle's nightmare. This is her memory. This is where the demon has trapped her."

"This is horrifying." Chrishtan paused. "I understand now why she was running. I see what she was running from, much worse than what I was running from."

"And some of the same." The guide interjected.

Chrishtan and his guide proceeded in their search around the outside of the cottage. They found nothing. *She has to be inside,* Chrishtan thought. A gut-wrenching feeling told him whatever waited inside of the cabin would be just as gruesome as the outside. He looked back at his guide, who was still leading Cohlen around by the hand. "You two stay out here. I'll go inside and look, all right?"

The guide seemed frightened as he nodded profusely.

Chrishtan painstakingly made his way up the wooden steps onto the porch. It looked as if everything had been knocked over. Chrishtan dragged his feet over the battered-down door that lay across the entryway of the cottage. Inside, he found a small kitchen and dining table. He gasped as he peered into the open room opposite the kitchen. One of the most horrific sights he had ever seen lay strung across the floor of the sitting room. He gagged at the pungent odor of decomposing flesh. The mutilated bodies of a man and woman sliced from the bottom of their torso up through their necks were lying in a pool of dark, coagulated blood. The sight sent Chrishtan rushing back out onto the porch.

Flashes of Framin's death stormed his memory. He held his stomach as he dry heaved. *Come on, Chrishtan, pull yourself together. You've seen plenty of this on the field of battle. This is no different.*

Chrishtan took a few moments to gain his composure before reentering the grisly cabin tomb. At the back of the kitchen, he eyed a door to another room and made his way toward it. Once inside, he found a bunk bed and an armoire, but no Raelle. He exited the vacant room and headed back out into the kitchen. At the back of the modest cabin beyond the sickening scene of the sitting room, Chrishtan discovered a washroom and another bedroom. Inside, he found a bed, a fancy armoire and bureau, but no Raelle.

Chrishtan fell back onto the bed and closed his eyes. He focused on his acute senses. His Lyre magnified every sound, smell, touch, and taste. As he fixated further, the faint sound of whimpering and labored breathing resonated above him. Chrishtan opened his eyes to see a small hatch in the ceiling directly above him. He stood up on the bed and poked his finger into a small hole in one of the logs and pulled open the trapdoor. Grasping both sides of the opening, Chrishtan hoisted himself up into the darkness of the attic. As he stood, he reached into his pocket and clutched the Opalz stone he had pilfered from Hazale's neck. He called upon the energy of the rare stone, using his Lyre to light the distinctive gem. Back in the possession of an un-tainted being, the Opalz stone glowed white, radiating a rainbow of colors. On the other side of the attic that lay over the grisly scene of the sitting room, he saw her. Raelle was curled up naked in the fetal position. She cried and scorned herself in a strange childlike voice.

"You did this. You know you did. It's entirely your fault, Raelle. You think you need to know everything, but you don't. Why can't you just be happy? What is wrong with you? You know you did this. All your fault, Raelle. All your fault. You may as well have murdered them yourself. You are a bad, bad girl, Raelle. You should be punished…"

Chrishtan hurried back down onto the bed and grabbed a blanket before climbing back up through the hatch. He tiptoed toward Raelle's shivering figure. "Raelle? It's me, Chrishtan." He said as he covered her with the blanket.

Raelle sluggishly sat up and pulled the blanket around her naked body. Her voice sounded soft and innocent as she shaded her eyes from the light. "Who are you? I don't know you. Don't hurt me, please. I didn't mean it, I swear. I didn't know what would happen."

Chrishtan lowered his light to the floor and squatted down in front of her. "It's all right, Raelle. He reached out to comfort her. Raelle gasped and backed away.

"I'm not here to hurt you. I'm here to help you. To take you somewhere safe, away from here."

In the light, Chrishtan was able to see remnants of blood from the horrific scene below, spattered over Raelle's face. Raelle grimaced and looked at him the same way a child would. "You are? Who are you? How did you find me? I don't know you. You want to take me away from my home?"

Chrishtan brushed a hand over Raelle's cheek. She flinched hard.

"But you *do* know me, Raelle. We are connected. I'm Chrishtan. The bothersome young man who wouldn't leave you alone, remember?"

Raelle shook her head and backed into the corner. "No, I don't remember. I'm bad. I did a terrible thing. Now my parents are dead. Now they're coming to get me. To punish me."

Chrishtan moved with her. He shook his head. "No Raelle. No one is coming to get you. What happened is not your fault, do you hear me? Not your fault. You are not bad. You didn't know. You are one of the most beautiful people I have ever met."

Raelle tilted her head as she shivered. "I am? No, I'm not. I killed my family. I'm horrible."

Chrishtan took Raelle's trembling hand and pressed it against his heart. "You are not bad, Raelle. You are beautiful.

Remember?"

With Raelle's hand over his heart, the same way his had rested on her hours ago on the Shimmering Coast, Chrishtan closed his eyes and surged his Lyre into her. When her eyes opened again, she looked deep into his before throwing both arms around him. Chrishtan prayed she would never let go. He looked into her soft green eyes as he examined her face to be sure it was really her.

"You just don't know when to give up do you, Chrishtan?" Raelle smiled.

"Oh thank the Architect, it's you." Chrishtan picked up the blanket and covered her once more. He took Raelle in his arms and held her tight before helping her rise on her wobbly legs.

"How did you find me? How did I get here? It's like being in a nightmare."

Chrishtan held her steady in his arms. "That is precisely what this is, a nightmare. Our most horrific memories and fears are used to trap us inside this evil place within the void of the Verge. I must say, I think yours has given me a whole new set of nightmares."

Raelle hung her head. "I'm sorry, I never intended for you to see any of this."

Chrishtan lifted her gaze to his. "No, Raelle, I'm glad I did. It has given me a true picture of what your life was really like. I know what haunts you, and so understand you at the deepest level. I know you better now than I could have any other way."

Raelle nodded. "I suppose you're right. I just don't think anyone should have to witness something like this."

"I understand. But right now the only thing we need to worry about is getting you out of here. Come on."

Chrishtan and Raelle headed for the hatch and climbed down onto the bed. Chrishtan turned his back as Raelle stole a nightgown from the bureau and slipped it over her head. Shielding their eyes, they made their way through the horrific living room massacre and out into the open where Cohlen and Chrishtan's guide greeted them.

"You've found her. Thank the Architect."

Chrishtan patted his guide on the back. "Indeed we have, my friend. Raelle, this is my guide. He helped me to find you. And *this* is my little brother Cohlen."

Raelle did not say a word as she stared at Chrishtan's guide.

"Raelle?" Chrishtan waved a hand in front of her.

Raelle shifted her gaze to Cohlen. "Cohlen… But I thought Cohlen had been taken?"

Chrishtan smiled. "He was taken, but we were able to find him here in the Verge. We have freed hundreds of souls of others who had been trapped as well."

Raelle shook her head. "But how? How did you free them?"

Chrishtan patted her shoulder. "It's a long story that I would love to tell you as soon as we leave this evil place."

Raelle nodded and shifted her eyes back toward Chrishtan's guide. "Hold on a moment. Do I know you? Have we met before? No, it can't be that we've met before. The only other people I have ever known my entire life besides Chrishtan are my fam—" Raelle swallowed hard and gazed into the guide's eyes. "It can't be."

The guide smiled and nodded his head. "It is me, sister. I'm here."

"Oh, Browden." Raelle threw her arms around her adopted brother and held him tight.

Chrishtan watched in disbelief as his guide transformed before his eyes inside Raelle's embrace.

Raelle stepped back to reveal a teenage boy. Browden had revealed himself and his true age. Raelle broke into tears. Her brother stepped forward and held her tight. "Browden, what are you doing here? Oh how I've missed you so."

Chrishtan stared at the two of them in amazement. It took everything in him to remember how to speak again. "This is Browden? This is my – my baby brother?"

Raelle nodded as she wiped elated tears from her face. "Yes, Chrishtan, this is your little brother, Browden."

Chrishtan shook his head. "Why didn't you tell me, Browden?"

Browden chuckled. "You can call me Brow. I couldn't tell you because it would have interfered with your focus, and we needed that to find Raelle. You needed my help to find her, as we both have a strong connection with her. But we really need to leave this place before Azmodil gets any ideas like Hazale. Raelle is still vulnerable here in this state. Let's head back to the light."

***

Within the heavenly glow and protection of the light region of the Verge, Chrishtan and Raelle basked in the reunion of their long lost brothers.

Tears cascaded from Raelle's green eyes as she hung her head. "I have missed you so much, Brow. I've thought about you every day since…"

Browden lifted Raelle's somber chin. "I know you have, Raelle, and I you. But I am with the Architect now. I'm all right. I am at peace. And thanks to you and your family, I have nothing but wonderful memories of my life on Lerim."

Raelle gleamed. "I know, Brow. I have just missed you so very much. We all have."

Browden shifted his sentimental gaze toward his brother. "Chrishtan, I have waited so long for this day. I thought it would never come."

"I know brother, I know." Chrishtan wept as he embraced his long-lost sibling. "I too, have been anxiously awaiting this day. I have been searching for you for years. Only now do I realize that I have been chasing a ghost." Chrishtan stepped back and looked in his brother's brown eyes. He could see his mother in them. "Now that I have found you, Browden, I never want to let you go. But I know I must. I just can't bear the thought of never seeing you again."

Browden giggled as he wiped the tears from his face. "I told you, call me, Brow." He smiled. "Have you forgotten already, brother? You have the Opalz stone now. You can come visit me in the Verge, remember? And Mother and Father as well."

Chrishtan reciprocated his brother's grin and laughed. "Once again you remind me of the obvious, little brother. What will I do without you on Lerim reminding me to use my head now and again?"

Browden made a face at Raelle. "I guess it will be up to *you*, sister, to remind Chrishtan to use his brain while back on Lerim."

Raelle laughed. "Oh, don't you worry your head about that, Brow. You know me. Have I ever let anyone slide for lacking a bit of common sense?"

Browden chuckled. "No, I suppose you're right. Chrishtan, you are in very good hands with my sister. I promise you that."

Chrishtan beamed. "Of that I have no doubt, Brow. She truly is a handful."

Raelle snickered. "Well, gee, thanks. Maybe Cohlen and I will go back to Lerim and leave you two here to bond over what a 'handful' I am."

They laughed in unison, reveling in the short-lived moment they had together before returning to Lerim. The inhabitants of the living world still needed them.

Browden's solemn tone cut into their merriment like a knife. "Unfortunately, it is time. I must return to my place with the Grand Architect and you all must return to Lerim. You have your whole lives ahead of you, and important ones at that. It is up to you to rescue the living world of Lerim and our continent of Mirilan from the evils that will stop at nothing to destroy it." A familiar grin transformed Brow's somber expression. "No pressure."

Chrishtan tried to grin over his sorrow. He did not want to leave his brother. "Thank you once again, brother. I will never forget this moment."

With their final words exchanged, the long-lost brothers embraced once more before parting. Chrishtan, Raelle and Cohlen waved goodbye as Browden faded into the white light of the Verge. Chrishtan focused his Lyre on their destination on Lerim where the Lady of The Realm awaited their return. Only this time, Raelle, and Cohlen would be joining him.

CHAPTER 27
KINGS AND QUEENS

Chrishtan's eyes fluttered open to the comforting sound of a familiar voice. His gaze met the luminous green eyes of the Lady of the Realm, Jenladra.

"Welcome home, warrior king."

Chrishtan tried to stand, but his weak and wobbling legs would not allow it. "Where are Raelle and Cohlen?"

Jenladra helped him to sit back down on her pearl throne. "Please, take a moment to rest, my young king. Traveling between planes has taken much from you. For now, your energy is drained and must be replenished." She backed away and stepped to the side to present what Chrishtan's heart so deeply desired to see. A beautiful young woman with long auburn hair wearing a new blue silk dress stood next to a young man with red hair and soft, blue eyes.

Jenladra bowed as she presented his prize. "You have succeeded, Chrishtan Vilgare. You have managed to rid Lerim of one of its most gruesome demons and meanwhile rescue the ones you love from a hideous fate. It is time for you to take back the throne of Abequa that is rightfully yours."

Chrishtan examined the young man with red hair. "Cohlen, is that you?"

The young man nodded. "It is I," he said as he walked toward the throne and up the stairs to greet Chrishtan.

"But, when I rescued you, you were just a boy—"

Jenladra cut in. "Fifteen years have passed since Cohlen was taken. Time does not exist within the Verge. Once Cohlen returned to Lerim, time caught up with him. It is as if he was never taken. Though, he has no memories to accompany his physical growth, as you do. He has lost fifteen years in what to him felt like only an instant."

Cohlen smiled at his surrogate brother. "It doesn't matter now, Chrishtan. What matters is that you came back for me. You have returned to me both my life and my soul. And for that, I am eternally grateful. Thank you, brother." Cohlen knelt down to embrace Chrishtan where he sat in Jenladra's throne.

"I had no other choice, Cohlen. I owe everything to you and Olee for rescuing me when I was lost."

"Well, what about me?" Raelle interjected. "You owed me nothing, yet you never gave up. I am thankful beyond words. To what do I owe this allegiance, King Vilgare of Abequa?" Raelle walked up the steps to take her turn with the young man who had so selflessly relived his harrowing past in order to rescue her.

Chrishtan's face lit up as she approached. "On the contrary, Queen Jowellia of Huronus, it is I who should be thanking you. You helped me remember who I am. It is you who led me here and set me back on my righteous path. It is you who taught me that I need not fear love and connection. I had long ago promised never to invest myself in anyone again so that if I lost them, I would not feel pain. I was a fool. You showed me this. You helped me find what I have been searching tirelessly for most of my life, my brother. You see, it is I who am in debt to you. Fate has brought us together, Raelle."

Raelle let out a deep sigh as she knelt before him. "Well, I suppose we may call it even then, my warrior king?"

Chrishtan grinned as he kissed Raelle's hand. "I am not king yet, but soon enough. And yes, we can call it even, my rogue queen."

Jenladra helped Raelle to stand as she addressed all three young mage royalties. "It is very important for you all to regain your strength before making your way to Ellios. Our spirit guide Jabrat has prepared a spectacular meal for you all in the main dining hall. I will join you there shortly."

Jabrat, who stood in the entry of Jenladra's chambers, nodded to acknowledge the dinner invitation. "You may follow me this way to the dining hall, young descendants of our lady Jenladra."

Raelle and Cohlen offered Chrishtan their hands to assist him from Jenladra's throne. Arms intertwined, the three followed Jabrat to the dining hall. The trek through the gorgeous views and seascape architecture of Jenladra's chateau left Cohlen and Raelle in awe as they admired every square inch of it.

"This is the most incredible place I have ever seen," Raelle declared as they walked barefoot over the white sand floors of the coral palace.

"I know. It is truly remarkable isn't it?" Chrishtan smiled.

"It is incredible. Our ancestors were amazing," Cohlen chimed.

Chrishtan hung his head at the thought of their first male ancestor, Hazale, who had transformed into a demon and took Cohlen's soul captive. "Yes, Cohlen, truly amazing."

The three young mages followed Jabrat through the elaborate seascape of the palace into a large, open room. They gazed up at the porous coral ceilings that allowed the sun to beam in. Its rays warmed the glittering white sand of the palace floor. The stunning purple leaves of the surrounding trees blended perfectly with the pearlescent hues of the coral.

Jabrat stopped at the back of a large table made of an enormous oyster shell. "We shall dine here with our lady, Jenladra. Please, have a seat and she will be along shortly with our feast."

Chrishtan, Raelle, and Cohlen took their seats at the oyster-shell table. Together, they admired the elaborate dishware and utensils made of pearl and glistening white gold. Their banter came to a halt as Jenladra entered the spectacular dining hall. Each one of them as they ogled at her intense beauty. Her bioluminescent blue skin looked almost white in the sunlight as she seemed to glide across the sandy floor. This time, she was not garbed in only her green scales and incredibly long locks of purple hair.

They all stared at her stunning dress, made of seashells and sheer silk. Together, small shells formed cups around her breasts leading to the center of her chest. A narrow trail of shells that ran through her mid-section and down to the bottom of her abdomen connected to a shell belt around her hips. The belt held a sheer silk dress bottom with a long train that floated in the soft sea breeze. Their gazes did not falter as Jenladra found her way to her seat at the table.

"Thank you all for dining with me on this beautiful afternoon. It has been many moons since I've dined in the company of friends and family." Jenladra nodded to acknowledge Jabrat's presence as he sat down next to her.

Chrishtan, Raelle, and Cohlen took their seats as they spoke in unison. "Thank you, Jenladra. We are truly blessed."

Jenladra nodded to acknowledge their appreciation. "Shall we feast then? I know you all must be very hungry."

Moments later, albino fairies floated in. They carried hefty trays of delicious breads and foods from the sea. As soon as the mouthwatering scent of the delicious sustenance wafted into their noses, all three young mages piled food on their plates and began feasting.

***

After receiving their fill of seafood, breads, desserts, and conversation, Raelle, Chrishtan, and Cohlen felt amazing. The feast had recharged their Lyre, and it flowed strong through their bodies once more.

"I trust you all enjoyed your meals?" Jenladra passed her empty plate to a cluster of fairies. The swarm bobbed up and down as they took the plate away.

"Yes, thank you," Chrishtan replied as the others did the same.

Jenladra smiled. "Very good. It is important for you all to remember that as Lyre-blood mages, you must feed your bodies much and often to remain in your strongest state. As you know, food gives us energy. Plants we eat get their energy directly from our great star that is the source of all life here on Lerim. Those plants get eaten by animals and in turn use that energy to sustain their own life. The Lyre force that lives within your blood and your cells is also an energy. So to keep that energy at its peak, you must feed it well. Especially you, Raelle and Cohlen. When you return to Ellios, you must both undergo training at the Ellios Academy of Interlyre Studies. There you will learn to harness your bloodline abilities, use them, and become the strongest and most powerful mages possible."

Cohlen shook his head. "Most powerful, but how? There are many Lyre bloods who train at the academy. What makes us so special?"

Jenladra opened her hand to reveal Raelle and Cohlen's Lyre harness rings. "Because your Lyre harnessing rings have been melded with the Opalz gemstone. As I explained to Chrishtan, Opalz will not only give you the ability to travel in and out of the Verge as you so wish, but will magnify your current Lyre-blood abilities in addition to blessing you with a new ability of the Opalz's choosing." Jenladra lifted her hand and focused on the rings. They levitated and floated to Raelle and Cohlen.

Cohlen and Raelle plucked their refurbished rings from the air, admiring the shards of reflective Opalz embedded within the white gold of the bands before sliding them onto their fingers.

Jenladra seemed pleased with their fit. She left her seat and walked over to one of the white treasure chests that decorated the chateau. From the chest she gathered three hooded cloaks of different colors of velvet. One red, one blue, and one green. "My dear mages, warrior, rogue, and hunter, it has come time for us to part ways. I have given you the tools you will need to defeat Lochran. You will also find strength in your growing numbers as the others join you. It is all that I can give at this time. I will meditate further still in request to the Grand Architect for assistance, but I fear I may go unheeded. I take every ounce of blame for your troubles and the evil that has plagued many on this continent. Go now and bring to me, and the rest of our people, hope for the future. I know deep within my soul that you are the answer. This is your purpose."

Raelle, Chrishtan, and Cohlen pushed back their chairs and stood as Jenladra handed them each a hooded cloak.

"In addition to your new gems, I offer to you these cloaks as a token of gratitude for your perseverance through the struggles you have already faced and will continue to face in the future. Keep them as a reminder of me. They are now yours."

Each of them shared an embrace of gratitude and reverence with their Lady of the Realm. But before letting Raelle go, Jenladra tucked a journal in her arms. "Raelle, this belongs to you now. It once belonged to your mother."

"Thank you, Jenladra." Raelle bowed as she took the journal and met her friends where they stood with Jabrat in the doorway.

Jenladra stopped them just before exiting. "It is your duty now, all of you, to help the others make it here and fulfill their destiny. Remember, the choice must be theirs, but it is up to you to guide them.

"Yes Milady. We shall not let you down. And thank you." Chrishtan bowed.

With their goodbyes in order and their hands fitted with the ultimate force of Lyre magic, all three mages followed Jabrat out of the palace. As they crossed over the oyster shell drawbridge, Pip and Sasha bounded through the plush green grass and onto the bridge to greet them.

"Pip! Sasha! You're well! I'm so happy to see you." Raelle picked them up one at a time and let them lick her face. She hugged each of them tight before setting them back on the ground. Off in the distance of the grassy field, Chrishtan and Raelle eyed Winston standing next to Boone.

"I took the liberty of bringing you your animals, young mages." Jabrat pointed at the horses who were fully packed.

He swatted at and shooed away the dogs who were jumping and begging for his attention.

"Thank you so much for taking care of my babies, Jabrat." Raelle smiled. "And you as well, Chrishtan. Who knows what would have happened to them if you hadn't been there."

"It was my pleasure, Raelle." Chrishtan grinned as he put his arm around her. "They kept me company. And Jabrat, thank you for taking care of them. I don't know what we would have done without you."

Jabrat bowed as they reached their mounts. "It was my duty, Sire."

Chrishtan laughed as he stepped toward the spirit guide. "Sire? I don't think I'm quite ready for that title yet, Jabrat."

Jabrat bowed again. "Yes, Sire."

Chrishtan shook his head and embraced his tall green friend. "Thank you, Jabrat. I will never forget all that you have done for us. I wish you the best."

"It was my pleasure, Sire." Jabrat bowed once more before heading back to the coral palace of the Lady of the Realm.

**

One of the last summer suns hung high in the southwest sky, warming the white shimmering sand that ran into the salty surf of the sea. Chrishtan stood silent in the wet sand with his arms folded, admiring his view of the Shimmering Coast. As the waves peacefully undulated, he dug his feet deeper beneath the surf. It was exactly where he wanted to be once they exited the Lantern Forest. He knew that autumn would soon be upon them, and winter soon after. It was his only chance to introduce Raelle to a proper beach experience before summer ventured back around again. Chrishtan took Raelle's hand as he looked out over the eastern horizon.

"This is it, the wonder of the sea, the Shimmering Coast.

It takes my breath away every time I look at it. You know Raelle, Huronus, your family's kingdom, is on the coast as well. Not this coast, but it sits beside the sea nonetheless."

Raelle scooted closer to him and dug her feet into the wet sand just as he had. "Yes, it truly is breath taking. I've never seen anything quite like it in my entire life. It makes me wish I could have lived in Huronus. That I could have spent time on the coast there."

Cohlen chuckled as he joined them. "Chrishtan, do you remember the last time we were here and you tried to catch crustaceans? You looked ridiculous chasing them all over the beach like a madman."

"Of course I remember." Chrishtan smiled and shook his head. "How could I forget? You and Olee allowed me to chase them around for at least ten minutes before deciding to intervene with your skills of animal hypnotism." Chrishtan laughed out loud. "I felt like an idiot. Here I am a simple warrior, trying to catch food for two actual hunters. I was so dimwitted."

"Well," Cohlen snickered, "let's hope you've learned a thing or two since then."

Chrishtan pulled his buried feet from the wet sand. "Oh, I have. I assure you I very well have." Chrishtan let out a long sigh. "Well, you two, the sun will be setting within the next four or five hours. It will take us at least that long to reach the Gates of Ellios."

Raelle followed suit and pulled her feet from the surf. "Then we had better be on our way gentlemen."

The young mages said goodbye to the sea and packed up their things. They mounted their horses, and headed west.

CHAPTER 28
LONG-LOST MIRACLES

The waning moon took refuge behind scattered clouds in the northeastern sky. Two horses with cloaked riders galloped over the lush grassy knoll just outside the Gates of Ellios. Fully-armored guards wearing bronze plates over brown leather, stood atop the bolt-studded bronze gates of their city. Each sentry was armed with a weapon made of the same metal. Around the outside of their massive metal gates, a translucent blue luminescent fog surrounded the large lakes on either side. As the moon peeked its head back out from behind its curtain of clouds, an older sentinel at the center of the formation raised his metal weapon and pointed it at the unauthorized riders headed toward the gate.

"In the name of Ellios, I command you to come no further or you will be rendered incapacitated." The sentinel signaled his company to draw their weapons alongside him. "Do not pull your trigger until I give the command." The company nodded in unison.

The leader focused his Lyre and accessed his ability to see long distances, like a bird of prey. "I still cannot make out their faces. They're wearing hooded cloaks. There seems to be three of them; two on a white stallion and the third on a painted horse." The sentry called out to the strangers in the distance once more. "This is your last warning. Do not ride any closer. Stop where you are, and we shall send men out to meet you."

The cloaked travelers did not stop. One of the sentries fired an accidental shot from his metal weapon. A bolt of what looked like blue lightning shot out from its barrel and over the travelers' heads as they ducked. Just barely avoiding the shot, they stopped dead in their tracks at the bottom of the grassy hill.

The leader turned to his company. "I said, do not fire! I think I've seen that white stallion before. You two will accompany me to meet them."

The leader and two of his fellow guardsmen swiftly exited down the bronze stairs of the gates and hopped onto bronze mechanized mounts lined up near the door. They took off their necklaces containing a chocolate colored gemstone and stuck the stone into a slot at the top of the vehicle. With the gemstone in the slot, the machine hovered a few feet off the ground, casting a light below it. The leader signaled a guard to open the bronze gate. With their exit clear, the three elven guards squeezed the handles of their bronze hovercrafts and flew off into the night toward the unidentified horsemen.

As the guards approached, one of the cloaked riders hopped down from the white stallion to greet them. He was followed by the rider of the painted steed. The guards parked their hovering cruisers and pulled out Diamoz lights to investigate the unexpected visitors. The lead sentry stepped toward the dismounted riders and his company aimed their metal weapons. "What business do you have here at the Gates of Ellios? These are dark times. We cannot allow you to enter without proper clearance."

The cloaked rider of the white stallion grinned as he removed his hood to reveal his face. "I see the force field is still holding strong, Zeell."

The guard's eyes grew wide as his jaw slackened. "Chrishtan, is it really you? You've returned? Have you found your brother? "

Chrishtan leaned in and hugged his old friend. "Yes, I have returned. And I did find my blood brother. He has passed on. He is with the Architect now."

"I am so sorry, Chrishtan," Zeell squeezed the arm of his long-lost friend.

Chrishtan's frown transformed into a smile. "But I also found someone I was not expecting, and I think you will be very pleased."

The rider of the painted horse stepped forward and

removed his hood to reveal a young man with red hair, freckles, and soft blue eyes.

Zeell took a step back. "By the Architect, it cannot be. We thought Master Cohlen dead."

"No, Zeell, I am not dead." Cohlen said as he approached. "My soul was trapped in the darkness, but Chrishtan came back for me, and now I am home."

Zeell stepped forward and embraced his long lost master.

Cohlen looked in his friend's hazel eyes. "Oh, how glad I am to be home, Zeell."

Zeell smiled. "Your mother and father will be made whole once again with your return. Please, let us enter the gates. As chance would have it, your mother and father are here in Ellios to inquire about some new weaponry and military technology that your brother Oleevar has been testing. I tell you, your brother's ability to harness and use Lyre energy to further advance the technology of Ellios and our army is limitless. He will be very surprised by your return. He tries very hard to pretend as if losing both of you is simply the way of the world, but we know that he has not been the same since you left."

Chrishtan stopped Zeell before he could walk back to his vehicle. "Zeell, first there is someone I would like you to meet."

Zeell brushed a piece of brown hair from his face and watched as the third rider hopped down from Chrishtan's white stallion. As Raelle stepped forward, she pulled her hood down onto her shoulders.

"Zeell," Chrishtan brought her forward, "this is Raelle. Daughter of the king and queen of Huronus."

Once again, Zeell found himself wide eyed and slack jawed. "Huronus? I thought she and her parents were murdered when Lochran took over."

Chrishtan shook his head. "No, they have been in hiding inside the Didumos Valley. As it turns out, the king and queen raised their children there to keep them safe. They were outside Lochran's reach."

"Where are the king and queen now? Are they not with you?"

Chrishtan shook his head. "No, I'm afraid that Raelle's parents and younger brother were murdered by Minotirr."

Zeell stepped in to embrace Raelle. "By the Architect, she can have a home here with us. Far too many have been lost to the evil that Lochran has called into this world."

Raelle nodded as their embrace ended. "Thank you, Zeell. It's wonderful to meet you."

Zeell smiled. "Indeed. It's quite the pleasant surprise to meet you as well. Any friend of Chrishtan's is a friend of mine. He and I go way back. I'm sure he's told you."

Chrishtan laughed. "Believe it or not, we haven't had much time for small talk, Zeell."

Zeell grinned as he bowed. "Of course not." With everything in order, Zeell hopped back onto his hovercraft with the other two guards. "Well, don't just stand there, young kings and queen, get on your horses and follow me."

***

The three young mages remounted their steeds and followed Zeell through the bolted bronze gates of Ellios. After passing through the enormous metal gates with two shimmering lakes on either side, Raelle felt overwhelmed at the sights and sounds of a place she had only ever heard about in her father's stories. The bustling streets were filled with people, some whizzing by on their peculiar, hovering mounts. It was a great deal for Raelle to take in. She had never witnessed anything like it.

All around her, shiny black marble streets reflected images of the tall bronze buildings and Diamoz street lamps that lined them. And though everyone looked human at a glance, their elven features were apparent in their pointy ears and some with strange-colored hair. Women and men crowded the walkways dressed in attire Raelle had never before seen. The men were garbed in brown leather with bizarre hats and the elven women in corsets with laced shoes. People stared at the cloaked strangers on horseback as they passed by. Raelle felt out of place in her cloak. While she sat behind Chrishtan as they rode, she buried her face in his back. She resented living her entire life secluded in the valley of the Didumos Mountains.

Chrishtan turned around to check on her. "How are you doing back there?" He hollered over the noisy streets.

Raelle squeezed him tight. "I'm fine. It's fine. Just a lot to take in, that's all."

Chrishtan gently squeezed one of her hands that clung to his waist. "We're almost there. Only a little further. Hang in there."

Raelle trusted Chrishtan and felt safe in his presence. She loosened her grip and attempted to take in the sights and sounds once again as they made their way to the Palace.

As they came upon the Ellios Academy Palace, the hustle and bustle of the city faded away. The large property of the academy sat far off from the noisy metropolis. Like the bronze metropolitan buildings, the Ellios Academy Palace sections were constructed in the shape of a skinny dome. But unlike the city's buildings, it was comprised of many dome shaped silos soldered and bolted together to form one large, brightly lit, bronze palace. Raelle was awed by its magnificence. Bronze statues of different elven figures lined the marble path leading to the front entrance. Each held a Diamoz crystal that lit their way to the entrance.

Finally, they arrived at the bottom of the black marble stairway leading to the enormous ornately welded, double doors, of the acropolis. A young elvish man rushed over to help them off their horses and take them to a stable.

Zeell dismounted his hovercraft, detached his chocolate-colored gemstone, and threw it back around his neck. "Welcome to the palace on the grounds of the Ellios Academy of Interlyre Studies. The first university of its kind to offer courses and training in any area of mage Lyre energy. Since Lochran's takeover, this has become the home of many young mages seeking to continue their training without the tyranny of Lochran and his push for black Lyre practices. It is also the only university to offer courses in lyre technology and have an entire school dedicated to the research and application of it."

Zeell stopped and placed his hands carefully inside a pair of hand prints welded into the doors of the palace. A large Emeralz jewel between the handprints lit up alongside Zeell's ring, and the bronze doors opened. Zeell walked backward and spread his arms through the entryway as he addressed his guests. "Welcome home, everyone."

Raelle's heart skipped a beat as she entered the miraculous palace. Leaves and vines of welded metal inserted with tiny diamoz gems decorated and lit the enormous domed ceiling. Raelle, Chrishtan, and Cohlen followed Zeell up a black marble staircase. The grand staircase forked at the top as it reached a balcony of bronze and iron railing around the entire dome. Around the balcony, open doorways carved in the shape of giant leaves led to elaborately decorated corridors.

Raelle found it difficult to take her eyes off the gorgeous architecture as she followed Zeell through the largest leaf-shaped entryway directly at the top of the stairs. Chrishtan took Raelle's hand as they continued down to the end of the hall to another bronze door decorated in intricately welded vines and leaves. Once again, Zeell placed two hands inside the prints to open the door. Inside, sitting at a large iron dining table with leafy iron vines for legs and a deep green marble top were three elven monarchs.

As soon as Zeell, Chrishtan, Raelle, and Cohlen entered the room, the king, queen, and prince froze. They stared in astonishment at their newly arrived guests.

Queen Lamoore was the first to stand. "By the grace of the Architect, it cannot be! Both of my sons have been returned home to me?" Tears welled up in her blue eyes. She made her way across the shiny black marble floor and stroked her soft white hands over Cohlen's cheeks. "Cohlen, it cannot be. Your soul was taken. This is not possible."

Tears flowed as Cohlen held his mother. "It is I, Mother. I've come home to you. Chrishtan came back for me. He destroyed the demon and rescued me. Hazale is gone now, Mother."

Lamoore nodded at Chrishtan as if to say thank you before gazing into the new face of her now twenty-one-year old son. "It is a miracle. The Architect truly has blessed us. Welcome home, my precious prince. How I've missed you every moment since you've been away."

It took a moment for Oleevar and King Adreahn to realize what was happening, but once reality sunk in, they too left their dinner to embrace their long-lost loved one.

The king turned to address Chrishtan. "You have truly saved us, Chrishtan. Our hearts have been restored to their full capacity." He took Chrishtan in his arms and held him tight. "Thank you, son."

Chrishtan was lost for words. He smiled as a tear trickled over his cheek.

Oleevar patted Chrishtan on the back. "Chrishtan, brother, you never cease to amaze me. You just can't stray from a good adventure, can you? Never know when to give up. Always looking for trouble." He embraced his surrogate brother. "We are truly blessed this day to have such an amazing and stubborn man back in our lives once again."

Raelle stood against the wall observing the reunion. She was overcome with emotion at the heartfelt scene. She desperately wished that she too could reunite with her brothers, but she also knew that her longing was in vain. Her brothers were gone forever, only to be reunited in death. Her eyes swelled with burning tears.

"And who might this be?" Oleevar gently grasped Raelle's palm and kissed the top of her hand.

Chrishtan immediately rushed to her side. "I am so sorry, Raelle." He said as he put an arm around her and kissed her on the cheek.

"Oleevar, Mother, Father, this is Raelle Jowellia of

Huronus. She is the true hero. Had I not met her during my travels, I am afraid that Cohlen may have never made it home."

Lamoore, Adreahn, and Oleevar immediately introduced themselves. They welcomed Raelle into their family with open arms. Their smiles of joy and acceptance quickly remedied some of Raelle's sorrows. They all sat down together at the extravagant dining room table. The rest of the evening was spent feasting and discussing the details of Chrishtan and Raelle's meeting leading up to the rescue and return of their beloved son and brother, Cohlen. A beacon of hope relit in such a dark time.

***

The startling sound of screams and cries woke Chrishtan from his peaceful slumber. He jumped out of bed and raced into the bedroom next to his chambers to find Raelle on the floor shaking violently. She was soaked in a cold sweat. Sasha and Pip licked their mistress's horrified face as Chrishtan rushed over and cradled her in his arms. Chrishtan wiped away the tears cascading down her sleeping face. "Raelle, Raelle, wake up. It's me Chrishtan. Please wake up."

Raelle let out a blood-curdling scream before her eyes shot open. "Oh Chrishtan, thank the Architect, it's you." She buried her wet face in Chrishtan's arms as he stroked her hair.

"It's all right, Raelle. You're safe. It's going to be all right."

Raelle rubbed her face as she sat up. "I saw them all. All of their deaths. Over and over again. Something was watching me. Following me. I couldn't escape it."

Chrishtan attempted to calm her. "I know, Raelle, I know. I used to have night terrors too when I was a boy. They began after Oleevar and I returned from the Red Lantern Forest. I know how real they can feel. And the fear is very real. But they're only dreams now. They are no longer reality. You're safe here in the palace. I promise. It's going to be all right."

Raelle looked at Chrishtan with vulnerable eyes. "I don't want to be alone ever again, Chrishtan. Please, would it be all right if I slept with you in your chambers? I can sleep on the floor."

Chrishtan smiled at one of the first signs of vulnerability Raelle had ever shown him. It pleased him that she was finally letting him in. "Of course you can. And you don't need to sleep on the floor. You can have my bed, and I can sleep on the floor. Whatever you need, Raelle. I promise we are going to get through this together, all right?"

Raelle smiled and nodded her head as Chrishtan embraced her once more. It was precisely what he longed for, yet completely unexpected.

Chrishtan helped Raelle off the floor and accompanied her back to his chambers. Pip and Sasha followed closely behind. His heart melted as Raelle crawled into his enormous canopy bed. With the summer nights turning cooler as autumn crept in, Chrishtan had a small fire crackling in the fireplace, giving the room a cozy and safe ambiance. The dogs wasted no time curling up in front of its warmth to sleep.

Raelle tucked herself in under the green silk sheets as Chrishtan pulled the quilt over her shivering body. "This is perfect, Chrishtan, thank you. I don't know what I'd do without you."

Chrishtan scooted in on top of the covers and rubbed Raelle's back to calm her nerves. As she drifted off to sleep, he felt more significant than he ever had in his entire life as a prince. In that moment he realized that he had become her everything. He was all she had in the world and it gave him purpose.

CHAPTER 29
THE ELITE ECHO

Soothing rays of morning sunshine warmed Raelle's soft rosy cheeks. She felt Chrishtan brush wisps of her hair away from her face before gently pressing his lips to her forehead. The comforting feeling of Chrishtan's lips prompted Raelle to open her eyes. A smile crept across her drowsy face as she looked deep into his blue eyes. "Good morning, my king." Raelle leaned forward and planted a kiss on his tender lips. The feel of his beard tickled her.

Chrishtan laughed. "Good morning, my stunning queen. Are you hungry? Because I am absolutely starving, but I wanted to wait for you. I didn't want you to wake up and find yourself alone."

Pip and Sasha perked their ears and wagged their tails at the mention of the word *hungry*.

Raelle chuckled. "Well, I suppose you have your answer. We are all most certainly ready for some breakfast."

Chrishtan kissed Raelle once more before leaving the bed and shuffling across the room to where a bronze-colored silk dress with an olive green floral corset hung on the wall. Raelle admired Chrishtan's shirtless physique as he walked away. His bulging triceps and lean muscular back seemed to glisten in the sunlight. It sent a strange feeling rushing through her body as she stared. She continued her penetrating gaze as Chrishtan turned around with the dress in hand. She admired his carved mid-section, cut with abdominal muscles and prominent pectorals. His bulging shoulders formed perfectly into his rounded biceps. Raelle's body throbbed like the large purple vein that ran from the top of Chrishtan's shoulder, through his bicep and down into his forearm. He was one of the most beautiful creatures she had ever seen.

Chrishtan gently laid the stunning dress on the bed before waving his hand in front of Raelle's face.

"Raelle? Hello? Are you in there?"

"Yes, sorry." Raelle blushed. "I uh – um – Yes the dress is lovely."

Chrishtan grinned as he sat back down on the bed. "Lamoore brought it for you this morning. I told her you didn't have anything. She said that later on you may go with her to the seamstress and have more made."

Raelle lifted the dress to admire it. As Chrishtan got dressed in his leather boots, sleeveless linen shirt, and sleeveless leather vest, he beamed at Raelle.

"I hope you like it, Raelle. I know it will look absolutely perfect on you. I'm going to head down and let them know we're ready for breakfast while you dress. I'll see you soon." He raced over and left a lingering kiss on her lips before exiting the room. The dogs ran out behind him.

Raelle dropped her feet to the smooth marble floor and left the bed to undress from the silk nightgown Queen Lamoore had given her. Near the bedroom door where she hung her new dress, she found a full-body length mirror with a frame of bronze vines and leaves. She silently studied her reflection from head to toe as she slipped the nightgown from her shoulders and onto the floor. She wondered if Chrishtan found her figure as breathtaking as she did his. Although she would never admit it, she prayed that he did. Hidden within her extravagant new dress, Raelle found strange silk undergarments that covered only the most necessary parts of her bottom half. She gently slipped them on before pulling the silk dress and corset over her head.

With the dress on and the corset buckled shut, Raelle was unsure of what to think. She had never worn anything so elegant or revealing in her entire life. The corset had no sleeves, leaving her chest, shoulders and top of her back completely exposed as it formed a perfect heart shape around the outline of her breasts. Under the corset, the bronze-colored silk of the dress gathered as it came down just above her knee in the front and trained onto the floor in the back. It was absolutely stunning, and Raelle started to feel stunning in it. The olive of the corset magnified the intense green of her eyes against her soft olive skin and rose-colored cheeks. As she stared at her reflection, for the first time in her life she thought herself capable of possessing beauty.

Raelle held back a satisfied grin as she walked over to a bureau. She noticed an ornate box with a parchment of paper on top that read, *for Raelle.* She unlatched the box to find a beautiful golden necklace and a lavishly decorated hair pin. She used it to pin her hair half up before donning the stunning necklace. She admired her own face in the hopes that Chrishtan would find hers as striking as she did his. And for the first time in her life, excited butterflies fluttered in her stomach as she buckled a pair of matching sandals before leaving Chrishtan's chambers.

Raelle swiftly made her way over the marble floors of the elaborate hallway and into the open dining room from the previous night. By the time she entered, she found Chrishtan and Oleevar already seated at the marble table. Both young men immediately paused their conversation to stand as Raelle entered the room. Chrishtan rushed to pull out the chair next to him.

"Thank you, Chrishtan." Raelle nodded, barely able to contain herself.

Chrishtan cleared his throat and stared at her as she took her seat. "You're very welcome. You look amazing, Raelle, you truly do. "

All three of them took their seats in front of their breakfast as Oleevar started the conversation right where he and Chrishtan left off. "Look, Chrishtan, even darker times lay ahead. Now, don't get me wrong, I am thrilled to have you back. You are my brother and I love you, but it is only a matter of time before word gets out that you have returned to Ellios and Lochran attacks our refugee camps or even Ellios directly. I feel safe enough behind our force field for the time being, but we cannot hide forever. Not to mention, word has come to us that Lochran has a new general. They call him the Elite Echo. He is a rogue mage supposedly of royal Huronus blood. They also say that he has been fitted with a black Opalz stone. They say he can emit a shriek from his mouth powerful enough to take down an entire army in less than a minute. I am not sure if these rumors are true, considering most of the Huronians were killed. But with you finding Raelle, I now see it as a possibility."

Chrishtan shook his head. "But who would it be? Raelle's blood brother was murdered years ago, probably by a Minotirr. Is it possible that Lochran had a son that no one knew about?"

Oleevar shrugged his shoulders. "It is not outside the realm of possibility, which means that it is time for me to put my new weaponry into effect."

Raelle eavesdropped on the conversation as she ate. It was strange to hear them speak of her family whom she knew almost nothing about. And the only thing she knew about Oleevar was that he was some sort of genius. She wished to be part of their elaborate plan. She too wanted to help save the people of Mirilan. "So, Oleevar, this new weaponry of yours, if you don't mind me asking, what is it exactly?"

Oleevar smiled. "You may call me Olee. No, not at all, Raelle. In fact, I would love to tell you about it. It is what I have worked my entire life to accomplish. I have developed a new technology harnessing the aquatic soil gem. It's the same gem we use to power our hovercrafts, among other things. This gem can only be found buried deep beneath the sediment of the lakes that surround our great kingdom of Ellios. With the energy of those stones, I have created a biomechanical suit for specially trained soldiers to wear in combat. These suits range from small add-ons, such as weapons attached to the face or limbs, all the way to a fully functioning suit of biomechanical armor. The full armored suit gives a soldier an additional height of a half meter over the average elf or man. It has lyre energy weapons built into it, of course. They are still in the test phase, but I have had five hundred of them made already just in case. A thousand more are coming over the next few months. I can take you down to see them this afternoon to show you, if you'd like."

Raelle smiled. "I would love to see them. I have never heard of such a thing."

Oleevar scoffed. "That is because I am the first to ever design such a thing. You will be impressed, I assure you."

Chrishtan rolled his eyes at Oleevar's typical cocky nature and smiled at Raelle. The two of them laughed until Zeell's startling voice sliced through their laughter like a guillotine.

"Oleevar, the force field is down! We have no idea how it happened. Someone may have sabotaged it from the inside. The enemy is at our doorstep. The Elite Echo himself, is outside with an army of Lochran's men demanding that Chrishtan come out and face him, or else he will destroy the entire city of Ellios."

Olee grabbed Chrishtan by the arm as they both stood. "Chrishtan, you do not need to do this, brother. I can have our army geared up and ready to go with the biomechanical suits within thirty minutes."

Zeell interrupted. "Milord, the Elite Echo has threatened that if he does not come out within the next five minutes that the destruction of Ellios is most certain."

Oleevar shook his head. "What an unreasonable way of conducting yourself –"

Zeell cut him off. "Milord, we are dealing with agents of evil here. They do not see reason."

Chrishtan stepped in between them. "I will go out there right now and face him. Olee, I will try to buy you enough time to get your biomechs ready. Zeell, I'll need my armor and my swords. You can help me suit up."

Raelle rushed over to the man that meant everything to her. "But, Chrishtan, this is dangerous. You can't do this alone. You could be killed. You must not go, please!"

Chrishtan looked deep into her troubled eyes. "I will

come back, Raelle, I promise. I am a strong and well trained warrior. Please, you must have faith. I must do this or all the people off Ellios could be killed, enslaved, or both. I cannot abandon the people of this city at a time when they need me most, especially not after they gave me a home when I had none. I know you can understand this."

Raelle closed her eyes to hide the tears damming up behind them. She nodded her head. "I understand."

"Thank you, Raelle." Chrishtan pulled her in and pressed his lips to hers before heading to the armory. "I *will* be back."

Fear and anxiety overwhelmed her. She could not bear the thought of losing Chrishtan. After all, he was all she had in the entire world. Chills shivered down Raelle's spine when she noticed she was all alone once again. Oleevar had already left to prepare the biomech suits. As she stood in the dining room by herself, Pip and Sasha looked up at her wagging their tails, begging for more scraps. Raelle envied their ignorance and ability to live in the moment.

Panic set in at the thought of Chrishtan being killed. Raelle was tired of everyone treating her like she was helpless. She refused to sit back and do nothing while everyone else did their part. She had to try and help Chrishtan. Raelle raced down the hall, through the main entryway and into the armory. As she rushed in, she swiftly removed her dress and corset and threw them onto the floor. She replaced them with a black and blue leather suit of armor she took from a glass case. Once fully dressed in Huronus rogue armor, she found two daggers and placed them in the sheaths on her hips.

Raelle set out in a dead run through the halls and out the bronze palace doors. She bolted down the palace steps in search of her horse, but soon remembered that a stable boy had taken him. In her desperation, she hopped onto one of the strange hovercrafts parked at the base of the staircase, but did not have the soil gem required to start it. She jumped at a startling voice of one of the palace guards behind her.

"Queen Jowellia, it is not safe for you out here. You must get back inside."

"No, I will not go back inside!" Raelle scolded the sentinel. "So you either help me to start this thing, or I will run to the Ellios Gates myself."

The guard swallowed hard and hopped onto the bronze craft. He powered it up and Raelle held him tight as they took off toward the Ellios Gates.

Hundreds of sentries and armed forces waited behind the Ellios Gates for their king to send them into battle. Raelle prompted the guard to park the craft behind the troops. She forced her way through the lineup of men and up the bronze stairwell to the top of the gates. Raelle's eyes darted around in search of Chrishtan among the new lineup of men with bronze weapons atop the gates. At the center of the lineup, stood King Adreahn and Queen Lamoore. Raelle heard the king's voice as he pleaded with someone outside the gate.

"If you will not see to reason, then Chrishtan will do what he must. But I know that it does not have to be this way."

Raelle heard a muffled voice echo from the ground in response to the king. "There is no more time for reason, Adreahn. My master was very clear when he expressed that anyone who harbored Chrishtan Vilgare would be at the mercy of his general and his armies. Lochran has kept his end of the bargain. It is only fitting that you should keep yours."

Raelle heard Chrishtan's voice as she made her way through the lineup toward the king and queen to get a better view. "You shall have what you have requested Echo, a fair duel with me. You will not harm the people of this city. That is our deal."

Raelle watched down below as Chrishtan approach the Elite Echo. The lean, muscular general wore sleeveless Huronus rogue armor with his hood up. A demonic-looking mask covered the rogue's face. He nodded in agreement with Chrishtan. Raelle thought her heart might beat out of her chest as Chrishtan got closer to his enemy. The fact that Chrishtan was fitted head to toe in a bolted bronze helm and armor with his warrior swords on each hip did not make Raelle feel any better.

It did not take long before the duel ensued. Raelle clenched her fists tight as the two Lyre-blood elites attempted to get at one another with their weapons. Chrishtan wielded dual swords, while the Elite Echo wielded dual daggers. As they struck and maneuvered, they seemed to be evenly matched. Chrishtan came close to making contact several times, but the Elite Echo avoided the blows, disappearing from one location to suddenly appear in another. Raelle knew this was because rogues had the ability to slow down time and move to a new location. She had done this when she defeated the dranogite. This Elite Echo shared her bloodline.

After what seemed like an endless array of swings, dodges, unfathomable high jumps, disappearing acts, and metal-to-metal clashing, the thing Raelle dreaded most occurred. While Chrishtan lunged forward to attack, in an instant the Echo appeared behind him and emitted a deafening screech, blasting Chrishtan back meters from where he once stood. The penetrating sound waves of the scream left a painful ring in everyone's ears. It felt as if the ground had been hit by a very small meteor. With Chrishtan attempting to recover from the blow, the Elite Echo suddenly appeared in front of him. He snickered as if playing some kind of game with Chrishtan before disappearing again. This time, he reappeared at Chrishtan's rear, slicing open both calves with his daggers. In Raelle's mind, it all happened in slow motion. Chrishtan fell back to the ground, dropping one of his swords as his face crashed into the grass.

***

With the agility of a cat, the Elite Echo jumped into the air and landed directly over Chrishtan with his legs straddled.

He triumphantly tugged off Chrishtan's helmet and threw it into the grass. He pressed one of his daggers to Chrishtan's throat. "Well, well, well," the Elite Echo snickered. "It looks like our beloved warrior prince isn't such a great warrior after all. You should have never been considered royalty."

The Elite Echo moved his blade out to the side to slice Chrishtan's throat, but before he could complete the motion, Chrishtan's free hand came up beside him. He focused his Lyre directly on the Elite Echo's throat. Chrishtan's hand trembled as the force he emitted from it choked his attacker without touching him. The Elite Echo grabbed at his own throat as he gasped for air. Chrishtan focused his Lyre even further as he lifted his enemy off the ground without laying a single hand on him. With his right hand still lifted in the air and his attacker floating above him gasping, Chrishtan grabbed his sword and sliced off the demonic mask worn by his arrogant enemy. To Chrishtan's surprise, the rogue general was young, much younger than he anticipated. He was just a teenager.

The crowd of infantry that surrounded them stared at the novel phenomenon. No one had ever witnessed a Lyre-blood with the ability to manipulate and harm his enemy without laying a single finger on him. With his enemy's face exposed, Chrishtan used his new Lyre ability to throw the young rogue across the field with incredible force. His juvenile adversary lay unconscious on the ground forty meters away. Despite the pain of his injuries, Chrishtan marched at an assertive pace toward his comatose foe. The screams of a woman echoed from the gates behind him.

"Chrishtan, no. Please stop!"

Chrishtan paused to turn around, but saw no one behind him. As he turned back around, he leapt into the air and landed with a loud thud that shook the ground in front of his enemy's unconscious body. Just as he reached for his weapons to slay the Elite Echo, he heard the woman's screams once more.

"Chrishtan, no. You can't. Chrishtan, please!"

He turned around to see Raelle running toward him with immense rogue speed. She screamed, emitting an explosive shriek that blew Chrishtan backward. Chrishtan's ears rang with pain as he lay on the ground. He felt as if he had been hit by the blast of a large explosive. As he sat up and tried to regain his bearings, he saw Raelle kneeling next to his enemy with tears streaming down her face. She sobbed wildly as she desperately tried to resuscitate the Elite Echo.

With his ability to hear slowly returning, Chrishtan crawled over to Raelle in her devastated state. "Raelle, what are you doing?"

Anger flooded her expression as she yelled. "Get away from us. You've killed him!"

Chrishtan scooted closer as he grasped Raelle's face and tried to turn her gaze toward him.

She slapped his hand from her face. "Don't you touch me!" She screamed as she pressed an ear to the Elite Echo's chest before returning to chest compressions.

Chrishtan was taken aback. "Raelle, what are you doing? What's going on with you?"

A look of deep hatred penetrated into him. "I'm trying to save my brother!" Raelle screamed.

Chrishtan's eyes grew two sizes. "What? What are you talking about? I thought your brother was killed!"

Raelle continued to press upon her brother's chest. "So did I, but this *is* my brother, Samuel. I don't know how it is, but it is. His face, his body, his voice, his energy, everything. The body we found in the woods was unrecognizable. We thought it was him. Maybe it wasn't. I mean, why else wouldn't he have come to see me in the Verge with Browden? It's because he wasn't dead."

Chrishtan knew deep within him that Raelle must be right. It made sense, especially since he could plainly see now that they had the exact same ability given to them by the Opalz gemstone. It had to be her brother. "Move, Raelle. I can do this. I know how to bring him back. If there is even the smallest bit of life and Lyre left in him, I can do it. You must trust me, please."

With tears gushing from Raelle's eyes, she nodded and allowed Chrishtan to take over. Raelle cradled Samuel's head, stroking his dirty blonde hair as she whispered in his ear. "It's going to be all right, Sam. We're going to be together again soon, I promise."

On the other side, Chrishtan pressed two fingers into Samuel's neck. "I can feel a pulse, a very faint one, but a pulse nonetheless." Chrishtan used one of Samuel's daggers to cut open his leather armor and expose his chest. Chrishtan pressed both palms to Samuel's pectorals as he focused hard and surged his Lyre energy into Samuel's flaccid body.

***

After a few moments, Samuel started to breathe again on his own. His eyes fluttered open to see Raelle's face hovering over him. "Rae- Raelle? I-is that you?" Samuel squinted his big brown eyes as he coughed.

Raelle's tear-soaked face managed a smile as she stroked her brother's dirty cheek. "Yes, Samuel. It's me."

Samuel continued to cough as he sat up with Raelle's help. He grinned as he looked into his sister's green eyes. "But how can this be?"

Raelle shook her head. "It is fate dear brother. We have found each—"

Samuel heard it before he saw it. An arrow pierced directly through Raelle's chest with another following through Chrishtan's shoulder. Raelle grew limp and fell face-first into Samuel's arms.

Samuel turned his sister's lifeless body over. "Raelle? Raelle please no." He bent his head down to listen for her breath. He shook his head as he looked into the devastated eyes of his warrior opponent. "She's not breathing."

Chrishtan felt Raelle's neck. "I don't feel a pulse. I must get her back behind the gates. She needs help."

Samuel was overcome with emotion as he stood. Holding his sister's wilting body in his arms, he cried out to the masses. "Whoever has done this, I promise you will pay with your life!"

Chrishtan stood beside his enemy. "It was one of yours, Samuel. Look at the fletching on this arrow." Chrishtan pulled the arrow from his shoulder. "Give her to me. She needs a healer as soon as possible if she is to have a chance." Tears ran down the warrior's face. Samuel nodded and handed his sister's unresponsive body over to his new ally.

Samuel's young mind reeled with the conflict of what he thought he knew to be the truth and what had recently presented itself as the truth. The hot, wild, wrath of his Lyre consumed him as his black Opalz gemstone amplified the rage within him. In an instant, a horrific and deadly screech blasted from Samuel's vocal chords, taking out the entire front half of the troops that he himself led to the gates of Ellios. Samuel marched forward as he emitted a second blast. The death of his dearly beloved sister would be unforgivable.

BOOK II of the *ON THE VERGE* series
AVAILABLE NOW on AMAZON.COM

When Deception & Murder,
Imprisonment & Suffering
Reign Over Truth & Light,
Trust Becomes a
Wavering Notion...
Will the young descendants
of Mirilan escape the
twisted web of lies & find
truth? Or will they let it
drag them to hell?

ABOUT THE AUTHOR

"*Ultimately, the On the Verge series is a story about dealing with trauma and loss. This is never an easy or pleasant task. As someone who has dealt with childhood PTSD and depression pretty much my entire life, I wanted to immerse readers in the realities of having to relive past traumas. On the Verge is truly an enormous metaphor for those experiences. Each and every character embodies a person or trait that helped me to make it through. They personify emotion and struggle. Like me, eventually, my characters will overcome what ails them, but first they must face their tragedies head on. And anyone who has ever hit rock bottom, knows that it always gets worse before it gets better. Healing is a process that occurs over time, not overnight. These characters are far from healed and their story is far from over.*"

— R. J. Jojola

To Keep Up With RJ On
SOCIAL MEDIA
LIKE HER at:
facebook.com/rjjojola
facebook.com/ontheverge
instagram.com/rjjojola
twitter.com/rjjojola

THANK YOU FOR READING
If you LIKED *ON THE VERGE*
Please RATE IT and/or LEAVE a REVIEW
at amazon.com or goodreads.com

COMING SOON!
A New Paranormal Thriller from
R. J. Jojola

*Once you lose
everyone & everything
the one thing left to lose is
your humanity...*

WANT to RECIEVE FREE CONTENT
& stay UP TO DATE on RJ's
latest BOOK RELEASES?
SIGN UP at WWW.RJJOJOLA.COM

35196247R00179

Made in the USA
Middletown, DE
23 September 2016